Linda Howard is an award winning *New York Times* bestselling author. She lives in Alabama with her husband and two golden retrievers.

D0808358

Cover of Night

Linda Howard

piatkus

PIATKUS

First published in Great Britain in 2006 by Piatkus Books
This paperback edition published in 2007 by Piatkus Books
First published in the US in 2006 by Ballantine Books,
A Division of Random House, Inc., New York, USA
Reprinted 2008 (twice), 2009, 2010

A CIP catalogue record for this book
is available from the British Library.

ISBN 978-0-7499-3771-3

Typeset by Action Publishing Technology Ltd, Gloucester
Printed in the UK by CPI Mackays, Chatham ME5 8TD

Papers used by Piatkus are natural, renewable and
recyclable products sourced from well-managed forests and certified
in accordance with the rules of the Forest Stewardship Council.

Mixed Sources
Product group from well-managed
forests and other controlled sources
www.fsc.org Cert no. SGS-COC-004081
© 1996 Forest Stewardship Council

Piatkus
An imprint of
Little, Brown Book Group
100 Victoria Embankment
London EC4Y 0DY

An Hachette UK Company
www.hachette.co.uk

www.piatkus.co.uk

Chapter One

The guest who was staying in room 3 of Nightingale's Bed and Breakfast, which Cate Nightingale privately thought of as the He-Man room because it was almost unrelievedly masculine, stopped in the doorway of the dining room, then almost immediately stepped back out of sight. Most of the patrons who were enjoying Cate's morning offerings didn't even notice the man's brief appearance; those who did probably didn't think anything about his abrupt departure. People here in Trail Stop, Idaho, tended to mind their own business, and if one of her guests wasn't in the mood for company while he ate, that was fine with them.

Cate herself noticed him only because she was bringing in a platter of sliced ham from the kitchen at the same time, and the kitchen door was directly opposite the open hall doorway. She made a mental note to go upstairs the first chance she got and see if he – his name was Layton, Jeffrey Layton – wanted her to bring up a breakfast tray. Some guests didn't like eating with strangers, plain and simple. Taking a tray up wasn't anything unusual.

Nightingale's B and B had been open for almost three years. The Bed part of the business was often slow, but Breakfast was booming. Opening her dining room to the public for breakfast had been a happy accident. Instead of having one large dining table where everyone would sit together – assuming all five of her guest rooms were occupied at the same time, which had never happened – she had placed five small tables, each seating four, in the dining room so that her guests could eat in relative privacy if they wanted. Folks in the little community had quickly realized that Nightingale's offered some fine eating, and before she knew it, people were asking if it was okay if they stopped by for coffee in

1

the mornings, and maybe for one of her blueberry muffins as well.

As a newcomer she wanted to fit in, so because she had the extra seats, she said yes, even though mentally she had groaned at the thought of the added expense. Then, when they tried to pay her, she had no idea what to charge, because the cost of breakfast was included in the room rental; so she'd been forced to hand-print a menu with prices and post it on the porch by the side door, which most of the locals used instead of walking around to the front of the big old house. Within a month she'd squeezed a sixth table into the dining room, bringing her total seating capacity to twenty-four. Sometimes even that wasn't enough, especially if she had guests in residence. It wasn't unusual to see men leaning against a wall while they drank their coffee and munched on muffins, if all the seats were taken.

Today, however, was Scone Day. Once a week she baked scones instead of muffins. At first the community folk, mostly from ranch and lumberjack stock, had looked askance at the 'fancy biscuits,' but the scones had quickly become a favorite. She had tried different flavors, but the vanilla was a runaway favorite because it went well with whatever jam the customer preferred.

Cate set the platter of fried ham down in the middle of a table, exactly halfway between Conrad Moon and his son so that neither could accuse her of playing favorites. She had made that mistake once, putting a platter closer to Conrad, and ever since then the two had kept up a running commentary about whom she liked best. Gordon, the younger Moon, would be joking, but Cate had an uneasy feeling that Conrad was looking for a third wife and thought she'd fill the position just fine. She thought otherwise, and made certain she never gave him any accidental encouragement with the ham placement.

'Looks good,' Gordon drawled, as he did every day, stretching out his fork to capture a slice.

'Better'n good,' Conrad added, unable to let Gordon top him in the compliment department.

'Thank you,' she said as she hurried away, not giving Conrad a chance to add anything else. He was a nice man, but he was about her father's age, and she wouldn't have picked him even if she weren't too busy to even think about starting to date.

As she passed by the Bunn double coffeemaker, she automatically checked the level of the coffee in the pots, and paused to start a fresh batch. The dining room was still full, and people were lingering longer this morning. Joshua Creed, a hunting guide, was there with one of his clients; folks always hung around when Mr. Creed was there, just to talk to him. He had an aura of leadership, of authority, that people naturally responded to. She'd heard he was retired from the military, and she could believe it; he radiated command, from his sharp, narrow gaze to the square set of his jaw and shoulders. He didn't come in very often, but when he did, he was usually the center of respectful attention.

The client, a handsome dark-haired man she judged to be in his late thirties, was just the sort of outsider she liked the least. He was obviously well off, if he could afford Joshua Creed, and though he was dressed in jeans and boots like most of the people in the room, he made certain, in some subtle and some not-so-subtle ways, that everyone knew he was Someone Important despite his show of camaraderie. For one thing, he'd rolled up his shirtsleeves and kept flashing the thin, diamond-set watch on his left wrist. He was also just a shade too loud, a shade too hearty, and he kept mentioning his experiences on a game hunt in Africa. He even gave everyone a geography lesson, explaining where Nairobi was. Cate managed to refrain from rolling her eyes at his assumption that *local* was synonymous with *ignorant. Weird,* maybe, but not *ignorant.* He also made a point of explaining that he hunted wild animals mostly to photograph them, and though on an emotional level Cate approved of that, her common sense whispered that he was just saying it to give himself an out in case he didn't kill anything. If he was any kind of photographer, she'd be surprised.

As she hurried on to the kitchen, she wondered just when she'd started looking at newcomers as 'outsiders.'

The dividing line between her life before and her life now was so sharply defined that sometimes she felt as if she weren't even the same person. There hadn't been a gradual change, giving her time to analyze and process, to slowly grow into the woman she was now; instead there had been jagged breaks, abrupt upheavals. The period between Derek's death and her decision to move to Idaho was a steep, narrow valley into which sunshine had never reached. Once she and the boys had arrived here, she'd been so busy getting the B and B open and settling in that she hadn't had much time to worry about being an outsider herself. Then, almost before she knew it, she was as much part of the warp and weave of the little community as she ever had been in Seattle; more, even, because Seattle was like all big cities, filled with strangers and everyone moving in individual little bubbles. Here, she literally knew everyone.

Just before she reached the kitchen door, it opened, and Sherry Bishop stuck her head out, a quick look of relief crossing her face when she saw Cate approaching.

'What's wrong?' Cate asked as she rushed through the door. She looked first to the kitchen table, where her four-year-old twins, Tucker and Tanner, were industriously digging into their cereal; the boys were sitting on their booster chairs exactly where she had left them. They chattered and giggled and squirmed, as usual; all was right in their world. Rather, Tucker chattered, and Tanner listened. She couldn't help worrying because Tanner talked so little, but their pediatrician hadn't seemed alarmed. 'He's fine,' Dr. Hardy had said. 'He doesn't need to talk because Tucker is talking for both of them. He'll talk when he has something to say.' Since Tanner was completely normal in every other way, including comprehension, she had to assume the pediatrician was right – but she still worried. She couldn't help it; she was a mother.

'A pipe burst under the sink,' Sherry said, sounding harassed. 'I turned off the valve, but we need the water back on fast. The dishes are piling up.'

'Oh, no.' Other than the obvious difficulty of having no water to cook or wash dishes with, another problem loomed even larger: her mother, Sheila Wells, was en route from Seattle for a week-long visit, and was due in that afternoon. Since her mother wasn't happy about Cate and the twins leaving Seattle to begin with, Cate could just imagine her comments about the area's remoteness and lack of modern conveniences should there not be any water.

It was always something; this old house seemed to need almost constant maintenance and repair, which she supposed was par for the course with old houses. Still, her finances were stretched to the breaking point; she could use just *one* week in which nothing went wrong. Maybe next week, she thought with a sigh.

She picked up the kitchen phone and from memory dialed the number of Earl's Hardware Store.

Walter Earl himself answered, catching the phone on the first ring as he usually did. 'Hardware.' He didn't need further identification, since there was only one hardware store in town, and he

4

was the only one who answered the phone.

'Walter, this is Cate. Do you know where Mr. Harris is working today? I have a plumbing emergency.'

'Mistuh Hawwis!' Tucker crowed, having caught the name of the local handyman. Excited, he banged his spoon against the table, and Cate stuck her finger in her ear so she could hear what Walter said. Both boys were staring at her in delight, quivering with anticipation. The community handyman was one of their favorite people, because they were fascinated by his tools and he didn't mind if they played with the wrenches and hammers.

Calvin Harris didn't have a phone, but he customarily stopped by the hardware store every morning to pick up whatever supplies he would need for the day's work; so Walter usually knew where he could be found. When she had first moved here, Cate had been taken aback that someone wouldn't have a phone in this day and age, but now she was accustomed to the system and didn't think anything of it. Mr. Harris didn't want a phone, so he didn't have a phone. Big deal. The community was so small, finding him wasn't a problem.

'Cal's right here,' Walter said. 'I'll send him your way.'

'Thanks,' said Cate, glad she didn't have to hunt him down. 'Could you ask him what time he thinks he can get here?'

Walter's voice rumbled as he relayed the question, and she heard a softer, indistinct mumble that she recognized as Mr. Harris's voice.

Walter's voice sounded clearly through the phone. 'He said he'll be there in a few minutes.'

Saying good-bye and hanging up, Cate breathed a sigh of relief. With any luck the problem would be minor and the water would soon be on again, with minimal impact on her finances. As it was, she needed Mr. Harris's fix-it genius so often she was beginning to think she would come out better to offer him free room and board in exchange for repairs. He lived in rooms over the feed store, and while they might be bigger than any of her bedrooms, he still had to pay for them, plus she could throw in meals. She would lose a bedroom to rent, but it wasn't as if the bed-and-break-fast had ever been filled to capacity. What held her back was the slightly unwelcome prospect of having someone permanently in the house with her and the twins. As busy as she was during the day, she wanted to keep the nights just for them.

Mr. Harris was so shy, though, she could easily see him mumbling something after supper and disappearing into his room, not to be seen again until the morning. But what if he didn't? What if the boys wanted to be with him instead of her? She felt small and petty for worrying about such a thing, but – what if they did? She was the center of their young lives, and she didn't know if she could give that up yet. Eventually she would have to, but they were just four, and all she had left of Derek.

'Well?' Sherry prompted, her brows raised as she waited for news, good or bad.

'He's coming right over.'

'Caught him before he got started on another job, then,' said Sherry, looking as relieved as Cate felt.

Cate looked at the boys, who were both sitting watching her, their spoons held suspended. 'You two need to finish your cereal, or you won't be able to watch Mr. Harris,' she said sternly. That wasn't exactly the truth, since Mr. Harris would be right there in the kitchen with them, but they were four; what did they know?

'We'll huwwy,' Tucker said, and both resumed eating with more energy than precision.

'Hu*rr*y,' Cate said, emphasizing the r sound.

'Hu*rr*y,' Tucker obediently repeated. He could say the sound when he wanted to, but when he was distracted – which was often – he fell back into babyish speech patterns. He talked so much; it was as if he didn't take the time to properly say the words. 'Mistuh Hawwis is coming,' he told Tanner, as if his brother didn't know. 'I'm gonna play with the dwill.'

'Drill,' Cate corrected. 'And you will not. You may watch him, but *leave the tools alone*.'

His big blue eyes filled with tears, and his lower lip trembled. 'Mistuh Hawwis lets us play with them.'

'That's when he has time. He'll be in a hurry today, because he has another job to do when he leaves here.'

When she first opened the B and B, Cate had tried to keep them from bothering the handyman while he was working, and since they'd been just one at the time, the job should have been easier, but they had shown remarkable skill in slipping away. As soon as she turned her back, both boys zoomed back to him like magnets to steel. They had been like little monkeys, poking into his toolbox, running off with anything they could pick up, so she knew they had been as severe a trial to his patience as they had been to hers, but he'd never said a word of complaint, and for that she blessed him. Not that his silence on the matter was surprising; he seldom said anything, period.

The boys were older now, but their fascination with tools hadn't waned. The only difference was that now they insisted on 'helping.'

'They don't bother me,' Mr. Harris would mumble whenever she caught them, ducking his head as his cheeks colored. He was painfully shy, rarely looking her in the eye and actually speaking only when he had to. Well, he did talk to the boys. Maybe he felt at ease with them because they were so young, but she had heard his voice mixed with the boys' higher-pitched, excited tones as they seemed to carry on real conversations.

She glanced out the kitchen door and saw three customers lined up to pay their bills. 'I'll be right back,' she said, and went out to take their money. She hadn't wanted to put a cash register in the dining room, but her breakfast business had made it necessary, so she had installed a small one by the outside door. Two of the customers were Joshua Creed and his client, which meant the dining room would soon be emptying out, now that Mr. Creed was leaving.

'Cate,' Mr. Creed said, inclining his head toward her. He was tall and broad-shouldered, his dark hair silvering at the temples, and his face weathered from the elements. His hazel eyes were narrow, his gaze piercing; he looked as if he could chew nails and spit out bullets, but he was always respectful and kind when he spoke to her. 'Those scones of yours just keep getting better and better. I'd weigh four hundred pounds if I ate here every day.'

'I doubt that, but thanks.'

He turned and introduced his client. 'Cate, this is Randall Wellingham. Randall, this lovely lady is Cate Nightingale, the owner of Nightingale's Bed and Breakfast, and incidentally the best cook around.'

The first compliment was debatable, and the second one a downright lie, because Walter Earl's wife, Milly, was one of those natural cooks who seldom measured anything but could cook like an angel. Still, it couldn't hurt business to have Mr. Creed saying things like that.

'I can't argue with any of that,' Mr. Wellingham said in his too-hearty tone, holding out his hand while his gaze swiftly raked down her before returning to her face, his expression saying that he was unimpressed with either her or her cooking. Cate forced herself to shake hands. His grip was too firm, his skin too smooth. This wasn't a man who did a lot of physical work, which would have been okay in itself if he hadn't plainly looked down on all the other people there because they *did*. Only Mr. Creed was spared, but then only someone blind and stupid would treat him with disdain.

'Are you staying long?' she asked, just to be polite.

'Just a week. That's all the time I can manage away from the office. Every time I leave, the place goes to hell,' he said, chuckling.

She didn't comment. She imagined he owned his own business, considering the wealth he flashed, but she didn't care enough to ask. Mr. Creed nodded, placed his black hat on his head, and the two men exited to let the next customer step up to pay. Two more people joined the queue.

By the time she had taken their money and refilled the coffee cups around the room, Conrad and Gordon Moon had finished, and she returned to the cash register, where she fended off Conrad's heavy compliments and Gordon's amusement. He seemed to think it funny that his father had developed a *tendre* for her.

Cate didn't think it funny at all when Conrad paused after his son had stepped out on the porch. He paused and swallowed so hard his Adam's apple bobbed. 'Miss Cate, I'd like to ask – that is . . . are you receiving visitors tonight?'

The old-fashioned approach both charmed and alarmed; she liked the way he'd done it, but was horrified that he'd asked at all. Cate did her own swallowing, then stepped up to the plate, on the theory that sidestepping the issue would only bring on more approaches. 'No, I'm not. I spend the evenings with my boys. I'm so busy during the day that night is the only time I have with them, and I don't think it would be right to take that away.'

Still, he tried again. 'You can't mean to give up the best years of your life—'

'I'm not giving them up,' she said firmly. 'I'm living them the way I think best for me and my children.'

'But I might be *dead* by the time they're grown!'

Now, there was a point of view that was sure to attract. She shot him an incredulous look, then nodded in agreement. 'Yes, you might. I still have to give the opportunity a pass. I'm sure you understand.'

'Not really,' he muttered, 'but I guess I can take rejection as well as any other man.'

Sherry poked her head out the kitchen door. 'Cal's here,' she said.

Conrad's gaze moved to her, and zeroed in. 'Miss Sherry,' he said. 'Are you by any chance receiving visitors—'

Leaving Sherry to handle the geriatric lothario as best she could, Cate dodged past her into the kitchen.

Mr. Harris was already on his knees with his head poked into the cabinet under the sink, and both boys were out of their chairs busily emptying his heavy toolbox.

'Tucker! Tanner!' She put her hands on her hips and gave them her best Mother glare. 'Put those tools back into the toolbox. What did I tell you about bothering Mr. Harris this time? I told you that you could watch, but to leave his tools alone. Both of you, go to your room, right now.'

'But, Mommy—' Tucker began, always ready to mount a spirited argument to defend whatever it was he'd been caught doing. Tanner merely stepped back, still holding a wrench, and waited for Tucker to either fail or prevail. She could feel the situation beginning to spiral out of control, her maternal instinct telling her they were on the verge of outright rebellion. This happened every so often, pushing at the boundaries to see how far she would let them go. *Never show weakness*. That was her mother's sole advice for facing bullies, wild animals, or disobedient four-year-olds.

'No,' Cate said firmly, and pointed at the toolbox. 'Tools in the box. *Now.*'

Pouting, Tucker threw a screwdriver into the box. Cate felt her back teeth grind together; he knew better than to throw his own things, much less someone else's. Swiftly she stepped over the toolbox, took his arm, and swatted his rear end. 'Young man, you know better than to throw Mr. Harris's tools. First you're going to tell him you're sorry; then you're going to your room to sit in the naughty chair for fifteen minutes.' Tucker immediately began to wail, tears streaking down his face, but Cate merely raised her voice as she pointed at Tanner. 'You. Wrench in the box.'

He scowled, looking mutinous, but he heaved a sigh and carefully placed the wrench in the toolbox. 'Oooookay,' he said in a tone of doom that made her bite her lip to keep from laughing. She had learned the hard way she couldn't give these two an inch, or they'd run roughshod over her.

'You have to sit in the naughty chair for ten minutes, after Tucker gets up. You disobeyed, too. Now, both of you finish picking up those tools and put them back in the box. *Gently.*'

Tanner's lower lip came out as he imitated a miniature thundercloud, and Tucker was still crying, but to her relief they began doing as they were told. Cate looked around to find that Mr. Harris had pulled his head from the depths of the cabinets and was opening his mouth, no doubt to defend the little culprits. She raised her finger at him. 'Not one word,' she said sternly.

He blushed scarlet, mumbled, 'No, ma'am,' and stuck his head back under the sink.

When the tools had been restored to the box, though probably not in their proper places, Cate prompted Tucker, 'What are you supposed to tell Mr. Harris?'

'I'm sowwy,' he said, hiccuping in the middle of the word. His nose was running.

Mr. Harris wisely kept his head inside the cabinet. 'It's o—' he started to say, then stopped. He seemed to freeze for a moment; then he finally mumbled, 'You boys should mind your mother.'

Cate seized a paper towel and wiped Tucker's nose. 'Blow,' she instructed, holding the towel in place, and he did with the excess energy he put into everything. 'Now, both of you go up to your room. Tucker, sit in the naughty chair. Tanner, you may play quietly while Tucker's in the chair, but don't talk to him. I'll come upstairs and tell you when to swap places.'

Heads down, the two little boys dragged themselves up the stairs as if they were facing a fate of unimaginable horror. Cate checked the clock to see what time Tucker would be released from punishment.

Sherry had come back into the kitchen and was watching Cate with a mixture of sympathy and amusement. 'Will Tucker actually sit in the chair until you go upstairs?'

'He will now. In the past his time in the naughty chair has been extended several times before so now he gets the idea. Tanner has been even more stubborn.' And that was the understatement of the year, she thought, remembering the struggle it had been to make him obey. Tanner didn't talk much, but he personified 'stubborn.'

Both boys were active, strong-willed, and absolutely brilliant when it came to finding new and different ways to get in trouble – and worse, danger. Once she had been horrified at the idea of even swatting their bottoms, much less spanking them, but before they turned two she had revised a lot of her former opinions on child-raising. They still had never had a spanking, but she no longer had confidence that they would get through their childhood without one. The thought made her stomach clench, but she had to raise them alone, discipline them alone, and keep them safe while somehow molding them into responsible human beings. If she let herself think too much about it, the long years stretching before her, she would almost drown in panic. Derek wasn't here. She had to do it by herself.

Mr. Harris cautiously backed out of the cabinet and looked up at her as if gauging whether or not it was safe to speak now. Evidently deciding it was, he cleared his throat. 'Ah . . . the leak is no problem; it's just a loose fitting.' Blood was climbing in his face as he spoke, and he quickly looked down at the pipe wrench in his hand.

She blew out a relieved breath and went toward the door. 'Thank God. Let me get my purse and pay you.'

'No charge,' he mumbled. 'All I did was tighten it.'

Surprised, she stopped in her tracks. 'But your time is worth something—'

'It didn't take a minute.'

'A lawyer would charge an hour for that minute,' Sherry observed, looking oddly amused.

Mr. Harris muttered something under his breath that Cate didn't catch, but Sherry evidently did because she grinned. Cate wondered what was so funny but didn't have time to pursue the matter. 'At least let me get you a cup of coffee, on the house.'

He said something that sounded like 'thank you,' though it could have been 'don't bother.' Assuming it was the former, she went into the dining room and poured coffee into a large take-out cup, then snapped a plastic lid in place. Two more men came up to pay their bills; one she knew, one she didn't, but that wasn't unusual during hunting season. She took their money, surveyed the remaining customers, who all seemed to be doing okay, and carried the coffee back into the kitchen.

Mr. Harris was squatting down, restoring order to his toolbox.

11

Cate flushed with guilt. 'I'm so sorry. I told them to leave your tools alone, but—' She gave a one-shouldered shrug of frustration, then extended the coffee to him.

'No harm,' he said as he took the cup, his rough, grease-stained fingers wrapping around the polystyrene. He ducked his head. 'I like their company.'

'And they love yours,' she said drily. 'I'll go up now and check on them. Thank you again, Mr. Harris.'

'It hasn't been fifteen minutes yet,' Sherry said, checking the clock.

Cate grinned. 'I know. But they can't tell time, so what does a few minutes matter? Will you watch the cash register for a few minutes? Everything looked okay in the dining room, no one needed coffee; so there's nothing to do until someone leaves.'

'Got it,' said Sherry, and Cate left the kitchen by the hall door, climbing the long, steep flight of stairs.

She had chosen the two front bedrooms for herself and the twins, saving the best views for the paying guests. Both stairs and hallway were carpeted, so her steps were silent as she turned to the right at the top of the stairs. Their door was open, she saw, but she didn't hear their voices. She smiled; that was good.

Stopping in the doorway, she watched them for a minute. Tucker was sitting in the naughty chair, his head down and his lower lip protruding as he picked at his fingernails. Tanner sat on the floor, pushing a toy car up an incline he'd made by propping one of their storybooks against his leg, and making motor noises under his breath.

Her heart squeezed as a memory flooded her. Their first birthday, just a few months after Derek's death, had brought them an avalanche of toys. She had never made motor noises to them; they were just learning how to walk, and their toys were soft, plush animals, or something to bang, or educational toys she was using to teach them words and coordination. They had been too young when Derek died for him to have played cars with them, and she knew her dad hadn't either. Her brother, who might have, lived in Sacramento and she had seen him only once since Derek's death. Without anyone having demonstrated motor noises for them, they had each seized one of their new, fat, brightly colored plastic cars and pushed them back and forth, saying something that sounded like 'uudddden, *uuddden*' – even capturing the gear changes. She

12

had stared at them in total astonishment, for the first time truly realizing that a large part of their personalities came preset, and she might fine-tune their basic instincts but she didn't have the power to shape their entire psyches. They were who they were, and she loved every inch, every molecule of them.

'It's time to swap,' she said, and Tucker hopped out of the naughty chair with a huge sigh of relief. Tanner released the little car and let his head droop as far as it would go, the complete picture of pitiful dejection. He dragged himself up, invisible weights attached to his feet so he could barely walk. He moved so slowly she was beginning to think he might become old enough to start school before he made it to that chair. But finally he reached it and dropped into the seat, his body slumped.

'Ten minutes,' she said, once again fighting the urge to laugh. He obviously thought he was doomed; his body language all but shouted that he had no hope of being released from the naughty chair before he died.

'I was good,' Tucker said, coming to lean against her legs. 'I didn't talk at all.'

'That was very brave of you,' Cate said, stroking her fingers through his dark hair. 'You took your punishment like a man.'

He looked up, blue eyes wide. 'I did?'

'You did. I'm so proud.'

His little shoulders squared, and he looked thoughtfully at Tanner, who showed every sign of expiring within moments. 'Am I bwavuh than Tannuh?'

'Braver,' Cate corrected.

'Brrrraverrr.'

'Very good. Tanner.'

'Tannerrrr,' he repeated, making the sound growl.

'Remember to take your time, and you'll have it down pat.'

Puzzled, he tilted his head. 'Who's Damn Pat?'

'Tucker!' Horrified anew, Cate froze and her mouth fell open. 'Where did you hear that word?'

If anything, he looked even more puzzled. 'You said it, Mommy. You said "Damn Pat."'

'*Down*, not *damn*!'

'Ohhh.' He frowned. 'Down Pat. Who's Down Pat?'

'Never mind.' Maybe it was just a coincidence; maybe he hadn't heard the word *damn* at all. After all, there were only

13

twenty-six letters in the alphabet, so how unusual was it that he would get some of them mixed up? Maybe he'd completely forget what he'd said if she just let the subject drop. Yeah, right. He'd savor it in private, then trot it out when it was certain to embarrass her the most – probably in front of her mother.

'Sit down and play while Tanner's in the naughty chair,' she instructed, patting his shoulder. 'I'll be back in ten minutes.'

'Eight,' said Tanner, reviving enough to give her a look of outrage.

She checked her wristwatch; damn if there weren't eight minutes left in his sentence. He'd already been in the chair for two of his punishment minutes.

Yes, sometimes her children definitely alarmed her. They could each count to twenty, but she certainly hadn't yet introduced them to subtraction, plus their concept of time tended to be either 'right now' or 'wait a long, long time.' Somewhere along the line, while he was observing instead of talking, Tanner had picked up some math skills.

Maybe he could do her taxes next year, she thought with amusement.

As she turned away, her gaze fell on the number *3* plainly lettered on the door across the hall from the stairwell. Mr. Layton! What with the plumbing emergency, plus the twins' disobedience, she had completely forgotten about bringing a breakfast tray up to him.

Swiftly she walked to the door; it was slightly ajar, so she knocked on the doorjamb instead. 'Mr. Layton, it's Cate Nightingale. Would you like me to bring up a breakfast tray?'

She waited, but there was no answer. Had he left the room and gone downstairs while she'd been in the twins' room? The door had a stubborn squeak, so she thought she would have heard him if he'd opened it.

'Mr. Layton?'

Still no answer. Gingerly she pushed the door open, and the squeak came right on cue.

The bedcovers were thrown messily aside, and the closet door stood open, showing several articles of clothing hanging from the pole. Each guest room had a small private bath and that door, too, was standing open. A small leather suitcase was on the folding luggage stand, the lid open and propped against the wall. Mr.

Layton, however, wasn't there. He must have gone downstairs while she'd been talking to the boys, and she simply hadn't heard the door squeak.

She started to back out of the room, not wanting him to return and think she was snooping, when she noticed the window was open, and the screen looked slightly askew. Puzzled, she crossed to the window and tugged the screen back into place, latching it. How on earth had it gotten unlatched? Had the boys been playing in here, and tried to climb out the window? Her blood ran cold at the thought, and she looked out at the drop to the porch roof below. Such a fall would break their bones, possible even kill them.

She was so riveted with horror at the possibility it was a moment before she realized the parking area was empty. Mr. Layton's rental car wasn't there. Either he hadn't come back upstairs at all, or – or he'd climbed out the window onto the porch roof, swung down to the ground, and driven off. The idea was ridiculous, but preferable to thinking her little boys might be climbing out on the porch roof.

She left room 3 and returned to the twins' room. Tanner was still in the naughty chair, and still looked in danger of imminent demise. Tucker was drawing on their blackboard with a piece of colored chalk. 'Boys, have either of you opened any of the windows?'

'No, Mommy,' Tucker said without pausing in his art creation.

Tanner managed to lift his head and give it a ponderous shake.

They were telling the truth. When they lied, their eyes would get big and round and they'd stare at her as if she were a cobra, hypnotizing them with the sway of her head. She hoped they'd still do that when they were teenagers.

The only explanation left for the open window was that Mr. Layton had indeed climbed out it, and driven away.

Why on earth would he do such a strange thing?

And if he had happened to fall, would her insurance have covered it?

15

Chapter Two

Cate hurried down the stairs, hoping Sherry hadn't been over-whelmed by an unexpected influx of customers while Cate had been upstairs dealing with the twins. As she approached the kitchen door, she heard Sherry's voice, rich with amusement. 'I wondered how long you were going to keep your head stuck under that sink.'

'I was afraid if I moved, she'd swat my ass, too.'

Cate skidded to a stop, her eyes wide in astonishment. Mr. Harris had said that? Mr. *Harris*? And to *Sherry*? She could see him saying something like that to another man – maybe – but when he was talking to a woman, he could barely put two words together without blushing. And there was an ease to his tone she'd never heard before, one that made her doubt her own ears.

Mr. Harris . . . and Sherry? Had she missed something there? It couldn't be; the idea of those two together was too outlandish to be real, like . . . like Lisa Marie and Michael Jackson.

Which told her that anything was possible.

Sherry was older than Mr. Harris, in her mid-fifties, but age didn't matter much. She was also an attractive woman, hefty but curvy, with reddish hair and a warm, outgoing personality. Mr. Harris was – well, Cate had no idea how old he was. Somewhere between forty and fifty, she guessed. She pictured him in her mind's eye; he looked older than he probably was, and it wasn't because he was wrinkled or anything like that. He was just one of those people who was born old, with a seen-it-all manner. In fact, now that she really thought about it, he might not even be forty yet. His nondescript hair, somewhere between brown and dishwa-ter blond, was always too shaggy, and she'd never seen him when he wasn't wearing a pair of grease-stained, baggy coveralls. He was so lanky the coveralls hung on him, looser than a prostitute's morals.

Cate felt ashamed; he was so shy she actually avoided looking at him or casually chatting, not wanting to stress him out, and now she felt guilty because not drawing him out was easier than getting to know him and putting him at ease, as Sherry had obviously done. Cate, too, should have put herself to the trouble, should have made the effort to befriend him, as everyone here had made the effort to befriend her when she'd first taken over the B and B. Some neighbor she'd been!

She went into the kitchen, feeling as if she were stepping into the twilight zone. Mr. Harris literally jumped when he saw her, his face turning red, as if he knew she'd overheard. Cate jerked her thoughts back to Mr. Layton's weird actions and away from the possibility of a romance going on beneath her nose. 'The guest in number three climbed out the window and left,' she said, then lifted her shoulders in an 'I don't know what the hell's going on' gesture.

'Out the window?' Sherry echoed, equally puzzled. 'Why did he do that?'

'I don't know. I have his credit card number, so it isn't as if he can run out on the bill. And his stuff's still here.'

'Maybe he just wanted to climb out the window, see if he could.'

'Maybe. Or he's nuts.'

'Or that,' Sherry agreed. 'How many nights is he staying?'

'Just last night. Checkout's at eleven, so he should be back soon.' Though where on earth he could have gone, she couldn't imagine, unless he'd felt a sudden urge to visit the feed store. Trail Stop didn't have any shops or restaurants; if he'd wanted breakfast, he should have eaten here. The nearest honest-to-God town was an hour's drive away, so he wouldn't have time to go there, eat, then get back before it was time to check out – not to mention that it would be self-defeating, if he simply hadn't wanted to eat with strangers.

Mr. Harris cleared his throat. 'I'll be ... um—' He looked around, clearly discomfited.

Guessing that he didn't know where to put his empty cup, Cate said, 'I'll take it,' and held out her hand. 'Thanks for stopping by. I wish you'd let me pay you, though.'

He stubbornly shook his head as he gave the cup to her. Determined to be more friendly, she continued, 'I don't know what I'd have done without you.'

'None of us know how we got along before Cal settled here,' Sherry said cheerfully, moving to the sink, where she began loading dishes into the dishwasher. 'Waited a week or more for someone from town whenever we needed repairs, I guess.'

Cate was vaguely surprised; she'd thought Mr. Harris had always been here. He certainly fit in with the locals as if he'd lived here all his life. The sense of shame rose in her throat again. Sherry referred to him by his first name, while Cate had always called him Mr. Harris, effectively putting him at a distance. She didn't know why she did it, but there it was.

'Mommmmy!' Tucker bellowed from the top of the stairs. 'Time's up!'

Sherry chuckled, and Cate saw a brief smile tug at Mr. Harris's mouth as he gave Sherry a two-fingered salute and picked up his toolbox, evidently intent on making a getaway before the boys came back downstairs.

Cate rolled her eyes heavenward, silently asking for a little peace and quiet, then stepped into the hall. 'Tell Tanner he may get out of the naughty chair.'

'Awwight!' The gleeful shout was followed by the sounds of jumping. 'Tannuh! Mommy said to get up! Let's build a fort and bawwicade me and you in it.' Caught up in his enthusiasm for his game, he ran back to their room.

Cate was torn between amusement at his Elmer Fudd pronunciation and puzzlement at his word choice. *Barricade*? Where had he come up with *that*? Maybe they'd been watching old westerns on television; she needed to keep a closer watch on their entertainment.

She checked the dining room: it was empty; the morning rush was over. After she and Sherry cleaned the dining room and kitchen and Mr. Layton returned to get his things, she could change the sheets on the bed and clean the room, then she'd have the rest of the day to get things ready for her mother's visit.

Mr. Harris had left. Going over to help with the dishes, Cate bumped her hip against Sherry's. 'So, what's up with you and Mr. Harris? Is there something going on between you two?'

Sherry's mouth fell open, and she gave Cate a look of absolute astonishment. 'Good God, no. What gave you that idea?'

Her reaction was so genuine that Cate felt foolish for having jumped to the wrong conclusion. 'He was *talking* to you.'

'Well, hell, Cal talks to a lot of people.'

'Not that I've seen, he doesn't.'

'He's just a little shy,' Sherry said, in what was probably the understatement of the month. 'Besides, I'm old enough to be his mother.'

'You are not – unless you were really, really precocious.'

'Okay, so that's an exaggeration. I do like Cal – a lot. He's a smart man. He might not have a college degree, but he can fix just about anything.'

Cate agreed with that. Whatever needed repair at the B and B, from carpentry to electrical work to plumbing, Mr. Harris handled it. He also filled in as a mechanic, if need be. If ever anyone had been born to be a handyman, Mr. Harris had been.

Ten years before, fresh out of college with her degree in marketing, she would have disdained people who did physical work – people with their names sewn on their pockets, as they had been described in her circle – but she was older and wiser now, she hoped. The world needed all types to make things work, from the planners to the doers, and in this little community someone who could fix things was worth his weight in gold.

She began cleaning the dining room while Sherry finished in the kitchen; then she vacuumed and dusted downstairs – at least in all the public areas. Thank goodness the huge old Victorian had two parlors. The front one, the big one, was for use by her guests. The small one in back was the den where she and the boys relaxed in the evenings, where they watched television and played games. She didn't bother even picking up their toys in there; for one thing, her mother wasn't due for hours yet and the boys would have their things dragged out again before she got here, so Cate didn't waste the effort.

Sherry poked her head out of the kitchen door. 'All through in here. I'll see you in the morning. Hope your mom gets here okay.'

'Thanks. I do, too; she'll never let me hear the end of it if she has car trouble or something.'

Trail Stop was so remote that there was no easy way to get there, no nearby airports for commercial flights, and only one road in. Because her mother hated the small propeller planes she could have flown on to get closer, and because renting any sort of vehicle at their tiny landing strip was almost 'mission impossible,' she chose to fly into Boise, where she knew there would be rentals available. That made for a long drive and yet another sore point with her concerning Cate's chosen home. She didn't like having her daughter and grandsons living in another state, she didn't like Idaho – give her a metropolitan area over a rural one any day – and she didn't like the inordinate trouble it took her to visit. She didn't like it that Cate had bought a B and B, which meant she seldom had any free time; in fact, Cate had visited her parents only once since buying the B and B.

All of those were valid points. Cate admitted it, and had even told her mother so. She herself would have preferred to stay in Seattle, if she'd had a choice.

But she hadn't, so she'd done what she'd thought was best for the twins. When Derek died, leaving her with nine-month-old twins, not only had she been devastated by losing him, she had been forced to face reality about their finances. Their combined incomes had provided a good living, but Cate had gone to part-time when the boys were born and most of her work she'd done from home. With Derek gone, she had to work full-time, but the cost of quality day care for the boys had been prohibitive. It almost didn't pay for her to work. Her mother couldn't help with their care, because she worked, too.

They had savings, and Derek had purchased a hundred-thousand-dollar insurance policy, intending to add to it as his income increased. They'd thought they had all the time in the world. Who could have anticipated a healthy, thirty-year-old man dying from a staph infection that attacked his heart? He'd gone rock climbing for the first time since the twins were born, scraped his leg, and the doctors said the bacteria had likely entered his body through the small wound. Roughly thirty percent of people carry the bacteria on their skin, they'd explained, and normally have no problems. But sometimes a break in the skin allowed infection to start, and maybe for some reason the immune system was temporarily depressed, say from stress, and the infection would roar through the body despite all efforts to stop it.

The how and why mattered, on an intellectual level, but emotionally all she knew was that she was suddenly a twenty-nine-year-old widow with two baby boys to care for. From there on out, all of her decisions had to be made with them in mind.

With their savings and the insurance money, and careful budgeting, she could have remained in Seattle, close to both her family and her in-laws. But there would have been nothing left over to pay for the twins' college education, plus she would have had to work such long hours she wouldn't have seen much of her own children. She'd gone over and over her options with her accountant, and the most logical plan he could devise was to move to an area with a lower cost of living.

She had been familiar with this area of Idaho, in the Bitterroots. One of Derek's college buddies had grown up here, and told him the rock climbing was great. He and Derek had spent a lot of weekends climbing. Then when she and Derek met at climbing club and began dating, it was only natural she would join the weekend climbs. She loved the area, its ruggedness, the staggeringly beautiful scenery, the peacefulness. She and Derek had stayed at the B and B she now owned, so she had even been familiar with the place. The former owner, old Mrs. Weiskopf, had been struggling to take care of it, so when Cate decided to go into the inn business and made an offer, the old lady had jumped at it and now lived in Pocatello with her son and his wife.

The cost of living in Trail Stop was certainly lower, and from the sale of their condo Cate had made a tidy profit, which she promptly set aside in the boys' college funds. She was determined not to touch that money unless it was a matter of life or death – theirs. She lived completely on the proceeds from the B and B, which didn't allow much room for extras. But the morning food business gave her a little leeway, if nothing went wrong and she had no unexpected expenses, such as this morning's plumbing emergency. Thank God it had been so minor – and thank God Mr. Harris had refused payment.

There were pros and cons to the life she'd chosen for herself and the boys. One of the pros, the biggest one, was that the boys were with her all day, every day. Their young lives were as stable as she could possibly make them, with the result that they were happy and healthy, and that was enough to keep her there. Another pro was that she liked being her own boss. She liked what she was doing, liked cooking, liked the people in the community. They were just people, maybe more independent-minded than their metropolitan counterparts, but with quirks, strengths, and weaknesses like everyone else. The air was clear and clean, and the boys were perfectly safe playing outside.

One of the items in the con column was the area's remoteness. There was no cell phone service, no DSL for the computer. Television was a satellite system, which meant a heavily snow-blocked reception. There was no such thing as a quick trip to the grocery to pick up a few items; grocery shopping involved a one-hour trip each way, so she made the journey every other week and bought mountains of supplies. The boys' doctor was also an hour away. When they started school, she would have to make that drive twice a day, five days a week, which meant she'd have to hire help. Even collecting the mail took effort. There was a long line of rural mail boxes down at the main road, more than ten miles distant. Anyone heading that way was obliged to take the community's outgoing mail and bring back whatever had been delivered – which meant keeping a supply of rubber bands handy to keep each person's mail separated from the others – and then deliver it to the recipients.

The boys were short on playmates, too. There was one child near their age: Angelina Contreras, who was six and in first grade, which meant she was in school during the day. The few teenagers often stayed with friends or relatives in town during the school year, coming home only on the weekends, because of the distance involved.

Cate wasn't blind to the problems caused by her choices, but overall she thought she'd made the best decision for the boys. They were her prime consideration, the underlying reason for every action she took. The responsibility of raising them, caring for them, fell on her shoulders, and she was determined they wouldn't suffer.

Sometimes she felt so alone she thought she would break under the stress. On the surface everything was completely normal, even mundane. She lived in this small community where everyone knew everyone else; she raised her kids; she bought groceries and cooked and paid bills, dealt with all the normal homeowner worries. Each day was almost completely like the one that had gone before.

But since Derek's death, she had constantly felt as if she were walking on the brink of a cliff, and one misstep would send her over. She alone had the responsibility for the boys, for providing for them, not just now, but in the future, too. What if the money she'd set aside for their college education wasn't enough? What if the stock market tanked when they were eighteen, what if interest rates plummeted? The success or failure of the B and B was totally on her shoulders – *everything* was totally on her shoulders, every decision, every plan, every moment. If she'd had only herself to worry about, she wouldn't have been terrified; but she had the boys, and because of them she lived on the edge of panic.

They were only four, little more than babies, and utterly dependent on her. They had already lost their father, and even though they didn't remember him, they had certainly felt his absence in their lives, and would feel it more keenly as they grew older. How could she make up for that? Was she strong enough to guide them safely through the headstrong, hormonal teenage years? She loved them so much she wouldn't be able to bear it if anything happened to them, but what if the decisions she'd made were all wrong?

There were no guarantees. She knew that, knew that even if Derek were still alive, there would be problems; but the big difference would have been that she wouldn't be alone in facing them.

Because of the boys, when Derek died she'd forced herself to function, forced the grief into an inner prison where she could keep it controlled until she was alone at night. She had cried through the nights for weeks, months. But during the day she had focused on her babies, on their needs, and in a way, three years down the road, that was still how she got by. Time had dulled the sharp edge of grief, but it hadn't disappeared. She thought of Derek almost every day, when she saw his expressions chasing across the lively faces of his sons. A picture of them together was on top of her dresser. The boys would look at it, and they knew that was their daddy.

She'd had seven great years with him, and his absence had torn a huge hole in her life, her heart. The boys would never know him, and that was something she couldn't make up to them.

Her mother arrived just after four that afternoon. Cate had been watching for her, and when the black Jeep Liberty pulled into the parking area, she and the boys ran out to meet her.

'There are my boys!' Sheila Wells cried, jumping out of the Jeep and squatting down to hug the twins to her.

'Mimi, look,' Tucker said, showing her the toy fire engine he held.

23

'Look,' Tanner echoed, displaying a yellow dump truck. Both boys had picked out a prized possession for her to admire.

She didn't disappoint. 'Goodness, look at that. I haven't seen a better fire engine or dump truck in – well, I don't think I ever have.'

'Listen,' Tucker said, turning on the siren.

Tanner scowled. His dump truck didn't have a siren, but the back did lift up and the gate swung open, dumping whatever was in the truck bed. He bent down, scooped some gravel into the bed, then held it over Tucker's fire engine and dumped the gravel all over it.

'Hey!' Tucker yelped indignantly, shoving at his brother, and Cate stepped in before a fight could break out.

'Tanner, that wasn't a nice thing to do. Tucker, you shouldn't shove your brother. Turn that siren off. Both of you give me the toys. They'll be in my room; you can't play with them until tomorrow.'

Tucker opened his mouth to protest, saw her eyebrows lift in warning, and wisely said to Tanner, 'I'm sowwy I pushed you.'

Tanner eyed her, too, and like his brother decided that after the morning's punishment he shouldn't push his luck this afternoon. 'I'm sorry I dumped on you,' he said magnanimously.

Cate set her back teeth together to hold back a burst of laughter, and her gaze met her mother's. Sheila's eyes were round and she slapped a hand over her mouth; she knew very well there were times when a mother Must Not Laugh. A snort escaped, but she quickly mastered it as she stood and hugged her daughter. 'I can't wait to tell your father this one,' she said.

'I wish he could have come with you.'

'Maybe next time. If you can't make it home for Thanksgiving, he'll definitely come with me then.'

'What about Patrick and Andie?' Patrick was her younger brother, and Andie – Andria – was his wife. Sheila opened the back of the Jeep and they began hauling out luggage.

'I've already told them we might be here for Thanksgiving. If we're welcome, of course. If your guest rooms are booked, there goes that plan.'

'I have two reservations for that weekend, but that still leaves three bedrooms, so there's no problem. I'd love it if Patrick and Andie could come, too.'

'Her mother would throw a fit if Andie came here instead of having Thanksgiving at her house,' Sheila said caustically. She liked her daughter-in-law a lot, but Andie's mother was another story.

'We want to help,' Tucker said, tugging at a suitcase.

Since the suitcase outweighed him, Cate pulled out a carry-on bag, which was surprisingly heavy. 'Here, you two take this bag. It's heavy, so be careful.'

'We can handle it,' he said, and they assumed expressions of determination as they each took a handle and grunted as they lifted the bag.

'Look how strong you are,' her mom said, and their little chests puffed out.

'Men,' Cate muttered under her breath. 'They're so easy.'

'When they're not being difficult,' Sheila added.

As they climbed the two steps to the porch, Cate looked around. Mr. Layton still hadn't returned. She didn't want to charge an extra night to his credit card; since she had no other guest coming in until tomorrow, he wasn't causing any problem by not checking out at eleven, but she was annoyed. What if he returned after she locked up for the night? She didn't give keys to her guests, so either he'd have to wake her – and maybe the boys, as well as her mother – or he could damn well climb back in the window the way he'd climbed out. Except she'd closed the window and locked it, so that wasn't possible. If he did disturb them after they'd gone to bed, she thought, she would definitely charge an extra night to his credit card. Besides, where else would he stay?

'What's wrong?' Sheila asked, noticing her expression.

'A guest left this morning and hasn't come back to check out.' She lowered her voice so the boys wouldn't hear her and get ideas. 'He climbed out the window.'

'Running out on his bill?'

'I have his credit card number, so he can't. And he left his things here.'

'That *is* weird. And he hasn't called? Not that he could, since cell phones won't work out here.'

'There are telephones,' Cate said wearily. 'And, no, he hasn't called.'

'If he hasn't gotten in touch by tomorrow,' Sheila said as she followed the boys inside, 'pack up his stuff and sell it on eBay.'

Now, there was a thought, though she should probably give him more than one day to claim his belongings.

Guests had made strange requests before, but this was the first one to walk off – well, drive off – and leave everything behind. She felt vaguely uneasy, and wondered if maybe she should alert the state police. What if he'd had an accident somewhere, driven off the road? But she didn't know where he could possibly have gone, and even though there was only one way out, there was an intersection about twenty miles away and he could have gone in any direction. Moreover, he'd climbed out the window, as if he were sneaking out. His absence might be deliberate, and there might be nothing wrong with him at all.

She had his telephone number on the form he'd filled out when he checked in. If he hadn't returned by tomorrow, she'd call it. And when this was straightened out, she'd make it plain to him he wouldn't be staying at her place again. The mysterious – or nutty – Mr. Layton was too much trouble.

Chapter Three

Cate got up at five am to begin preparations for the day. The first thing she did was look out her side window into the parking area below, to see if Mr. Layton had returned during the night and was perhaps sleeping in his car, since she hadn't been awakened by any pounding on the front door. The only vehicles there were her red Ford Explorer and her mother's rental, which meant Mr. Layton was still a no-show. Where on earth was that blasted man? The least he could have done was to call and tell her . . . something: when he'd be back or, failing that, what to do with his stuff.

She was so annoyed she decided she would pack up his things and charge him a second night's stay for her trouble. It wasn't as if she had a lot of free time on her hands today – or any other day, come to that.

But first she had to start the coffee and get ready for the morning influx of customers. The big house was silent except for the ticking of the grandfather clock in the hallway, and though she had a lot to do, she treasured the peacefulness of these early hours when she was the only one awake and she could be alone. Only this early did she have the opportunity to think without the constant interruptions of children and customers; she could talk to herself if she wanted or listen to music while she worked. Sherry would arrive shortly before seven, and at almost seven thirty on the dot the twins would come galloping downstairs, as hungry as bears emerging from hibernation, but for these two hours she could sneak in a little time for Cate the woman. She even got up a little earlier than she really needed to so she wouldn't be rushed and could have an extra few minutes to savor.

As sometimes happened, she found herself wondering if Derek

would have approved of her decision to move to Trail Stop.

He had really liked this area, but as a visitor, not an inhabitant. And they both had adored this B and B when they'd stayed here. The memories of the good times they'd had – going on muscle-burning, treacherous climbs during the day, then coming back here both exhausted and exhilarated and falling into the soft bed, only to discover they weren't *that* exhausted after all – had definitely influenced her when she'd been looking for someplace less expensive than Seattle to live.

She felt close to Derek here. Here, they'd known only happiness. And while she had also been happy with him in Seattle, that was where he had died and it held a host of bleak associations with those last terrible days. Sometimes, when she still lived there, the memories would overwhelm her and she would feel as if she were living the nightmare all over again.

This street was the one she had driven down on the way to the hospital. *There* was where she had stopped to pick up his dry cleaning, never dreaming she was picking up the suit he would be buried in. *Here* was where she'd bought the dress she'd worn to the funeral, the dress she had thrown in the trash as soon as she'd removed it, sobbing and cursing and trying to tear the hateful garment from neck to hem. Their bed was where he'd lain, burning with fever, before he became so sick he agreed to let her take him to the ER – and by then it was too late. After he died, she had never slept in that bed again.

The memories, as much as sheer economics, had driven her from Seattle. She missed the city, missed the cultural entertainments, the bustle and character, the Puget Sound and the ships. Her family was there, and her friends. But by the time she was able to go back the first time for a visit, she had spent so much time here in Trail Stop, working on the house, getting herself and the boys settled, trying to improve business by every means she could think of, that she had somehow become more of *here* than of *there*. She was now a visitor to her home city, and home was ... here.

To the boys, of course, this had always been home. They'd been so young when she moved that they had no memories of living anywhere else. When they were older and the B and B was – please, God! – more successful, she intended to take them to visit her parents more often instead of the other way around. While in Seattle she could take them to concerts, to ball games, to plays and museums, and round out their experiences so they knew there was more to life than this little end-of-the-road community.

She didn't dismiss the good aspects of living here. In a place so small that everyone knew everyone else, the boys could safely play outside while she kept an eye on them from the window. Everyone knew her and the boys – knew where they belonged, and wouldn't hesitate to bring them home if they were seen wandering too far from the house. Their days consisted of one chore – putting away their toys at the end of the day – and hours and hours of playing, finishing up with story time and brief, repetitive lessons on their letters, numbers, and colors and the few short words they could read. Baths at seven thirty, bedtime at eight, and when she tucked the covers around them, she saw little boys who were both tired and contented, and utterly secure. She had worked hard to give them that security and was happy that, right now, they had everything they needed.

The other big plus of living here was the beauty that surrounded her. The landscape was majestic and awe-inspiring, and almost unbelievably rugged. Trail Stop was, literally, the end of the trail. If you went any farther, you went on foot – and not easily.

Trail Stop existed on a little spit of land that rose from the sloping valley floor like an anvil. To the right rushed the river, wide and icy and treacherous, with sharp, jagged rocks jutting above the spray. Even white-water rafters didn't try the rapids here; they started their adventures about fifteen miles downriver. On both sides rose the Bitterroot mountains and the vertical expanses of rock that she and Derek had climbed, or attempted to climb and abandoned as too difficult for their level of expertise.

Trail Stop was basically in a box, with one gravel road linking it to the rest of the world. The peculiar geography protected them from snowslides, but sometimes during the winter she would hear the roar of snow collapsing and rushing down the steep slopes, and she would shiver in reaction. Life here was complicated, but the inconveniences and lack of cultural opportunities were offset by the breathtaking natural beauty surrounding them. She missed being close to her family, but her money went much further here. Maybe she hadn't made the best possible decision, but overall she was satisfied with her choice.

Her mother came yawning into the kitchen and, without a word, went to the cabinet to retrieve a cup then back out into the dining room to get some coffee. Cate glanced at the clock and sighed. Five forty-five; her two hours of solitude had been cut short this morning, but the payoff was she'd get to spend some time with her mother without the boys clamoring for their Mimi's attention. Here, too, there was balance. She missed her mother, wished they could see each other more often.

Her face practically buried in the coffee cup, Sheila reentered the kitchen and, with a sigh, sat down at the table. She wasn't a morning person, so Cate suspected she had set the alarm in order to have some mother-daughter time before the twins got up.

'What kind of muffins today?' Sheila finally asked in a hoarse tone.

'Apple butter,' Cate said, smiling. 'I found the recipe online.'

'Bet you didn't find the apple butter at that dinky little store across the road.'

'No, I ordered it online from a place in Sevierville, Tennessee.' Cate ignored the dig because, first of all, it was true, and second, she knew that even if she'd moved to New York City, her mother would have found something wrong there, too, because her core problem was that she wanted her daughter and grandchildren nearby.

'Tanner's talking more,' Sheila observed a moment later, pushing her blond hair out of her face. She was a very pretty woman, and Cate had often wished she'd inherited her mother's looks instead of the mishmash of features she sported.

'When he wants. I've almost decided he hangs back so Tucker can be the one who gets in trouble.' Grinning, she related the tale of Mr. Harris's tools, and how Tanner had somehow figured out the basics of simple math so he knew he had only eight minutes left in the naughty chair.

Her mother laughed, but her expression was full of pride. 'I've read that Einstein didn't talk until he was six, or something like that. Maybe I'm wrong on the age.'

'I don't think he's the next Einstein.' Cate would settle for healthy and happy. She had no ambitions for her sons; standards, yes, but not ambitions.

'You never can tell.' Sheila yawned. 'My God, I couldn't face getting up this early every day. It's barbaric. Anyway, you can't tell how a child will turn out. You were a total tomboy, always playing softball and climbing trees, plus you were in that climbing club, and now look at you: your entire career is domestic. You clean, you cook, you waitress.'

'I run a business,' Cate corrected. 'And I like cooking. I'm good at it.' Cooking was, for the most part, a pleasure. Nor did she mind waiting tables for her customers, because the one-on-one contact helped bring them back. On the other hand, she hated cleaning, and had to force herself to do it every day.

'No argument there.' Sheila hesitated. 'You didn't cook much when Derek was alive.'

'No. We split it about evenly, plus we'd order in. And we ate out a lot, at least before the boys were born.' Carefully she poured milk into a large measuring cup, bending down to eye the level markers. 'But after he died, I spent every night at home with them and I got bored with the fast food I'd pick up, so I bought some recipe books and started cooking.' It was difficult to remember that that was only three years ago; the processes of measuring and mixing were so second nature now she felt as if she'd been cooking forever. The early experiments, when she had tried all sorts of exotic dishes, had also been a way to occupy her mind. She had also thrown out a lot of those efforts, judging them inedible.

'When your dad and I first married and you kids were little, I used to cook every night. We didn't have the money to eat out; a burger from a fast-food joint was a luxury. But I don't do it much now, and I don't miss it.'

Cate eyed her mother. 'But you still make those huge meals for Thanksgiving and Christmas, and you always baked our birthday cakes.'

Sheila shrugged. 'Tradition, family; you know the drill. I love everyone getting together, but to be honest, I'd just as soon skip the huge meals.'

'Then why don't I do the cooking for our get-togethers? I like it, and you and Dad can play with the boys and keep them occupied.'

Sheila's eyes lit up. 'Are you sure you wouldn't mind?'

'Mind?' Cate gave her a look that questioned her sanity. 'I'm getting the best end of the deal. They find new ways every day to get into trouble.'

'They're just being boys. You were adventurous, but Patrick's first ten years came close to turning my hair white – like the time he set off that 'bomb' in his room.'

Cate laughed. Patrick had decided firecrackers weren't loud enough, or powerful enough, so one Fourth of July he somehow collected over a hundred of them. With a knife filched from the kitchen he had carefully split open each firecracker and dumped the gunpowder contents onto a paper towel. When he had all the gunpowder in a pile, he asked for an empty tin can, which, thinking he intended to make a can-and-string 'telephone,' Sheila had cheerfully provided.

He had read about the old muzzle-loading rifles, so he figured his bomb would follow the same premise, except he hadn't been exactly certain what went where. He'd packed the tin can with toilet paper, tiny gravel, and the gunpowder, then twisted a length of thread together and soaked it with rubbing alcohol to make his fuse. To keep the floor from burning, he set his 'bomb' on a cookie sheet – and as a finishing touch, he took his old fishbowl and turned it upside down over the can, with one side of the bowl propped up just a little bit so the thread could run under the rim and up to the can. His thinking had been that the bowl would contain everything and he'd get the noise and flash without having to clean up a mess.

Not.

The one good thing Patrick had done was to take cover behind his bed after lighting the fuse.

With a loud bang the fishbowl shattered, sending glass and gravel flying around the room. The wad of toilet paper, having caught on fire, disintegrated into small flaming pieces that floated down to cover the bed, the carpet, even getting inside the open door of Patrick's closet. When his parents burst through the door, Patrick was busily stamping out sparks on the carpet and trying to put out the nice little flame spreading on his bedspread by spitting on it.

It hadn't been funny at the time, but now Cate and Sheila looked at each other and burst into laughter.

'I'm afraid that's what I have to look forward to,' Cate said, torn between amusement and horror. 'Times two.'

'Maybe not,' Sheila said, a trifle dubiously. 'If there's any justice in the world, though, Patrick will have four kids who are just like him. My dearest wish is that he'll call me in the middle of the night because his kids have done something horrendous and he'll *sob* while he apologizes from the bottom of his heart.'

'But poor Andie will have to suffer, too.'

'Well, I do love Andie, but this is about *justice*. If she has to suffer, too, my conscience will hold up under the burden.'

Cate snorted with laughter as she sprayed the muffin pans with butter-flavored nonstick spray, and then began spooning batter into the cups. She adored her mother; she was strong-willed, a bit irascible, and she loved her family to distraction while letting her children get away with nothing. A line Cate fully intended to use on the twins when they were older was one she'd heard her mother shout at Patrick after listening to him whine for an hour because he had to mow the lawn: *Do you think I carried you for nine months and suffered through thirty-six hours of agonizing labor to bring you into this world so you could sit on your butt? Get out there and mow that lawn! That's what I had you for!*

Sheer genius.

After another hesitation, Sheila said, 'There's something I want to talk to you about, let you think on it while I'm here.'

That sounded ominous. Her mother *looked* ominous. Cate felt an automatic tightening in her stomach. 'Is something wrong, Mom? Is Dad sick? Are *you* sick? Oh, my God, you aren't getting divorced, are you?'

Sheila stared at her, eyes wide, then in tones of awe said, 'Good God, I've raised a pessimist.'

Cate's cheeks flushed. 'I'm not a pessimist, but the way you said it, as if something is wrong—'

'Nothing's wrong, I promise.' She took a sip of coffee. 'It's just that your dad and I would like to have the boys come home with me for a visit, since he hasn't seen them since Christmas. They're old enough now, don't you think?'

Played. Cate rolled her eyes. 'You did that on purpose.'

'Did what on purpose?'

'Made me think something terrible was wrong' – she held up her hand to halt her mother's protest – 'not by what you said but how you said it, and your expression. Then, by comparison to all the horrible things I thought, the idea of the boys going home with you would seem minor. Harmless. Mom, I know how you operate. I took notes, because I intend to use the same tactics on the boys.'

She took a breath. 'It wasn't necessary. I'm not categorically against the idea. I'm not crazy about it, either, but I'll think about it. How long did you have in mind?'

'Two weeks seems reasonable, considering how difficult the trip is.'

Let the negotiations begin. Cate recognized that ploy, too. Sheila probably wanted a week with the boys, and to make sure she got it, she was asking for twice that. It might teach her a lesson if Cate sweetly agreed to the two weeks. Fourteen days of unrelieved supervision of rowdy four-year-old twins could break even the strongest person.

'I'll think about it,' she said, refusing to be drawn into a discussion about the length of the visit when she hadn't yet agreed to let the boys go. If she didn't stay on her toes, Sheila would have her so tied up in the details that the boys would be in Seattle before Cate realized she hadn't said 'yes.'

'Your dad and I will pay for their plane tickets, of course,' Sheila continued persuasively.

'I'll think about it,' Cate repeated.

'You need a little break, yourself. Taking care of this place and those two little hooligans doesn't give you much time for yourself. You could get your hair cut, get a manicure, pedicure . . .'

'I'll think about it.'

Sheila huffed out a breath. 'We really need to iron out the details.'

'There'll be plenty of time for that later . . . *if* I decide they can go. You might as well give up, because I'm not committing myself until I think about it for more than the two minutes you've given me.' Just for a second, though, she thought longingly of the hair salon in Seattle she had used. It had been so long since she'd had her hair done that she no longer had a recognizable style. Today, her wavy brown hair was simply pulled back and secured by a large tortoiseshell clip at the back of her neck. Her fingernails were short and bare, because that was the most practical way to keep them given how much her hands were in dough, and she couldn't remember the last time she'd painted her toenails. Just about the only extra grooming she had time for these days was keeping her legs and underarms shaved, which she did because – well, just because. Besides, all it took was an an extra three minutes in the shower.

The boys were so excited about their Mimi visiting that they came thundering downstairs in their pajamas a full half hour before their usual time. Sherry had just arrived, three customers followed her in, and Cate was glad to hand the boys off to her mother to entertain and feed them their breakfast. Her own breakfast was one of the muffins, which she snatched a bite of whenever she could.

It was a beautiful day, the early September air crisp and clear, and it seemed as if almost every inhabitant of Trail Stop came in that morning. Even Neenah Dase, a former nun who, for reasons of her own, had left her order and now owned and operated the small feed store – which meant she was Mr. Harris's landlady, since he lived in the tiny apartment over the store – came in for a muffin. Neenah was a quiet, self-possessed woman in her mid-forties and one of Cate's favorite people in Trail Stop. They didn't often have a chance to chat, and this morning was no different, because they each had a business to run. With a wave and a cheerful hello, Neenah was out the door and gone.

What with one thing and another, it was after one o'clock before Cate had a chance to get upstairs. Her mother was still keeping the boys occupied so Cate could get things ready for the guests coming in that afternoon. Mr. Layton still had neither returned nor called, and she was now as much worried as she was annoyed. Had he had an accident? The gravel road could be treacherous if an inexperienced driver took one of the mountain curves too fast. He had been gone for over twenty-four hours without word.

She made a swift decision and went to her room, where she called the county sheriff's department and after a brief hold was transferred to an investigator. 'This is Cate Nightingale in Trail Stop. I own the bed-and-breakfast here, and one of my guests left yesterday morning and hasn't returned. All of his things are still here.'

'Do you know where he was going?' the county investigator asked.

'No.' She thought back to the morning before, when she'd seen him step back from the dining room door. 'He left sometime between eight and ten. I didn't talk to him. But he hasn't called and he was supposed to check out yesterday morning. I'm afraid he might have had an accident.'

The investigator took down Mr. Layton's name and description, and when he asked for the car's license plate number, Cate went downstairs to her office to pull the paperwork. The investigator, like her, thought Mr. Layton might have had an accident and said he would first check the local hospital and would get back to her later that afternoon.

She had to be satisfied with that. Going back upstairs, she went into Mr. Layton's room and looked around to see if he'd left any clue as to where he might have gone. The top of the dresser in room 3 was bare except for some small change scattered across the polished surface. A change of clothes was hanging in the closet, and the open suitcase on the luggage stand revealed underwear and socks, a small plastic shopping bag from Wal-Mart with the handles tied in a knot, a bottle of aspirin, and a silk tie rolled up. She wanted to look in the shopping bag, but was afraid the county investigator would disapprove. What if Mr. Layton had been the victim of a crime? Cate didn't want to leave her fingerprints on his things.

In the small attached bathroom, a disposable razor and a can of shaving cream lay on the edge of the sink, and a can of spray deodorant sat next to the cold-water handle. An open Dopp Kit sat on the back of the toilet, and inside it she could see a hairbrush, a tube of toothpaste, and a toothbrush holder, as well as a few loose Band-Aids.

There was nothing here of value that she could see, but people tended to cling to their things. If he'd left all this behind, surely he'd intended to return. On the other hand, he *had* climbed out the window, for all the world as if he'd been escaping instead of simply leaving.

Maybe that was it. Maybe he wasn't simply nuts. Maybe he'd escaped.

The question was: from what? Or whom?

Chapter Four

Yuell Faulkner considered himself, first and foremost, a businessman. He was in operation to make money, and since he gained clients by word of mouth, he couldn't afford screwups. His reputation on the street was that he got the job done ... whatever the 'job' was, efficiently and without fuss.

Some jobs he refused outright, for a variety of reasons. Number one on his list was that he didn't take any job that had a high probability of bringing the Feds swarming down on him. That meant for the most part he stayed away from politics, and he tried never to do anything that would make national news. The real trick was to do a newsworthy job but pull it off so slickly that it was passed off as an accident.

With that in mind, the first thing he did when receiving a job offer was research it thoroughly. Sometimes clients weren't entirely truthful when presenting an offer – fancy that. It wasn't as if he dealt with people of pristine character. So he always double-checked the information he'd been given, and then would decide whether or not to take the job. He tried to never let his ego enter into the decision, never let the adrenaline rush of finessing a difficult situation sway him. Yeah, he could take all the hot jobs and pit his brains and organizing skill against the odds, but the reason the casinos in Vegas didn't go bust playing the odds was that the long shot usually didn't win. He wasn't in business to gratify his ego; he was in business to make money.

He also wanted to stay alive.

When he walked into Salazar Bandini's office, he knew he'd have to take this job, no matter what it was, or he wouldn't be walking out.

He knew about Salazar Bandini, or as much as anyone did. Yuell knew that wasn't the man's real name, but where he'd come from before arriving on the Chicago street scene and adopting that name was up in the air. *Bandini* was an Italian name; *Salazar* wasn't. And the man sitting behind the desk looked maybe Slavic, maybe German. Hell, maybe even Russian, with those broad cheekbones and prominent brow ridges. Bandini had pale hair, of a thinness that allowed pink scalp to show through, and brown eyes as soulless as a shark's.

Bandini leaned back in his chair and didn't invite Yuell to sit down. 'You're very expensive,' he remarked. 'You think highly of yourself.'

There wasn't anything to be said to that, because it was true. And whatever Bandini wanted, he wanted it badly, or he wouldn't have summoned Yuell past the barricades, both human and electronic, that surrounded him. Based on that, Yuell had to assume his price wasn't too high; in fact, maybe he should increase his fees.

After a long minute in which Yuell waited for Bandini to tell him why his services were needed, and Bandini waited for Yuell to betray any hint of nerves – which wasn't going to happen – Bandini said, 'Sit.'

Instead, Yuell leaned over the desk, took a pen from the expensive set beside the phone, and looked for a piece of paper. The polished expanse was clear. He lifted his eyebrows at Bandini, and without expression, the other man opened a drawer and drew out a legal pad, which he pushed across to Yuell.

Yuell tore off a sheet of paper and pushed the pad back across to Bandini. On the single sheet Yuell wrote: *Has the room been swept for bugs?*

He hadn't yet said a word, hadn't been identified by name, but caution was a good thing. The FBI had to have at least tried to get a wire in here, as well as tap the phones. Someone might be camped in a room across the street with a supersensitive parabolic microphone aimed at the window. The lengths to which the Feds would have gone depended on how large Bandini loomed on their radar. If they'd heard even half of what was said on the street, then Bandini was the size of an aircraft carrier.

'This morning,' Bandini said, looking grimly amused. 'By myself.'

Which meant that even though Bandini had any number of

people in his employ who could have done the chore, he didn't trust any of them not to betray him.

Smart man.

Yuell returned the pen to its slot, folded the sheet of paper, and slipped it into his coat pocket, then sat down.

'You're a cautious man,' Bandini observed, his gaze like chips of frozen mud. 'Don't you trust me?'

That had to be a joke, Yuell thought. 'I don't even trust myself. Why would I trust you?'

Bandini laughed, a humorless grating sound. 'I think I like you.'

That was supposed to make his day? Yuell sat quietly, waiting for Bandini to look him over and get to the point.

No one looking at Yuell would have taken him for the janitor he was. He cleaned up messes, left things looking pristine. And he was very, very good at his job.

He was aided by his looks. He was very average: average height, average weight, unremarkable face, brown hair, brown eyes, indeterminate age. No one noticed him as he came and went, and even if someone did notice him, he or she would be hard put to give more than a vague description that would match millions of other men. Nothing about his appearance was threatening, so it was easy for him to get close to someone without ever being tagged.

He was, ostensibly, a private investigator – a very expensive one. The know-how came in handy when he was tracking someone. He even took regular PI jobs, which usually consisted of getting the goods on a cheating spouse, and which made him good with the IRS. He reported every penny of income that was paid by check. Luckily for him, the majority of the jobs he took were ones no one wanted a paper trail on, so he received cash. It took a bit of fancy laundry work to make the income usable, but the majority of it was stashed offshore in a healthy retirement account.

Yuell had five carefully chosen men working for him. Each one could think on his feet, wasn't given to mistakes, and wasn't hotheaded. He didn't want any cowboys fucking up the operation he'd spent years building. He'd hired the wrong type once, and had been forced to bury his mistake. Only a fool made the same mistake twice.

'I have need of your services,' Bandini finally said, opening a desk drawer again and extracting a snapshot, which he slid across the glossy expanse toward Yuell.

39

Yuell looked at the photograph without picking it up. The subject was dark-haired, eye color not discernible, possibly late-thirties. He was dressed in a conservative gray suit, getting into a gray late-model Camry. A briefcase was in his hand. The background was suburban: brick house, lawn, trees.

'He took something from me. I want it back.'

Yuell pulled at his ear and glanced at the window. Bandini grinned, showing eyeteeth as sharp as a wolf's. 'We're safe. The windows are acoustic. No sound gets in or out. Walls are the same.'

Come to think of it, there was no street noise. The only sound was that of their voices. No air-conditioning hum, no water rushing through pipes – nothing penetrated. Yuell relaxed, or at least stopped worrying about the FBI. He wasn't stupid enough to relax around Bandini.

'What's his name?'

'Jeffrey Layton. He's a CPA. *My* CPA.'

Ah, the book-cooker. 'Embezzlement?'

'Worse. He took my records. Then the little fucker called me and said he'd give them back when I deposited twenty million in his numbered account in Switzerland.'

Yuell whistled between his teeth. Jeffrey Layton, certified public accountant, had either balls the size of Texas or brains the size of a pea. He voted for the pea.

'And if you don't give him the money?'

'He downloaded them on his flash drive. He said he'd turn it over to the FBI if the money isn't in his account in fourteen days. Nice of him to give me time to get that much together, right?' Bandini paused. 'Two of those fourteen days are already gone.'

Bandini was right; this was way worse than just taking money. Money could be replaced, and getting Layton would be a matter of saving face, no more. But the downloaded files – and Bandini had to be talking about his true financial records, not the second set of books kept for the IRS – would not only give the FBI indisputable evidence on tax evasion, but would also give them a wealth of information on the people Bandini did business with. Not only would the IRS be on Bandini's ass, so would the people who would blame him for the whole mess.

Layton was a dead man. He might not have reached room temperature yet, but it was just a matter of time.

'Why did you wait two days?' Yuell asked.

'My people tried to find him. They failed.' His flat tone didn't bode well for the continued good health of the failures. 'Layton had already skipped town before he called. He made it to Boise, rented a car, and disappeared.'

'Idaho? He from there, or something?'

'No. Why Idaho? Who the hell knows. Maybe he likes potatoes. When my guys hit a dead end, I decided I needed a specialist. I asked around, and your name surfaced. Word is you're good.'

This was one time Yuell wished he hadn't so assiduously built his reputation. He could happily have spent the rest of his life not having a face-to-face with Salazar Bandini.

The way Yuell saw it, this was a lose-lose proposition. If he turned down the job, his body would turn up either in little pieces or not at all. But if he took it, Bandini would have to figure he downloaded the flash drive onto his own computer before turning it in; knowledge was power, no matter which world you lived in. Bandini wouldn't hesitate to backstab anyone, so he expected it from everyone. What to do in such a case? Kill the messenger. You can't blackmail someone if you're dead.

The thing was, Yuell hadn't built his rep by being stupid – or by being a coward. He met Bandini's cold, empty gaze. 'You'd have to figure anyone who found the flash drive would copy the files before giving it back to you, so it follows you'll kill whoever finds it. That being the case, why would I take the job?'

Bandini began his grating, humorless laugh. 'I really do like you, Faulkner. You *think*. Most assholes don't know how. I'm not worried about anyone copying the file. It's coded to wipe clean if anyone tries to access the file without the password. Layton had the password.' He leaned back in his chair. 'Any future files will have to be coded not to allow downloading, but you learn from experience, right?'

Yuell thought about that. Bandini might be telling the truth. He might not. Yuell would have to do some research on computer files to find out if it was possible to write a program that would erase itself from the drive if anyone tried to access it without the password. Maybe. Probably. Damn hackers and geeks could probably make a program sit up and bark if they wanted.

Or maybe the file would be emptied, but the info would still be on the drive somewhere. He'd been thinking about recruit-

41

ing a computer forensics expert, and now he wished he'd already taken on the expense. Too late now; he'd have to go with what he could find out on his own, and he wouldn't have enough time for a thorough investigation.

'Get that flash drive,' Bandini said, 'take care of Layton, and the twenty million is yours.'

Holy shit. Fuck. Yuell managed not to show any reaction, but he was as alarmed as he was enticed. Bandini could have offered half that – hell, one-tenth that – and he would have felt overpaid. For Bandini to offer twenty million, the flash drive had to hold some explosive stuff – probably more than just his financial records. And whatever it was, Yuell didn't want to know.

Or Bandini planned to kill him anyway, so it didn't matter how much he offered.

The thought niggled at him. He couldn't ignore it, but from a business standpoint it didn't make sense. If Bandini got the reputation for reneging on deals, he was gone. Fear could take you so far, but it didn't trump the bottom line. You start pissing on people's money, and they'll find a way to piss back.

But he was in it now, and he'd do the job.

'You got Layton's social security number?' he asked. 'Save me a little time if you do.'

Bandini smiled.

Chapter Five

Yuell called in his two best men, Hugh Toxtel and Kennon Goss, because he didn't want any mistakes on this job. He also sent another man, Armstrong, to Layton's house in the suburbs to look for information such as credit card bills that might have arrived since Layton had bolted. Hell, Layton might even have left stuff like that lying around. People did stupid shit every day, and Layton had already demonstrated he wasn't the most logical person in the galaxy.

While Yuell was waiting for the men to arrive, he ran several search programs on his computer, digging up every bit of information on Jeffrey Layton that he could find, which was a lot.

Most people would have a stroke if they knew how much of their personal information was out in cyberspace. From public records he got the dates of Layton's marriage and subsequent divorce, and he noted down the ex–Mrs. Layton's name for further investigation. If she hadn't remarried, it was possible Layton would run to her for help. Yuell also noted how much Layton's property taxes were, and some other details that were probably useless but which he wrote down anyway. You could never tell when something that looked trivial on the surface would turn out to be crucial.

Some of the programs he used weren't exactly legal, but he'd paid through the nose for them because they worked, allowing him to get into databases that were otherwise closed to him. Insurance companies, banks, Federal programs – if you could make the computers think you were a legitimate user, you could go anywhere in their systems. By logically starting with Illinois's largest health insurer, he discovered that Layton had high blood pressure for which he took medication, and that he also had a two-year-old prescription for Viagra – which he'd never had refilled or renewed, which meant he wasn't getting laid very often, if at all. Nor had he had the foresight to refill his hypertension medication before absconding with Bandini's files. Running for your life was bound to be stressful; the fucker could stroke out if he wasn't careful.

Exiting from the insurer's system, Yuell logged in to the state system and soon netted Layton's driver's license number. Going into the social security system took a bit more finesse, because he had to piggyback on another, legitimate user, but he persisted until he had it because the payoff was worth the risk. The social was the magic key to a person's life and information; with it, Layton's entire life was his.

Armstrong called on his cell from Layton's house. That was one of the first things Yuell told his guys: Never use the phone in someone else's place. That way no cop could hit 'redial' and find out the last number called. That way no information connecting you to the place turned up in the phone company's records. Yuell's rule was ironclad: Use your own cell. As an extra precaution, they all used disposable cells. If for any reason they thought the number had been compromised, they simply bought another phone.

'Jackpot,' Armstrong said. 'This fucker kept everything.'

Yuell had hoped that Layton, being an accountant, would. 'What do you have?'

'Practically his whole life. He kept the important shit, like his notarized birth certificate, his social security card, his credit card accounts, in a wall safe.'

That was why he'd sent Armstrong, on the chance Layton might be cautious enough to have some kind of safe; the small, commercial safes were child's play to Armstrong, and most custom jobs merely slowed him down. 'I already have the social. Give me his credit card numbers, then put everything back and leave it the way you found it.'

Armstrong began reading off the various credit cards, their numbers and security codes. Layton had a ton of cards, the hallmark of someone who was likely to spend more than he could afford. Maybe that was why he was taking the desperate chance of blackmailing Bandini, but Yuell didn't really care *why*. The dumb fuck had sucked him into Bandini's orbit, and now Yuell had to do the job or go into hiding himself.

For a minute he thought of doing just that; telling his men to scatter, taking his money, and disappearing, maybe in the Far East, for a few years. But Bandini's arms were long and his well-earned reputation was brutal. Yuell knew he'd spend the rest of his life looking over his shoulder, waiting for the shot into the back of his head or the knife slicing into his kidney, and Layton's life wasn't worth it to him. Layton was a dead man, one way or the other. If Yuell didn't do the job, someone else would.

He set to work with the list of card numbers. Layton had two American Express cards, three Visas, a Discover, and two MasterCards. Yuell began methodically piggybacking into the credit card databases so he wouldn't set off any alarms, looking for any new charges. On the second Visa account he found a hit: a charge at a bed-and-breakfast in Trail Stop, Idaho, for the day before.

Bingo.

Just how stupid was this guy? He should have paid cash, stayed under the radar and given himself some time to hide his tracks. The only reason to use a credit card was if he was running critically low on cash, which again was stupid because who the hell would start something like this without a sizable roll of cash at hand?

Yuell sat back, thinking hard. Maybe the credit card charge was a feint. Maybe Layton had booked the room, then neither called to cancel nor showed up to claim his reservation; most places charged a night's stay for holding the room, whether you showed up or not. Maybe Layton was acting stupid but thinking smart.

He noted the name of the bed-and-breakfast, and pulled up the telephone number. Checking whether or not Layton had showed up was easy enough. He picked up his own cell phone.

A woman answered on the third ring. 'Nightingale's Bed and Breakfast,' she said pleasantly. Yuell liked her voice, which was melodic and cheerful.

He thought fast; she might not give out information on a guest to just anyone. 'This is National Car Rental,' he said. 'A customer hasn't returned his car on schedule, and he left this as a contact number. His name is Jeffrey Layton. Is he there?'

'I'm afraid not,' she said in a regretful tone.

'Has he been there?'

'Yes, he was, but – I'm sorry, but I think something may have happened to him.'

Yuell blinked. That wasn't what he'd expected to hear. 'What do you mean, something happened to him?'

'I'm not certain. He left yesterday, and never returned. All his things are still here, but – I've called the sheriff's department and reported him missing. I'm afraid he might have had an accident.'

'I hope not,' Yuell said, though it would be very convenient for Yuell if the man had driven off a mountain and killed himself, taking the flash drive with him. That would greatly simplify matters: he'd get paid and Layton would be gone. 'Did he tell you where he was going?'

'No, I didn't get to speak to him.'

'Well, this is bad news. I hope he's okay, but – I'll have to notify our insurance company.'

'Yes, of course,' she said.

'What will you do with his things? Has the sheriff's department notified his next of kin?'

'Mr. Layton isn't officially missing yet. If he doesn't turn up soon, I assume someone will find his family and I'll send his things to them. Until then, I suppose I'll just keep them.' She didn't sound happy about the prospect.

'Maybe someone will take them off your hands. Thank you for your help.' Yuell hung up, smiling; he couldn't have been happier to find that Layton had left his luggage behind, and that the woman still had everything. His mind was racing. Would Layton carry the flash drive around with him? The thing could be anywhere. Some people put them on their key chains, so the little gadgets wouldn't get lost. Or Layton could have stashed it somewhere, maybe in a safe-deposit box in his bank, in which case it would be out of Yuell's hands. On the other hand, maybe he'd simply put it in his suitcase.

If he was lucky, Yuell thought, the flash drive was at the B and B, just waiting for his men to go through Layton's things and find it. Whether it was there or not, he felt good. Layton was probably dead, in circumstances that were legitimately accidental. So long as he found the flash drive, he'd get paid. It didn't matter if Layton was dead or alive.

Hugh Toxtel was the first to arrive. He was in his early forties, seasoned and patient, methodical. He would go anywhere the job took him, without comment or fuss. Like Yuell, he was of average height and had dark hair, but his features were sharper. He was, in fact, the first man Yuell had hired, a decision that neither man had ever regretted.

'I'm pulling you off the Silvers job, and sending you and Goss to Idaho.'

'What's in Idaho?' Hugh asked, taking a seat and hitching up his sharply creased trouser legs. He usually dressed as if he held an executive position in a Fortune 500 company, and occupied a corner office, which was maybe his dream but was a far cry from reality.

'Salazar Bandini's runaway accountant,' Yuell replied.

Hugh winced. 'Stupid fucker. Took the money and ran, huh?'

'Not exactly. He copied all the financial files – the real ones – onto a flash drive and he's trying to blackmail Bandini. Bandini traced him to Idaho, lost track of him there, then called me.'

'Why Idaho?' Hugh asked. 'If I was dumb enough to try blackmailing Bandini, I'd at least leave the country. On the other hand, if you're dumb enough to screw Bandini, you're too fucking dumb to leave the country, right?'

'Or you're smart enough to lay a false trail.' Or you were desperate, Yuell suddenly thought. Layton was a CPA, for God's sake. He might be inexperienced, even naive, but he wasn't stupid. It wouldn't do to underestimate him. He could have bought a change of clothes and an extra bag and left it at the bed-and-breakfast as a diversion, while he hightailed it somewhere else. Even knowing that the things Layton had left behind could be just time-killing bait, Yuell would still have to send his men to check them out and search for the flash drive.

'You think that's what he's done?' Hugh asked.

Yuell shrugged. 'I don't know. It's possible. I want you to be on your toes tomorrow; if even one tiny thing looks unusual, I want to know about it. The clothes that were left behind, see if they're new. Ditto the bag.' He handed over the file of information he'd spent the last couple of hours compiling. 'This is everything I've got on the guy.'

Hugh spent a long time looking at the photo Bandini had provided, committing Layton's face to memory. Then he read over Layton's background, education, everything Yuell had been able to find above and beyond the dryness of numbers. Watching his face, Yuell saw Hugh come to the same conclusion he himself had reached. 'In over his head,' Hugh finally said, 'but not stupid.'

'That's what I think. He charged a room at a bed-and-breakfast in Trail Stop, Idaho; now, you have to figure he knows he can be traced by anything he charges on a credit card, right? So why did he do it?'

Before Hugh could answer, Kennon Goss arrived. There was a cold, unemotional, completely ruthless streak in Goss, though he usually hid it well; he was like a bulldog in accomplishing his assignment. Yuell used Goss when he needed someone to get close to a woman; he was blond and handsome, and something about him caused women to blindly respond to him. Because his looks also made him memorable, Goss had to be doubly alert, doubly agile in eluding suspicion. He made no bones, though, about preferring to have all modern conveniences available for his use. To him, a hotel was a dump if it didn't have Ethernet connections, twenty-four-hour room service, and a chocolate on his pillow every night.

Yuell brought Goss up to speed on Jeffrey Layton. Goss bent forward and buried his head in his hands. 'Podunk, Idaho,' he groaned. 'It'll take us two days to get there. We'll have to take a wagon train from Seattle.'

Yuell fought a grin. He'd love to be along for this one, just to watch Goss handle Mother Nature. 'You can get closer than Seattle. There are airstrips all over Idaho. You'll have to take a prop job from Boise, probably, but the drive once you're on the ground shouldn't be too bad. I'll arrange something with four-wheel drive for you.'

There was a muffled groan, and Goss pleaded, 'Not a pickup truck. I beg you.'

'I'll see what I can do.'

While he listened to Yuell delineate the situation and possibilities, Kennon Goss felt satisfaction begin to well as other possibilities occurred to him.

He hated Yuell Faulkner with every cell in his body, yet for more than ten years he had worked with and for the man, pushing his hatred aside so he could function while he looked and waited for the perfect opportunity. While he waited, he had in many ways become like the man he so hated, an irony that hadn't escaped him. Over the years his own emotions had withered, and now he was just as cold and unfeeling, capable of snuffing out a human life with no more thought than he would give to stepping on a cockroach.

He'd known it would be like this, known the price he would pay, but his hatred was so strong he'd considered the cost well worth the result. Nothing had mattered except getting close to Yuell, and biding his time.

Sixteen years ago, Yuell Faulkner had killed Goss's father. Goss was under no illusions now about the type of man his father had been; he'd been a hired killer, just like Faulkner, just like Goss himself. But there had been something electric about him, something bigger than life. A complicated man, his father; on the one hand he had been a loving husband, a stern but just parent – while on the other, he killed people. In some way his father had separated that in his mind and life, a way that Goss himself hadn't been able to manage.

His father had worked for Faulkner for a little over three years. All Goss had been able to find out, and that only after he himself had connected with Faulkner and joined his stable of killers, was that Faulkner had decided Goss's father was a weak link, somehow – so he had executed him. What had triggered the action was something Faulkner kept to himself.

To Yuell Faulkner, it had been a business decision. To Goss, it had been the destruction of his life. His mother had been devastated by her husband's murder; on the day Goss returned to his college classes, a week after the funeral, she swallowed a bottle of pills. Goss had found her body when he got home that afternoon.

Something in him, something human, had died when he stood in the kitchen doorway and saw his mother's body on the floor. Coming so brutally close on the heels of his father's murder, losing her, too, had pushed him to the wall.

He'd been nineteen, too old to go into the foster system. He dropped out of college, walked away from the suburban house that he never wanted to reenter, and wandered. He supposed the house had long since been sold for back taxes. He didn't care, had never gone back, had never driven by out of curiosity to see if someone else lived there now or if it had been torn down to make room for a service station or something.

After about a year, the idea of revenge, which had bubbled on the edge of his consciousness since his father's murder, began to firm and take shape. Until then he'd been too numb to plan, to have a direction, but now his life once again had a purpose – and that purpose was death. Yuell Faulkner's death, to be precise – though for a long time he hadn't had a name for his father's killer – and if it meant his own death, too, Goss didn't worry about that.

First, though, he'd had to reinvent himself. The boy he'd been, Ryan Ferris, had to die. Figuring out how to accomplish that was easy. He looked for a street kid, an addict, roughly his height and age, and stalked him; when he saw his chance, he jumped the guy from behind and knocked him out, then beat the hell out of his face before killing him. He put his own identification on the body, dumped it in a neighborhood where the corpse wasn't likely to be robbed, and took off for another part of the country.

He knew, with that first killing, that he'd crossed a line he would never be able to step back over. He was on his way to becoming what he hated.

Send a thief to catch a thief. To deal with death, he had to become death himself.

Building his new identity took time and money. He didn't immediately return to Chicago and try to find his father's killer. He established the new self, Kennon Goss, with multiple layers of certification. He ruthlessly pushed aside his own identity and became Kennon Goss, not only to others but to himself.

By the time he returned to Chicago, not even the FBI could have proven he was anyone other than who he said he was.

Finding out who had been behind a murder over five years old hadn't been easy. No one had fingered Yuell. Finding out his father had been a hired killer had been yet another shock to a psyche already battered beyond recovery, but it gave him a direction. From there, he was able to find out that his father had worked for a man named Faulkner, and it had seemed to Goss that maybe the best way to find out what his father had been involved in would be from the inside of Faulkner's organization.

He'd managed to bring himself to Faulkner's attention, because he was too streetwise to just walk in and ask for a job. Let Faulkner approach him.

Once on the inside, Goss had done his job and taken care not to screw up. Over time he had earned trust, not just from Faulkner but from the other men who worked for him. It was Hugh Toxtel, who had worked for Faulkner the longest, who had given him the piece of information he wanted. It had been more in the way of some friendly advice: *Don't let a target get to you. Get in, do the job, get out. Don't listen to some sob story.* One guy, Ferris, had let someone soft-soap him and hadn't done the job, and Faulkner took him out because he'd let his emotions get the best of him and, by letting the target live, established a trail that led back to Faulkner's company. *Not only that, not doing the job was bad for business.*

So Ferris had been disposed of, and Faulkner himself had finished the job Ferris had muffed.

Yuell Faulkner had killed Goss's father. He could even see that it had been a good business decision, which in no way changed Goss's mind about anything.

Faulkner was going to die, but Goss was looking for the perfect opportunity. He could have walked into the office and fired a nine millimeter into Faulkner's brain a hundred times, but he didn't want it to be that clean, that fast. He wanted it messy, wanted Faulkner to suffer, wanted him to squirm.

This situation with Salazar Bandini might be just what he'd waited for all these years. Bandini's viciousness was exceeded only by his vindictiveness. If Goss could somehow turn Bandini on Faulkner . . .

He'd have to think about the possibilities, how he could manage it without getting caught in the riptide of Bandini's vengeance. Maybe something would occur to him during this trip to Nowhere, Idaho, looking for a runaway accountant who might or might not already be dead.

'Do we leave today?' Goss asked.

Chapter Six

Cate completely stripped the bed in number 3, removing even the blankets and mattress cover. She intended to wash everything. Mr. Layton might not be dead, but she suspected he was, and she thought it would be slightly ghoulish to remake the bed without washing all the bed linens, top to bottom. The next guest wouldn't know, but she would.

Her mother had taken the boys on a picnic, so the house was quiet for once. They were just a quarter of a mile away, at the picnic table Neenah Dase had installed under a big tree in her backyard, but to the boys they were on a grand adventure. Cate had watched from the window as they walked off down Trail Stop's one real road, her mother carrying a small basket loaded with peanut-butter-and-jelly sandwiches and lemonade, with the boys circling around her in a frenzy of excitement. For every step she took, they each took at least five, hopping and skipping and darting away to examine a bug, a rock, a leaf, then returning to their grandmother like satellites to a planet. Cate hoped they'd be nice and tired when they returned; since her mother's arrival they'd been in high gear, and she suspected her mother was as ready for a little quiet time as she herself was.

The phone call she'd received from National Car Rental made her feel both vaguely uneasy and vaguely depressed. The depression was because the call only verified that Mr. Layton was missing and now she felt bad that she'd been so annoyed when he didn't return on schedule. The uneasiness ... she couldn't pinpoint the cause of that. Maybe it was just this entire situation; she'd never before had a guest go missing, and she had a growing sense that whatever had happened to Mr. Layton, it wasn't good.

Because she felt as if she should, she called the sheriff's department again to report the call she'd received. She was put in touch with the same investigator, Seth Marbury. For all she knew, he was the county's *only* investigator.

'I know I'm being a bother,' she said apologetically, and explained about the phone call. 'He not only didn't come back yesterday, he didn't return his rental car. The rental agency called here asking to speak to him, since he didn't turn the car in. Have you found anything?'

'Nothing. He hasn't been reported in any accidents, and there aren't any unidentified victims. He hasn't been reported missing by any friends or family, either. You said he left his clothes behind? What else?'

'It's actually just one change of clothes. Some underwear and socks, disposable razor, some toiletries. And a plastic bag from Wal-Mart. I don't know what's in it.'

'It sounds as if he didn't leave anything important.'

'No, nothing looks important.'

'Mrs. Nightingale, I know you're worried, but no crime has been committed and there's no evidence that Mr. Layton's had an accident. Sometimes people just walk away, for no good reason. You have his credit card number, so he didn't run out on his bill, right?'

'That's right.'

'He left under his own steam. He didn't bother to check out, and he left some unimportant things behind. We'll keep checking for an accident site along the most likely routes, but in all likelihood he just – left.'

She couldn't see Marbury, but Cate knew he'd shrugged. 'But what about his rental car?'

'That's between him and the rental agency. The car hasn't been reported stolen, so there's nothing we can do about that, either.'

She thanked him and hung up. There was no help there; as Marbury had pointed out, no crime had been committed. If Mr. Layton had family, either he'd been in touch with them or they hadn't expected to hear from him yet, so he wasn't officially missing. He had just vanished.

Maybe she *was* making too much of this. Maybe Mr. Layton was fine, and he simply hadn't bothered to come back for the few possessions he'd left here.

She thought back over the sequence of events. Yesterday morning he'd briefly come downstairs, but as soon as he realized the dining room was full, he'd stepped back from the door and returned to his room. Sometime between then and when she'd gone upstairs to check on the twins, he'd climbed out of his bedroom window and driven away.

At the time she'd thought he simply hadn't wanted to eat with strangers, but given his method of departure and the fact that he hadn't returned, she now had to wonder if perhaps he'd recognized someone in the dining room that he hadn't wanted to let know he was here. Yesterday morning had been unusually busy, but the only stranger she could remember was Joshua Creed's client – she couldn't remember his name. Had Mr. Layton known him? And if he had simply wanted to avoid the man – for which she couldn't blame him – why hadn't he just remained in his room until Creed and his client left?

This line of reasoning at least made her feel better, because looking at it that way made it seem far more likely Mr. Layton had done exactly as Marbury thought, and simply left without bothering to take his possessions with him. If he'd wanted to avoid what's-his-name bad enough to climb out a window and sneak away, then leaving his stuff behind probably hadn't bothered him at all.

But why hadn't he turned in his rental car, if not in Boise at least in some other town where National had an office? Cate wasn't normally a conspiracy theorist, but Trail Stop wasn't exactly the most-traveled-to place in the state; if someone Mr. Layton wanted to avoid had followed him here, that someone, logically, had found out he'd rented a car and where he was going. There were probably all sorts of rules against that kind of information being given out, but information was bought and sold every day, and a lot of those transactions were against the rules. So Mr. Layton had to know the car was a liability; if he wanted to continue avoiding whoever had followed him, surely he would want to get rid of it. Maybe he'd parked it somewhere and walked away, since that seemed to be his modus operandi, figuring he'd just deal with whatever extra charges were tacked onto his credit card bill –

Something the county investigator had said rang in her mind. She had already charged Layton's credit card, so he hadn't run out on the bill. The same circumstance applied to the rental agency; in fact, she didn't think you could rent a car without having a credit card. So why was the rental agency trying to track Mr. Layton down? Was that standard? She had no idea what their policy was, but a reasonable person would think they'd just keep applying charges against his credit card for at least a couple of days.

On impulse she checked Caller ID, and frowned when she read 'Unknown Name, Unknown Number.' That was inconvenient. And since when did a business block its number from showing? Not only that, the caller hadn't given her his name. Still, she thought she should pass along what Investigator Marbury had said.

She called Information, got National's number, then waited for the automatic connect. On the second ring a woman's voice said, 'National Car Rental, Melanie speaking. How may I help you?'

'Someone from your company called me a little while ago about one of my guests,' Cate said, 'Jeffrey Layton. Mr. Layton didn't return the car yesterday and this person was trying to track him down. I'm sorry, but the man who called didn't give me his name.'

'Someone from here called to ask about . . . What did you say his name was?'

'Layton. Jeffrey Layton.' Cate spelled it for her, even though the names seemed common enough.

'A *man* called you?'

'That's right.'

'I'm sorry, ma'am, but there are only women working here today. Are you certain he called from this location?'

'No, I'm not,' Cate admitted, wishing she'd thought to ask. 'The name and number were blocked on Caller ID, but I assumed the call would have come from the office at the Boise Airport.'

'The number was blocked? That's unusual. Let me call up the file on Mr. Layton.'

Cate heard the sound of computer keys being tapped. There was a short wait, then more tapping. The woman said, 'That's J-e-f-f-r-e-y L-a-y-t-o-n? Is there a middle initial?'

'No, no middle initial.' Cate was certain about that, because she had verified his identification before accepting his credit card. She'd commented on the lack of a middle name or initial, and Mr. Layton had smiled as he explained that he didn't *have* a middle name.

'What date was he supposed to have rented a vehicle from us? I

55

don't have anything under his name.'

'I don't really know,' Cate said slowly, taken aback by that information. 'I got the impression Mr. Layton had just arrived in Idaho, but I may be mistaken.'

'I'm sorry, but I'm not showing anything. He isn't in our system.'

'No, it's my fault. I must have misunderstood the name of the company,' Cate said, then thanked the woman and hung up. Cate had been polite because she hadn't misunderstood; she knew exactly what the caller had said – and he had obviously lied about being with National Car Rental. Even the twins could have figured out he'd just been trying to find Jeffrey Layton, who must be involved in something nasty and who really had driven away and left his possessions behind.

She was definitely curious about what was going on, but above that she was infinitely relieved that Mr. Layton was probably alive somewhere, and not rotting away at the bottom of a gorge. She felt okay about resurrecting her annoyance with him.

After tossing the dirty bed linens into the hallway, she vacuumed and dusted, cleaned the bathroom, and remade the bed with clean sheets and blankets. She then took the single change of clothing from the closet and neatly folded the garments before placing them in the suitcase Mr. Layton had left behind. The plastic Wal-Mart shopping bag rustled as she moved it aside to make room for the folded clothes, and she eyed it with more than a little curiosity.

'If you didn't want me to look in it, you shouldn't have left it behind,' she muttered to the absent Mr. Layton, seizing the bag and picking with her fingernails at the knots he'd tied in the handles. The knots loosened and she pulled the bag open, peering inside.

A TracFone was lying loose inside the bag. There was no receipt in the bag, so she didn't know if he'd bought the phone recently and just left it in the bag, or if he'd put it inside the bag to protect it, in case his suitcase got wet while being loaded on the plane. On the other hand, most people kept their cell phones with them, not in their suitcase.

For all she knew, he could have had the phone on him until he got here and realized there was no cell phone service, therefore no reason to carry the phone around, and put it in the bag rather than leave it lying around in the open. Cate, under ordinary circumstances, didn't go into her guests' rooms from the time they checked in until they checked out, though a few did request that she make the bed and clean the bathroom every day – but Mr. Layton wouldn't have had any reason to trust her, because he didn't know her.

Double-checking the closet, she found a pair of black wingtip shoes that she had overlooked before, so she put the shoes inside the plastic bag and added them to the suitcase. In the bathroom, she put all of the toiletries inside the leather Dopp Kit, zipped it, and tried to wedge it into the suitcase beside the shoes. The suitcase was a small one, though, and the kit simply wouldn't fit.

Mr. Layton must have had more than one suitcase, she thought, and left the other one in his car overnight. She had seen his luggage when he checked in, and he'd been carrying only this one bag. Since the possessions he'd left behind wouldn't fit inside the suitcase, that meant he'd gone back to the car and retrieved something from the other bag – either the Dopp Kit or the shoes. Following that line of thought, she realized, he hadn't left *all* his possessions behind, just left the ones that hadn't been important enough for him to make the effort to carry them with him. After all, he could have packed the suitcase and heaved it out the window, then retrieved it when he was on the ground. He hadn't taken the time, so she doubted he would ever bother to come back for his abandoned stuff.

Which brought up the question of just what she was supposed to do with it. How long should she store the suitcase? A month? A year? She intended to put it in the attic, so it wasn't as if the case would be in the way, but ever since Derek had died, she'd tormented herself with what-if scenarios. What if she didn't get rid of the suitcase and a few years down the road something happened to her? Whoever went through the things in the attic would find this suitcase full of men's clothing and the normal assumption would be that they'd belonged to Derek, and she'd kept them for sentimental reasons. The most logical thing then would be to keep the suitcase and its contents for the twins, and she didn't want her boys mistakenly treasuring items from some idiotic stranger who'd gotten himself in trouble and disappeared.

Just in case, she got a sheet of the stationery with the B and B's letterhead on it, which she put in all the rooms, and quickly wrote out Mr. Layton's name and the date, and the information that he'd left his belongings behind, then tucked the sheet inside the suitcase. If the worst happened and she got killed, this would explain things.

She hadn't used to be such a worrier, but that was before she'd become, in short order, a mother and then a widow. Bad things did happen. She had quit rock climbing the moment she'd learned she was pregnant, and though she'd been an even more avid climber than Derek, she hadn't considered returning to the sport, because she had the boys to consider now. What would happen to them if she suffered a bad fall and died? Oh, she knew that physically they'd be well-cared for; her family would see to that, as well as Derek's family, though they weren't as close to the boys as she wished. But what about the twins' emotional well-being? They would grow up feeling abandoned by their parents, and no amount of logic would offset that primitive response.

So she took what precautions she could, shied away from risky behavior, but she couldn't offset the hand of fate: accidents happened. And no way would she let her children think Jeffrey Layton's things had belonged to their father. Besides, Derek had had better taste in clothes.

Smiling at the thought, she hefted the suitcase in one hand and the Dopp Kit in the other and carried them to the hallway, then set them down. She went to her room to get the key to the attic stairwell.

Because she didn't want the boys going into the attic by themselves, she kept the door locked and the key in her makeup bag, which was in a drawer of the bathroom vanity. On the way into the bathroom she passed by her dresser, on which sat several framed photographs. She paused, suddenly heart-struck, staring at the freeze-frame moments of her life.

It happened once in a while; enough time had passed that she could usually walk by the dresser and not really even notice the photographs. When the boys came into her room on those rare days when she could sleep a little late, they would almost always ask questions about the photographs and she could answer with equanimity. But sometimes . . . sometimes it was as if a razor-sharp memory reached out of the past and squeezed her heart, and she would stop in her tracks, almost felled by the rush of grief.

She stared at the picture of him, and for a moment she could hear his voice again, the timbre of which she had almost forgotten. He'd bequeathed so much of himself to the boys: the blue, mischievous eyes, the dark hair, the easy grin. It was the grin that had gotten her, so cheerful and sexy – well, that and the lean, athletic body.

He'd been an advertising executive; she'd worked in a large bank. They were young and single and had enough money to do the things they wanted. After they'd gone on their climb together, they'd begun seeing each other in locations other than on a sheer rock face, and things had grown from there.

She moved on to a picture of them on their wedding day. They'd done the traditional ceremony; he'd worn a tux; she'd worn a romantic satin-and-lace gown. How young she'd looked, she thought, suddenly catching a glimpse of herself in the mirror and comparing the two images. Her shoulder-length brown hair had been in a sleek, sophisticated style; now it was merely long, and the style was a clip or ponytail. She'd worn makeup then; now she was lucky if she had time for a swipe of lip balm. Then she hadn't had a care in the world; now the constant strain of worry caused faint shadows under her eyes.

Her mouth hadn't changed; she still had a duck-mouth, with the upper lip fuller than the lower. Derek had thought her mouth was sexy, but she had obsessed about its shape all through her teenage years and she never quite believed him. Michelle Pfeiffer's duck-mouth was more subtle, and way more sexy. Cate's mouth had often caused her little brother, Patrick, to go into such prolonged fits of quacking that she had once thrown a lamp at him.

Her eyes were still brown, a lighter, more golden shade of brown than her hair, but ... brown. Unexciting brown. And her body was still the same shape it had always been, except during her pregnancy, when she'd actually had full breasts. She was lanky to the point of thinness, with the sort of build that made her look taller than her ordinary five-foot-five. The only curvy part on her body was her butt, which looked too prominent for the rest of her body. Her legs were muscular, her arms thin and sinewy. All in all, she was no bombshell; she was just an ordinary woman who had loved her husband very much and, at times like this, missed him so acutely his absence was like a knife in the heart.

The third photograph was of the four of them together: Derek, her, and their three-month-old babies. They had each held one of the twins, whose tiny faces were identical, and she and Derek had such wide, proud, sappy smiles as they looked down at their children that, looking at them all now, she wanted to both laugh and cry.

Oh, God, their time together had been so short.

Cate shook herself back to the present and blinked the tears from her eyes. She let herself cry only at night, when there was no one to notice. Her mother and the boys could return from their picnic at any time, and she didn't want them to catch her with her eyes red. Her mother would be worried, and the boys would cry if they thought Mommy had been crying.

She got the old, long key out of her dresser, slipped it into her jeans pocket, and retraced her steps down the hall to where she'd left the suitcase and Dopp Kit outside room 3. She turned on the hallway light, then picked up the suitcase and kit and took them all the way to the end of the hall, where the attic stairs were, plunking them down again.

The stairwell door opened outward, revealing three steps up to a landing; then the stairs made a right turn and ended at an awkward spot in the attic, so close to the slanted ceiling that she had to duck to take that last step. At least, the door was *supposed* to open outward. She inserted the key and turned it, and nothing happened. The lock was a little tricky, so she wasn't surprised. She pulled the key out a little and tried again, with no success. Muttering to herself about old locks, she pulled the key all the way out, then reinserted it a little at a time, trying repeatedly to turn it. The key had to hit the pins just right . . .

She thought she felt a tiny click, and triumphantly turned the key with a brisk motion of her wrist. There was a snap, and half the key came away in her hand. Which meant, obviously, that the other half was stuck in the lock.

'Son of a bitch!' she swore, then hastily looked around to make certain the twins weren't standing silently behind her. Not that there was much chance of them silently doing anything, but if they ever did, it would be when she was swearing. Seeing that she was safe, she added – for good measure – 'Damn it!'

Okay, the door needed a new lock anyway. And locks weren't hideously expensive, but still, there was always something that needed repairing or replacing. She also still needed to get that door open, so she could store this suitcase somewhere out of the way.

Swearing under her breath, she stomped downstairs and into the kitchen. She was just reaching for the phone to call the hardware store to locate Mr. Harris when she heard a car stop outside. Looking out the window, she saw – miracle of miracles – Mr. Harris himself, climbing out of his battered pickup.

She didn't know what had brought him here, but his timing couldn't have been better. She jerked open the kitchen door as he was coming up the steps, both relief and frustration evident in her voice as she said, 'Am I glad to see you!'

He stopped in his tracks, his cheeks already firing with color as he glanced back at his truck. 'Will I need my toolbox?'

'A key broke off in the attic door – and I need the door unlocked.'

He nodded and went back to the truck, reaching over the side of the bed and one-handing the heavy toolbox up and over. She had the fleeting thought that he must be stronger than he looked.

'I'm going into town tomorrow,' he said as he trudged up the steps. 'Thought I'd stop by and let you know, in case you need anything.'

'I have some mail that needs to go out,' she said.

He nodded as she stepped aside to let him enter. 'This way,' she said, preceding him into the hallway and up the stairs.

Even with the light on, the hallway was dim, because there were no windows at either end. The open bedroom doors let some daylight in, enough to see unless you had some specific task, such as manipulating a cantankerous old lock or retrieving a broken key from it. Mr. Harris opened his toolbox, took out a black flashlight, and handed it to her. 'Shine the light on the lock,' he muttered as he moved the suitcase out of the way and went down on one knee in front of the lock.

Cate turned on the flashlight, amazed at the powerful beam that shot out. The flashlight was surprisingly lightweight, with a rubberized coating. She turned it in her hand, looking for a brand name, but she didn't see one. She turned the beam on the door, directing it just below the knob.

Using needle-nose pliers, he retrieved the broken key, then took some kind of pick from the toolbox and inserted it into the lock.

'I didn't know you knew how to pick locks,' she said with amusement.

His hand froze for a moment, and she could almost hear him wondering if he needed to actually reply to her comment; then he made a 'hmm' noise in his throat and resumed manipulating the pick.

Cate moved so she was directly behind him and leaned closer, trying to see what he was doing. The bright light illuminated his hands, etching every raised vein, every powerful sinew. He had good hands, she noticed. They were callused, stained with grease, and his left thumbnail sported a black mark that looked as if he'd banged it with a hammer, but his nails were short and clean and his hands were lean and strong and well-shaped. She had a soft spot for strong hands; Derek's hands had been very strong, because of the rock climbing.

He grunted, withdrew the pick, and turned the doorknob, pulling the door open a few inches.

'Thank you so much,' she said with heartfelt gratitude. She indicated the suitcase he'd pushed to the side. 'That guy who left without taking his things still hasn't come back, so I have to store his suitcase for a while, in case he decides to come back for it.'

Mr. Harris glanced at the suitcase as he took the flashlight from her, turning it off and placing both it and the pick back in his toolbox. 'That's weird. What was he running from?'

'I think he wanted to avoid someone in the dining room.' Odd that the handyman had so swiftly picked up on something that hadn't immediately occurred to her. Initially, she'd just thought Layton was nuts. Maybe men were more naturally suspicious than women.

He grunted again, an acknowledgment of her comment. He dipped his head at the suitcase. 'Anything unusual in there?'

'No. He left it sitting open. I packed his clothes and shoes, and put his toiletries in the kit.'

He stood and nudged the toolbox to the side, opening the door wide, then bent and picked up the suitcase. 'Show me where you want to put it.'

'I can do that,' she protested.

'I know, but I'm already here.'

As she led the way up the steep staircase, Cate reflected that she'd probably heard him say more in the past ten minutes than she had in months, and it was certainly one of the few times she'd heard him utter an unsolicited comment. Usually he'd give a brief answer to a direct question, and that was it. Maybe he'd joined Toastmasters, or taken a loquacious pill.

The attic was hot and dusty, with that moldy smell abandoned possessions all seemed to have even when there wasn't any mold present. Light from three dormer windows made it a surprisingly sunny place, but the walls were unfinished and the floor was made of bare planks that creaked with every step.

'Over here,' she said, indicating a bare spot against the outer wall.

He put the suitcase and Dopp Kit down, then glanced around. He saw the climbing gear and paused. 'Whose is that?' he asked, pointing.

'Mine and my husband's.'

'You both climbed?'

'That's how we met, at a climbing club. I stopped climbing when I got pregnant.' But she hadn't gotten rid of their gear. It was all still there, neatly arranged and stowed: the climbing shoes, the harnesses and chalk bags, the belaying and rappelling devices, the helmets, the coils of rope. She'd made certain direct sunlight never reached the ropes, even though she knew she'd never go climbing again. It just wasn't in her to mistreat the equipment.

He hesitated, and she could see his face turning red again. Then he said, 'I've done a little climbing. More mountaineering type stuff, though.'

He'd actually volunteered information about himself! Maybe he had decided she was as nonthreatening as the boys, so she was safe to talk to. She should note this day on her calendar and circle it in red, because any day that shy Mr. Harris began talking about himself had to be special.

'I just did rocks,' she said, trying to keep the conversation going. How long would he keep talking? 'No mountaineering at all. Have you climbed any of the big ones?'

'It wasn't that type of mountaineering,' he mumbled, edging toward the top of the stairs, and she knew his unusual talkativeness was over. Just then, two stories below, she heard the sound of childish voices raised in an argument, and she knew her mother and the boys were home.

'Uh-oh. Sounds like trouble,' she said, bolting for the stairs.

She knew something was wrong just from the looks on their faces when she reached the bottom floor. All three looked angry. Her mother was holding the picnic basket, her mouth compressed, and she had the boys separated, with one on each side of her. The twins were red-faced with anger, and their clothes were dirty, as if they'd been rolling in the dirt.

'They've been fighting,' Sheila reported.

'Tannuh called me a bad name!' Tucker charged, his expression mulish.

Tanner glared at his brother. 'You pushed me. Down!' His outrage was evident. Tanner didn't like losing in any situation.

Cate held up her hand like a traffic cop, stopping both of them in the middle of continued explanation. Behind her, Mr. Harris came down the stairs, carrying his toolbox, and the boys began shifting in agitation; their hero was here, and they couldn't swarm him as they usually did.

'Mimi will tell me what happened,' Cate said.

'Tanner got the last piece of orange, and Tucker wanted it. Tanner wouldn't give it to him, so Tucker pushed him down. Tanner called Tucker a "damn idgit." Then they started rolling around and punching each other.' Sheila looked down at both of them, frowning. 'They knocked my lemonade over and it soaked my clothes.'

Now that she looked, Cate could see the dark, wet patches on Sheila's jeans. She crossed her arms and looked as stern as possible as she did her own frowning. 'Tucker—' she began.

'It wasn't my fault!' he burst out, clearly furious at being singled out first.

'You pushed Tanner first, didn't you?'

If anything, he now looked even more mutinous. His little face turned red, and he was all but jumping up and down. 'It was – it was Mimi's fault!'

Mimi! Cate echoed, thunderstruck. Her mother looked just as stunned by this turn of events.

'She shoulda watched me better!'

'Tucker Nightingale!' Cate roared, galvanized by his blame-shifting. 'You get upstairs and sit in the naughty chair right now! How dare you try to blame this on Mimi! I'm ashamed of the way you're acting. A good man never, never blames someone else for something he did himself!'

He shot a pleading look for understanding and backup at Mr. Harris. Cate wheeled and gave the handyman a gimlet stare, just in case he was thinking of saying anything in the least sympathetic. Mr. Harris blinked, then looked at Tucker and slowly shook his head. 'She's right,' he mumbled.

Tucker's little shoulders slumped and he began dragging himself up the stairs, each step as ponderous as a four-year-old could possibly make it. He began crying on the way up. At the top he paused and sobbed, 'How long?'

'*Long.*' Cate said. She wouldn't leave him up there any longer than half an hour, but that would seem like forever to someone with Tucker's energy. Besides, Tanner would have to spend some time in the naughty chair, too, for calling his brother a 'damn idgit.' Okay, this meant they both knew the word *damn,* and how to use it. Her children were swearing already.

She tucked her chin and scowled at Tanner. He sighed and sat down on the bottom stair, waiting his turn in the naughty chair. Nothing more had to be said.

Mr. Harris cleared his throat. 'I'll pick up a new lock tomorrow while I'm in town,' he said, and beat a path to the door.

Cate drew a deep breath and turned to her mother, who now seemed to be sucking really hard on her cheeks.

'Are you sure you want to take them for a visit?' Cate asked wearily.

Sheila, too, took a deep breath. 'I'll get back to you on that,' she said.

Chapter Seven

Because of the time change, Goss and Toxtel arrived in Boise early in the evening. Goss figured the plane tickets had cost a fortune, purchased at the last minute as they were, but that wasn't his problem. Rather than make the rest of the trip that night, which would have meant they'd have been driving the last leg on unfamiliar mountain roads when they were both tired, they booked into a hotel close to the airport.

In the morning they would procure weapons, then take a prop plane to an airstrip about fifty miles from their destination. The plane was a private hire, so they'd have no problems taking the weapons aboard. Faulkner had arranged for some model of four-wheel-drive vehicle to be waiting for them at the airstrip. They'd drive the rest of the way to Trail Stop, where he'd booked them a reservation at Nightingale's Bed and Breakfast. Staying in the place they'd be searching was only logical, because that gave them a reason to be there.

After they ate dinner in the hotel's restaurant, Toxtel went up to his room, while Goss decided to see something of Boise – specifically, something female. He caught a cab and hit a crowded singles bar, fending off a few women who didn't appeal to him before settling on a pretty, wholesome-looking brunette named Kami. He hated cutesy names like that, but time was short and it wasn't as if she were going to be in his life for any longer than it took for him to scratch his itch, then put on his clothes and leave.

They went to her condo, a cramped two-bedroom. He was always amazed when women he'd just met invited him to their homes. What were they thinking? He might be a rapist, a murderer. Okay, so he *was* a murderer, but only if he was paid.

The ordinary citizen was perfectly safe with him. But Kami didn't know that, and neither had any of those other women.

When they were lying exhausted and sweaty, side by side but no longer connected by even the pretense of emotion, he said, 'You should be more careful. You lucked out with me, but what if I'd been some nutcase who collected eyeballs, or something like that?'

She stretched, arching her back and pushing her breasts toward the ceiling. 'What if *I'm* the nutcase who collects eyeballs?'

'I'm serious.'

'So am I.'

Something in her tone made his eyes narrow. They stared at each other in the lamplight, her dark gaze going flat, and he let his own gaze show his cold emptiness. 'Then I guess we both lucked out,' he finally said.

'Yeah? How do you figure?'

'I warned you – and *you* warned *me*.' Meaning that she couldn't get the jump on him now, and if she valued her life she wouldn't try. So what if he was naked; so was she. She might have a knife stuck under the mattress – shades of *Basic Instinct* – but he was prepared to break her neck if he saw either of her hands start to inch under the pillow or toward the side of the bed.

Slowly, deliberately, she spread her hands wide . . . and smiled, her head cocked and her eyes flirting with him. 'Had you going there for a minute, didn't I?'

'Just keep your hands where they are,' he said coolly, sliding out of bed and reaching for his clothes. He didn't turn his back on her for even a second.

'Oh, please. I'm no more a killer than you are.'

Wasn't that reassuring? If she only knew. But the prickling on the back of his neck told him not to let down his guard, no matter what she said or how convincing she was. 'Maybe you've hit on the perfect way to kick a man out of your bed after you've finished fucking him,' he said as he pulled on his shorts and pants. 'In which case, congratulations – unless the next guy you pull it on thinks you're about to pop his eyeballs out of his skull and freaks on you. That's a good way to get the shit kicked out of yourself.'

She rolled her eyes. 'It was just a joke.'

'Yeah, hah hah. I'm laughing my ass off.' He put on his socks and shoes, shoved his arms into the sleeves of his shirt, and showed her his teeth in what could have been a smile. 'Let's just say that if I hear of any eyeballs being cut out, I might have to give the cops your description.' A thought occurred to him; he quickly glanced around, saw the small shoulder bag she'd dropped on the floor, and quick as a cat snatched it up.

'Give me that,' she snarled, lunging for it, but he caught her and tossed her facedown onto the bed, planting one hand in the middle of her back and leaning his weight on it to keep her in place while with the other hand he emptied the bag onto the bed. She wheezed, trying to suck in air as she bucked and twisted, but he didn't let up. Cursing, she slung her arm back, trying to hit him in the crotch; he twisted sideways, deflecting the blow with his hip.

'Watch it,' he warned. 'You don't want to make me mad.'

'Fuck you!'

'Been there, done that, don't want the T-shirt.'

With his finger he poked through the things he'd dumped out of the bag. She didn't have a wallet – at least, she didn't have one in the bag, just a money clip. That struck him as odd, because how many women carried money clips? There was also a little leather thing with credit card slots on both sides. One of those slots held her driver's license. He thumbed the card out of its slot and looked at the photo to make certain the license was really hers, then checked out the name.

'Well, well ... Deidre Paige Almond. So you really *are* some kind of nut.' She must not have thought his little joke was funny, because she cursed again. Goss grinned, enjoying himself more than he had in a while. What was even funnier was that he'd given *her* a false name, as well. Twisted minds evidently thought alike. 'Let me guess – "Kami" is a nickname, right?' He tossed the license on the bed beside her.

She bucked under his hand, her tousled dark hair falling across her face as she turned her head to glare at him. 'You son of a bitch, let's see if you think this is so funny when I press charges against you!'

'On what grounds?' he asked, sounding bored. 'Rape? Too bad I got in the habit of carrying a voice-activated tape recorder with me whenever I'm with a woman – just in case.'

'Bullshit!'

'Actually, it's a Sony.' He patted his right pants pocket, where his cell phone made a nice little bulge. 'The sound quality is top-notch. Besides, what name would you give the cops?' He made a *tsk*ing sound. 'You can't trust anything anyone tells you these days, can you? It's been fun, gotta go now, won't be seeing you around. Just remember what I said about the eyeballs. And if you *were* fooling around, you might want to rethink the routine.' He released her and moved swiftly out of her reach. 'Don't bother getting up,' he said as he went out the door.

She didn't – or at least, she didn't bother coming after him, maybe because she was naked. Goss let himself out of the condo and walked down the cracked sidewalk. She had driven them here, so he was temporarily stranded, but he wasn't perturbed. He had a phone, and he had a card in his pocket with the number of the cab company he'd used earlier. He walked until he came to an intersection where there were street signs, then called for a taxi.

He wouldn't have been surprised if Deidre-Kami had come speeding down the street in her five-year-old Nissan and tried to run him over, but she had evidently decided not to look for more trouble. Goss didn't know if she was just some kind of flake who thought it would be funny to pretend she was a psycho serial killer, or if she was a real psycho, but his instincts had been telling him he'd better get his ass out of there. All in all, it was one of his more interesting evenings.

After a fairly reasonable length of time – coming close to what he would consider unreasonable – the cab arrived and he climbed in. Twenty minutes later he was whistling softly as he walked down the hotel hallway toward his room. It was after one AM; he wouldn't get much sleep, but the evening's entertainment was worth it.

He showered before climbing into bed, where he slept like a baby until the bedside alarm went off at six. There was nothing like a clear conscience – or, better yet, *no* conscience – for a good night's rest.

A box containing their weapons was supposed to be delivered by seven AM, but that time came and went without the delivery. Toxtel got on the phone to Faulkner, who had arranged everything, and then they waited. Goss used the time to order breakfast. Shortly after nine, and half an hour after they were supposed to have been in the air, a bellman brought up a box marked 'Printed Material' and sealed with masking tape. Toxtel took the delivery; he looked like some sort of executive, or maybe a salesman, in his suit and tie. Goss had chosen to dress with more comfort, in slacks and a raw silk shirt, no tie. He imagined people who went to B and B inns were there on vacation, not to work, but Toxtel was going to wear his suit and tie regardless of the circumstances.

The handguns inside the box were clean, the registration numbers filed off. Silently they checked the weapons, the routine just that – routine. Goss's weapon of choice was a Glock, but in situations like this you took what was available on short notice. The two handguns provided were a Beretta and a Taurus, with a box of cartridges for each. Goss had never used a Taurus before but Toxtel had, so Toxtel took it and let Goss have the familiar Beretta. They transferred the weapons to their bags, then called the pilot of their rent-a-plane to tell him they were on the way.

Because they were flying on a private plane, they didn't have to go through security at the airport. The pilot, a taciturn man with the weathered skin of someone who'd never bought sunscreen, grunted a greeting and that was that. They stowed their own luggage, which was fine, and climbed aboard. The plane was a small Cessna that had seen its best days maybe ten years ago, but it met the two most important qualifications: it flew, and it didn't need a long runway.

Goss didn't care for scenery, at least not the country kind. His idea of a good view was one from a penthouse. Still, he had to admit the sparkling, boulder-filled rivers and jagged mountains were pretty, as those things went. They were definitely best viewed from the air, though. That opinion was reinforced when, an hour later, the small plane was set down on a bumpy, dusty strip over which rocky, jagged mountains loomed like malevolent giants. There was no town, only a corrugated tin building; three vehicles sat outside it. One was a nondescript beige sedan, one was a rusty Ford pickup that looked older than Goss, and the last was a gray Chevy Tahoe. 'I hope the pickup isn't our four-wheel-drive,' Goss muttered.

'It won't be. Faulkner took care of us; you'll see.'

Toxtel's stolid confidence in Faulkner never failed to irritate Goss, but he didn't let it show. For one thing, he didn't want anyone to have the slightest inkling that he despised Faulkner, but the main reason was Hugh Toxtel was the only one of Faulkner's stable of hired killers that Goss wouldn't want to go up against. It wasn't that Toxtel was a superman or anything; he was just good at what he did – good enough that Goss respected him. And Toxtel had a good ten years of experience that Goss didn't have, maybe more.

As they climbed out of the plane and began pulling their bags out of the storage compartment, a chunky guy in stained coveralls ambled out of the tin building. 'You the guys wanting the rental?' he asked.

'Yeah,' Toxel said.

'They've been waiting for you.'

'They' turned out to be two young guys from the rental company; one had driven the Tahoe out, followed by the other. Evidently patience wasn't their strong suit, because both of them were irritated by the wait. Toxel signed some papers; the two guys jumped into the beige sedan and were gone in a cloud of dust.

'Damn kids,' Toxel groused, glaring after them as he waved the dust out of his face. 'They did that on purpose.'

Toxel and Goss put their things in the back of the Tahoe, then climbed into the big vehicle. There was a map folded on the driver's seat, with the route to Trail Stop obligingly traced in red and the destination itself circled. After looking at the map, Goss wondered why someone had bothered to circle the name, since the road stopped there and they couldn't go any farther. Trail Stop – wonder how it got its name, har-dee-har-har.

'Pretty country,' Toxel offered after a few minutes.

'I guess.' Goss looked out the passenger window at the sheer drop to the bottom of a rocky gorge. Had to be three or four hundred feet straight down, and the road wasn't the best, a narrow, roughly paved two-lane with battered guardrails at some of the worst parts. The problem was, the places he thought needed guardrails evidently didn't jibe with what the Idaho department of transportation considered dangerous. The sun was bright, the sky overhead a deep, cloudless blue, but when they passed from a sunny stretch of road to one shadowed by the mountain, he noticed that the temperature on the Tahoe's gauge dropped a good ten degrees. He'd hate to get caught out in these mountains at night. They hadn't seen a single structure or another vehicle since leaving the airstrip, and even though they'd been on the road fewer than ten minutes, that just struck Goss as deeply unnatural.

After half an hour they came to an actual small town, population four thousand and something, with streets and traffic lights – a couple of them – and everything, and he relaxed somewhat. At

71

least there were people around.

Then they took a left turn onto the road indicated on the map, and all signs of civilization vanished again.

'Jesus, I don't know how people live like this,' Goss muttered. 'If you run out of milk, it's a damn day's expedition to the grocery store.'

'It's what you get used to,' Toxtel said.

'I think it's more a case of not knowing anything different. You can't miss what you've never had.' The next turn of the road brought them out into the bright sun again, and the glare on the windshield made him squint his eyes, which made him yawn.

'You shoulda got some sleep last night, instead of going out looking for pussy,' Toxtel observed, a hint of disapproval in his tone.

'I didn't just look, I found some,' Goss said, and yawned again. 'Weird chick. She looked like some small-town poultry queen, or something, but when I told her she shouldn't take strangers home with her, it was too dangerous and I could have been some kind of psycho, she said that *she* might be the psycho. The look in her eyes right then gave me the shivers, like she might really be nuts. I put my clothes on and got out of there.' He left out the part about the struggle, and the fake name.

'You're gonna get your throat cut one of these days,' Toxtel warned.

Goss shrugged indifferently. 'Always possible.'

'You didn't kill her or anything, did you?' Toxtel asked after another few minutes, and Goss could tell he'd been worried by the thought.

'I'm not stupid. She's fine.'

'We don't want to draw attention to ourselves.'

'I said, she's fine. Alive, breathing, unhurt.'

'That's good. We don't need any complications. We find what we're looking for at this place, and we leave. That's it.'

'How will we know where to look? Are you going to say, 'Where'd you put the stuff that stupid accountant left behind?' '

'Might not be a bad idea. We could say he sent us.'

Goss considered that possibility. 'Simple,' he admitted. 'Might work.'

The road had so many twists and turns that he began to get nauseated. He let his window down to get some fresh air into the vehicle. There were No Passing signs all along the road. After they went by what seemed like the fiftieth sign, he muttered, 'No shit.'

'No shit, what?'

'All these No Passing signs. First, how could you pass anything on this damn road? It's one curve after another. And second, there's nothing *to* pass.'

'City boy,' Toxtel said, grinning.

'Damn straight.' He looked down at the map. 'The next turn should be coming up on the right.'

'Coming up' took another long ten minutes. The temperature had dropped another five degrees, and the air felt thin. Goss wondered what the elevation was.

The road they were looking for was marked by a line of thirty or more mailboxes, leaning at all angles like a row of drunken soldiers. There was also a sign that said 'Trail Stop,' and an arrow, and just past that a neatly lettered sign that read 'Nightingale's Bed and Breakfast.'

'That's the place,' Toxtel said. 'Shouldn't be hard to find.'

The road had been steadily climbing, but shortly after they turned onto the narrow, one-lane road, it began winding downhill. The way down was even steeper than going up had been. Toxtel shifted into a lower gear, but still had to ride the brakes.

On one curve, they could see what had to be Trail Stop down below, sitting out on a wide spit of earth with a river roaring down the right side. The number of buildings looked as if it might match the number of mailboxes back on the road.

At the bottom of the mountain they went over a narrow wooden bridge that creaked under the weight of the Tahoe. Goss looked down at the wide, rushing stream coming off the mountain on its way to join the river, the water churned white by the black boulders that jutted above the spray, and a chill went down his spine. The stream wasn't as rough as the river they'd seen, but something about it spooked him.

'Don't look now, but I think we're in *Deliverance* territory,' he muttered.

'Wrong section of the country,' Toxtel said blithely, not at all perturbed by the wildness around them.

The road curved up and over a small hill, and when they crested it – Goss briefly closed his eyes, in case another vehicle was coming over the hill from the opposite direction – Trail Stop was laid out before them, a cluster of buildings that stretched along either side of the road. There were some houses, most of them small and rundown, a feed store, a hardware store, a general store, another few houses, and at the end on the left was a big Victorian-style house with wide porches, gingerbread trim, and a sign out front proclaiming it to be the bed-and-breakfast. There were two other cars in the side parking area, and one parked in the rear in a separate garage building. The single bay door was open. To the right of the garage door was a regular door. That might be a good place to look for Layton's stuff, Goss thought.

'Well, you were right,' he said. 'The place isn't hard to find.'

As they parked, a woman came down the steps toward them. 'Hello,' she said. 'I'm Cate Nightingale. Welcome to Trail Stop.'

Toxtel got out of the SUV first, smiling as he introduced himself and shook hands, then opened the rear door so they could get their luggage. Goss followed more slowly, though he did the smile-and-handshake deal, too. They introduced themselves as Huxley and Mellor – he was Huxley and Toxtel was Mellor. Faulkner had taken care of the bill with a credit card under some generic company name, so they wouldn't have to show identification.

Goss didn't attempt to hide the interest in his eyes as he surveyed the bed-and-breakfast's owner. She was younger than he'd expected, with a lanky build that didn't lend itself to curves, though she had a nice ass. She didn't show it off, dressing in black pants and a white shirt with rolled-up sleeves, but he could tell it was there. Her voice was good, too, warm and friendly. Thick brown hair was pulled back in a ponytail, and her eyes were brown – nothing outstanding there. Her mouth, though, was one of those oddly shaped ones, with the top lip fuller than the lower one. It gave her a soft, sensual look.

'Your rooms are ready,' she said with a friendly smile that completely lacked any response to the interest he'd shown. He checked out her ass as she turned away. He'd been right about its niceness.

Inside the house, he saw a teddy bear lying outside a room, indicating the presence of a child. That might mean Mr. Nightingale was in residence, too. She wasn't wearing a wedding band, though; he'd noticed that when he'd shaken her hand. Goss glanced at Toxtel and saw that he, too, had spotted the teddy bear.

She stopped at a desk in the hallway, positioned against the side of the staircase, and picked up two keys. 'I've put you in rooms three and five,' she said as she led the way upstairs. 'Each room has its own bathroom, and good views from the windows. I hope you enjoy your stay here.'

'I'm sure we will,' Toxtel said politely.

She gave him room number 3, and Goss got room number 5. Looking around, Goss saw two rooms to the right, on the front of the house, and four more doors to their left. Considering the vehicles in the parking area, at least two of those rooms were occupied, maybe more, depending on how many people had been in each car. Searching the place might not be as easy as they'd hoped.

On the other hand, Goss thought with a smile as he unpacked his things, knowing there was a kid in the place opened up some interesting possibilities.

Chapter Eight

Cate didn't know what was going on, but she suspected that the man who had called late yesterday afternoon to book rooms for Messrs. Huxley and Mellor was the same man who had called earlier, pretending to be someone working at the car rental agency and asking about Jeffrey Layton. She couldn't be certain, and if she hadn't already been suspicious, the possibility would never have occurred to her, but both the accent and the voice had seemed familiar and after she'd hung up the phone the familiarity worried at her subconscious until she made the connection.

The two men were obviously looking for Layton, which was also suspicious. If they'd been *worried* about him because he'd disappeared, obviously they would have said so at the beginning, told her they were looking for their friend and asked questions about the morning he'd left. That they hadn't done so told her they weren't worried about his well-being at all. Mr. Layton was in trouble, and these two men were part of that trouble.

She shouldn't have let them stay here. She knew that now. If she had recognized the voice on the phone in time, she would have told him she didn't have any rooms available – not that she could have stopped the men from coming to Trail Stop, but at least they wouldn't be staying here in this house with her and the boys. A chill went down her back at the thought of the kids, and her mother, and even the three young men who had arrived yesterday afternoon for a couple of days of rock climbing. Had she inadvertently put them all in danger?

At least Mimi and the boys were out of the house right now. She had taken Tucker and Tanner for a walk, telling them that she was giving them another chance to prove they knew how to behave, and if they let her down this time ... Of course, her mother never finished that line, but as a child Cate had imagined that letting her mother down a second time would come close to causing the end of the world. Tucker and Tanner had looked suitably grave. Cate just hoped the walk was a long one.

There was the possibility that these two men had no connection with Jeffrey Layton at all. Cate couldn't completely dismiss the idea that her imagination was running away with her. The voices on the phone had been similar, but that didn't mean the calls had come from the same person – though Caller ID had once again shown no number in the phone window. She felt silly for letting herself think something sinister was going on, but at the same time she was alarmed.

The two men had been perfectly polite. The older one, Mellor, looked out of place in his suit and tie, but that in itself didn't mean anything. Maybe he'd been to a business meeting, flew in, and hadn't had a chance to change into more casual clothing. The other one, Huxley, was tall and handsome, and on the make. He'd checked her out, but she hadn't responded and he'd let it go instead of pushing. Maybe they had a perfectly innocent reason for being here –

That was where her thoughts turned back on themselves. Trail Stop wasn't on the main route; people had to deliberately come here; they didn't stop by on their way to somewhere else. If Huxley and Mellor weren't here to look for Jeffrey Layton, then why *were* they here? Her usual guests were vacationing families, hikers, couples on romantic getaways, fishermen, hunters, and rock climbers. She'd bet the house that neither of these men fished, hunted, or climbed, because they hadn't brought along any equipment or gear. Neither were they lovers – not after the way Huxley had been looking at her. Hikers, maybe, but she doubted it. She hadn't seen them carry in any hiking boots, walking sticks, backpacks, or any of the other paraphernalia serious hikers carried when they were going into remote areas.

The only logical reason left for their presence was Layton – and she didn't know what to do about it.

She went into the kitchen, where she had started making a batch of peanut butter cookies for the boys. Neenah Dase was sitting at the table, sipping a cup of tea. Business at the feed store was slow, so Neenah had put a sign on the door saying that she was at Cate's;

anyone needing feed would come get her.

Neenah was a native, born and bred in Trail Stop. Neenah's father had started the feed store more than fifty years before. Her older sister hadn't liked rural living at all, and had 'gone city' as soon as she got out of high school; she was now living, very happily, in Milwaukee. Cate didn't know Neenah's story, other than the bit about her being a former nun – or novice (Cate didn't know if one could leave an order after becoming a full-fledged nun) – who had come home some fifteen years ago and taken over the day-to-day running of the feed store. When her parents died, Neenah inherited the store. She'd never married and, to Cate's knowledge, never dated.

Neenah was one of the calmest, most peaceful people Cate had ever met. Her light brown hair had such an ashy undertone that it had a silvery sheen. Her eyes were lake blue, and her skin was porcelain. She wasn't beautiful; her jaw was too square, her features too unsymmetrical, but she was one of those people who made you smile when you thought of her.

Cate liked most of the people in Trail Stop, but Neenah and Sherry were the ones she was closest to. Both of them were comfortable people to be around – Sherry because she was so upbeat, Neenah because she was so placid.

Placid didn't mean lacking in common sense, though. Cate sat down at the table and said, 'I'm worried about my two new guests.'

'Who are they?'

'Two men.'

Neenah paused with her teacup almost at her lips. 'You're afraid to be in the house with them?'

'Not in the way you mean.' Cate rubbed her forehead. 'I don't know if you know—' Since Trail Stop was so small, gossip seemed to be as fast as instant messaging. '—but one of guests climbed out his bedroom window yesterday, drove away, and didn't come back. He left his things here, maybe because he couldn't carry a suitcase and climb off the roof at the same time. Yesterday, a man supposedly from a rental car agency called here looking for him, but when I called the agency later to give them an update, they had no record of Mr. Layton ever renting a car from them. Then late yesterday afternoon someone called and reserved rooms for the two men who just arrived and I think it was the same man who called pretending to be from the rental agency. Are you following this?'

Neenah nodded, her blue eyes serious. 'Guest disappeared, people looking for him and lying about who they are, and now those same people are here.'

'Essentially.'

'It's obvious he was up to no good.'

'And neither are the people looking for him.'

'Call the police,' Neenah said decisively.

'And report what? They haven't done anything wrong. No laws have been broken. I've reported Mr. Layton missing, but because he didn't run out on his bill, other than check hospitals and ravines for him, there's nothing they can do. It's the same situation here. Just because I'm suspicious of these two is no reason for the police to even question them.' Cate leaned over to retrieve her own cup of tea from where it was sitting, beside the bowl of cookie batter, and took a sip, then cocked her head as a faint sound from the hallway made her pulse jump. 'Did you hear that?' she whispered urgently, getting to her feet and moving swiftly toward the hallway door.

'Don't—' Neenah said, looking alarmed, but Cate was already jerking the door open.

No one was there. No one was in the hallway, or on the stairs. She stepped closer to the stairs and looked up; from there she could see the doors to rooms three and five, and both were closed. She stuck her head into the dining room, but it, too, was empty. She turned back to the kitchen, where Neenah was standing anxiously in the doorway. 'Nothing.'

'Are you sure?'

'Maybe I'm just jumpy.' Cate closed the door, rubbing her arms as chills roughened her skin. She picked up her teacup and sipped, but the tea had cooled and she made a face. Taking the cup to the sink, she dumped the remainder of the tea down the drain.

'I didn't hear anything, but you're more familiar with the sounds of the house. Could it have just been a creak?'

Cate replayed the sound in her mind. 'It wasn't a creaking sound; it was more like someone brushed against the wall.' She was too on edge to sit down again, so she resumed spooning up the cookie batter and dropping dabs onto the prepared cookie sheet, then flattening and shaping the dough with the flat of the spoon.

79

'Like I said, maybe I'm just jumpy. The sound could have come from outside.'

Beyond the closed kitchen door, Goss stepped silently out of what looked like a den, complete with toys strewn on the floor. That had been a close call, but he'd learned something important. Going up the stairs, he stayed close to the outside edge of the risers, testing each one before he put his full weight down, and he made it to the top without any betraying squeaks. He didn't knock on Toxtel's door, just opened it and slid inside. When he turned around, he was looking down the barrel of the Taurus.

Toxtel scowled as he lowered his arm. 'You trying to get killed?'

'I overheard the Nightingale woman talking to some other woman downstairs,' he explained in a low, urgent tone. 'She's on to us. She mentioned calling the cops.' That wasn't exactly what she'd said, but this was an opportunity he didn't intend to pass up.

'Shit! We need to find Layton's crap and get out of here.'

Goss had hoped Toxtel would have that reaction. Neither he nor Toxtel were wanted, but they had checked in under assumed names and that, coupled with Layton's disappearing act, might strike some local yokel lawman as suspicious. Faulkner would be pissed beyond description if a hayseed cop traced them back to him, and even worse than that, Bandini would be even more unhappy that they'd brought that sort of attention to Layton. In a situation like this, caution went out the window and speed was important.

Toxtel began throwing the things he'd unpacked back into his bag. Goss went next door and did the same. Pulling the pillowcase off one of the fat pillows on the bed, he wiped down every surface he'd touched, including the doorknobs. Things might go down the way he hoped, they might not, but he believed in protecting himself. Now, if Toxtel would just escalate this beyond retrieval –

Less than two minutes after he'd entered Toxtel's room, they met in the hallway.

'Where are they?' Toxtel murmured. The Taurus was in his hand.

Goss leaned over the stair railing and pointed. 'That door. The open door is the dining room, so the next one is probably the kitchen.' Like Toxtel, he kept his voice down.

'Kitchen. That means knives.' And because the availability of weapons was something they now had to factor in, that meant Toxtel would be even more alert. 'Is anyone else in the house?'

'I don't think so. I didn't hear anyone else.'

'No kid?'

'Toys in the den downstairs, but no kid. Maybe in school.'

Quietly they carried their bags downstairs and set them by the front door so they could grab them on the way out. Goss's veins were burning with adrenaline. A couple of bodies; a credit card charge that might not lead directly back to Faulkner, but a smart cop would eventually dig deep enough to find him; and a botched job for Bandini ... the setup couldn't get any sweeter than this. And Toxtel's finger, not his own, was on the trigger. Even if he got caught up in the heat, he could plea-bargain, give up Toxtel, and be a free man in a few years. He'd have to change his name and disappear again, but that was no big deal. He was tired of being Kennon Goss.

Signaling for Goss to take his back, weapon in his hand, Toxtel pushed open the kitchen door. 'Sorry to do it this way, ladies,' he said calmly, 'but you have something we want, Ms. Nightingale.'

Cate froze, a spoonful of cookie dough in her hand. The older, suit-clad man stood just inside the door, an ugly black weapon in his hand. The only thought that sprang into her mind was a desperate prayer: *God, please don't let Mom and the boys come back right now!*

Neenah's face washed white, and she, too, was frozen, with the teacup still in her hand.

'W-what?' Cate stammered.

'The stuff Layton left here. We want it. Give it to us and there won't be any problem.'

Cate felt as if her brain were mired in quicksand. Sheer disbelief that this was actually happening made her shake her head.

'I think you will,' Mellor said softly. The weapon in his hand hadn't wavered, and it was pointing right at her head. She could see the black hole of the barrel.

'No, I didn't mean' – she swallowed – 'of course—'

'Someone's coming' came a soft call, and she thought she would faint. *Dear God, dear God, please don't let it be Mom and the boys* – 'A guy in an old truck.'

'See who it is,' Mellor snapped, shifting the weapon so it

pointed at Neenah, 'and get rid of him.'

Cate turned her head as she heard tires crunching on gravel outside the kitchen window. She recognized the truck, and the lanky figure crawling out of it. Relief was just as overwhelming as panic had been. She dropped the spoon into the bowl and grabbed the edge of the table as her knees threatened to buckle. 'It – it's the handyman.'

'Why's he here?'

For a moment she drew a blank; then she gave herself another little shake. 'The mail. He's here for the mail. He's going into town.'

Mellor reached out and grabbed Neenah by the collar of her shirt, dragging her out of the chair and out into the hall. 'Get rid of him,' he warned Cate again as steps sounded on the wooden porch, then the knock on the kitchen door. Mellor pulled the hallway kitchen door almost shut.

Her scalp was prickling with fear and she thought her hair must be standing on end, but she had to keep it together or that man would kill Neenah, she knew he would. He might kill both of them anyway, just for the fun of it, or to eliminate witnesses who could identify them. They needed help, but with Mellor standing there listening to everything she said, she didn't know what she could do, how she could alert Mr. Harris without alerting Mellor.

Trying to school her face to blankness, she opened the door.

'I'm on my way to town,' Mr. Harris mumbled, looking down as his cheeks started coloring. 'You have your mail ready?'

'I'll need to put postage on,' she said, fighting to keep her voice from trembling. 'It won't take but a minute.' She didn't invite him in as she usually did, but dashed into the hallway where her desk was stationed by the stairway. Mellor jerked Neenah out of the way, keeping the barrel of his gun jammed against her temple. Out of the corner of her eye, Cate saw the other man, Huxley, stationed at the front door.

With shaking hands, Cate grabbed the four bills and hurriedly stuck stamps on them, then dashed back out. 'Sorry to keep you waiting,' she said as she handed the envelopes out the door to Mr. Harris.

He looked down at the envelopes, his dirty-blond hair falling over his eyes, and he shuffled them in his hands. 'No problem,' he said. 'I'll bring that new lock by when I get back.' Then he turned and went down the steps, climbed into his truck, and backed out of the driveway.

Cate closed the door, leaning her head against the frame. He hadn't noticed anything. There went her hope for help.

'That was good,' Mellor said, opening the hallway door wider. 'Now, where is Layton's stuff?'

She turned around, sucking in quick little gasps of air as distress constricted her lungs. He had shifted his grip to Neenah's hair, holding her head pulled back at an unnatural angle and keeping her off-balance, unable to help herself. Neenah was gasping for breath, too, her mouth open, her eyes wide with horror.

Cate tried to think, tried to marshal her turgid brain into action. Which was best, to delay or to give them what they wanted and hope they would just leave? But if she delayed, what would that gain them? Any delay would only increase the chances that her mother and children would walk right into the middle of this, and she would do anything, anything, to prevent that from happening.

'Up – upstairs,' she gasped. 'In the attic.'

Mellor pulled Neenah back, gesturing with his head. 'Show us.'

Her knees were trembling so violently Cate could barely walk, much less climb the stairs, and the terrified glance she shot behind her at Neenah told her Neenah wasn't in any better shape. Her friend was very quiet, not making a sound other than the panicked rasping of her breath, but she was visibly shaking.

Cate grasped the railing and hauled herself up, willing her legs to carry her. The staircase had never seemed so steep, or so high. The Victorian house had twelve-foot ceilings, so the stairs were higher than usual, and every one was an effort as she concentrated on not falling. 'Hurry,' the man behind her growled, shoving Neenah forward so that she hit Cate's legs and they both stumbled.

'Stop it!' Cate flared, whirling to face him, an unreasoning anger burning through the panic. 'You're just making things more difficult. Do you want the damn suitcase or not?' Her own voice sounded distant to her, the tone oddly familiar. With a faint sense of shock, she realized it was the same tone she used with the boys when they became too unruly.

The man stared back at her, no expression in his eyes. 'Keep moving.'

'*You* stop shoving before you make us all break our necks!'

There was no color at all in Neenah's face, even her lips were white, and her eyes were so wide that white showed around the blue irises. She must have wondered what Cate had been thinking, snapping at the man who was grinding a gun barrel into her temple, but still not even a whimper escaped her. Oh, God, Cate thought in despair, what on earth was she doing? Without another word she turned around and began climbing again, but at least the brief surge of anger had steadied her knees.

At the top of the stairs she turned to the right and led the way to the dark end of the hall, and the door to the attic stairs. They might be killed up here, she thought as her blood turned to ice water at the thought. The delay in finding their bodies would give Mellor and his pal plenty of time to get away.

What would happen to her babies if she were killed? They wouldn't lack for love; her parents would take them, or Patrick and Andie, even though they were expecting their own baby now, but their lives would be forever scarred by violence. How much would they remember her? In ten years, would they have any memories of her at all? Would they ever truly realize how much she loved them?

Damn Jeffrey Layton for bringing this to her house! she thought with fierce, sudden violence. If she ever got her hands on him, she would choke him to death.

Laboriously they made their way up the steep, narrow attic stairs. His eyes narrowed, Mellor surveyed the crowded space as he pushed Neenah forward. 'Where is it?'

'Here.' Cate went to the suitcase and pulled it out. She started to tell him that whatever he was looking for, he was wasting his time, because there was nothing in the suitcase except clothing, but she choked the words back. Maybe it was better to let him think he had what he wanted. Maybe he wouldn't kill them; maybe he'd leave her and Neenah up here and leave.

Gripping the handle of the suitcase, she turned to face him, and froze.

Calvin Harris stood at the top of the stairs, a shotgun raised to his shoulder as he aimed directly at the back of Mellor's head.

Cate jerked back, her head banging against the top of the sloping ceiling as she instinctively tried to get out of the line of fire.

Alerted by her actions, Mellor swung around, taking Neenah with him.

'Let her go,' the handyman said calmly. The big weapon in his hands was as steady as a rock, his cheek nestled against the stock, and the eyes she had previously thought of as 'washed out' were as pale and cold as ice.

Mellor smiled a little. 'That's a shotgun. You kill me, you kill the women, too. Not a good choice of weapon.'

Calvin's smile matched Mellor's. 'Except it's loaded with a slug, not shot. At this distance, it'll take your head off and not touch Neenah at all.'

'Yeah, sure. Put the shotgun down, or she's dead.'

'Analyze the situation,' Calvin said softly. 'Your buddy isn't coming up those stairs to help. You can get off a shot, yeah, but not in time to stop me from pulling the trigger. I use this shotgun for deer hunting, so believe me when I say it's loaded with slugs instead of pellets. You might get me, you might get Neenah, but the bottom line is you'll be dead, too. So we can either have two dead people, or everyone can live and you get your buddy and get out of here.'

'You can have the suitcase, too,' Cate choked out. Anything to keep them from coming back.

Mellor inhaled deeply as he did the math. The fact was, they were at a stalemate, and the only way he could get out of it alive was to drop his weapon. Cate tried to follow what was going through his mind, but all she could think was he'd have to trust Calvin wouldn't shoot him after he was disarmed. Mellor himself would probably kill them all in cold blood, but Calvin wouldn't.

Very deliberately, Mellor released Neenah and clicked the safety on the automatic. She slumped to the floor, unable to even stand. Cate started toward her, but Calvin threw an icy glance at her, and she halted, belatedly understanding that he didn't want her any closer to Mellor.

'Now drop it,' Calvin instructed.

The weapon hit the floor with a heavy thud. Cate flinched, thinking it would go off, but nothing happened.

'Get the suitcase and leave.'

Slowly, not making any sudden moves, Mellor retrieved the suitcase from Cate. Cate stared at him, her eyes wide. Their gazes met for a brief moment. His was still calm and expressionless, as if this was all in a day's work.

'Cate,' said Calvin. She blinked at him. 'Pick up the pistol.'

She scrambled for the weapon, gingerly picking it up. She'd

never touched a gun before, and she was surprised by the weight.

'See that button on the left side? Push it.'

Holding the pistol in her right hand, she used her left forefinger to push the button.

'Okay,' Calvin said, 'you just took the safety off. Don't pull the trigger unless you mean to shoot. Go down the stairs first, and stay far enough away from him that he can't reach you. We'll be behind you. Go past the head of the stairs, and keep the gun aimed at him until I'm out of the stairwell and behind him again. You got that?'

The logic of it made sense. If he'd let Mellor go first, either he'd have had to be so close behind that Mellor could grab the shotgun, or Mellor would be out of sight for a few seconds after he reached the bottom of the stairs. Cate couldn't imagine what Calvin thought Mellor could do in those few seconds, but if he thought there was danger, she was willing to go along with him.

Where was the other man, Huxley? What had Calvin done with him?

She went down the stairs much faster than she'd gone up them, not entirely on purpose. Her knees were still wobbly and she half-ran, half-stumbled down them. She kept a death grip on the weapon, all the while sending up a prayer that Mellor wouldn't try anything, because she had no idea what she was doing. She went past the head of the stairs and turned, pointing the barrel at Mellor and using both hands to hold the weapon as steady as she could. It wobbled because she was still shaking, but she thought – she hoped – she was aiming it close enough to him that he wouldn't take any chances.

Calvin followed Mellor at a safe distance, and in contrast to her own trembling, he seemed ice cold and impervious to stress.

'Keep going,' he told Mellor in that same soft tone. They headed down the stairs.

After a moment Cate moved forward to follow. Neenah came down the attic stairs then, moving very slowly and clinging to first the bannister and then the door frame. Her gaze met Cate's and she swallowed. 'I'm okay,' she said in a thready tone. 'Go help Cal.'

Cate went down the stairs to the bottom floor. She saw the other man lying on the floor in front of the front door, his hands tied behind him. He was groggily trying to sit up.

'I can't manage him and three bags at the same time,' Mellor said.

'So untie him. He'll be able to walk.' Calvin kept the shotgun at his shoulder.

Mellor untied Huxley and helped him to his feet. The other man swayed, but stayed upright. His blue eyes glared hatred at Calvin, but he might as well have saved the effort for all the reaction Calvin showed.

Between them, the two men picked up the three bags and went out onto the front porch, Huxley stumbling and weaving but managing to walk. Following Calvin onto the porch, Cate watched them stow the bags in the Tahoe, then climb into the front seats. Just before Mellor cranked the engine, she heard the faint, high-pitched sound of her children's voices, and knew her mother was returning with the boys. She almost burst into tears at the realization of how close they had come to walking into a deadly situation.

Huxley shot both of them a deadly glare as the Tahoe went past. She and Calvin watched until it was out of sight.

'You okay?' he finally asked, still looking down the road. She wondered if he thought they might come back.

'I'm fine.' Her voice was thin with shock, almost soundless. She cleared her throat and tried again. 'I'm fine. Neenah—'

'I'm okay,' Neenah said, appearing in the doorway. She was still white, still shaky, but she was no longer clinging to things to walk. 'Just shook up, I think. Are they gone?'

'Yeah,' Calvin said. He held the shotgun easily in one hand, the barrel now pointing downward, as he gave Cate a searching look. 'That was a good idea, turning the stamps upside down.'

It had worked; her pitiful attempt at signaling for help had worked! 'I read ... I read that an upside-down flag is a distress signal.'

He dipped his head in a brief nod. 'You were nervous and shaky, too. I drove down the street and circled back on foot, figured I'd check things out and make sure everything was okay.'

'I didn't think you'd noticed.' He'd glanced at the envelopes, shuffling them in his hands, but hadn't even blinked his eyes to show any reaction.

'I noticed.'

His calmness made her feel her own shakiness even more acutely. She looked at Neenah and saw that she, too, was trembling as she tried to hold things together. With a choked sob Cate dropped the gun she was holding and grabbed Neenah in a tight hug and they clung together for comfort and support. She felt Calvin putting his arms around both of them, murmuring something soft and probably comforting, if she'd been able to understand what he was saying, but the actual words didn't matter. A part of her brain noticed that he was still holding the shotgun, and that was definitely comforting. For a long moment they leaned into his surprising strength; then she heard Tucker's piping shout as he raced toward them, Tanner keeping pace beside him.

'Mr. *Hawwis*! Is that a *gun*?'

Her children's voices had Cate straightening and wiping her face dry of the tears that had seeped under her lashes, and she went down the steps to grab both of them and pull them tightly to her.

Chapter Nine

Goss and Toxtel drove all the way back to the main road before they spoke. Goss had been content to let the silence continue because his head hurt like a son of a bitch and his ego had been squashed like a bug. How in fuck had a damn handyman taken him from behind like that? He couldn't remember hearing anything, seeing anything, just the back of his head exploding with pain and the lights going out. Bastard must have hit him with the shotgun butt.

The best thing about Toxtel was that he wasn't chatty. He didn't waste time asking what the hell had happened, either, when it was obvious what had happened.

Hot nausea boiled in Goss's throat and he said, 'Pull over, I gotta puke.'

Toxtel whipped the Tahoe to the side of the road and stopped. The two left wheels were still on the pavement, since there wasn't much of a shoulder, and when he got out, Goss almost fell into a gully or ravine or whatever the hell they were called. Balancing himself with a hand on the side of the SUV, he made his way to the rear bumper and bent over with his hands braced on his knees. The position made his head throb even worse, and all the trees and bushes and other green shit did a slow, sickening whirl.

He heard the driver's door slam, and Toxtel came around the side. 'You okay?'

'Concussion,' Goss managed to say. He sucked in deep breaths, fighting the nausea. Letting a handyman get the jump on him was bad enough; he didn't want to puke in front of Toxtel, too.

Toxtel wasn't exactly a touchy-feely guy. He didn't so much as grunt in sympathy. Instead he opened the back cargo door and pulled Layton's suitcase to him. 'Let's see what we have,' he said. 'I want to make certain the flash drive is here before I call Faulkner.'

Goss managed to straighten as Toxtel unzipped the bag and began pulling things out. Every garment was examined, every pocket and seam felt, then dropped to the ground. A plastic shopping bag yielded a TracFone, which looked promising, but when Toxtel popped the back off, it revealed nothing more interesting than batteries. Determinedly, he dismantled the entire phone and still came up empty.

There was a pair of black wingtips in the suitcase, and Toxtel turned his attention to them. Holding each shoe with the heel pointing out, he beat them against the truck frame until the heels came off. No flash drive.

Next was the suitcase itself. Toxtel ripped out the lining, felt every inch of the bag, even cut the stitching on the handles and examined them.

'Fuck!' he swore, sending the suitcase sailing. 'It isn't here.'

'Maybe Layton took the flash drive with him. All he had to do was slip it into his pocket,' Goss said. He was disappointed this opportunity to screw Faulkner hadn't worked out, but right now his head hurt too much for him to think of another plan.

'That's if he wasn't planning to come back. Hell, he could have carried it in his pocket all the time anyway. I'd buy that, if there wasn't something suspicious about this suitcase.'

'Like what?' Goss asked tiredly. 'You've taken it apart, and didn't find anything.'

'Yeah, and it's what I didn't find that makes me think that bitch held out on us.'

'Like what?' Goss asked again.

'Do you see a razor, toothbrush, comb, deodorant, anything like that?'

Goss surveyed the scattered contents, and even with a pounding headache came to the obvious conclusion. 'She didn't give us everything.'

'Most men carry their crap in a shaving kit. There aren't a lot of clothes here, either. I think there's another suitcase.'

'Fuck.' Goss sat down on the bumper and gingerly felt the knot on the back of his head. The lightest touch sent spikes of pain spinning through his skull, and little twinkling lights danced in front of his eyes. A second chance was presenting itself, but he couldn't think clearly enough to grasp what it was.

'We can't go back in,' Toxtel said grimly. 'She knows us now, and she probably called the cops.'

Through the haze of pain, Goss saw Toxtel's dilemma. He could call Faulkner and tell him what had gone down, tell him to send in someone else – but that would be quitting, and neither of them had ever quit, ever said they couldn't do the job.

It wasn't just ego. They made their money taking care of things. They both had the reputation of getting the job done no matter how much shit went down, and because of that Faulkner sent more jobs their way. Let their reliability slide, even once, and the doubt would always be there. It wasn't as if they were on salary, for fuck's sake. They got a percentage of whatever the kill fee was, and since they got the tougher jobs, the fee was higher, which meant their take was higher.

'I've got the beginnings of an idea,' Toxtel said, turning to look back down the road. 'Let me think about it some. First, do you need a doctor?'

'No.' The response was automatic. After it came out of his mouth, Goss mentally took stock of his condition, and said again, 'No – unless I go to sleep and you can't wake me up.'

'I'm not sitting by your fucking bedside shaking you awake every hour,' Toxtel said flatly. 'So you better be damn sure you're feeling okay.'

That was Toxtel: all heart. 'Let's go,' Goss snapped. 'Let me know when this grand plan takes shape.'

The problem was: Go where? They needed at least a temporary place to stay, and he couldn't remember seeing even a fleabag motel since landing at the airstrip. Toxtel got out the map and opened it on the hood of the Tahoe, while Goss dug in his own luggage to see if he'd brought anything for pain. His own shaving kit yielded one of those sealed-plastic individual doses of ibuprofen that you bought in airports, and he popped both pills, swallowing them dry. That was another thing; they needed something to eat and drink, too. At least that little town they'd gone through would be able to provide that, and if they were lucky it *might* have a motel on some side street.

'This map doesn't tell me shit,' Toxtel growled, folding it up and tossing it back into the Tahoe.

'What are you looking for?' Goss asked as he carefully made his way back to the passenger door and got in. One slip of the foot and he'd fall a good hundred feet or so. It wasn't a straight drop, and he'd probably bounce into a tree and stop instead of going all the way down, but he wouldn't like the experience. Something was *wrong* with all those fools who liked the great outdoors. As far as he was concerned, fuck nature.

'I need one of those maps that shows mountains, shit like that.'

'Topographical,' Goss said.

'Yeah. That kind.'

'Why do you need to find a mountain? Look around you,' he growled, waving a hand to indicate the world beyond the windshield. There were plenty of mountains out there. Look in any direction, nothing but fucking mountains.

'What I need,' Toxtel said slowly, 'is to figure out if there's any way we can box that place in. We know there's just the one road, and it ends there. Can we block it so no one can leave?'

Goss's headache was suddenly unimportant as he grasped the basic idea Toxtel was proposing. If he'd ever heard of a situation fraught with possibilities for escalation, this was it. 'We'd need aerial shots, too,' he mused. 'Make sure there's not some pig trail the locals use that isn't on any state map. The terrain is pretty rough; I'm thinking that if we could block a few spots, the rest would be too rugged for them to get out.'

Toxtel nodded, his face taking on that narrow-eyed, set expression that said he was committing himself to a course of action. This would take money, Goss thought, and more people. He and Toxtel couldn't handle this on their own. And they'd also need someone who knew the area and the type of people they'd be up against. Goss knew his limitations. He was at home on concrete, not dirt. Put him out here against some yahoo who was used to deer hunting and crap like that, and who probably had an entire wardrobe of camouflage clothing, and he'd be severely disadvantaged. His biggest asset was his brain, so he intended to use it.

'We'd have to make certain all the guests at the B and B were gone,' he muttered, thinking aloud. 'People would be expecting them back, expecting them to call in, something.'

'How would we know that?'

'Someone will have to go in and check, someone local – or at least someone who won't look suspicious.'

Toxtel started the engine and put the vehicle in gear. 'I know someone I can call.'

'You know people here?'

'No, but I know someone who knows someone, if you get my drift.'

Goss got it. He leaned his aching head back against the headrest, then winced at the pressure and instead eased sideways until he could lean against the side window. The glass was cool, and gave him a tiny bit of relief. He closed his eyes. They didn't want to rush into anything; they'd take the time to think things over, hammer out the details. He dozed off imagining tick marks placed beside items on a list: power lines cut, *check;* telephone service out, *check;* bridge blocked, *check;* breaking that bastard handy-man's neck, *check.* Just like counting sheep, only better.

Chapter Ten

The house was full of locals, all wanting to know what had happened. Almost automatically Cate put on coffee and began serving it, but Sheila looked at her daughter's tense expression and firmly said, 'Sit. People can serve themselves.'

Cate sat. Tucker and Tanner were in the dining room, too; she normally didn't allow them in when customers were there, but this was different. This was neighbors gathering in a time of trouble, not customers. She watched the boys' expressions, trying to see if they were picking up on any of the undercurrents. They were excited, but that was all. When they'd asked Calvin why he had the gun, he said there'd been a snake in the attic and he'd had to get rid of it. Naturally they were fascinated by both the shotgun and the snake, demanding to see both, and they'd been disappointed that the snake was gone. As far as they were concerned, all this talk and excitement was over the snake – and Cate supposed they weren't wrong. They just didn't know the snake had been human. Now they were right in the middle of things, their gazes ping-ponging from person to person as the situation was discussed.

'You should have held them until the rest of us could get here,' Roy Edward Starkey groused to Cal. He was eighty-seven, and his opinions often reflected a time when interlopers who dared harm one of the town's own would have been strung from the nearest tree.

'Seemed smarter to give them what they wanted and get them out of here before someone got hurt,' Cal said calmly.

'We need to call the sheriff,' said Milly Earl.

'Yeah, but I'm the one most likely to be arrested,' Cal pointed out. 'I hit one of them on the head.'

'I agree with Milly,' put in Neenah. 'We have to call the police right away. I'm not hurt, but I was scared half to death.'

'Did the snake almost bite you?' Tucker asked, going to her and leaning against her legs. His big blue eyes were round with excitement.

'It came close,' she said gravely, brushing a hand over his dark hair. Tanner leaned close, too, never taking his gaze from her face, and he also received one of those gentle caresses.

'Wow,' Tucker breathed. 'And Mr. Hawwis *saved* you?'

'He did.'

'With the shotgun,' Tanner prompted, sotto voce, when she didn't continue.

'Yes, he saved me with the shotgun.'

Roy Edward looked down at the boys, distracted by their alikeness, and asked of no one in particular, 'Which one's which?'

'That's easy,' Walter Earl said with a laugh. 'If one of them has his mouth open talking, that's Tucker.'

Everyone in the room chuckled, and the atmosphere relaxed a little.

Cate's heart ached with love, and a fierce sense of protectiveness welled inside her. They were so little, their heads craned upward as they tried to catch every word in a room full of chattering adults. They were just four, and the big accomplishment in their lives right now was learning how to dress themselves. They were completely dependent on her for their safety and well-being. She turned to Sheila and said, 'I want you to leave tomorrow, and take them with you. Keep them until this all dies down.'

Sheila reached for her hand, squeezing. 'Do you think they'll come back?' she asked, her eyes narrowing. She'd been quiet since returning from the walk with her grandchildren to find her daughter had been held at gunpoint, and belatedly Cate realized Sheila was feeling her own sense of protectiveness.

'I'm terrified,' she admitted. 'But why would they come back? They don't have any reason to, since I gave them the suitcase, and I know this is probably nothing more than reaction to the shock, but I'll feel better if you have the boys safe. The most awful thing about the whole situation was thinking that the three of you could have walked into the middle of things.' She felt sick to her stomach all over again, the remembered terror almost as debilitating as it

95

had been while the situation was happening. 'I don't know what I'd have done—' Her voice broke and she clenched her jaw to control the tears that hovered just on the edge of breaking free.

'You know how much I want to take them for a visit, but sleep on this tonight and see if you still feel the same way tomorrow.' Sheila paused, then added, 'You *don't* know how much it irks me to play fair.'

The comment was so Sheila that it pulled Cate back from tearfulness, and the look she gave her mother was full of both love and appreciation. 'I do, actually.'

Sherry Bishop came over to pat Cate's shoulder. 'You need to call the sheriff.'

'It isn't that I'm against the idea,' Cate said, managing a smile that was only slightly wobbly. 'I just don't think there's anything they can do. Those men probably gave me false names, and are long gone anyway. This proves Mr. Layton was up to no good, but even though threatening someone with a pistol is against the law, the bottom line is, no one was hurt. So I could file a report, but that would likely be the end of it. Why bother?'

'They had guns! They robbed you! That's a felony! You *have* to call the police! It has to be on record, in case they come back.'

'I guess you're right.' She swiftly glanced over at Calvin. 'Though I don't think I'll mention Mr. Harris hitting one of them on the head.' She looked away just as quickly, oddly disturbed. One memory kept popping into her head with shattering clarity, and that was the way he'd looked with that shotgun aimed right at Mellor's head. She'd had no doubt he would pull the trigger, and she realized Mellor had come to the same conclusion. In that single moment she'd seen a part of Calvin she'd never dreamed existed, and she couldn't reconcile the painfully shy, gentle handyman with the man whose eyes had been so cold and his hands so steady on that deadly weapon.

No one else seemed surprised by what he'd done, so maybe she was the only one who'd been blind. The simple fact was, since Derek's death she had focused completely on raising the boys and running the bed-and-breakfast, and nothing else had impinged on her awareness. She hadn't felt curious about any of her neighbors, hadn't asked any questions that would have given her information about who and what they were beyond the surface of daily living. She had got through the years alone by pulling in and plowing on, dealing with what she had to, and blocking out everything else. Overwhelmed as she'd been, that was the only way she could have survived.

What else lay behind the kindness of her neighbors? Neenah was her closest friend here, but Cate really didn't know anything about her. She didn't even know why she'd left the religious order. Was that because Neenah didn't want to talk about it, or because Cate had never asked? She felt ashamed, and ached inside because of the years of friendship wasted, when she could have reached out and hadn't.

They were all here now, her neighbors, gathering as soon as they'd heard there was trouble. She had no doubt that, had they known in time, they'd have faced down Mellor and Huxley with whatever weapons they had at hand. After knowing these people for three years, she felt as if she was for the first time actually *seeing* them. Right now Roy Edward had sat down and was taking things out of his pocket to show Tanner, trying to entice him into talking. Her dealings with Roy Edward before had made her think he was crotchety and impatient, but he seemed to be connecting because Tanner had taken his finger out of his mouth and was leaning close, interest written on his face as he examined a pocketknife and a buckeye.

Milly came over to pat Cate's shoulder. 'If you don't mind my taking over your kitchen, I'll brew a little tea for you and Neenah. Tea's more the thing than coffee when you're upset. Don't know why, but there it is.'

'I'd love some tea,' Cate said, dredging up another smile, though she really didn't want any tea. She and Neenah had been drinking tea when Mellor had come into the kitchen and pointed his gun at them. She suspected Milly felt the need to do something, and cooking was her chosen arena. Neenah had heard Milly's offer; Cate glanced across the room and their gazes met. Neenah made a little grimace, then looked rueful. She felt the same way as Cate about drinking tea again just now.

Rather than put the call off, and also because she wanted to be able to tell everyone gathered there what Seth Marbury said, Cate slipped away to the family den and called the sheriff's department one more time. He didn't answer the phone, so she left a voice mail message, then leaned back on the sofa and closed her eyes, using the relative peace and quiet of the room to steady her frayed nerves. She could hear the rise and fall of voices in the dining room, sometimes sharp with anger on their behalf, but for the most part the discussions had calmed down.

The phone rang before she could gather the strength to return, and it was Marbury returning her call.

'I'm not certain I understood exactly what you said.' His tone was crisp and alert, which made her think he'd understood, but wasn't certain he believed.

'Two men checked in today,' she explained, 'then came downstairs a short while later and held a pistol on Neenah Dase and me, demanding I give them the things Jeffrey Layton left behind. I did, and they left. I think it's safe to say Mr. Layton was up to no good, and neither were these two men.'

'What were their names?' Marbury asked.

'Mellor and Huxley.'

'First names?'

'Let's see.' She got up to go into the hall and get her guest book, and hesitated when she saw Calvin Harris standing just inside the room, listening to her side of the conversation. He had a vested interest, so she waved him farther into the room as she fetched the guest book and brought it into the den.

'They're listed as Harold Mellor and Lionel Huxley.'

'How did they pay?'

'The man who called yesterday afternoon and made the reservations for them gave me a credit card number. I think it was the same man who called pretending to be from the rental car agency. I can't be certain, but I think the voice was the same. And the Caller ID said Unknown Name, Unknown Number both times.'

'What's the name on the credit card?'

'The name he gave me was Harold Mellor, but I know it wasn't the same man who was here today; their voices were completely different.'

'Have you run the charge through yet?'

'Yes, and it went through.'

'It could still be a fake card. That's something we can check, though. Did you get their license plate number?'

'No.' Writing down tag numbers wasn't something she normally did when a guest checked in – though she thought she might start.

'And they left without harming anyone after you gave them Layton's things?'

'That's right. They didn't harm anyone.'

Calvin made a motion that said he wanted to speak to Marbury. Cate raised her eyebrows in question, silently asking if he was certain, and he nodded. 'Hold on,' she said to Marbury. 'Mr. Harris wants to speak to you. This is Investigator Seth Marbury,' she said to Calvin as she extended the phone to him.

'This is Cal Harris,' he said, sounding his usual normal, quiet self. Cate felt an unsettling moment of shifting reality, as if she had lost her balance. She stared at him in disbelief that he could be the same man who had been so calm and cold as he aimed his shotgun at someone's head. It was too much to take in, and almost in self-defense she found herself focusing on the strong hand that held the phone. Luckily for her and Neenah, he'd handled a shotgun as competently as he handled a hammer or a wrench.

Marbury must have asked what he did for a living. He said, 'Whatever needs doing. Carpentry, plumbing, mechanic work, roofing.'

He listened for a minute. Cate could hear the rumble of Marbury's voice, but couldn't make out the words. Calvin said, 'When Mrs. Nightingale gave me her mail to take to town, she'd put the stamps on upside down. You know – the kind that come in a roll of a hundred. It's the American flag.' More rumbling from Marbury. 'Yeah. I thought she looked kind of upset, so I took the chance I was acting like an idiot and came back. Just to be on the safe side. Brought my shotgun with me. That's the reason the two left without hurting anyone.' More rumbling and a moment later he said, 'No, no shots were fired, by anyone. My Mossberg trumped his Taurus – which, by the way, he left behind.' A faint thread of amusement ran through his tone.

'Tomorrow's okay,' he finally said, and handed the phone back to her.

'Mrs. Nightingale,' Marbury said, 'I'm coming tomorrow to take Mr. Harris's statement. Is it convenient for you to give one, too?'

'Sure. After ten o'clock would be best,' she said.

'No problem. I'll be there at eleven.'

Cate clicked the 'off' button and stood there, knowing she needed to rejoin the group in the dining room, but inertia held her feet rooted to the spot. 'How could this happen?' she finally said.

'It's going to be okay.'

She realized he hadn't mumbled at all during those awful, tense moments in the attic, nor had he blushed once. He must be one of those people who rose to the occasion when he had to, then settled back into his comfort zone when the crisis was over. She would never again be able to look at him in the same way, she thought. 'Calvin, I—' She stopped, and to her confusion felt her own cheeks turn hot. 'I haven't told you how grateful I am—'

He looked shocked, staring at her as if she had two heads. 'You don't have to tell me. I know.'

Because of the boys, she thought. He knew how petrified she'd been that Sheila would bring the boys back while Mellor and Huxley were still there. Grateful that she didn't have to explain, she turned and hurried back to the dining room. He followed more slowly, and suffered a thigh-level mugging from two four-year-olds demanding once again to know how big the snake was and what he'd done with it.

She told the gathered neighbors what the detective had said, and that he was coming out tomorrow to take statements. By then Milly had the tea brewed to her satisfaction and Cate was obliged to sit and sip, as was Neenah. To her surprise, her nerves did begin to settle and the faint sense of everything being out of place began to fade. It wasn't until her three rock-climbing guests returned, tired and windburned and happy, that the gathering dispersed.

Because there was no restaurant in Trail Stop, the nearest one being over thirty miles away, at extra cost Cate provided an evening meal of sandwiches, chips, and dessert if the guests asked for it. Her climbers had, so she got busy with the cold cuts and cheese. Her mother kept the boys occupied, though they kept asking to go to the attic so they could hunt snakes, too, and got them fed while Cate was serving the climbers. By the time she and Sheila sat down, Cate was so tired she could barely eat. She knew it was her body's reaction to the day's stressful events; she was as exhausted as if she'd climbed all day, then hiked ten miles.

'Mom, I'm so sleepy,' she muttered, covering a yawn with her hand.

'Why don't you have an early night for a change,' her mother suggested, in a tone that made it sound more like an order. 'I can get the boys to bed.'

Cate surprised her, and perhaps even herself, by agreeing. 'I'm dead on my feet. While you're putting them to bed, why don't you broach the subject of going home with you? They've never spent the night away from me, so they may be resistant.'

'Leave them to me,' Sheila said smugly. 'By the time I get through with them, they'll think Mimi's home is better than Disneyland.'

'They haven't been there, either, so they may not get the comparison.'

'Never mind the details. By morning, they'll be begging you to let them go. That's if you're certain you want them to go. I still think you should sleep on it, make certain you aren't saying this just because of what happened today.'

'Of course I am,' Cate said. 'I want my children safe, and right now I don't feel they are. Maybe I'm overreacting, but I don't care.'

Sheila hugged her. 'It's your prerogative to overreact. And I won't hold it against you if you change your mind in the morning ... much.'

'Oh, thank you, that's reassuring,' Cate said, and laughed. She hugged the boys and kissed them good night, explaining that Mommy was tired and was going to bed early, but that Mimi would put them to bed tonight, and they were satisfied. All the excitement had worn them out, too; they were already yawning and rubbing their eyes.

Cate brushed her teeth and showered, then fell into bed. She was so tired her body felt boneless, but her thoughts chased around like crazed squirrels, darting hither and yon, unable to settle on anything. She kept reliving snippets of the day, flash-card images: Neenah's white face, the look in Calvin's pale eyes as his finger tightened on the trigger of the shotgun – She hadn't really noticed it at the time, but now she saw it over and over, the slight twitch of his finger that meant he intended to shoot.

Mellor must have seen the same thing, she thought, that telltale little motion, and decided to do things Calvin's way. She shivered, feeling cold, and curled up in the bed so she could tuck her feet closer to her body for heat. She was often cold at night, and sometimes it wasn't so much her reaction to the temperature as it was her aloneness, which seemed more acute in the dark. Tonight she huddled under the blanket with fear as a companion, fear for her children, fear of the violence that had come to her home that day, and she was made colder by the company.

Her subconscious replayed the look in Calvin's eyes. She had known him for three years, but she felt as if she had seen him, really *seen* him, for the first time today. She had discovered a lot of things about her neighbors today, appreciated them in new ways, but this was different. Her perception of Calvin hadn't undergone an adjustment; it had suffered a sea change.

Never again could she look at him and see just a painfully shy, good-hearted handyman.

Even worse, she felt as if more had changed than she realized, as if there had been a major shift in her life, but she hadn't yet found exactly where, or how much the foundations had moved. She didn't know how to react, what to think, because she didn't know if she stood on solid ground or on quicksand.

The memory of Calvin's pale eyes, the expression in them, arrowed into her with piercing clarity, and she went to sleep while trying to puzzle out if she should feel safer now, or more in peril than before.

Cal Harris had long ago discovered that if he stood at the window in his darkened bedroom, he could see the light in the window of Cate Nightingale's bedroom. The B and B was perhaps the equivalent of a block and a half down the road, but the road had a dogleg angle in it that let him see the windows of the two front bedrooms. The first set of windows was the twins' bedroom. The second set was Cate's.

He'd been in her bedroom when he was working on the plumbing in the attached bath. She liked pretty things, like fancy throw pillows on the bed, and in the bathroom were thick cotton rugs that matched the shower curtain and the thing that covered the lid of the john. Her bedroom smelled good, too, like a faint perfume . . . and like a woman. He'd looked at her bed and his imagination had gone wild.

His reaction to her was so strong he couldn't control it. He blushed and stammered like a fourteen-year-old, to the endless amusement of their neighbors. For three years they'd been urging him to ask her out, but he hadn't. From the way she called him 'Mr. Harris' and looked at him as if he were her grandfather, he knew she was nowhere near ready to start dating.

It had been a while since he'd aimed a weapon at another human being with the intention of pulling the trigger, but that bastard,

Mellor, had come within a hair of having his head blown up like an exploding pumpkin. Only the realization that Cate was watching, and that she would have been even further traumatized, had stayed Cal's finger on the trigger. He never wanted her to look at him with the sort of terror that had been in her eyes when she'd looked at Mellor.

Tonight her bedroom window was dark. He saw the twins' light come on, then go off about fifteen minutes later, but Cate's light never came on. Intuitively he guessed she was exhausted, and was already in bed; her mother must have put the boys to bed.

For three years he'd waited, and common sense had long since told him to give up and move on, but he hadn't. Whether it was bone-deep stubbornness that held him, or the little boys clinging to his legs and his heart, or Cate herself, he hadn't been able to say, 'That's enough, I'm through.'

The day's terror had broken down some barricades. He sensed it, knew it. Today, for the first time, she'd called him 'Calvin.' And she'd been the one blushing.

He went to bed feeling as if the world had shifted, and he would start tomorrow standing in a new place.

Chapter Eleven

The next morning, Goss and Toxtel sat in Toxtel's motel room, a map spread out in front of them on the rickety round table. They were drinking bad coffee made in the motel's cheap, tiny four-cup maker, and eating stale honey buns bought in a convenience store. The town had a mom-and-pop restaurant that served breakfast, but they couldn't discuss business in the middle of a local gathering place.

Toxtel pushed a sketch across the table toward Goss. 'See, here's the layout of the place, as I remember it. If you remember something different, say so. This has to be accurate.'

Toxtel had made a rough drawing of Trail Stop and the road leading to it, putting in stuff like the bridge, the stream, the river roaring on the right, the mountains looming tall on the left.

'I think there's a pig trail coming in from the right somewhere along that sorry excuse of a road,' Goss said. 'Couldn't tell if it was a driveway or some sort of hunting trail.'

Toxtel made a note of that, then checked his watch. He'd called someone who called someone, and a local who knew the area – and was supposedly good at taking care of problems of a certain type – was supposed to meet them here in Toxtel's room at nine. Goss was smart enough to know they were in over their heads and without expert help they wouldn't be able to contain those hayseeds in Trail Stop. They needed someone who was wilderness-savvy and who was good with a rifle. Goss did okay with a pistol, but he'd never fired a rifle. Toxtel had, but many years ago.

This local guy they were to meet supposedly had a couple of other guys he could call on to help. Goss wasn't an expert, but even he could tell there were more avenues of escape than just three people could cover – not to mention the fact that those three people also needed to sleep occasionally. For Toxtel's plan to work, he figured they'd have to have at least two more people, though three more would be better.

Goss was content to play along with whatever wild idea Toxtel came up with; the wilder the better, in fact, because that increased the chances the whole situation would blow up in Toxtel's face and Salazar Bandini would get a lot of attention he wouldn't want – like the Federal kind – which would make him very unhappy with Yuell Faulkner.

Goss had tried to come up with a concrete idea, but there were too many variables. The best he could hope for was that situations would present themselves in which he could surreptitiously foul things up, maybe make them worse. The best outcome would be that they got Bandini's flash drive and no one got hurt or killed – the best outcome for Bandini, that is, and by extension, the best outcome for Faulkner. Therefore he had to make certain the first thing didn't happen, and the second one did. He also wouldn't mind if that bastard handyman was one of the ones who got shot.

The fact that Goss hadn't died during the night meant he probably didn't have brain damage, but he still had a bitch of a headache. He'd taken four ibuprofen when he woke up, and while that had taken the edge off enough for him to be able to concentrate, he hoped he wouldn't be required to do anything more strenuous today than sit and talk.

At nine o'clock sharp there was a single rap on the door, and Toxtel got up to answer it. He opened the door and stepped aside for their visitor to enter.

'Name,' the man said briefly.

Hugh Toxtel was no one's flunky, but neither was he so full of himself that he took umbrage at every little thing. 'Hugh Toxtel,' he said as matter-of-factly as if the guy had asked what time it was. 'This is Kennon Goss. And you are—?'

'Teague.'

'Got a first name?'

'Teague will do.'

Teague looked like the Marlboro Man gone junkyard-dog mean. His face was so weathered it was impossible to tell how old he was, but Goss guessed maybe in his fifties. His hair was salt-and-pepper, and cropped close to his head. There was American Indian blood there, a few generations back, evidenced in the high cheek-bones and dark, narrow slits for eyes. If he'd let himself go soft, it didn't show anywhere.

He wore jeans, hiking boots, and a green-and-tan-plaid shirt tucked neatly into his waistband. A serious-looking knife rode in a sheath at his right kidney, the kind of knife used for skinning deer. It sure as hell would never qualify as a pocketknife. He was also toting a worn black canvas bag. Everything about Teague shouted 'serious badass,' and it wasn't anything he said or wore, it was the utter confidence with which he carried himself, the look in his eyes that said he'd gut someone with no more concern than if he were swatting a fly.

'I got word you need somebody who knows the mountains,' he said.

'We need more than that. We're going hunting,' Toxtel said neutrally, and indicated the map on the table.

'Just a minute,' said Teague, and hauled an oblong electronic device out of the canvas bag. He turned it on and walked around scanning the room. When he was satisfied there were no listening bugs, he turned it off and turned the television on. Only then did he approach the table.

'I appreciate a careful man,' Toxtel said, 'but tell me up front if you have the feds dogging you. We don't need a complication like that.'

'Not that I know of,' Teague replied, face expressionless. 'Doesn't mean things can't change.'

Toxtel regarded him silently. In the end, Goss thought, it came down to trust: Did Toxtel trust his contact? Trust was a commodity in short supply in their business, because there was no such thing as honor among thieves – or killers, as the case may be. What trust existed was there because of a sort of mutual-assured-destruction thing. Goss knew enough to bury Toxtel, and Toxtel knew enough to bury Goss. He felt safer with that than he would have with friendship.

Finally Toxtel shrugged and said, 'Good enough.' He turned back to the map and quickly outlined the situation, without mentioning Bandini's name; he just said that something very important had been left at the B and B and the owner wasn't inclined to give it to them. Then he laid out his plan.

Teague bent over the map, his hands braced on the table and his

106

brows drawn together in a frown as he worked things around in his mind. 'Complicated,' he finally said.

'I know. It'll take some people who know what they're doing.'

'That's why you're here,' Goss said drily. 'Hugh and I aren't exactly loaded with wilderness experience.' It was the first thing he'd contributed to the conversation, and Teague flashed him a quick glance.

'Smart of you to see that. Some people wouldn't. Okay. There are several things to consider. First, how do you cut off contact with the outside world? Not just physical contact, but phone, computer, satellite?'

'Cut the phone and power lines,' said Goss. 'That takes care of phones, computers, and satellite e-mail.'

'What if one of them has a satellite phone? You considered that?'

'Satellite phones aren't real common,' replied Goss, 'but just in case one of those yahoos does have one, we'll need to know. Should be easy enough to find out in a place that small. Likewise, it'll be easy to spot any vehicles new enough to have OnStar or something like it.'

'OnStar won't work out there,' Teague said. 'No cell phone service. You're safe on that.'

That was good; the situation was already complicated enough.

Since there were only two chairs, they dragged the table over to the bed. Toxtel sat on the bed, while Goss and Teague took the chairs. They spent an hour leaning over the map, with Teague pointing out topographical details.

'I'll have to reconnoiter, make sure the land lies the way I think it does, but I think this is a doable plan,' Teague finally said. 'Trail Stop is a dead end for the utility lines, the phone company and power company might not know service has been interrupted – and even if they do, taking out that bridge means they won't be able to do anything about it. So we put up 'bridge out' signs here' – he pointed to where the road to Trail Stop joined the large road – 'and block the road with construction sawhorses, and we should be good. This won't take forever, probably just a day or so. Put enough pressure on that woman and she'll cave. Hell, the rest of them there may throw her to the wolves; you never know. You said she's got a kid?'

'Toys were lying around. Never saw one, though.'

'Could be in school. So we make sure the kid is at home, start

107

this dance late in the afternoon or on Saturday. People tend not to risk their kids. After you get what you want, you gotta disappear fast. My men and I can slow them down, but at some point I'll have to pull out and fade into the woodwork, too. If you aren't gone by then, that's your ass on the line.'

'Understood,' said Toxtel. Then he frowned. 'If the bridge is out, how will we get what we came for?'

'The creek can be forded at other places. What we have to do is keep people from crossing at those places until we want them to. Now, let's talk money.'

When Teague left the motel room an hour later he had his money, and he was both satisfied and so amused it was all he could do to keep from laughing in their faces. Toxtel's plan was one of the most idiotic things he'd ever heard in his life, but if Toxtel wanted to pay him a small fortune for making this Rube Goldberg farce work, he was glad to take the man's money.

The plan was workable, with a lot of trouble and expense. It was also unnecessarily complicated. If it had been left up to Teague, he would have taken two men with him and gone in on foot about two AM; the woman would give up whatever it was she had or her kid would die. Simple. Instead, Toxtel had dreamed up this elaborate scheme to hold the entire community hostage.

Toxtel and Goss must have gone in there and had their asses handed to them. Teague had no doubt those two were bad men to cross, but they were out of their element. They were probably used to being the only ones with weapons; out here, everyone and his grandmother had a weapon. Now, wounded ego and hurt pride had come into play and clouded their judgment, which was never good.

On the other hand, making this work would be a challenge, and Teague dearly loved a challenge. There was so much to consider, so many pieces that had to fall into place, that he'd have to be at the top of his game. Maybe Toxtel and Goss weren't the only ones who'd let pride sway their decisions. The difference between them was, Teague recognized the element of pride in his motivation, and would allow for it. His biggest motive, though, was greed: he liked the numbers they'd been talking.

He was familiar with the Trail Stop area. The land surrounding it was rugged, almost impassable. In places the jagged mountains were almost vertical, with sheer rock faces and treacherous ravines. On the other side, the river blocked the way, and it was a bitch of a river. He didn't know of anyone, even white-water rafters, who put a raft in this far upriver. Trail Stop existed only because it had been needed by miners who excavated for gold in the mountains in the nineteenth and early twentieth centuries, leaving the place riddled with abandoned mines. That jut of land between the river and the mountains was the only reasonably flat piece of land for miles, so that was where a general store to serve the miners had been based. The general store was still there, the miners were long gone, and other than the handful of people who didn't have better sense than to live there, the only people ever there were tourists, hunters, or rock climbers.

Hmm. Rock climbers. That was something else to add to his list: he had to make certain there were no visiting rock climbers staying in the bed-and-breakfast, because they could conceivably offer a way out that he couldn't block. He didn't think so, because even if someone scaled the rock faces of the mountains to the northeast, they were still miles and miles of rugged territory away from help, but he preferred to cover all possibilities.

The way he saw it, his biggest problem would come from Joshua Creed. There weren't many people Teague respected, but Creed topped the list. The former Marine major had a cabin in the Trail Stop area, so it stood to reason he'd get some of his supplies there rather than drive thirty miles to another store. If anyone could throw a monkey wrench into the works, it would be Creed.

There were two options: bottle Creed up with the others inside the contained area and take the risk he would not only organize them but somehow mount a counteraction, or seal off the area with Creed outside it and hope the pretense of working on the bridge would fool him. Teague figured he'd have to be on his toes to manage Creed if he was with the others, but at least Teague would know where he was. If Creed wasn't in Trail Stop, then Teague had no way of keeping tabs on him – and Creed could well take it into his head to see what he could see.

Teague decided he was better off with Creed contained. That meant he'd have to take extra steps, bring in special equipment, to make certain Creed *stayed* contained.

Timing was everything. Everyone who belonged in Trail Stop had to be there and anyone who didn't belong had to be gone when the trap was sprung. An outsider would have people who expected to hear from him, or that he'd return home at a certain time. A local would certainly ask uncomfortable questions if he couldn't get to his home. Of course, said local could also meet with an accident, so that was more easily controlled than if the trap accidentally caught someone who didn't belong.

First on his list of things to do, however, was reconnaissance.

Cate overslept and as a result had to rush the next morning to get the muffins baked and ready for the usual onslaught of customers. Of course, after the excitement of the day before, it seemed as if everyone in Trail Stop felt the need for a muffin, even Milly Earl, the best cook in town.

As soon as the twins got up, they started pestering Cate about visiting Mimi's house, so it appeared Sheila had done a good job selling the idea to them. Cate pretended reluctance, to whet their appetite even more. The last thing she wanted was to have to physically manhandle the boys into her mother's SUV when they left. At the same time, neither did she want to act so reluctant that they would think she'd be unhappy if they went. Hoodwinking four-year-olds was a balancing act.

Sheila called the airline to see about changing her departure date, as well as purchasing tickets for the boys. The only flight she could get was at eleven AM the next morning, which meant she and the boys would be leaving by six in the morning, at the latest. She had to drive to Boise, return her rental, and shepherd the twins and their belongings to the gate, as well as find time to feed them before they got on the plane. She also called Cate's dad, letting him know she was coming home ahead of schedule and bringing the boys with her. 'Brace yourself,' Cate heard her mother say, laughing.

Investigator Marbury was due at eleven, so as soon as the morning crowd was gone, Cate rushed to get the kitchen and dining room cleaned up. The climbers had each grabbed a muffin and left early, eager for another day on the rocks. Cate could remember when she and Derek had been like that, with nothing more on their minds than testing their strength and skill on the rocks. These guests were leaving the next morning, so this was their last day to enjoy their sport.

At a quarter to eleven, she dashed up the stairs to change clothes, brush her hair, and swab on some lip gloss. Halfway up, she heard thuds and the boys shrieking with laughter in their room. Since experience told her they generally found things such as burst pillows and flying feathers hilarious, Cate was at a dead run by the time she hit the top of the stairs.

She skidded to a stop in the doorway, blinking at her children. They were both stark naked, jumping up and down, and laughing so hard they kept collapsing on the floor. Behind her, she heard Sheila running up the stairs, too, calling, 'Are they okay?'

'What on *earth* ... what are you two *doing*?' Cate asked, completely bewildered. She turned her head and said to Sheila, 'They're fine. They've pulled off all their clothes and they're jumping up and down.' She looked back at the boys. 'Stop – boys, stop jumping! Tell me what you're doing.'

'We're making our goobies shake,' Tanner said, for once speaking before Tucker could, but mainly because Tucker was laughing too hard to talk.

'Your—' Cate tried to say, then burst out laughing. They looked so funny, jumping up and down and pointing at each other's 'goobies,' and they were having such a good time all she could do was shake her head and laugh with them.

A flash went off beside her, and she jumped. It was Sheila, a digital camera in her hand.

'There,' she said with satisfaction. 'Something to blackmail them with when they're sixteen.'

'Mom! That'll embarrass them!'

'You bet it will. I'd have given anything to have had something like this to hold over Patrick's head. I'll print out a couple of copies when I get home. Just wait; you'll thank me someday.'

The doorbell rang downstairs, and Cate looked at her watch. If that was Marbury, he was early, and now she had no time to freshen up. Groaning, she said, 'Will you get them back in their clothes while I answer the door? It's probably the county investigator.'

She ran back down the stairs and pulled open the front door. Calvin Harris stood there, a box from Earl's Hardware Store in one hand and his toolbox in the other; beside him stood a stocky guy she didn't recognize, but since he had a holstered pistol on his belt she was certain this was Marbury. He had medium brown hair, and he wore jeans and a polo shirt, with a dark blue windbreaker. 'Mrs. Nightingale?' Without waiting for her to answer he said,

'I'm Seth Marbury, investigator with the sheriff's department.'

'Yes, come in, please.' As Cate stepped back, she cast a harried glance up the stairs, where childish peals of laughter were still unabated. She could hear her mother, though, sounding increasingly frustrated, as she told the boys to stop shaking their goobies and put their clothes back on, and evidently was being ignored. The thuds from their jumping echoed from the ceiling.

Both men looked upward.

Cate felt color heat her cheeks. 'Um . . . I have twin boys,' she explained to Marbury. 'They're four.' And that should definitely have been all the explanation needed.

'Tannuh, look!' she heard Tucker say in his clear, piping voice. 'I can make mine *zigzag*!'

Zigzag?

Evidently losing patience with the unproductive cajoling, Sheila said in her sternest voice – which was drill-sergeant stern – *'All right! I don't want to see any more zigzagging goobies. I don't want to see your goobies shake, dance, skip, yodel, or anything else you can make them do. I want to see those goobies inside your shorts. Got it? If you're going home with me, we have to make plans, and I can't do that if I can see your bare goobies.'*

Truer words had never been spoken, Cate thought, as she swallowed a bubble of laughter. She tried not to look at either man's face, because if she did she knew she'd lose it completely. Yodeling goobies? Sheila was in fine form.

Evidently she wasn't the only one trying not to lose it. Calvin sidled toward the stairs, carefully not even glancing at her. 'I – uh – I'll just go put this lock on the attic door,' he said, and all but bolted up to the second floor.

Cate drew a deep breath, then blew it upward in an attempt to cool her hot face. 'Let's go into the den. My mother should have the uproar quieted in a minute.'

Marbury was chuckling as she led him into the back den. 'They must keep you on your toes.'

'Some days more than others. Today is one of those days,' she said ruefully. Thank God, the uproar from their bedroom had subsided as the lure of making plans to go to Mimi's house must have outweighed the entertainment of shaking goobies.

To her everlasting gratitude, Marbury didn't ask what had been going on upstairs, but then that must have been fairly obvious.

He'd also been a little boy himself, once. She didn't want to think about him doing anything even remotely like that. She wanted to think of Marbury strictly as a law enforcement officer.

'I've already taken Mr. Harris's statement,' he said, and abruptly Cate saw the pitfalls of making any statement at all, because she didn't know exactly what Calvin had told him. Had he told about bashing the other guy, Huxley, in the head? She took a gamble that he hadn't, and in fact she hadn't seen him do it, so she started at the beginning and even told about having thought someone was listening to Neenah and her talking about the two men and her suspicions about them.

When she finished, Marbury sighed and rubbed his eyes. He looked tired, she realized; he must have had a lot on his plate, but he'd still taken the time to come out here and take their statements. 'These two are probably long gone. You didn't see anything else of them yesterday, did you?'

Cate shook her head. 'I should have called you sooner yesterday,' she admitted, 'but I just didn't think of it. We were okay but kind of stunned, if you know what I mean. Everyone stood around talking about it, and the twins were listening, and I—' She spread her hands helplessly. 'If I had, you could have cut them off at the pass, so to speak.'

'I could have brought them up on charges, yeah, but they'd have made bail, walked, and we'd never see them again. I hate it, but the county doesn't have the resources for us to spend a lot of time looking for out-of-state felons, especially when no one was hurt and nothing was taken except a suitcase that didn't belong to you anyway. Are you sure nothing of value was in the suitcase?'

'The most valuable thing was the pair of shoes, and I put them in there myself. They weren't originally in the suitcase.'

Marbury flipped his pad closed. 'That's it, then. If you see them again, call immediately, but they got what they came for, so I think they're long gone.'

With the distance of a night's sleep between now and then, Cate agreed with him. She was much calmer today, and beginning to wish she hadn't asked her mother to take the boys home with her, but she had started that train rolling, so she would let their plans proceed, since the boys were so excited about going to visit Mimi.

Shrieks abruptly splintered the air, and Cate, long used to the different qualities in her children's yells, interpreted these as

113

shrieks of joy. 'They must have spotted Mr. Harris,' she told Marbury. 'They love his toolbox.'

'That's understandable,' he said, grinning. 'A boy, a hammer – what's not to love?'

They went out of the den and watched Calvin coming down the stairs, preceded by the twins who jumped and danced in front of him. 'Mommy!' Tucker said, spotting her. 'Mr. Hawwis let us hold his dwill!'

'Drill,' Cate automatically corrected, meeting Calvin's gaze, which was as calm and steady as always.

'Drill,' Tucker repeated, grabbing the hammer loop on the side of Calvin's pant leg and tugging at it.

'Stop pulling at Mr. Harris's clothes,' she said, 'before you tear them off.'

No sooner were the words out of her mouth than she felt her face begin to heat. What was wrong with her? She hadn't blushed in years, but it seemed as if she'd done nothing *but* blush since yesterday. Everything seemed to have a double meaning, or seem overtly sexual, and, yes, the prospect of tearing Calvin's clothes off definitely seemed sexual.

The realization stunned her.

Calvin? Sexual?

Because he'd saved them yesterday? Was she casting him in a heroic role and, in the time-honored male-female way, subconsciously responding to that display of strength? She'd taken some anthropology courses, because they'd seemed interesting, so she knew the dynamics of sexual instincts. That had to be it. Women responded to strong, powerful, or heroic men. In caveman days, that had meant higher chances of survival. Women didn't have to do that now, but the old instincts remained; how else could one explain the allure of Donald Trump for so many women?

The rationalization relaxed her. Now that she knew what was causing this unusual sensitivity, she could deal.

She introduced the twins to Marbury, and of course they immediately noticed his pistol and were wide-eyed with awe that he was a policeman, though they were disappointed he wasn't wearing a uniform. At least they were distracted long enough for Cate to ask Calvin, 'How much do I owe you?'

He fished the receipt for the lock from his pocket, and gave it to her. Their fingers brushed, and she fought a quiver that wanted

114

to shake her entire body, as abruptly she remembered those strong hands holding the shotgun, his finger tightening on the trigger. She also remembered the way he'd held her and Neenah afterward, his arms warm and reassuring around them, his lean body surprisingly hard and sturdy inside the baggy coveralls.

Oh, damn. She was blushing again.

And he wasn't.

Chapter Twelve

'So,' her mother said casually that night as they were sitting on the boys' beds and packing their things, 'is something going on between you and Calvin Harris?'

'No!' Stunned, Cate almost dropped the pair of jeans she'd been folding and stared at her mother. 'What gave you that idea?'

'Just ... something.'

'Like what?'

'The way you two are together. Sort of awkward, and sneaking looks at each other.'

'I haven't been sneaking looks.'

'If I weren't your mother, that righteously indignant tone might work. As it is, I know you too well.'

'Mom! There's nothing going on. I'm not – I haven't—' She stopped and laid her hands in her lap, smoothing her fingers over the small garment. 'Not since Derek died. I'm not interested in going out with anyone.'

'You should be. It's been three years.'

'I know.' And she did – but knowing something and doing it were two different things. 'It's just – so much of my time and energy is taken up with the boys and this place ... adding something else, someone else, to the mix would be more than I could handle. And I haven't been sneaking looks,' she added. 'I was worried today about giving a statement to Marbury because I didn't know if Calvin had told him about hitting Huxley on the head. If I "sneaked" a look at him, it was because of that.'

'He looks at you.'

Now Cate had to laugh. 'And probably blushes while he looks

away as fast as he can. He's very shy. I think I've heard him say more in the past two days than I have in the rest of the time we've lived here. Don't read more into it than is there. He probably sneaks looks at everyone.'

'No, he doesn't. I haven't noticed he's particularly shy, either. When he was putting the new lock on the attic door and the boys were practically crawling all over him, he was chatting with me like he does with Sherry and Neenah.'

Cate paused, remembering that she'd overheard Calvin chatting with Sherry. Evidently there were some people he felt comfortable with, but she herself obviously wasn't one of them. The thought caused an odd little pain in the pit of her stomach. Instinctively shying away from examining the cause, she forced herself back to the conversation. 'Anyway. Before you start scheming to throw us together, think for a minute: neither of us is exactly a good catch. I'm chronically broke, and I have two children. He's a handyman. No one is beating down our doors.'

Sheila's lips twitched as she fought a smile. 'Then you'd probably make a good couple, since you're so evenly matched.'

Cate didn't know whether to feel amused or horrified. She was now on a handyman's level? She hadn't been raised to be a snob, but she'd worked in the corporate world, and she had ambitions. They weren't great ambitions, but they did exist. As far as she could see, Calvin was perfectly content to be what he was. On the other hand, given her chosen occupation of owning and operating a bed-and-breakfast, what could be handier than having her own handyman? God knows she couldn't have survived without him these past three years.

She gave a spurt of laughter. 'Well, I *have* considered asking him to move in.'

Her mother blinked in surprise.

'Giving him room and board in exchange for free repairs,' Cate explained, laughing again as she got up to get the boys' underwear out of their dresser drawers. While she was up she stuck her head out the door to check on the boys, who were playing with their cars and trucks in the hallway. She had put them out there so she and her mother could get their clothes packed without them helping, which would have guaranteed mayhem. They were building some sort of fort with their blocks, and crashing their cars into it. That should keep them safely occupied for a while.

'Sweetheart, it *is* time to consider beginning to go out with men again,' Sheila continued. 'Though God knows the pickings here are so slim Calvin is just about all there is. If you moved back to Seattle—'

Ah, there it was, the real reason behind her mother's sudden interest in Calvin. Cate made a rueful face. This was just another campaign to convince her to leave Idaho.

Cate waited until she paused for breath, then reached out and touched her hand. 'Mom, of all the advice you've ever given me, do you know what I treasure the most?'

Sheila drew back a little, her eyes narrowing suspiciously. 'No, what?'

'When Derek died, you told me a lot of people would be giving me advice about living and dating and so on, and not to listen to any of them, not even you, because grief had its own timetable and it was different for everyone.'

If there was anything Sheila hated, it was having her own words turned back on her. 'Well, good God!' she said in a tone of total disgust. 'Don't tell me you fell for that profound claptrap!'

Cate burst out laughing and pitched backward across Tanner's bed, both fists raised in victory.

Sheila threw a pair of balled-up socks at her. 'Ungrateful wretch,' she muttered.

'Yes, I know: you were in labor for twenty days—'

'Twenty *hours*. It just seemed like days.'

Both boys came running in. 'Mommy, what's funny?' Tucker demanded, jumping onto the bed with her.

'What's funny?' Tanner echoed, jumping to the other side of her.

Cate wrapped her arms around them. 'Mimi is. She's been telling me funny stories.'

'What kind of stories?'

'About when I was a little girl.'

Their eyes got big and round. Their mommy being a little girl was a concept that was just too unbelievable. 'Mimi knew you then?' Tucker asked.

'Mimi is Mommy's mommy,' Cate said, glad she didn't have to say that ten times really fast. 'Just like I'm your mommy.'

She saw Tanner's lips move as he silently repeated the words *Mommy's mommy*. He stuck his finger in his mouth as he regarded

Sheila with laser-beam intensity.

'I feel like a zoo animal,' Sheila complained.

'Zoo?' Tanner asked around his finger, his interest caught.

'Zoo! Mimi's taking us to the zoo!' Tucker shouted with glee.

'Trapped,' said Cate, grinning at Sheila.

'Ha ha. I happen to think that's a great idea. We certainly will go to the zoo,' she promised firmly. 'If you behave and go to bed when you're supposed to.'

Once the boys saw her putting their clothes in their suitcases, the jig was up, as Cate had known it would be. Their excitement almost fizzed out of control. They started dragging out the toys they wanted to take with them, which of course would have required chartering a plane for that purpose alone. Cate let Sheila handle the situation, since she would be in charge of them for the next couple of weeks and the boys needed to get even more in the habit of listening to her.

Finally they were packed, with a limit of two toys each. By then they were winding down, and Cate left Sheila to the chore of getting them bathed and into their pajamas while she went downstairs and tackled the job of switching their car seats from her Explorer to Sheila's rental. She should have done that in the daylight, she thought after wrestling with the straps and buckles in the overhead dome's dim light. Finally the seats were secure, and she trudged back inside to make name and address tags for the seats, since they would have to be checked in to the plane's luggage hold. She made another trip outside to put the tags on the seats.

The September night was chilly, and Cate wished she'd grabbed a jacket before going out. She paused for a moment, staring up at the star-shot sky. The air was so clear there seemed to be thousands of stars hanging overhead, many more than she'd seen anywhere else.

The night surrounded her, but it wasn't silent. The roar of the river was constantly in the background, accompanied by the rustle of leaves as the wind whispered through the trees. The uppermost branches were already starting to turn color; fall was coming fast, and as winter took hold, business would slack off to the point that some weeks she wouldn't have any paying guests at all. Maybe she should start serving lunch during the slow season, she thought. Just simple stuff, like soups and stews, sand-

119

wiches; they were easy to make and would keep some money coming in. When snow was two and three feet deep on the ground, the promise of hot soup or stew or chili would bring the citizens of Trail Stop over. Heck, it might even bring Conrad and Gordon Moon in from their ranch.

Sheila's question about Cal swam back into her mind. She had never even remotely connected him with anything romantic – but then, she hadn't thought romantically about anyone. She still couldn't get her mind around that concept, but she felt that odd little pain in her stomach again as she wondered once more why he was so closemouthed around her. If he could chat with other people, why not her? Was something wrong with her? Did he shy away from her because he didn't want her to get ideas about *him*? The idea was almost laughable – and yet it wasn't. She had two small children. A lot of men didn't want to get involved with women who had children from a previous marriage.

But why was she even thinking this way about Cal? She had no basis for that supposition. She'd never been interested in him in that way, and if he had any such ideas about her, then he was the world's best actor, because he'd revealed nothing.

She shoved the whole subject away. It was nuts, and she was nuts for letting herself obsess about it. She should be making plans for the next two weeks.

While the boys were gone, she could get some things done, such as clean out the freezer and pantry, and pile rocks around the circumference of the parking lot to make it more official-looking than just some gravel spread around. She could go through their clothes and pack up the things that were too small or too worn, and put them in the attic. She should probably donate the clothes to a shelter or something, but she couldn't bring herself to part with their things yet. She still had all their baby clothes, the tiny onesies, the bibs and socks and adorable little shoes. Maybe by the time they started school, she would get over this ridiculous attachment to their outgrown clothing; if she didn't, she could foresee the entire house being used as storage.

Yes, she had a lot with which to occupy herself while the boys were gone. Maybe she'd be so tired at the end of the day she wouldn't be in tears from missing them so much.

That reminded her that if she didn't get inside in a hurry, they would already be asleep. She wouldn't have the opportunity to tuck them in and read them a story for the next two weeks, so she didn't want to miss tonight.

Sheila was just getting them into their pajamas when Cate entered the steamy bathroom. 'All clean,' Tucker said, beaming up at her.

She bent to kiss the top of his head, hugging him close and then straightening with him in her arms. He snuggled close, his head on her shoulder, making her heart squeeze at the knowledge that these days were flying by and soon they would be too big for her to pick up – not that they'd want her to. By then they probably wouldn't want her hugging and kissing them, either.

Cate picked up Tanner, who wound his arm around her neck and smiled winsomely at her. She pulled back a little, narrowing her eyes at him, which might have been a little more effective if she hadn't been patting his back at the same time. 'You're up to something,' she said suspiciously.

'Not,' he assured her, and smothered a yawn.

They were tired and ready for bed, but too excited to settle down. First they couldn't decide what story they wanted to hear; then Tanner wanted one of his dinosaurs to hold, which meant Tucker had to decide which toy he wanted, too. Finally he settled on his Batman figure, which he bounced around on the covers.

Tanner laid down his dinosaur and gave her a very serious look. 'I'm going to be in the army when I grow up,' he announced.

Tucker nodded, too caught up in a yawn to say anything.

Last week they'd been set on being firemen, so Cate could only wonder at how fast they changed. 'Do you know where kings keep their armies?' she asked in wide-eyed seriousness.

They both shook their heads, their own eyes going big.

'In their sleevies.'

For several long seconds they stared at her in silence, then began giggling as they got the joke. Sometimes she had to explain jokes to them, but that frustrated them and they loved it when they caught on all by themselves. Behind her her mother gave a soft groan, probably because she remembered that at the twins' age repetition was the name of the game and now she could count on hearing that joke at least a hundred times over the next two weeks.

Cate read them their story, which lulled them to sleep within five minutes. She kissed them good night, then tiptoed out of the room.

Sheila saw the tears in her eyes and hugged her. 'You'll be all right, I promise. Just wait until the first day of school; *that's* when you'll cry your eyes out.'

Through her tears Cate had to laugh. 'Thanks, Mom, that's such a comfort to know.'

'Yes, but if I told you it wouldn't bother you at all, when the day came you'd know I'd lied and you wouldn't trust me again. Of course,' Sheila said thoughtfully, 'I didn't cry at all when Patrick started school. As I remember, I turned handsprings on the lawn.'

Sheila continued to reminisce about Patrick, keeping Cate smiling, until they went to bed. As soon as Cate told her mother good night and closed her bedroom door, however, her eyes filled and her chin wobbled. The boys had never been away overnight before. She was devastated by the prospect. They'd be so far away; if anything happened it would take her hours and hours to get to them. She wouldn't be able to hear them playing during the day, their shouts and squeals and laughter, the pounding of their feet as they raced around. She wouldn't be able to hug them tight, feel their little bodies close to her own and know they were okay.

Bitterly she wished she'd kept her mouth shut about them going home with her mother, but at the time she'd been panic-stricken – which had been a perfectly normal reaction to having had a gun pointed at her. Her only thought had been to get her children away from any possible danger.

She hadn't known cutting the apron strings would be so difficult. Nor had she intended to cut them now. When they were five would have been about right. Or six. Maybe even seven.

She had to laugh at herself, a watery gurgle that caught in a hiccup. Part of her had wanted them to be more independent, because being a single parent of two active little boys wasn't easy. She felt as if she never had any downtime, as if she had to be alert every minute of every day, because they could get into trouble in a second. If they were older, more responsible, she could relax a little. She just didn't want them to be older and more responsible right *now*.

Giving herself pep talks didn't help; neither did reasoning with herself. She cried herself to sleep, already missing the boys so much she ached.

The next morning Cate got up even earlier than usual so she could help her mother get the boys and their stuff loaded in the SUV, as well as do her normal morning cooking. She made hot oatmeal for the boys, because the predawn air was downright cold, but they were too sleepy to eat more than a few bites. Knowing they'd never last all the way to Boise without getting hungry, she prepared each of them a zippered plastic bag of cereal, and sent along two apples just in case.

Dawn hadn't yet arrived when they shepherded the boys outside. Even the cold air didn't rouse them very much. They climbed into their seats, looking adorable in their jeans and sneakers, their little flannel shirts left unbuttoned over their T-shirts. They had resisted wearing jackets, so Cate had gone outside and started the SUV ahead of time, turning the heater on high, and the interior was nice and warm. They settled in, each clutching a chosen toy. Cate kissed each of them, told them to have fun and that they should do what Mimi told them to do, then hugged her mother. 'Have a safe trip,' she managed to say without her voice quivering too much.

Sheila hugged her in return, patting her back just as she had when Cate was little. 'You'll be fine,' she said soothingly. 'I'll call when we get home, and I'll call or e-mail every day.'

Cate didn't want to mention the word *homesick* where the boys might hear her – she didn't want to plant a seed, in case they knew what the word meant – so she said, 'If they get teary—'

'I'll handle it,' Sheila interrupted. 'I know you agreed to this when you were scared and then nothing happened and you're thinking you were worried for no reason, but ... tough. You agreed, and I'm holding you to it. I don't like cutting my visit short, but I'll get the rest of my time when I bring the boys home.'

Nothing like some of her mother's no-nonsense commentary to brighten her world, Cate thought, laughing as she got in another hug. Then her mother got behind the wheel, and Cate leaned down for a last look at the boys. Tucker was already asleep. Tanner looked drowsy, but he gave her an impish smile and blew her a kiss. Cate pretended to be staggered by the impact and he giggled.

They would be okay, she thought as she watched the taillights disappear down the gravel road. She had doubts about herself.

From his observation point, Teague watched the SUV slow as it approached the bridge, then pick up speed. The lights from the dashboard showed a middle-aged woman behind the wheel. The passenger seat was empty.

The logical supposition was that, leaving this early, the woman had a flight to catch. He couldn't imagine why a lone woman would come to the middle of nowhere for a solitary vacation, but maybe she was some high-powered executive who just wanted to get away from everything, and Trail Stop was certainly a good place to do that.

During the wee hours he'd reconnoitered the community. Two rental vehicles had been parked on the far side of the B and B, meaning just one was left now. He'd watch for it. Slipping among the houses, he'd looked at angles, deciding the best positions his men could take for the most effective lines of fire. A couple of dogs had barked, but he was very good at clandestine movement and neither of them had taken real alarm; no lights had come on, so he guessed the inhabitants were accustomed to the occasional bark.

These people wouldn't roll over and play dead. They would fight back as well as they could, and probably every house had some sort of weapon in it. Out here, with bears and snakes and other wildlife, it paid to keep at least a pistol handy. He wasn't worried about the pistols; they wouldn't have the distance. Ditto the shotguns. It was the rifles that would give him problems, and it was a sure thing that some of the men would hunt deer, so they'd have powerful weapons that shot powerful rounds.

He marked the buildings from which the locals would be able to effectively return fire, which, if he positioned his men right, would be few. The houses were too spread out, with a lot of open ground that they couldn't safely cross. There were maybe thirty, thirty-five buildings total. The road angled to the left side of the roughly comma-shaped area, putting most of the houses on the river side, on the right, which was good because it clustered people on the side where they had literally nowhere to go. Not only was there a seventy-foot bluff on that side, but the river itself was an effective barrier.

Any escape attempts would necessarily come from the left, where there were fewer houses for cover. The mountains on that side were mostly impassable, but before he started this dance, he intended to explore them himself, looking for possible escape routes. These people would know their own backyard; there might be an abandoned mine that cut all the way through a fold of the mountain. If there was, he wanted to know about it.

Then the next step would be to locate Joshua Creed.

Chapter Thirteen

When Teague opened the porch door into the B and B's dining room, the delicious aroma of fresh baking assailed him. He paused, inhaling deeply. The room was big but filled with small tables and with people, some of whom stood around with a cup of coffee in one hand and a muffin in the other, instead of taking a seat – not that there were many vacant seats.

He took a good look around, marking one or two faces that looked familiar. He could put a name to one face, that of Walter Earl, who owned the little hardware store here. In all likelihood, that meant Earl could put a name to Teague's face, which in turn meant he had to be extra careful not to do or say anything suspicious, and when the plan actually came down, he couldn't let any of the locals see him.

The buzz of conversation died down as his presence was registered and everyone got a good look at him, not being shy about it, either. Some even turned around in their chairs to eye him. Probably whatever dustup the two city boys had caused made the locals a little antsy, not that they would ever have been shy about looking over an outsider.

Their interest died fairly fast. The city boys would have stood out like sharks in a pool of guppies – though they'd found out pretty quick that these guppies had teeth. Teague, on the other hand, looked like one of them, because he *was* one of them. He was wearing old boots, jeans worn white from years of use, and a faded flannel shirt against the sudden chill the weather had taken. On his head was a green John Deere cap, definitely not new. He could have been any one of them.

A woman came into the dining room, bearing a tray containing muffins and butter that she unloaded on one of the tables, deftly placing a muffin-filled plate in front of each person while the butter went in the middle. Each table already bore an assortment of jams and jellies. She smiled at Teague in passing, saying, 'I'll be right with you.'

From Goss's description, he knew this was the owner. Funny how Toxtel and Goss had given such different descriptions. Toxtel had shrugged and said, 'She's nothing extra. Brown hair, brown eyes. Average.' Goss, on the other hand, had smiled and said, 'She's got a great ass, like an athlete. Round and muscular. Small tits. Lanky build, except for that ass. Like a runner, maybe. Long, wavy hair, and this funny-looking, kissable mouth.' Toxtel had snorted at that, but Goss had ignored him. The difference told Teague as much about each man as it did about the B and B owner.

Her name was Cate Nightingale. Dumb name, Nightingale. What kind of a name was that? He'd done some checking, so he knew she wasn't a local. How had she ended up at Trail Stop? If you weren't born here, why would *anyone* come to Trail Stop? The few little businesses had to be barely hanging on, providing service to the community and the neighboring ranches, but God knows, they couldn't be making much. Still, for the folks born here, this was home and a few of them had stayed when common sense said they should have moved on years ago.

Having finished delivering the tray full of muffins, she came back to him. 'What can I get you? A muffin, or just a cup of coffee?'

She had a nice voice. She didn't look like someone who would take what didn't belong to her, but that wasn't his problem.

As if suddenly remembering his manners, he grabbed the cap off his head and stuck it in his back pocket. 'Uh – I'm looking for Joshua Creed, but those muffins do look good. One, please, and a cup of coffee.'

'Coming right up.' She looked around. 'Take any seat you like; we're very informal here. Just ask any of the men about Mr. Creed, and if one person doesn't know where he is, someone else will.'

He nodded and she whipped through the door into the kitchen, where he glimpsed another woman working. No sign of a kid, though, and in his experience a kid made its presence known. If there was one, it was probably old enough to be in school, and would be home this afternoon.

One of the tables was occupied by a group he recognized by their clothes as outsiders. Climbers, he thought, catching enough of their conversation to confirm his guess. And from the way they were dressed, they weren't going out climbing. Were they going home today? The weekend was just starting, but maybe they had a climb planned at another location. They bore watching, to see if their vehicle was packed up when they left.

He approached the table where Walter Earl was sitting, and gravely nodded his head in acknowledgment. 'Sorry to interrupt,' he said, 'but do any of you know where I can find Joshua Creed?'

'Don't I know you?' Walter Earl asked with a slightly puzzled expression.

Teague pretended to study him. 'Maybe. Your face looks familiar. My name's Teague.' Lying wouldn't be smart, because Earl might remember his real name later.

Walter's face cleared. 'That's it. You've been in the store a time or two, haven't you?'

Once, to get some shotgun shells, but in a place like this people tended to remember anyone they didn't normally see every day. 'I have,' Teague said. Maybe it was good the old man remembered him; it placed him in the others' minds as someone who belonged.

'Josh took a client deer hunting,' Walter offered. 'Monday, wasn't it?' He looked at the others for confirmation.

There were several nods. 'Sounds right,' another man said. 'I don't remember when he said he'd be back.'

'Should be today or tomorrow, though; he usually keeps his hunts to four or five days. Says that's about his limit on tolerating most of them.'

'In that case, he should have brought this one back yesterday,' another man said, and they all laughed.

Teague allowed himself a small smile, to go along. 'A bad one, huh?'

'Let's just say he thought highly of himself. Isn't that right, Cate?' Walter said as the Nightingale woman approached with Teague's muffin and coffee.

'Isn't what right?'

'This last client of Josh's, the one who was in here with him on Monday, was a real likable guy.'

She snorted. 'Yeah, I just loved the geography lesson he gave

127

us.' She turned to Teague. 'Where're you sitting?'

'I'll just stand,' he said, taking the plate and cup from her. 'Thank you, ma'am.'

She smiled and whisked away. He watched her take note of the level of coffee in every cup she passed and then go straight to the coffeemaker, where she lifted a pot off the heating plate and then went around the room providing warm-ups. Because he was a man, he also watched her ass. Like Goss said, it was an eye-catcher.

'Cate's a sweet woman,' Walter said, and Teague looked around to find all the occupants of the table watching him with various levels of aggression. Protective of her, were they?

'No need to look at her like that,' an old man who looked close to ninety said. 'She's spoken for.'

What was up that they felt the need to warn him away from Cate Nightingale? Teague manufactured another smile, which was about his limit, and lifted one hand. 'I was just about to say she reminds me of my daughter,' he lied. He didn't have a daughter, but these old farts didn't know that.

It worked. They all relaxed, and the smiles came back out. Walter leaned back in his chair and returned to the original subject. 'Josh might come in here when his client leaves, might not. He's not a regular like the rest of us. Did you leave a message on his answering machine?'

'No, I didn't bother. Someone told me I might find him here,' Teague answered. 'This guy I know is trying to find a guide for some important client who decided out of the blue he wanted to go hunting, so I thought of Creed. Since the guy needs someone pronto, no need to leave a message. I'll just tell him to move on to the next name on the list.' He paused. 'Unless Creed has a satellite phone, maybe?'

Walter rubbed his jaw. 'If he does, he's never mentioned it. Can you call a satellite phone from a regular phone?'

'Have to be able to; otherwise there's no point in 'em,' the old man said testily.

'Guess you're right,' Walter admitted. He looked back at Teague. 'Josh is the best guide there is, no doubt about it. His clients bag trophies more often than anyone else. Too bad your friend missed him.'

'His loss,' Teague said briefly. Holding his coffee in one hand and balancing the plate on top of the cup, he lifted the muffin and took a big bite. His taste buds exploded with delight. He could detect walnuts and apple, cinnamon, and something else he couldn't identify. 'Damn,' he muttered, and took another bite.

Walter laughed. 'Cate bakes a mean muffin, doesn't she? Every time I have one I think, no way can her scones top her muffins – but then on Scone Day I wish she'd make scones more often.'

Teague had heard of scones, but he'd never tasted one, and wasn't really certain what one was. He hated fancy food, and usually wouldn't even touch a muffin, but he was glad he'd taken this one. Assuming Ms. Nightingale lived through Toxtel's plan for Trail Stop, Teague thought he might have to stop by the B and B again; these muffins were tasty.

He'd found out what he needed to know about Creed, so there was nothing else to do now except keep watch and see what happened. Did a kid show up after school? Did the climbers leave? Did anyone else come to stay at the B and B? And if Creed didn't come to Trail Stop often enough to be considered a regular, then Teague would have to come up with some way to neutralize him, which could get messy.

After the breakfast bunch had cleared out and she and Sherry had cleaned up, Cate checked out her climbing group and saw them on their way. She didn't have anyone else coming in until the following weekend – another group of climbers – which she now realized wasn't good. With the boys gone, she would have preferred to stay busy.

Sherry left after the cleaning was finished, and Cate was alone in the house.

The silence was painful.

Because no one was arriving immediately, she didn't have to hurry to clean up all the rooms, but she threw herself into it with a vengeance. After stripping the beds and getting started on the mound of laundry, she cleaned the bathrooms, vacuumed, dusted, and even cleaned the windows.

Then she got started on the boys' room, which might or might not have been a good idea. It really needed cleaning, but being in there – putting away their toys, cleaning out their closets, and straightening their clothing – reminded her of their absence. She tried not to watch the clock, but she kept glancing at her watch anyway, trying to gauge where they were by the time. It was impossible, of course; she didn't know if the plane had been delayed for an hour or two, though she hoped her mother would have called her in that case, knowing she'd be worried if she didn't receive their safe-arrival call on time.

She didn't pause for lunch, because preparing something just for her didn't seem worth the effort. Several times she had to sniff back tears. This felt like grief, which was silly; she *knew* what grief really was. Still the feeling of having lost part of herself persisted, even though her apron strings hadn't been cut, just stretched a little ... if several hundred miles could be considered 'little.'

'Apron strings, my ass,' she muttered to herself. 'More like the *umbilical* cord.' And that comparison was extreme enough to make her laugh, just a little. They were fine. Her parents might not be fine by the end of the twins' visit, but the boys would sail through. She'd worked hard to make certain they felt utterly secure, which had given them the self-confidence to fly off with their grandmother for a two-week visit. They were eager to be on an airplane. They'd flown before, of course, but they'd been infants and didn't remember. She should be glad they were such brave little hearts.

Except two weeks was too long. She should have agreed to just one week.

When the phone rang shortly after three, she lunged for it.

'We made it,' her mother said, sounding exhausted.

'Is everything all right? Was there any trouble?'

'Everything's great; there weren't any problems. They loved pushing the luggage cart. They loved watching the planes take off and land. They loved the tiny bathroom, which they both had to use. Twice. The pilots stopped by to talk to them before takeoff, and both boys now have a set of wings, which they haven't taken off.'

They would probably still be wearing those wings when they came home, Cate thought, tears sparkling in her eyes even as she smiled at the thought.

'The first thing they saw when we got home was the riding lawn mower,' her mother continued. 'Your father is out there now with both of them in his lap, riding them around and around. The blades are disengaged,' she added.

Cate could remember riding with her father on the lawn mower, and she got a mushy feeling around her heart knowing that now he was doing that with her children.

'So now you can stop sniffling,' Sheila said. 'They're not only having a blast, they've exhausted me and are now working on your father, which should give you a nice warm sense of revenge.'

'It does,' Cate admitted. 'Thanks.'

'You're welcome. Do you want me to send pictures? We've already taken a bunch.'

'No, it takes too long for them to download, since I just have dial-up. Print them out and bring copies when you come back.'

'Okay. How did *you* do today?'

'Been cleaning like a maniac.'

'Good. Now that you have afternoons free, go get your hair done.'

Cate laughed, and for the first time truly realized she *could* get a haircut. A trim, at least, wouldn't cost all that much, and she desperately needed one. 'I think I will.'

'Spend some time on yourself. Read a book. Watch a movie. Paint your toenails.'

After they hung up, Cate realized that her parents' intention had been to give her a little break as much as it had been to have the boys to themselves for a while. She appreciated their concern, she really did, and would try to spend some time on herself. With that in mind, after she'd checked her e-mail and handled the reservations that had come in via the Web site, after she'd finished the laundry, after she'd copied down a list of ingredients for her next shopping trip – for some recipes she wanted to try – and after she had prepared supper for herself – a grilled cheese sandwich – she took her mother's advice to heart and painted her toenails.

Chapter Fourteen

That night Teague met with Toxtel and Goss again. The three men he'd called in came, too: his first cousin, Troy Gunnell; his nephew, Blake Hester; and an old friend, Billy Copeland. Troy and Billy were almost as good in the mountains as Teague was himself; Blake was pretty good, but his main accomplishment, and the reason he was included, was his marksmanship. If there were any tough shots to be made, Blake would be the triggerman.

The six of them went over the plan again and again. Teague had spent most of the day mapping it out, literally, using a combination of road maps, topography maps, satellite images, and maps he himself had made of the area. While he'd been in Trail Stop, he'd also surreptitiously taken pictures, using a digital camera, and printed out the photos on his computer. Using the photos and his own memory, he'd drawn a rough map of Trail Stop, showing the placement of the houses and their distance apart.

'Why do we need to know where the houses are?' Goss asked, staring intently at the map. There was no impatience in his tone, but a genuine interest. He was looking better than he had the day before; when Teague had commented on that, he'd admitted he'd been bashed in the head by Trail Stop's handyman, whom Toxtel described as a skinny-assed bastard with a big shotgun.

'Because these aren't people who'll just throw up their hands and surrender,' Teague explained. 'One or two might, but for the most part they'll get mad, and they'll try to fight back. Don't underestimate them. These people have grown up hunting in these mountains, and there'll be some damn fine marksmen among them. By choosing our spots, we can neutralize most of their avenues of effective fire; plus we need to get them congregated as much as possible. Makes them easier to watch. See how the houses are spread out?' he asked, tapping the map. 'With the firing platforms I've selected, we have direct lines of fire at twenty-five of the thirty-one houses.'

'What about the bed-and-breakfast?' Toxtel asked.

Teague drew a dotted line from one of his selected firing positions to the bed-and-breakfast. There was a clear shot only to the upper-right corner room; everything else was blocked by another building.

Toxtel frowned at the dotted line. He'd evidently hoped for something more. 'You can't move your position and get a better angle?'

'No, not without repositioning way the hell up on this slope.' Teague tapped a spot on the map, at the northeast corner of Trail Stop.

'Why don't you, then?'

'First, I'm not a damn mountain goat; that's an almost vertical slab of rock. Second, it isn't cost effective, because any attempts to escape won't go in that direction. We've left them only one way out, and it's through here.' He traced a route that ran roughly horizontal to the land peninsula on which Trail Stop was situated, then angled northwestward through a deep cut in the mountains.

'Why don't you close that gap, too?' Goss asked.

'Last time I looked, there are only four of us. Six, counting you two, but I gather neither of you has any experience with a rifle. Am I right?'

Goss shrugged. 'I don't. Can't say about Toxtel.'

'Some,' Toxtel said grudgingly. 'Not much.'

'Then, what it comes down to is the four of us will have to split the watches into twelve-hour shifts. That's tough enough as it is. At first there will be one of us with a rifle on each of these three firing positions, but after we drive most of the people to the far left corner, the position here at the bridge will be turned over to you two. They won't know the rifles have been concentrated on the other two firing positions, and on the right the river makes an effective barrier anyway.'

'What about the nights? Do you have night-vision goggles?' Goss asked.

Teague gave a feral grin. 'I have something better than that. FLIR scopes.'

'Flur? What the hell's that?'

'Forward-looking infrared. FLIR. Picks out body heat. Camouflage can fool night vision, but it can't fool the heat seekers. Our field of vision will be limited with scopes, so we'll have to be on our toes, but by limiting the places where we'll have to look, we can offset that shortcoming.'

Teague had put some thought into the scopes. For one thing, they were heavy, three pounds at least. That meant he and the others couldn't hold the rifles for any length of time; they'd have to be on rests. And the battery packs lasted only about six hours – in optimal conditions, meaning around eighty degrees. He thought they'd be lucky to get five hours out of them. Given that daylight hours were shrinking daily, it was a given each man would have to change battery packs at least once a shift, and probably twice if the weather turned cold. Last night the temperature had dipped into the low forties. Snow wasn't all that unusual in September, so the weather could turn bad without notice. To be on the safe side, he'd gotten twelve rechargeable battery packs, plus heavy-duty rechargers capable of handling more than one pack at a time.

'Billy got some collapsible sawhorses, painted them up to look like the ones used by the state, to block the road and keep nosy people out. We've also put a magnetic construction company sign on a pickup we can use, to make it look like work is being done on the bridge. I'm not worried about the state people. What worries me are the power and telephone companies. Everything they have is computerized. Are they gonna know when Trail Stop goes dark?'

Blake spoke for the first time. He was twenty-five, a six-footer, with short dark hair and eyes, a lot like his uncle. 'Not necessarily. They don't know if an individual customer is having trouble, even when it's line trouble; someone has to report the problem. Trail Stop is the end of the line; there's nothing beyond. And if they do show up – hell, the bridge is out, they can't get across. What they gonna do? Wait for the state to fix the bridge, that's what.'

Teague thought that over and gave a short nod. 'That should work. All you two guys have to do' – he glanced at Toxtel and Goss – 'is convince them you work for either the state or the construction company hired to rebuild the bridge. Neither of you looks like a construction worker, so state would be more believable – but you have to lose the suit.' That last was targeted at Toxtel. 'Khakis, boots, flannel shirts, jackets. That's what you wear on this job. And get a couple of hard hats, to make it look official.'

'Time line?' Goss asked.

'There's one more little detail I need to take care of.' Creed wasn't so 'little,' but they couldn't put the plan into action until Teague had located the guide. 'You two take tomorrow to get the clothes and gear you need. I'm good with my supplies. And while you're buying, don't forget camping gear. None of us are leaving Trail Stop until the dance is over, so that means food, water, lanterns, and heaters. It can get damn cold at night, and the weather's changing. Thermal underwear. Extra socks and underwear. Whatever else you can think of. Get all of that packed and ready, so we can move in tomorrow after midnight. I'll have the power and telephones off by two o'clock, and then we take out the bridge.'

There hadn't been any point in calling Creed's cabin when he didn't expect Creed to be there, but by Saturday morning Cal Harris judged Creed should have sent his client home by now and would be kicked back for some downtime. Old Roy Edward Starkey had judged the client to be a major pain in the ass, and Roy Edward was a good judge of character. That meant Creed would need even more alone time than usual, to reward himself for not choking the son of a bitch to death.

First Cal treated himself to a muffin and cup of coffee at Cate's house, just to watch her move among the customers and to hear her voice. Her mother had taken the twins home with her for a visit, and he was of two minds about that. On the one hand, he missed the little stinkers. On the other, this was the first time in the three years he'd known Cate that the boys weren't close at hand, the first real opportunity he'd had for some private conversation – provided he could string two words together without stammering and turning beet red like some idiot.

Cate barely glanced at him as she served his muffin, though when he darted a look at her, he saw that her cheeks were pink and she seemed flustered. He didn't know if that was good or bad. He wanted her to be aware of him, but he didn't want her feeling uncomfortable. That couldn't be good, could it?

The entire community was aware of, and amused by, his

predicament. Everyone was also unfailingly on his side, though he'd warned them to stop deliberately sabotaging Cate's plumbing, wiring, Explorer, or doing whatever else their fertile brains could concoct to throw the two of them together – as if having his head stuck under her sink with his ass in the air was going to ignite her interest. Besides, all those little 'repairs' caused her added stress, and she was under enough of that without their help. She was a young widow with four-year-old twins, trying to make a go of an old Victorian bed-and-breakfast in the middle of nowhere, for God's sake.

When he was certain that what he was repairing was one of those little sabotage jobs, like Sherry's loosening the connection beneath the sink to make it leak, he refused to let Cate pay him. Even when it was a legitimate repair, he cut his charge down to expenses. He wanted Cate to succeed in business; he didn't want her to close down and move back to Seattle. He wouldn't have charged her anything at all, except he had to live, too. There was a surprising amount of work for him to do here, considering how small the community was; he'd become the go-to guy for just about any kind of repair work or odd job that needed doing. He'd always been good with his hands, and though his strength was mechanics, he'd found he could repair a windowsill or put up a screen door as well as the next person. Neenah had asked if he could refinish her old cast-iron tub, and he'd been reading up on that, so he guessed next he'd be a tub refinisher, too.

Hell of an occupation for a man who'd spent most of his life with a rifle in his hands.

That thought brought him back to the reason he needed to call Creed.

The two of them were a pair, he thought with amusement. Give them weapons, point them at the enemy, and they functioned like Swiss clockworks. Throw a woman they wanted in front of them, though, and apparently neither of them could find his ass with both hands and a flashlight. Creed was even worse than Cal; at least Cal had a reason for waiting, because Cate had still been shell-shocked from losing her husband. Three years was a long time to wait, but grief took its own sweet time; even after she had recovered from that and could laugh again, she had protected herself by building a wall between her and any eligible man. He understood, and because he'd judged the prize worth the wait, he'd hung in there.

His patience had been rewarded; now that wall was showing signs of cracking, and he was ready to help it along with a few nudges.

Creed, though, when it came to the woman he cared about, the toughest man Cal knew had proven himself a coward.

About ten o'clock, figuring Creed could sacrifice a little of his downtime, Cal called. And got the answering machine.

'Major, this is Cal. Give me a call. It's important.' He could picture Creed scowling at the machine as he listened, trying to decide whether or not to pick up. Normally Creed would ignore a call until he was damn good and ready to respond, so Cal had tacked on the 'it's important' to whet his curiosity. Creed knew there was damn little Cal would consider all that important; if he was there, he should call back in a few minutes.

Cal waited for the call. The telephone remained silent.

Well, shit. It was possible, after being on a hunt for five days, Creed had gone into town to restock his supplies so he'd be ready for the next client. Small stuff he would pick up here in Trail Stop, but a full-bore restocking called for more than the community could offer. Hell, he might even be meeting a new client, though Cal doubted it. Creed seldom did back-to-back hunts. He offered guiding trips, at outrageous prices, so he could afford the solitary but small-scale luxurious life he wanted; too many trips would have meant he wouldn't have time to enjoy that life. The irony of it was, the higher he set his prices, the more he was in demand. Creed was turning down jobs left and right, which in turn made him seem even more requested, and the people doing the asking responded by asking earlier and more often.

As Cal had once told him, success was a vicious circle – to which Creed had replied with a suggestion that Cal do something anatomically impossible. Cal had responded that while Creed's dick might be floppy enough to do that, *his* wasn't, and from there the conversation had disintegrated to the point that even two old battle-hardened former marines had been wincing in disgust.

After waiting as long as he could, Cal left to attend to his current job of replacing the sagging step on old Mrs. Box's back porch. When that was finished, he helped Walter put up a new shelving unit in the hardware store. He then went back to his place over the feed store to check his answering machine, but Creed still hadn't returned his call.

Neenah was moving bags of feed around, and though she was

stronger than the average woman, Cal took over the job. Some days he didn't get around to using the free-weight set he had in his bedroom, so lifting fifty-pound bags of feed helped keep him in shape.

Neenah had been quiet and a little withdrawn since the episode with the two men in Cate's house. She was a quiet, serene woman anyway, but friendly. Cal suspected that had been the first time she'd experienced violence firsthand, and she'd been left reeling. She was trying to handle it herself, and he didn't think she should, but he wasn't the person to help her.

Night had fallen when Creed finally returned his call, and Cal was pissed. 'Took you long enough,' he snapped.

Creed paused, and Cal could almost see his eyes getting squinty, and his back teeth grinding together. 'I've spent six days with the biggest fucking asshole this side of the Rockies,' he finally said. 'He was supposed to have left yesterday, but the son of a bitch sprained his fucking ankle, and I had to fucking carry him five fucking miles to camp, then hold his fucking hand until I could get him to a clinic and get him X-rayed and on a fucking plane home at five fucking o'clock this afternoon. So what's so fucking important?'

Over the years, Cal and the others on their team had learned that Creed's mood could be measured by how many times he inserted the word *fuck* into a sentence. Judging from the number of F-bombs he'd just spit out, his mood was a centimeter short of homicidal.

'Two guys got rough with Neenah and Cate,' Cal said. 'A couple of days ago.'

The silence on the line was black and icy; then Creed said softly, 'What happened? Were they hurt?'

'Scared, mostly. One jammed a pistol against Neenah's temple and she's sporting a bruise. I bashed the other one in the head with my Mossberg, then got a bead on the guy holding Neenah.'

'I'll be right there,' Creed said, and crashed the phone down in Cal's ear.

Chapter Fifteen

Teague was almost in position outside Creed's cabin when the front door banged open. He froze in place, wondering if the place was rigged with motion sensors or night-vision cameras that he hadn't spotted during his reconnaissance, and whether or not Creed would shoot first and try to identify him later. As a result, Creed had slammed into his pickup truck and was fishtailing down the rutted lane that was his driveway before Teague could react.

'Shit!' Teague grabbed his Motorola CP150 two-way hooked to his belt, thumbed the 'talk' button. 'The subject just left in his pickup, coming toward the road. Follow him.'

'What about you?' came Billy's reply, his tone very quiet but his voice clear.

'Send someone back for me. Don't let him give you the slip – and don't let him see you.'

'Roger that.'

Still swearing, Teague carefully reversed the path he'd taken. He could have made better time if he'd moved down into the lane, but he would also leave boot prints, and he preferred staying in the rough. He wondered what had happened to cause Creed to take off like a cat with its tail on fire, and whether he'd be better off waiting here and taking his shot whenever Creed returned, instead of following.

The problem was, Creed might be gone for days, and Teague had no intention of sitting on his ass that long. He wanted to know where Creed had gone. Even more to the point, he'd rather chase the action than wait for it to come to him – more fun that way.

Less than half an hour after Creed had hung up on him, a thunderous pounding on his door made Cal wonder if the thing would come off its hinges before he could get it open. It wasn't locked, so he yelled, 'For God's sake, turn the doorknob!'

Creed powered into the room like an avalanche, his jaw set and his fists clenched, just as Cal had known they would be. 'What happened?' Creed demanded in a hoarse growl.

'It started last Monday,' Cal said, turning away to grab a couple of long necks from his beat-up, avocado-green refrigerator. He popped off the tops and handed a bottle to Creed, who took it in a grip that made Cal wonder if he intended to crush the bottle in his bare hand. 'A guy staying at Cate's bailed out the window and drove off, left his stuff behind.'

Immediately Creed's hazel eyes took on the analytical expression Cal knew so well. 'I was there Monday morning,' Creed said. 'She was busier than usual. Who was he running from?'

'Don't know who or why. He didn't come back. On Tuesday, Cate reported him missing, but because he left under his own steam, the sheriff's department didn't do much more than check the area hospitals and instruct deputies to be alert for signs of an accident. Also on Tuesday, some guy called Cate pretending to be from a car rental agency, trying to track this guy down. Later Cate called the rental agency but found they had no record of this guy ever renting a car from them.'

'Caller ID record?' Creed asked.

'Unknown name and number. I guess the phone company could give us more info than that, but why would they? No crime was committed, no threats made. Same with Cate's customer – he hadn't run out on his bill, so no crime was committed, so the cops aren't interested.'

'What was the guy's name?'

'Layton. Jeffrey Layton.'

Creed shook his head. 'Never heard of him before.'

'I hadn't either.' Cal tipped back his head and poured down some cold beer. 'Then, on Wednesday, these two guys checked into Cate's.' He explained why Cate had been suspicious, and that one of the men had evidently overheard her and Neenah talking in the kitchen. 'Next thing they knew, the guy calling himself Mellor came through the door with a pistol in his hand, demanding Cate give them the stuff Layton had left behind.'

'I hope she didn't argue,' Creed said grimly.

'She didn't. In the meantime, I was going into town to pick up some stuff, and I stopped by to get her mail. I thought she was acting weird, kind of jumpy and distracted, and when she gave me her mail, she'd put the stamps on upside down.'

He saw Creed make the leap. 'Smart girl,' he said approvingly.

'I took the chance I was jumping into idiot-land, parked the truck down the road, and got the shotgun out from behind the seat. Then I sneaked back and went in. Found one guy in the foyer, pistol in his hand, sneaking peeks out the window. Clubbed him in the head, and went looking for Cate. I heard voices upstairs, followed them to the attic. Cate was hauling Layton's suitcase out, and this other guy was holding Neenah by the hair, her head jerked sideways, with the barrel of his pistol jammed against her temple. I got the drop on him, convinced him his only way out alive was to drop his weapon and let Neenah go. Cate gave him the suitcase, and I saw them on their way.'

He'd left a lot out of the telling, but Creed had known him a long time and could read between the lines; he knew exactly how Cal had sneaked up on the two men.

'This was Wednesday?'

'Yeah,' Cal reaffirmed.

'Fuck.'

That needed no response. Creed's instinct was to hunt them down and make them pay – very painfully – but the incident had happened three days ago and they were long gone.

Creed made a frustrated sound in his throat, then sagged onto Cal's secondhand sofa. 'Are they okay?' he asked. 'Neenah and Cate?'

'Cate was shaky, but her mother was here to help, plus Cate had the twins to take her mind off things. Neenah didn't have anyone – in private, I mean. All the neighbors gathered round, but you and I both know the reaction kicks in when everybody leaves and you're alone.'

Creed leaned forward to prop his elbows on his spread knees, his hands dangling down. Cal watched him closely as he continued, 'I can tell she's having a tough time dealing. She's withdrawn, and she's got circles under her eyes like she isn't sleeping. Plus there's that big bruise on her face.'

Creed's hands knotted into fists, but he didn't move from Cal's sofa.

Cal leaned down, looked his former commanding officer in the eye, and very softly said, 'You're a candy-ass coward if you don't go hold that woman now when she needs holding.'

Creed shot to his feet and opened his mouth to deliver a blistering tirade, then abruptly shut it. 'Fuck,' he said again. *'Fuck!'* Then he stomped to the door and was gone, the stairs thudding beneath his boots as he went down them two at a time.

A slight smile curving his mouth, Cal shut the door.

Teague couldn't believe his luck. Sometimes the sunshine just poured down on a man, now didn't it? That bastard Creed had driven straight to Trail Stop, of all places.

They weren't likely to have a better opportunity than this. The hour wasn't as late as he'd like, but most people in Trail Stop were middle-aged, at least, with a few old geezers, so it wasn't as if they were hitting the singles bars every night and staying out until the wee hours. There were a few younger people, like the Nightingale woman, and one couple looked about the same age as her, but that was about it. He'd bet every inhabitant was at home, snug as a bug. Come to think of it, he *was* betting on that – betting the success of this plan on what he knew from observing people and his skill in reading them.

'Hurry up,' he whispered into the two-way.

'I'm hurrying,' Billy whispered in return. He was under the bridge, putting detonators into the packages of explosives they'd stolen from a construction site some months before. Teague believed in being prepared; you just never knew when you might need to blow something to hell and back. Billy had to move carefully because the slabs of rock under the bridge were wet with spray, and slippery; one false step and he was in the swiftly moving creek, being swept toward that murderous river.

Slowly Billy made his way out from under the bridge, carefully unrolling the reel of wire in his hand. Teague could have gone with wireless detonators, but in his experience they weren't as reliable – not to mention they could be accidentally set off by a signal from someone else. Not good. Playing out the wire in this terrain took time, time during which Creed might leave, but like almost everything else in life, using wire was a judgment call and Teague had made it.

His nephew Blake was set up at the nearest firing position,

infrared scope attached to his hunting rifle. As soon as Billy had turned over the wire to Teague, he would get into position at the next firing position over.

Troy, his cousin, was up the nearest utility pole with his insulated cutters, waiting for Teague's signal. Because Trail Stop was so small and so isolated, the power company and the phone company shared the poles. Troy would cut the power line first, then the phone line – and then Teague would blow the bridge.

Creed hesitated on Neenah's porch, his fist raised to pound on her door. He was so wound up that instead of driving he'd walked to her house, which was about a hundred yards from the feed store with another house tucked between them, but the hundred yards had done nothing to ratchet down the tension coiling in him.

Only the knowledge that he would scare her half to death if he started beating on her door stayed his hand. Hell, she'd probably heard him stomp across the porch with all the lightness and grace of Paul Bunyan and had run out the back door in fear for her life. He grimaced. What in hell was wrong with him? He'd spent a lifetime, two lifetimes, moving soundlessly behind enemy lines and across this damn mountain range; now all of a sudden he was stomping?

He knew what was wrong. It was the sudden, gut-wrenching knowledge that Neenah could easily have died on Wednesday – and not only was there nothing he could have done to save her, she would have died without knowing how he felt. He'd have lived the rest of his life knowing he hadn't taken the chance and now it was too late. All the excuses he'd given himself over the years – very good excuses – suddenly seemed pretty lame. Cal was right. He was a candy-ass coward.

Creed had felt fear before; every good soldier had. He'd been in situations so tense he'd given up hope of ever relaxing his sphincter again – but he'd never before been frozen into inaction.

He tried to bolster his nerve. What was the worst that could happen? Neenah could reject him, that was all.

And just the thought of that was enough to curdle his blood and make him want to run. She could reject him. She could look at him and say 'No, thanks' as if she were turning down nothing more important than a stick of chewing gum. At least if he never asked, he'd never have to face the sure knowledge that she didn't want him.

But what if she did? What if she would say yes, if only he dared ask?

Shit. Piss. *Fuck*. He sucked in a deep breath and knocked – gently.

A moment of silence stretched out so long he fought a deep surge of despair. Her lights were on; why wasn't she answering the door? Maybe she'd peeked out a window while he'd been dithering there and seen who it was, and didn't want to talk to him. Hell, why should she? He was nothing to her; he'd made damn sure of that, by giving her a wide berth for years. He'd never said anything to her other than a few pleasantries whenever he was in the feed store, which wasn't that often.

What the hell. He knocked again.

'Just a minute,' came a faint call, and he heard the sound of approaching footsteps.

A couple of feet from the door she hesitated, and said, 'Who is it?'

That was probably the first time she'd asked who it was before opening the door, at least here in Trail Stop, he thought grimly, and he hated that her sense of security had been shattered.

'Joshua Creed.'

'My goodness,' he heard her mutter to herself; then the lock clicked and she opened the door.

She'd been getting ready for bed. She wore a white nightgown and a long blue robe that she'd belted snugly around the waist. He'd never seen her wear her silvery brown hair any way except pulled back from her face and held with a scarf, which struck him as very old-fashioned, or pinned up in a knot. It was loose now, straight and sleek, falling around her face and over her shoulders.

'Is something wrong?' she asked anxiously, stepping aside so he could enter. She closed the door behind him.

'I just heard about what happened Wednesday,' he said, his tone a little rough, and he watched all expression fade right out of her face. She lowered her eyelids, closing herself off; his heart pinched as he realized Cal was right, she wasn't handling the incident well and had no one to turn to. She'd been alone a long time, he thought, which was strange because everyone in Trail Stop thought of her as a friend. She'd been here when he'd retired from the Corps, changing little over the years. To his knowledge, she didn't date at all. She ran the feed store, occasionally she would visit with a friend, and at night she came home alone. That was it. That was her life.

'Are you all right?' he asked, his deep voice coming out in little more than a rumble. Before he could stop himself, he reached out, gently brushing her hair back from her right temple so the dark bruise there was fully revealed.

She quivered, and he thought she might jerk back, but she didn't. 'I'm fine,' she said automatically, as if she'd already provided the same answer many times over.

'Are you?'

'Yes, of course.'

He moved closer, his hand touching her back. 'Why don't we sit down,' he suggested, urging her toward the sofa.

Two lamps were all that lit her cozy living room, so he wasn't certain, but he thought her color warmed. 'I'm sorry, I should have—' She broke off and would have veered toward a chair; with a subtle shift of his body he prevented that, steering her back toward the sofa. She sat down on the middle cushion, hard, as if her legs had suddenly gone out from under her.

Creed sat beside her, close enough that his thigh would touch hers if he shifted just a bit. He didn't, remembering suddenly that she'd been a nun.

Did that mean she was a virgin? He broke out in a sweat, because he didn't know. Not that he would be having sex with her tonight or anything like that, but – had any man *ever* touched her? Had she ever dated at all, as a teenager? If she was completely inexperienced, he didn't want to do anything to scare her, but how in hell was he supposed to find out?

And why had she stopped being a nun? The only thing he knew about nuns was that line 'Get thee to a nunnery,' which told him exactly nothing. Well, he'd watched a couple of episodes of *The Flying Nun* when he was a kid, but all that had told him was that when lift and thrust exceeded drag, flight was achieved. Big help that was.

All right, so he was scared shitless. But this wasn't about him. This was about Neenah. Neenah being terrified and having no one to talk to.

He relaxed, sitting back and letting the overstuffed cushions cradle him. This was very much a woman's room, he thought, looking at the lamps and the plants, the photographs, the books and

145

knickknacks, some kind of sewing clamped in a round wooden frame and laid aside. There was a television, a nineteen-incher, wedged among books on top of what looked like an antique sideboard. A fireplace occupied the left wall, and glowing embers told him she'd lit a fire against the early chill.

She hadn't relaxed; she was still sitting upright; he couldn't see anything except her back. Good enough. Maybe she needed that sense of anonymity.

'I was career Marine Corps,' he finally said, watching her shoulders straighten in surprised attention. 'In for twenty-three years. I saw a lot of action, was in a lot of tight situations. Some of them I thought I wouldn't get out of, and when I did, sometimes I'd shake so hard I thought my teeth would crack. The combination of shock and adrenaline crash can do a number on you, take you a while to get over it.'

A moment of silence ran between them, as palpable as a touch. He could hear her breathing, every soft inhale-exhale, the faint rasp and slither as she rubbed a fold of her robe between her thumb and finger. Then she murmured, 'How long does it take?'

'Depends.'

'On what?'

'On whether or not you have someone to hold you,' he said, reaching out and gently grasping her shoulders, easing her back.

She didn't actively resist, but he could sense her surprise, her initial reluctance. He gently tucked her into the curve of his arm, drawing her close. She blinked up at him, the expression in her pure blue eyes solemn, questioning, hesitant. 'Shhh,' he murmured, as if she'd protested. 'Just relax.'

Whatever she saw in his face must have reassured her – God, how could she be so blind? – because with the barest hint of a sigh, she let the steel flow out of her bones, let herself sink and mold against his side, into his warmth, as he pulled her closer.

She was soft and warm and she smelled good. His senses swam at her nearness, at the delirium of finally holding her, feeling her, smelling her. She buried her face in his shoulder, trembling. Her shoulders jerked a little, and he murmured something soothing as he cuddled her closer.

'I'm not crying,' she said, her voice muffled and faintly forlorn.

'Go ahead if you want to. What's a little snot between friends?'

She burst out laughing, the sound muffled against him, and tilted her head back to look at him. 'I can't believe you said that.'

He kissed her. He'd wanted to for, God, years, and when she turned her face up, her lips were just inches from his, so, what the hell, he did it. He cupped her face in his hand and kissed her as gently as he could, giving her plenty of space to pull back if she wanted to – but she didn't. Instead she gripped his shoulder with one hand and kissed him in return, her lips parting, her tongue easing out to touch his.

The earth shook; a gigantic boom rocked the entire house. A tiny part of Creed credited the upheaval to the kiss, but the bigger part of him knew better, and he wrapped both arms around her as he rolled the two of them off the sofa to the floor, covering her protectively with his body.

Chapter Sixteen

As soon as Teague blew the bridge, Billy, Troy, and Blake began laying down fire into the outer rim of homes. They weren't deliberately trying to hit anyone, but neither did they care if they did. The only thing that kept their aim a little high was the knowledge that a bloodbath would bring every law officer in Idaho down on them when it was discovered, which could be bothersome.

Blake was using a Weatherby Mark V Magnum .257, a truly sweet piece of work that packed a heavy punch. Billy had a Winchester; Troy, a Springfield M21. The Weatherby and Winchester were good hunting rifles; the Springfield was more suitable for sniping. Teague's chosen weapon was a Parker-Hale M85, with a bipod system for stability. Both the Springfield and the Parker-Hale were long-distance rifles, capable of reaching out and touching someone a mile distant, if the person pulling the trigger had sufficient skill.

Teague had chosen the weapons with their differences in mind. Blake and Billy would take the night shifts, when the infrared scopes would be needed. The scopes had a physical limit; anything beyond four hundred yards just wasn't going to show up. So their rifles were best for the middle ranges. Troy and Teague could use high-powered binoculars during the day, and their long-range rifles would put the fear of God into anyone they saw moving about the community. These, too, had infrared scopes, but Troy and Teague wouldn't have to depend solely on them.

Goss and Toxtel were positioned to move in close to where the bridge had once spanned the rushing mountain stream, once the debris had settled. With their handguns they were responsible for any close-range action, which Teague didn't expect at all.

The roar of the explosion and the subsequent rain of debris hadn't yet settled when people began running out of their houses to see what was happening. Calmly and deliberately, the four men began shooting, driving the good citizens of Trail Stop farther and farther back.

As soon as the lights went out, Cal was moving, reaching for his weatherproof flashlight and heading for his door. If the electricity was out at the feed store, which was one of the first buildings on the way into Trail Stop, then it was almost certainly out for the entire community – and Cate was alone in her house. He was at the door when the explosion knocked him off his feet; he was already rolling when he landed, the flashlight gripped tight in his hand so he wouldn't lose it.

Bomb.

The darkness, the explosion, the blast of the percussion, threw him straight into battle mode. Adrenaline roared through his body, and he didn't stop to think, didn't have to think, because this was not second nature at all but first nature, *his* nature. Thrusting the flashlight into his front pocket, he opened the door and crawled out onto the landing of the outside stairs. There were no vertical safety railings around the landing, just a frame made of weathered two-by-fours. He gripped the edge of the landing and swung himself over, hanging for a split second before dropping into the darkness. Since he couldn't see the ground, it was difficult to anticipate and control his landing, but familiarity let him judge it within a cat's whisker. He bent his knees to absorb the shock, tucked into a roll, and came up behind his parked pickup.

He was already on the ground when the first shot was fired.

His ears were ringing from the explosion, but he could still pinpoint the direction the shots were coming from ... correction: directions ... four different firing locations. Rifle fire, from across the stream. The explosion had come from the direction of the bridge; maybe a vehicle had exploded while crossing the bridge, but he didn't think so, the sound was all wrong. Since there was nothing else in that direction, instinct told him the bridge had been blown. Why and by whom were questions that would wait. He had to get to Cate.

A heavy round punched at an angle through the walls of his living room, blowing splinters of wood over the pickup as it exited.

Whoever was on the other side of the stream was systematically shooting into the houses.

From the bridge, the feed store was the third building on the right; Neenah's house was the first, and was one of the most exposed. Creed had gone to her house, which meant Cal had to consider that his former commanding officer might be dead, or at least wounded. He couldn't count on help from that quarter.

He rose to a low crouch, staying behind the pickup's engine block, and jerked open the passenger door. The Mossberg shotgun was behind the seat, along with a couple of boxes of shells. He tore open the cargo pocket on the right leg of his pants, dumped the shells in it, then closed the pocket by pressing the Velcro tight. There was one other item he was certain would be needed, and he grabbed the small green tackle box containing his first-aid gear.

Almost drowned out by the rifle fire, shrill screams of fright and pain reached his ears. Everyone would have come out of their houses, he realized, maybe even been deliberately driven out of them. Now they were out in the open, and sitting ducks.

'Down!' he roared as he angled back and to the right, trying to keep a building, a tree – anything – between him and where those rifles were situated. 'Everybody take cover! Get behind your cars!'

There were fairly large open gaps between the houses; Trail Stop was a loosely constructed community. When he had to cross a gap, he put his head down and ran like hell, zigzagging like a champion tailback. One of the shooters picked him up almost immediately and sent a bullet whining behind his head. He rolled and darted and finally dived headlong behind the next house, scraping his arms on loose gravel and fetching up hard against an outdoor faucet that dug into his shoulder.

Fuck! The shooters had night-vision scopes, or maybe even infrared. What the fucking hell was going on? Who were these guys? Cops? Some kind of military action? Maybe some sort of survivalist group with a hard-on for somebody in Trail Stop? Didn't matter. They weren't just shooting blind. They could see him; they could see everyone.

They couldn't see through walls, though.

To minimize their clear shots, he needed to get as many houses, vehicles, trees, any solid object at all, between him and their positions. That meant angling away from Cate, because the road didn't bisect Trail Stop down the middle; it curled to the left, leaving

complete darkness around her. Then she woke up enough to look at the clock, only to discover no red digital numbers were in their accustomed place. The power was off.

'Damn it,' she muttered, because her clock didn't have battery backup, which meant she would have to get up and find the little battery-operated travel clock she'd had for years – otherwise she might oversleep in the morning. It was either that or sit up until the power came on. She lay there wondering if the booming noise had been a transformer exploding, which would explain why there was no electricity. Or maybe there was a really fierce thunderstorm and lightning had struck something.

Then she heard more loud noises, different from the booming sound, in that the house didn't shake. These noises weren't as loud, and they were sharper, with a sort of flat echo. There were a lot of them, too. She wished they would stop, because she was so sleepy . . .

Realization hit her like a slap in the face, and tilted her world on its side. Oh, my God, that was gunfire!

From the twins' bedroom came the sound of breaking glass.

She bolted out of bed, feeling blindly for the flashlight she always kept on her bedside table in case one of the boys needed her in the middle of the night. Her hand brushed it and knocked it sideways; it hit the floor with a clatter and thump, rolling.

'Shit!' She had to have a flashlight; the interior of the house was as dark as Tut's tomb; she'd fall on something and break a bone if she tried navigating it in total darkness. She went down on her hands and knees and crawled around the bedroom floor, slowly sweeping her hands out in front of her. After a couple of panicky sweeps in which she touched nothing more interesting than her bedroom slippers, her fingers found cool metal. She thumbed the switch, and a bright beam shot out, the light restoring her surroundings to familiarity and banishing that disturbing sense of disorientation.

She ran out into the hall, instinct turning her to the left, toward the twins' room. The sound of more breaking glass made her skid to a stop. The boys weren't there, they were safely in Seattle with her parents, and . . . and . . . *was someone shooting at her house?*

Her blood ran so cold she thought she might faint, and she swayed against the wall, putting her hand out for support. Without knowing the particulars of what was going on, her mind made a huge, instinctive jump and shouted '*Mellor*!' at her.

Mellor and Huxley. They had come back.

She had been terrified they would; that was the reason she'd sent the boys away. She didn't know why the two men were back or what they wanted, but beyond any doubt, she knew they were the ones doing this. Were they downstairs, even now, waiting for her? Was she trapped up here?

No. They had to be outside, if they were shooting into the house. This was *her* house, her home, and she knew every nook, every weird angle, every way out. They couldn't trap her in here. She could get out, somehow.

She realized that the flashlight pinpointed her position, and switched it off. The night seemed even darker than before, her vision ruined by the brief time she'd had the flashlight on. She had to risk it, she thought, and switched the light on again.

First things first. She had to put some clothes on and get to the ground floor.

She raced back to her room, grabbed some clothes, listening hard for a betraying noise that would tell her they were in her house. The gunfire continued and it actually sounded somewhat distant. From outside came shouts and screams, cries of fear or pain. She couldn't hear anything inside.

When she reached the head of the stairs, she shone the flashlight down them. She couldn't see anything unusual, so she went down the first few steps, flashing the light around the hallway and foyer. Empty, as much as she could see. She took the rest of the stairs faster, feeling horribly exposed and vulnerable, almost leaping down the last three steps.

Weapon. She needed some sort of weapon.

Damn it, she had two four-year-olds in the house; she didn't keep weapons around.

Except for her knives. She was a cook. She had a lot of knives. She also had that cliché woman's weapon, a rolling pin. Fine. Anything would do.

Keeping the flashlight aimed at the floor so the beam would be more difficult to see, she eased into the kitchen and went straight to her block of knives, pulling out the biggest one, the chef's knife. The handle fit into her hand like an old friend.

Silently she moved back into the hallway, which was centrally located in the house. This was where she would be least trapped, where she could go in any direction.

She turned off the flashlight and stood there in the dark, listening, waiting. How long she stood there didn't matter. She could hear her own harsh breathing, feel it rasping in her throat. Her head swam. She could feel her heart racing in panic, feel the almost painful thud of her heartbeat against her ribs. No, she couldn't panic – she *wouldn't* panic. Drawing in a deep breath, as deep as she could manage, she held it and used her inflated lungs to compress her heart and hold it, force it to slow. It was an old trick she'd used while climbing, whenever she'd caught her body's automatic responses overpowering her discipline and focus.

Slow ... slow ... already she could think better ... slower, slower ... she gently released that breath and took another, more controlled one. The dizziness faded. Whatever happened, she was readier to face it now than she had been a moment before.

Thudding on the front porch, fast and heavy, and the doorknob rattled violently.

'Cate! Are you all right?'

She took a step forward, then froze. A man. She didn't recognize the voice. Mellor and Huxley both knew her first name, because she'd introduced herself to them.

'Cate!'

The entire front door shuddered as something was slammed hard against it, then slammed again. The door frame seemed to groan.

'Cate, it's Cal! Answer me!'

Relief swept over her in a huge surge and a cry burst out of her. She started forward as the door gave up its resistance and banged back against the doorstop. A flashlight suddenly came on, sweeping across her face and blinding her. She threw up an arm to shield her eyes, skidding to a stop as she tried to see. She could make out only the vague outline of a man behind the glare of the light, and he was moving fast, too fast for her to get out of his way.

Chapter Seventeen

It was like hitting a wall. His body collided with Cate's with enough force to knock the knife from her hand and send it clattering down the hall. The blinding beam from his flashlight waved wildly back and forth in a strobe effect before spinning to the side. She staggered back, grabbing wildly for something, anything, to break her fall and found herself clutching a hard, lean waist. She couldn't have fallen anyway, because a steel band clamped around her back, steadying her against him.

A sharp sense of unreality made her head swim again as time collapsed and the world shrank to a tiny point of focus, poised on the edge of a cliff. None of this was real; it couldn't be. She was just Cate, an ordinary woman living an ordinary life; people didn't *shoot* at her.

'It's okay,' Cal murmured against her hair. 'I've got you.'

She heard the words, but they didn't make sense because he was part of the whole unreality. This man was not the man she'd known for three years. Mr. Harris wouldn't hold her this way, wouldn't have broken in her door and come charging across the floor like some avenging warrior badass dude, holding a shotgun in one hand –

Except he had.

The body she was clinging to so tightly was hard and muscled, almost steaming with heat. He was breathing fast, as if he'd been running, and his head was bent down to press against hers. And the way he was holding her was – She hadn't been held this way in so long that she was stunned, disbelieving. *Mr. Harris? Cal?*

Her body whispered, *yes*. That was even more disconcerting, tipping her further and further off balance. What kind of pervert

156

was she, to have some sort of weird sexual response to the *handyman* when the entire community was evidently under some sort of attack? It still sounded like a war out there, but she felt as if the two of them were contained in a small private cone of existence where reality didn't intrude. For a moment his arm tightened, arching her even closer, so that she felt the bulge of his genitals pushing, seeking ... then he released her and eased away, bending to pick up the flashlight.

Cate stood unmoving, desperately trying to put herself back in time to the way things had been just half an hour before, before explosions and shooting and the upheaval of all she knew or had thought she knew.

Hooking the strap of the shotgun over his shoulder, Cal also picked up the chef's knife she'd dropped, studying the wide blade with a sort of grim approval. He held the flashlight pointed at the floor, the powerful beam reflecting enough for her to see him, and her senses reeled again.

She had never seen him wearing anything other than baggy coveralls, stained with grease, paint, dirt, or whatever else he'd been working with that particular day. She'd had him firmly fixed in her mind as a skinny shy handyman, backward but useful. That view had taken a hit when she'd seen the expression in his eyes as he looked down his shotgun barrel at Mellor, and now it was shattered forever.

He was wearing his usual work boots, but nothing else was the same. The khaki cargo pants were belted at his waist, and despite the chilly weather, he was wearing only a dark T-shirt that clung to wide shoulders and a lean, rock-hard body. Even with just the light from the flashlight she saw the gleam of sweat on his bare arms, arms that were sinewy and powerful. His shaggy hair was still shaggy, but there was no hint of shyness in his grim, set expression.

Cate could barely breathe. She was standing on the edge of some internal cliff and she was afraid to move, afraid she would ... would what? She didn't know, but the sense of instability frightened her almost as much as all those guns shooting outside.

Someone appeared in the broken doorway, and to Cate's amazement he, too, was carrying either a shotgun or a rifle. 'Is Cate all right?' he asked, and Cate recognized Walter Earl's voice.

'I'm fine, Walter,' she said, moving toward the door. 'Is Milly okay? Is anyone hurt?'

'Milly's sitting on your back lawn. Staying low seemed smart to me, so that's where she is. People are pulling back. Someone said that's what you said to do, so that's what they're doing. Are we out of range here?'

'No,' Cal said. 'Not of the rifles, anyway.'

'The window in the boys' bedroom was shot out,' Cate said softly, and the horror of it hit her all over again. What if they'd been here? They'd have been terrified, possibly hurt ... possibly dead. Her heart squeezed in anguish at just the thought.

'Then what are we doing here?' Walter asked.

'Putting as many walls as possible between us and them, plus I'm pretty sure they have either night-vision or infrared spotters. Infrared is limited to about four hundred yards, so we need to get beyond that. Won't stop the bullets, but at least they'll be shooting blind – and they may not want to waste the ammunition.'

Cal had placed his hand on Cate's back as he answered Walter's question, urging her outside. As soon as she stepped onto the porch, she stopped. Some twenty or thirty people were in her back-yard, most of them sitting on the chilly ground. Almost all the men and some of the women carried some sort of weapon. The darkness enveloped them, making her sharply aware that seeing lights shining in nearby windows at night had made her feel comfortable and secure.

Cal urged her off the porch; then his hand on her shoulder forced her to the ground. 'The foundation is sturdier than walls,' he said quietly. 'Better protection.' Raising his voice, he said, 'Everyone, we need to save the batteries in the flashlights. Turn most of them off. We only need one or two.'

Obediently the people around her clicked off their flashlights, and the darkness almost swallowed them. Cal left his powerful light on. She began to shiver as the cold air seeped through her flannel pajamas, and she wished she'd thought to get a coat. From somewhere in the darkness she heard someone mutter 'I'm cold,' but without any real complaint.

'Right now, we need to determine two things,' Cal said. 'Who's missing, and is anyone hurt?'

'I'd like to know just who is shooting at us,' Milly said angrily.

'First things first. Who isn't here? Look for your neighbors.

Creed went down to Neenah's house; has anyone seen either of them?'

There was silence for a moment, then a voice behind Cate said, 'Lanora was right behind me when we were running, but I don't see her now.'

Lanora Corbett lived in the second house from the bridge, on the left.

'Anyone else?' Cal asked.

There was murmuring as they looked around and took stock, and names began to surface: the elderly Starkeys, Roy Edward and his wife, Judith; the Contreras family, Mario, Gena, and Angelina; Norman Box; and others. A cold hand squeezed Cate's heart as the horrible possibility began to creep in: Would she ever see these people again? And Neenah. *Neenah!* No. She couldn't lose her friend. She absolutely refused to think it even possible.

'All right,' Cal finally said when no more names were forthcoming. 'Let me get a head count, and we'll know where we stand.' He shone the light around, briefly touching on each face, and in every one Cate saw the same raw mixture of horror, disbelief, and anger that must be on hers. She saw people clinging to each other, huddling together for comfort and warmth, and dimly she began to think of practical matters: blankets, coats, other things she could get from the house. Coffee would be nice, but the electricity was off. On the other hand, she did have a gas stove ... The thoughts were laborious, emerging from her brain with effort, but at least the daze was beginning to wear off.

'Is anyone hurt?' Cal asked one more time, after he had an accurate count of those grouped in Cate's yard. 'I'm not talking sprained ankles, or a scraped knee. Has anyone been shot? Is anyone bleeding?'

'You are,' Sherry Bishop said with some tartness.

Cate's head whipped around. Cal was hurt? Shocked, she looked hard at him as he held his arms out and looked down to examine himself, as if he didn't know what Sherry was talking about. 'Where?' he asked.

Cate spotted the black-red streaks on his arms. 'Your arms,' Cate said as she began to climb to her feet.

In a flash he was beside her, his hand on her shoulder, pressing her down. 'Stay down,' he said in a low voice intended just for her. 'I'm fine, it's just a couple of glass cuts.'

To her way of thinking, cuts should be taken care of no matter what caused them. And if sitting was safer than standing, why wasn't *he* sitting? 'If you don't sit,' she said in the same tone of voice she used with the boys, 'then I'm standing. Your choice.'

'I can't sit, I have a few things to do first—'

'*Sit.*'

He sat.

Cate got to her knees and moved behind him. 'Sherry, can you help me here? Hold the light and let's see how bad these cuts are. And I need to get some bandages from—'

'My first-aid kit is on the porch,' he said. 'I dropped it there.'

'Someone get it, please.' Cate raised her voice a little, and Walter moved to obey.

'Keep low,' Cal added. Walter obediently bent at the waist.

The back of Cal's T-shirt was damp and sticky. Sherry took Cal's flashlight and trained it on him as Cate rolled the shirt up. Blood was welling from what looked like several pinpricks, while there was a larger cut on his right triceps and another one across the top of his left shoulder. She pushed the T-shirt over his head so it was draped over his arms and his entire back was bare.

Walter arrived with a tackle box and flipped the latches, opening it up to reveal compartments full of first-aid supplies. Sherry switched the light beam to the contents of the box, allowing Cate to pick out the individually packaged antiseptic wipes. She tore one envelope open and unfolded the wipe to its full four-by-six inches, and began swabbing. 'I don't know what we'll do if these two bigger cuts need stitches,' she muttered to Sherry.

'I have sutures in the box,' Cal said, trying to turn his head to judge the damage for himself.

'*Ahnt!*' She made one of those wordless warning sounds that were a mother's specialty, and he froze, then carefully faced forward again.

In silence she cleaned the wounds, and pressed gauze pads over the deepest cuts. Unfortunately, the blood seepage kept them in place, which allowed her to apply antiseptic ointment to the smaller wounds and cover them with adhesive strips. His skin was cold and damp under her hands, reminding her not only that he wore nothing more than a T-shirt and pants on this chilly night, but he'd been sweating – and now she'd cleaned his back with damp wipes. He must be freezing, but somehow he kept still.

'He needs something to wear,' she murmured to Sherry.

'It's okay,' he said over his shoulder.

Cate felt something rising in her, some great big bubble of tension that almost choked her. 'No, Calvin Harris, it is *not* okay!' she said fiercely. 'It is not okay for you to run around half naked and wounded on a cold night. We'll find something for you to wear, and that's that.' Many things had happened that night that were far worse, but she couldn't do anything about those. She was damned, however, if Cal would take another step without a coat or at least a shirt.

He fell silent again, and she wondered if she'd lost her mind. Events were swimming out of focus again, so that small things seemed vitally important and large things were fading into the background. She looked at the strong length of his back, the deep furrow of his spine and the layers of muscle, and wanted to weep. Instead she took a deep breath and concentrated on cleaning the two deeper cuts. They were still oozing a little watery blood, but that was all. She put antibiotic on them, then held the edges together with one hand while with the other she painstakingly placed a row of butterfly bandages over each cut. When she was finished, the cuts no longer gaped open. Maybe they wouldn't have needed stitches, because neither of the gashes was truly severe, but she didn't want to take the chance.

'That's the best I can do,' she finally said, restoring the first-aid kit to the way he'd had it and gathering the soiled wipes and torn paper she'd thrown on the ground. She hesitated, not knowing what to do with the trash now that she'd gathered it, and finally dropped it back on the ground. She would worry about neatness later.

Cal started to rise and she put her hand on his right shoulder to hold him still. 'Cal needs something to wear,' she called out to the people gathered on her lawn. 'A shirt, a jacket, anything. Do any of you have something you can spare?' Then she added, 'I'm going to get blankets from inside, so we can be warmer.'

'Why don't we go inside?' Milly asked, her voice trembling with cold.

'Cate's house may be a little too close to the action,' Cal replied. 'There are other houses farther away, and out of the line of fire. I think it's safe here, but I'm not certain. A high-caliber bullet can go through several houses unless it hits something like a refrigerator to slow it down. I'll check distances after daylight. Until then, we need to pull even farther away, put more structure between us and the shooters. Thanks,' he added as a flannel shirt was passed to him. Cate hadn't seen who made the donation. Cal quickly put on the shirt and buttoned it; he was shivering now.

'The coat closet is just inside the front door, on the right,' she said to him. 'I have several coats hanging in there, and the linen closet with extra blankets is just this side of the laundry. I'll run in, gather everything I can, and be back out here within one minute.'

'I'll do it,' he said instead, turning toward the porch.

Cate stopped him with her hand on his arm. 'You can't do everything. Go find Creed and Neenah, and the others. I'll get the blankets and coats. Where should we go, so you'll know exactly where we are?'

For a moment she thought he would argue, but he said, 'Pull back to the Richardsons' place,' naming the house that was farthest from the bridge. 'The shooting was coming from at least three separate locations, so they have different angles of fire. Stay low, try to keep some sort of structure between you and the mountain, from the bridge to the Notch. Got it?' He'd raised his voice so he was speaking to all of them, not just to Cate.

'Yes.' Her breath was frosty as it hung in the air between them.

'If you do have to cross an open space, do it in a hurry. Don't stay in a line or the last ones are just asking to be picked off. Vary your routes, your timing, everything you can. Keep the flashlights off, if possible; you're just pinpointing your position if you have one on when you're in the open.'

Heads nodded in the dark.

'How long will you be?' Cate asked, trying to keep her anxiety out of her tone. She didn't want him going out into the night by himself, though she understood they needed to know what was going on. And he was armed; he wasn't helpless.

'I don't know. I don't know what I'll find.' He turned his head and looked at her in the darkness, a long, quiet gaze as potent as a touch. 'But I *will* be back. Depend on it.' Then he was gone, melting into the darkness with just a few steps.

Chapter Eighteen

Neenah shrieked, terror clamping her arms convulsively around Creed as his heavy body crushed her to the rug. The percussion from the explosion shook the entire house, raining dust down on them in a choking cloud. Creed covered her head with his arms, trying to tuck her completely beneath him to shelter her from any falling debris.

Then it was quiet, a strange, ear-ringing silence.

'E-earthquake?' she gasped.

'No. Explosion.' Creed lifted his head, and saw nothing but darkness. The lights were out – big surprise there. The explosion must have taken out the power lines that crossed the stream at the bridge.

Then there was a sharp, deep *crack!* that made his blood go cold, and simultaneously the front window imploded with a shower of glass slivers. He felt several stings but disregarded them as more booming shots rang out. He was already moving, twenty-three years of training kicking in at the sound of rifle fire even though he'd been out of the Corps for almost eight years, dragging Neenah along beneath him as he scrambled, half-crawling and half-slithering, out of the exposed living room and toward the short, more protected hallway he'd noticed when he came in. He couldn't see shit in the sudden darkness, but he had an excellent sense of direction.

Neenah was utterly silent except for the harshness of her breathing. She clung to him like a monkey and tried to help by pushing with her feet. She'd recognized the sound of rifle fire, too; after all, she'd grown up around people who still hunted for some of their food.

He wasn't certain where the shots were coming from, didn't know if he was the target or if Neenah was, or if neither of them was the specific target and this was more a case of being in the wrong place at the wrong time. Right now the 'why' didn't matter, only the 'where' – the location the shots were coming from. He couldn't just blindly run out; he had to keep Neenah safe.

'Where's the kitchen?' he rasped, listening to round after round being fired. It sounded like a fucking war out there. The kitchen would offer the most protection, with its array of metal appliances. A high-caliber bullet from a powerful rifle would punch through multiple walls unless it was stopped by something like a refrigerator. He still intended to stay on the floor, even if Neenah happened to have a whole row of refrigerators lining her walls.

'I – I don't know,' she stuttered, gasping for breath. 'I – where are we?'

She was disoriented, which wasn't surprising. Creed tightened his left arm around her. 'We're in the hall; your feet are pointing toward the front door.'

She was silent for a moment, breathing hard, as she struggled to order the position of her rooms. 'Ah – okay. To your right. Ahead, and to the right. But I need to go to the bedroom.'

He disregarded that; a bedroom wouldn't offer as much protection. 'The kitchen is safer.'

'Clothes. I need clothes.'

Creed paused. There had been some sort of powerful explosion, someone was shooting at them, and she wanted to change clothes? The same sort of acid comment that had taken strips off some very tough Marines boiled to his tongue, but he held it back. This wasn't one of his men; this was Neenah ... and she'd been a nun. Maybe former nuns were extremely modest. God, he hoped not, but –

'What you have on will do,' he ventured, cautiously feeling his way lest he run afoul of some nun rule.

'I can't run in this nightgown and robe, much less in bedroom slippers!'

Unfortunately, that made sense, not to mention that the nights were getting cold. He would have preferred to retreat to a safe position where he could assess the situation, but he was acutely aware he couldn't command her as he had his men. Faced with that reality, Creed shifted his priority to helping her do what she wanted as safely as possible.

'Okay, one change of clothes coming up.' Another round punched through the living room wall, followed by the deep crack of the rifle shot. Creed flattened her in case the next shot was lower, letting his weight crush her against the floor. She was so soft beneath him, the way he'd spent years imagining, and the thought of one of those powerful rounds tearing into her was horrifying. He'd fought wars, lost men to every kind of violence possible, whether it was a bullet, a bomb, a knife, or a training accident, and every loss had been a scar on his soul; he himself had killed, and that was a different sort of scar – but all of that he'd borne with an inner stoicism that had allowed him to function. If anything happened to Neenah, though, he simply couldn't bear it. Because of that he said, 'You stay in the kitchen – lie flat on the floor where it's safest. I'll get your clothes and bring them to you.'

'You don't know where they are; you'll be exposed longer—' Before she finished speaking, she was trying to wriggle away from him.

Stunned, he realized *she* was trying to protect *him*. Shock made him a little rough with her as he blocked her effort to wriggle free, keeping her firmly beneath him.

She pushed on his shoulders, her breasts straining into his chest. 'Mr. Creed ... Joshua – I need to breathe!'

He eased his weight off her, but not enough that she could slide out from under him. He could piss her off, he thought, or he could keep her alive. To his way of thinking, the choice was crystal clear. He bent his head to her ear. 'Here's the way it is: Someone is shooting at us with a high-powered rifle, which makes this my game, not yours. My job is to get us out of here alive. Your job is to do what I say the second the words are out of my mouth. After we're safe, you can slap my face or kick my shins, but until then I'm boss. Got it?'

'Of course I've got it,' she said with remarkable cool, under the circumstances, one of which was not being able to draw a deep breath. 'I don't believe I'm an idiot. But it's only logical that I would be able to get my clothes faster than you would, thereby making it safer for both of us, because if you get shot while you're hunting for my shoes, then my own chances for getting out of here alive go down. Am I right?'

She was arguing with him. The experience was both novel and infuriating. Even more frustrating was the fact that she made sense – again. He hung there over her, torn between logic and his overpowering instinct to protect her at any cost.

With a sudden fierce movement he rolled off her and snapped, 'Be fast. If you have a flashlight, get it, but don't turn it on. Don't stand up. Belly crawl if you can, get to your knees if you have to, but under no circumstances are you to stand up. Clear?'

'Clear,' she said. Her voice shook a little, but she was in control of herself. Creed forced himself to let her move away from him, tracking her by the sounds she made as she pulled herself along on her elbows, and dug into the carpet with her toes to push. Once he heard what sounded like a muttered curse, but he was pretty sure nuns, even ex-nuns, didn't swear, so he was probably wrong about that.

He broke out in a fine sheen of sweat, waiting for her, knowing that at any second another round could rip through the walls as if they were made of paper. So far the shots had been placed about head high, designed to catch people who were standing. The people of Trail Stop were civilians; they hadn't been trained to automatically hit the ground. Instead they would try to run, and not necessarily in the best direction. They might even try to look out the windows, which was about the dumbest thing to do in this situation. Or they might grab their flashlights and turn them on, pinpointing their positions for the shooters. He needed to get out there, get them organized, stop them from doing stupid shit.

At least Cal was there, unless he'd been taken out in the first minute – and that wasn't likely. That damn ghost had a sixth sense about survival. The entire team had learned to pay acute attention to him, because time after time he would do something that looked senseless in that exact second but five seconds later had either saved his life or put him in a much stronger strategic position. If Cal jumped, the entire team jumped with him. And when it came to moving covertly from point A to point B, Creed had never seen anyone better. Cal would get the survivors rounded up, organized, and in the safest position possible; then he would come looking for the stranded and the wounded.

Neenah was taking too long. 'What are you doing?' he asked sharply, barely containing his urge to follow and drag her into the kitchen.

'Changing clothes' came her equally sharp reply. His eyebrows lifted a little. The nun had a temper. For some reason, that seemed a tad kinky; he liked it. Creed knew himself well enough to realize he'd never be able to tolerate a doormat.

'Just get the clothes and bring them into the kitchen to change. Don't leave yourself vulnerable any longer than necessary.'

'I can't change in front of you!'

'Neenah.' He took a deep breath, managed to inject patience into his tone. 'It's dark. I can't see anything. And even if I could . . . so what?'

'So what?'

'Yeah, so what. I plan to get you naked pretty soon, anyway.'

Okay, so he had the finesse of a gorilla. If she exploded in his face, he'd know right now that he was wasting his time.

She didn't explode. Instead she went very, very quiet, as if she were even holding her breath. The pause went on so long despair began to rise in his throat. Then came the unmistakable sounds of her crawling toward him.

His heart almost seized, literally almost stopped beating.

He'd lied about not being able to see. At first, before his vision adjusted, he hadn't been able to see shit, but now he could dimly make out the shapes of doorways and windows, the darker bulk of furniture. If he could see, then she could see – so she knew exactly how much he was seeing. No detail, of course, but definitely the pale length of bare leg. She already had her shirt on, but she was dragging her jeans and shoes and coat with her. Maybe she had on underwear, maybe she didn't. He fought the urge to slide his hand over her ass to find out. He fought the even stronger urge to roll her onto her back and make a place for himself between those bare legs. If ever there'd been a bad time, this was it, but for once his libido didn't want to listen to his training.

She crawled past him into the kitchen, and in the darkness he made out the whiteness of panties in front of him, which solved the question of underwear or no underwear. He was following before he realized it, as if drawn by a magnet. Any red-blooded man would follow a woman's panty-clad ass crawling in front of him, he thought, and once again he fought the urge to pounce. Get her to safety first, pounce later.

In the kitchen, she sat on the floor and pulled on socks, then her jeans and shoes. Her shirt was light-colored, but there was no help for that now because he sure as hell wasn't sending her back to change; she'd be wearing her coat anyway.

'Flashlight?' he asked, wondering if she'd forgotten.

'I put it in my coat pocket.' She pulled the flashlight out and passed it to him.

He stifled a sigh as his big hand closed around the slender tube; it wasn't much larger than a penlight. He couldn't use it until they were safe, of course, but lights this size were basically made for a single task directly in front of the holder, not for helping them safely make their way across rough ground. Still, any light at all was better than none.

'All right, let's slip out the back door and get away from here.'

Teague's two-way crackled to life, a faint voice coming from the radio speaker.

'Hawk, this is Owl. Hawk, this is Owl.'

Owl was Blake, manning the farthest firing position. Teague moved away from Goss and Toxtel, taking care to remain behind cover. Those people on the other side of the stream had rifles, and he hadn't forgotten it for a minute. He had the volume on the two-way turned down because noise carried at night; he sure as hell didn't want to pinpoint his position for some lucky shot. With a large outcropping of rock securely between him and the community, he thumbed the 'talk' button to reply. 'This is Hawk. Go ahead.'

'Hawk, that guy you had Billy follow? I've sort of kept an eye on him, just in case you needed to know where he was. He went in that two-story building, third on the right—'

That was the feed store, Teague thought, pulling up his mental layout of the place. The place closed at five PM, so what was Creed doing there? Not that it mattered; he was just curious. 'Yeah, what about it?'

'He stayed just a few minutes; then he came out and walked down to this first house on the right. Never came out, at least not before you started the dance. I've been pretty busy since then, but I've still tried to keep a lookout for him and I haven't seen anything move. I put a few rounds in the place, maybe I got him.'

'Maybe. Thanks for the info. Keep putting rounds into those houses, and anything you see moving.' Teague clipped the radio onto his belt again, then worked his way back to his position near

Goss. Going prone on the ground for the most stable firing platform, he lifted his weapon and put the scope on the house in question.

Carefully he panned the infrared scope from left to right, looking for a telltale heat signature. The house itself glowed from its interior heat, making it more difficult to differentiate body heat – more difficult, but not impossible. Blake might be optimistic that he'd gotten a round in Creed, but Teague wasn't of that opinion. Creed would have hit the floor before the shooting ever started, and immediately sought the most cover available.

At least one other person, maybe more, would be in the house. Teague had no idea who lived there, didn't care. What mattered was that Creed would assess the situation and then pull back to a more secure location. He sure as hell wasn't going to simply walk out the front door – so that meant he'd be going out the back.

Teague's pulse jumped at the idea of being able to pick off Creed like a cherry on a tree. Of course, he might already have pulled an Elvis and left the building, but not that much time had elapsed, maybe ten minutes, and being Creed, he would have first organized the people inside the house. Teague chewed his lip, then made a decision and pulled out the radio, keyed his buddies' radios. 'This is Hawk. I'm moving to the right, trying to get into position to see behind this first house.' Keeping them apprised of his movement was a good idea, so one of them wouldn't accidentally blow his head off.

He repeated the same information to Goss, who gave one sharp nod of the head before returning his attention to his post. Teague was sort of impressed by Goss, not because he'd done anything spectacular, but because he seemed to immediately grasp the why of anything Teague did.

Teague couldn't move all that far to the right, maybe seventy yards or less, before the ground sharply dropped away to the river. This side of the road was nothing but treacherous boulders on a steep incline; if he put a foot wrong, he was risking a sprained ankle or knee at the least, and maybe a broken bone. Moss made the boulders slippery, and the going slow, plus he had to carry the rifle and take damned good care of the heavy scope mounted on it. He couldn't use a flashlight without pinpointing his own position, which made the going even slower. With every passing minute, he was aware that Creed could be slipping away, but there was

169

nothing he could do to hurry. Damn it, if Blake had just told him where Creed was before the bridge blew –

At last, when he put the rifle to his shoulder to check the angle, he could see the back of the house, or at least part of it. The angle wasn't the best, but he'd gone about as far as he could go. He settled behind a boulder and rested the rifle barrel on the rock to steady it, put the scope on the house, and waited.

No shots had come from this location. Creed would have automatically noted where the rounds were being fired from, so if he wanted to eyeball the situation, the most logical position would be from the near back corner of the house. He might allow for the possibility that they'd have starlight scopes, but he wouldn't expect infrared because it was so damned expensive, and not exactly convenient. He would be moving cautiously as he approached the corner . . .

An enormous heat signature burst out of the house, moving fast, then diving behind something and vanishing. Swearing under his breath, Teague tracked with the scope, trying to get the crosshairs settled, but he'd been caught off guard and if he fired now, he would essentially be firing blind – and alerting Creed to his position. He'd have to wait for a better shot.

Jesus, that heat signature had looked weird, like some huge spider. Still unsettled, Teague's brain took another moment before it interpreted the signal his eyes had sent and translated it to *two* people, moving practically in lockstep, with the big one in back right against the smaller one in front. Four legs, four arms, extra-thick body: two people.

Right now he could have used a starlight instead of the infrared, so he could tell exactly what they'd dived behind. A car, maybe; made sense to park one there, close to the back door. No heat signature emanated from the black bulk that was all he could see, though, so if it was a car, it had been sitting there long enough for the engine to get cold. Too bad; the engine block of a car was damn good armor, certainly enough to stop any round they had.

But by holding his fire, he'd given Creed a false sense of security, Teague figured. Thinking they were unseen, Creed wouldn't be as careful in his next movement. This time, Teague would be ready.

A sliver of light in the scope caught his attention; then it bobbed out of sight. Shit. What were they doing? Changing position maybe, shifting around and getting ready for another run. They wouldn't be running back toward the house, and they wouldn't be coming toward the bridge, so that left only two directions. Creed had someone with him, someone he was trying to protect – someone smaller. A woman? Logically he would be trying to put more cover, more walls, more distance, between them and the shooters, which meant he would be pulling back, toward the river.

Time passed – way too much time. What the fuck was Creed waiting for – Christmas? Teague checked the luminous dial of his watch and saw that thirty-four minutes had passed since Blake had radioed with the info about Creed, making it maybe forty-four, forty-five minutes since the bridge blew. The rifle shots now weren't being fired at anyone, because all the inhabitants were either down, behind cover, or had withdrawn beyond the range of the scopes. The occasional shot now was meant to remind them to stay where they were. Maybe that was what Creed had decided to do.

No, the cover of the vehicle – Teague was almost certain that was what they were behind – was too restrictive, and offered no shelter from the cold, no food, no water. Creed would move, but he was a patient bastard, more patient than Teague would ever have guessed.

The minute hand on his watch clicked off another minute, then another, then another. Fifty minutes since the bridge blew. He could be just as patient, Teague thought – more patient, because he *knew* they were there.

Fifty-three minutes.

Yes. There! The heat signature filled his scope, clear and bright, both of them bent low and moving fast. He took a breath, let half of it out, and pulled the trigger just as the glowing figures disappeared.

A split second later, a flare of light brighter than any he'd seen appeared in the bottom half of his scope, and the boulder in front of him exploded in his face.

Chapter Nineteen

Creed heard the crack of the rifle and felt a hard blow to his left leg, just above his ankle, while he and Neenah were still literally in the air. The next split second there was a deep-throated *BOOM!* and they landed with a teeth-jarring thud on the ground behind the pump house, landed so hard he couldn't keep his arms locked around her and the impact sent her rolling. His leg felt as if a giant had taken a hammer to it, and a harsh grunt of pain tore from his throat, past his gritted teeth. Instinctively he rolled, grabbing for his leg even though he dreaded what he would find. 'Shit! *Fuck*!'

His pant leg was already sticky with blood, and he could feel the wet warmth pooling in his boot. He clamped his hand as hard as he could over the wound, mildly surprised his foot was still attached. He'd seen too many wounds from high-caliber weapons, seen arms and legs literally blasted away, and in that first moment of realization that he'd been hit, he was outraged but curiously resigned to the damage he expected to find. Even though his foot was still at the end of his leg and not lying several feet away, the damage could still be severe and what he'd find when he cut away his boot remained to be seen.

The boot was interfering with his ability to apply pressure to the wound; it needed to come off, fast.

Neenah crawled to him, her hands patting over his chest and shoulders. 'Joshua? Are you all right? What happened?'

'Fucker tagged my left leg,' he ground out through the pain; then a whisper from his conscience managed to make itself heard. 'Uh – sorry.'

'I've heard the word *fuck* before,' she said briskly. 'I've said it a time or two myself. Where's that flashlight?'

'In my right pocket.' He lay back on the ground and fished in his pocket, removing both the flashlight and his knife. 'Cut my boot off so I can apply pressure.'

'I'll do it.' They both jumped in shock as the third voice sounded behind them.

Creed's right hand automatically reached for a weapon that wasn't there; then a dark figure went down with a sodden plop on one knee beside him, spraying drops of water over them as he did. Creed's subconscious pulled out that second shot he'd heard, the deep boom, and the pieces fell into place. 'You sneaky son of a bitch, where were you?'

'In the edge of the stream,' Cal replied, his teeth chattering with cold. He laid his shotgun on the ground, reached for Creed's knife, and gave the little flashlight to Neenah. 'Shine this on his foot,' he directed, and Neenah promptly obeyed.

'Why didn't the shooter see you?' Creed asked.

'I figure they have infrared instead of night vision; they lose their specific targets at about the effective range for infrared. So I got wet and cold.'

Thereby losing his heat signature, Creed thought. Shafts of white-hot pain stabbed through his leg as Cal sliced off the boot, unavoidably jarring him. To distract himself Creed thought about the risk Cal had taken, gambling that the shooters didn't have night-vision devices. What if he'd guessed wrong? 'You lucky son of a bitch,' he said, and bit back a groan as Cal pulled off the ruined boot.

'Not lucky,' Cal replied absently. 'Good.' The same old smart-ass but inarguable reply that Creed had heard a hundred times before threw him years back in time, to when they'd run countless missions in the dark and got their asses in some tight jams, which they'd escaped by a combination of skill, discipline, training, and pure luck. Creed was almost surprised to see Neenah on her knees beside Cal, her expression worried but her hands steady as she held the light; for a moment, he'd expected to see some of his men gathered around.

He glanced at his leg, and was genuinely surprised. He was bleeding like a son of a bitch, but the wound, while bad enough, didn't look half as bad as he'd expected. 'Must have ricocheted and shattered,' he said, meaning the bullet. He'd taken a partial instead of a full round.

'Probably.' Cal turned his leg. 'Here's the exit wound. Looks like the fragment hit bone and went sideways.'

'Just wrap it up so we can get the hell out of here.'

Likely the bone had been fractured by the force of the bullet. Creed knew he wasn't out of danger, because the bleeding still had to be stopped and there was the possibility of infection, problems from torn muscles, and so on; but overall, he wasn't in bad shape compared with how bad he could have been. He'd seen men lose legs from being shot in the thigh. Hell, on reflection, he was feeling downright cheerful.

'What will we wrap it with?' Neenah asked, an edge of panic beginning to show in her tone. So far she'd held up admirably, but the bad guys were still out there and could be getting closer to them by the minute, he was hurt, and Cal couldn't run interference for them and help him all at the same time.

Silently Cal peeled out of his wet jacket and shirt, his torso gleaming wetly in the slight reflection of light. Using Creed's knife, he sliced one arm out of his shirt, then made a cut and tore the fabric almost to the end. He placed the untorn end over the exit wound, which was bleeding worse than the entry, and began wrapping the torn ends around and around Creed's leg, crisscrossing the fabric and pulling it snug, then finally tying the ends in a knot with the knot placed firmly over the wound.

'Best I can do right now,' he said, slipping back into what remained of his shirt. Cal should be taking his wet clothes off, Creed knew, to fight off hypothermia; the night was cold, and wearing wet clothes leeched the warmth from someone faster than wearing nothing. The only reason Cal wasn't doing so was to keep those infrared devices from spotting him.

'Did you get the shooter?' Creed asked.

'If I didn't, I scared ten years off his life.' Cal took the flashlight from Neenah and clicked it off, slipping it into his own pocket. 'This is going to be tricky, at least the first part, because even if I got that one, the others still have some good angles on us when we start moving. We have to go that way,' he said, indicating the river. 'Get more houses between us and them, plus distance.'

Cal was shaking with cold as he helped Creed upright, positioning himself on Creed's left to take the weight off the wounded leg, then picking up the shotgun with his left hand. Creed would have been worried if he hadn't seen Cal shoot left-handed before. All of his men had cross-trained, for circumstances such as this.

'He can't walk!' Neenah said with alarm.

'Sure he can,' Cal replied. 'He still has one good leg. Neenah, put my wet jacket over your head. I know it'll be uncomfortable, but it'll block a lot of your heat signature.' Not all, but maybe enough to momentarily puzzle a shooter.

'Come on, Marine,' Creed said, bracing himself for what he knew was going to be a long, cold, and painful trek. 'Let's get moving.'

Cate and the others had made it to the Richardsons' house without sustaining any injuries or losses, though several times the whine of bullets nearby had made them hit the dirt. Stumbling, running, falling, and immediately jumping up to run again, they were like panic-stricken refugees – which wasn't far from the mark. They carried what they could, the blankets and coats Cate had grabbed, the first-aid box Cal had left behind. Cate carried that, despite its weight and despite how it banged against her legs. She hoped the kit didn't make the difference between life and death for someone, but was painfully aware that it might, and she didn't dare leave it behind.

The Richardsons' house was built on land that sloped down toward the river and, as a result, was the only house in Trail Stop that had a full basement. Some of the older houses had pits dug beneath them for storing vegetables, but the root cellars didn't qualify as basements and, if push came to shove, would hold a handful of people but not the twenty or so who made their way to the Richardsons'. The house loomed before them in the night, all pale walls and dark windows.

'Perry!' Walter called as loudly as he could as they approached the house. 'It's Walter! Are you and Maureen all right?'

'Walter?' The voice came from the back of the house, and they turned in that direction. A flashlight shone across the rough ground, danced briefly across their faces as if Perry wanted to reassure himself of their identities. 'We're in the basement. What in thundering hell is going on? Who's doing all that shooting, and why is the electricity off? I tried to call the sheriff's department, but the phone's dead, too.'

The lines must be cut, Cate realized, shivering with horror as she realized the lengths to which Mellor and Huxley had gone in their quest for vengeance. This all seemed so unreal, so out of proportion to the provocation; those men couldn't be sane.

'Come on in with us,' Perry said, indicating the way with his flashlight. 'Get in out of the cold. I lit the kerosene heater; it's taking the chill off the air.'

Gratefully the group stumbled forward, crowding through the basement's outside door. Like most basements, this one was filled with a jumbled assortment of cast-off furniture, clothing, and outright junk. The smell was musty; the floor was bare concrete. But the kerosene heater was putting off wonderful heat, and the Richardsons also had an oil lamp lit. The yellow light was dim and threw enormous shadows into the corners, but after the cold darkness the light seemed miraculous. Maureen hurried forward, a short, plump, gray hen of a woman, clucking in sympathy.

'My goodness, what do you make of this?' she asked of no one in particular. 'I have some candles upstairs, and another lamp. I'll get those and some more blankets—'

'I'll do it,' her husband interrupted. 'You stay down here and help them get settled. Do you know where that old coffee kettle is? Might take some time, but we can make coffee on top of the kerosene heater.'

'It's under the sink. Wash it out good – no, wait, we don't have water. We can't make coffee.' Like everyone else in Trail Stop, the Richardsons had a well, and an electric motor pumped the water from it. No electricity, no pump. Walter Earl had a generator that he used when the electricity went off, and then he generously allowed his neighbors to get water from his well; but his house was on the side that was closest to the shooters and going there now for water was too dangerous.

Perry Richardson wasn't stymied for long. 'We have a bucket,' he stated, 'and there's some rope around here somewhere. I reckon I still know how to draw water. If someone wants to help me, we'll have that coffee going in no time.'

He and Walter went off to accomplish that chore, and Maureen promptly took a flashlight and disappeared up the stairs. Cate hesitated a bare moment, then followed.

'I'll help you carry things, Mrs. Richardson,' she said as she got to the top of the stairs and stepped into the kitchen.

'Why, thank you, and call me Maureen. What *is* going on? What

176

was that loud noise? It shook the whole house.' She set the flash-light on a cabinet, balancing it on end so it was shining at the ceiling and illuminating the whole room, then got an empty laundry basket from a room off the kitchen.

'Some kind of explosion. I don't know what they blew up.'

'"They"? You know who's doing this?' Maureen asked sharply as she bustled around the kitchen gathering supplies and putting them in the laundry basket.

'I think it's those two men who pulled guns on Neenah and me last Wednesday. You heard about that, didn't you?' Belatedly Cate tried to remember if Maureen had been one of the throng of neighbors in her dining room that afternoon. She didn't remember seeing her if she had been.

'My goodness, everyone heard about it. Perry had some tests done at a hospital in Boise that day—'

'I hope he's all right.'

'He's fine, just some stomach problems from eating too much spicy stuff and then going to bed. That man never listens to a thing I tell him. This time the doctor told him the same thing I've been saying for years, and all of a sudden it's the gospel. Makes me want to kick him sometimes, but there you go, that's a man for you.' She removed a plastic sleeve of polystyrene coffee cups from the cabinet, and added it to the basket. 'Now, let's get some blan-kets and cushions rounded up. We can take the dining room chairs down, give people a place to sit, but I'll let the guys bring them down. Why would those two men come back?'

It took Cate a moment to realize Maureen's mental train had switched tracks. 'I don't know, unless they were angry that Cal got the best of them. I just don't know what they could want.'

'That's the thing about mean and crazy people; unless you're mean and crazy yourself, they just don't make sense to you.'

Despite everything, Cate found herself oddly comforted by the woman's cozy philosophy regarding people, life, their current circumstances, and just about everything else as she followed her around the house, gathering blankets and towels, throw pillows, seat cushions, and everything else they could carry to make things more comfortable in the basement. She remembered to stay low and cautioned Maureen to do the same, which made walking espe-cially awkward, laden as they were, but she knew bullets could go a long way and she wasn't certain this house was completely safe.

They made multiple trips to the top of the basement stairs, handing things off to volunteers who then passed them on down.

'Good,' Maureen finally said, 'that just leaves the sofa cushions.' She started toward the living room.

Cate's stomach twisted with sudden panic, and she grabbed Maureen's arm. 'No, don't go in there.' She was taller than Maureen, stronger, and she began pulling her toward the stairs. 'The room's too exposed, and we've pushed our luck being up here this long, shining the flashlight around.' She was suddenly desperate to get belowground again, her skin prickling as if she felt a bullet speeding her way, the projectile boring its way through the barrier of air and walls faster than the speed of sound, heading straight for her as if it had a mind of its own, so that no matter how she twisted and turned it followed her.

With a sharp cry she plowed into Maureen, leading with her shoulder, legs driving, and took them both down to the floor as the living room window shattered and she heard the faint whine of an angry metal hornet a split second before it tore through the wall with a *thhttt!* sound.

Belatedly came the flat, deep crack of rifle fire.

Maureen shrieked. 'Oh, my God! Oh, my God! They shot out the window!'

'Maureen!' came Perry's panicked bellow from the basement, then the thunder of his feet on the stairs as he rushed upward.

'We're okay!' Cate yelled. 'Move back, we're coming down!' Without thinking, she was on her feet with her hand clutching the back of Maureen's shirt, lifting her up and pushing her forward at the same time, terror giving her a strength she hadn't known she possessed. She all but shoved Maureen at Perry, who of course hadn't moved back, and he staggered and nearly went down but was saved by the press of people behind him, all of whom had been rushing upstairs with him. Cate hurled herself through the doorway and down several steps, where she crouched to make certain her head was below ground level. She was shaking wildly, her nerves shattered by how close that had been.

'Cate wouldn't let me go in the living room,' Maureen sobbed on her husband's chest. 'She saved my life, she *tackled* me. I don't know how she knew, but she did—'

Cate didn't know either. She sat on the step and buried her face in her cupped hands, trembling so violently her teeth chattered. She couldn't seem to stop, even when someone – Sherry, she thought – wrapped a blanket around her and gently but determinedly urged her off the stairs and settled her on a cushion on the basement floor.

Her mind went a little fuzzy after that, worn out by shock and fatigue. She listened to the hum of conversation around her without really hearing it, she watched the blue flame of the kerosene heater, she waited for the old-fashioned camp percolator they'd placed on top of the heater to start boiling and making coffee, and she waited for Cal. He should have been back already, she thought, switching her gaze to the door and willing it to open.

At least an hour later – she thought it had to be an hour, unless something had gone seriously wrong with the progression of time – the outside door finally opened and a trio of people staggered in. She saw a head of shaggy, dark blond hair, a face pinched and blue with cold; she saw Mr. Creed, his arms thrown around Cal's and Neenah's shoulders –

Cate threw her blanket off and leaped forward, joining all the others who reached out to stop the three from hitting the floor. There was a confusion of exclamations and questions as Mr. Creed's weight was taken from Cal and Neenah and he was lowered to some cushions; then Cal swayed and stumbled and Cate found herself desperately gripping him, wedging her shoulder into his armpit and trying to hold him up.

'Joshua's shot,' Neenah gasped, sinking to her knees and sucking in huge gulps of air. 'And Cal's freezing; he's been in the water.'

'Let's get him out of these wet clothes,' said Walter, easing Cal away from Cate. Living where they did, they all knew how to treat hypothermia. Within seconds someone was holding up a blanket in front of Cal while he managed, with aid, to strip out of his freezing wet clothes. He was roughly dried, to which he made no protest; then a warmed blanket was wrapped around him and he was seated beside the heater. At some point the percolator had started perking, so Cate put some sugar in one of the polystyrene cups and poured coffee over it. The coffee was still a little weak, but it was hot and it was coffee, and it would have to do.

Cal was shaking convulsively, his teeth chattering; there was no way he could hold the cup. Cate sat beside him and carefully held the cup to his lips, hoping she wouldn't spill the coffee and scald him. He managed a sip and made a face at the sweetness of the brew.

'I know you don't like sugar in your coffee,' she said softly. 'Drink it anyway.'

He couldn't manage much in the way of a response because his entire body was engaged in battling the cold, but he dipped his chin in a nod and took another sip. She set the cup aside and stood behind him, rubbing his back and shoulders and arms as vigorously as she could without completely dislodging the blanket.

His hair was wet, and the night had turned so cold ice crystals had begun to form on his head. She warmed a towel over the heater, then used it to rub his head until his hair was merely damp. By the time that was accomplished the shudders had subsided a bit, though occasionally a violent shiver would rattle his bones and teeth. She gave him more of the coffee; he reached to hold the cup himself and she let him.

'How are your feet?' she asked.

'I don't know, I can't feel them.' His voice was flat, utterly drained. The savage shaking his body had given him in an effort to get warm had completed his exhaustion. He swayed where he sat, his eyelids heavy.

Cate moved to sit at his feet, and then folded the blanket back. Taking one cold foot in her hands, she rubbed and chafed and blew on his toes, then repeated the effort with his other foot. When they were no longer white with cold, she wrapped them in a warm towel. 'You need to lie down,' she told him.

With bleary effort he shook his head, and looked toward where Neenah was taking care of Mr. Creed. 'I need to see what I can do for Josh.'

'You can't do anything right now, considering the shape you're in.'

'Yeah, I can. Get me another cup of coffee – black this time – and something to wear, and I'll be good to go in five minutes.' His pale eyes flickered up at her and she read the steely determination in them.

He really did need to sleep, but in an instant of unspoken communication she knew he wouldn't until he'd done what he thought he needed to do. The fastest way to get him to lie down, then, was to help him.

'One cup of coffee, coming up.' She poured more coffee, and as she did she looked around the basement at her neighbors and friends. They had been alarmed, disoriented, but already they were settling down to take care of business. Some were arranging cushions and pillows and distributing blankets, some were taking inventory of the number of weapons and amount of ammunition they had, Milly Earl was getting some food organized, and Neenah was overseeing Mr. Creed's care. They had cut away his pants and covered him with a blanket except for his injured leg, which was propped on a pillow. Neenah had carefully washed the wound but seemed at a loss for what to do next.

Cate went to Maureen and mentioned Cal's need for clothes. The jeans Maureen unearthed from a box were too big in the waist, but they would do. Perry made an upstairs raid – on his hands and knees, in the dark – and returned with clean underwear and socks, and a thermal-knit pullover shirt. Cal pulled on the underwear under the cover of the blanket, then threw it off to finish dressing as fast as he could.

Cate didn't let herself stare at his mostly naked body, though she couldn't resist one look, during which she noticed that all her carefully placed butterfly bandages were gone and the two cuts were oozing blood again. Sherry noticed her looking, and leaned close to whisper, 'That's a *man.*'

'Yes,' Cate murmured in agreement, 'he is that.'

When Cal finished dressing, he moved slowly to where Mr. Creed was lying, and asked for his first-aid box. Cate braced herself, told her suddenly queasy stomach to take a hike, and went to help him.

'What can I do?' she asked, going down on her knees beside him.

'I'm not sure yet. Let me see what the damage is.'

Neenah moved to Mr. Creed's head, her face white as Cal studied the two wounds and carefully prodded the bone beneath. Creed bit off a curse, his back arching, and Neenah reached for his hand. His big fingers closed around hers with a force that made her wince.

'I think the bone's cracked,' Cal said, 'but I don't feel any displacement. I have to look for any bullet fragments—'

'The hell you do,' Creed snapped.

'—or an infection could cost him his leg,' Cal finished.

181

'Fu—' Creed darted a look from Neenah to Cate and clamped his jaw shut.

'You're tough, you can stand it,' Cal said with a remarkable lack of sympathy. Then he glanced at Cate. 'I need more light, a lot more.'

The light from candles and an oil lamp wasn't suitable for probing, so Sherry stood behind Cate with Cal's powerful flashlight and shined it on Creed's leg. Taking a pair of forceps from his tackle box, Cal probed, and Creed cursed. He found one sliver of bullet fragment, and a chunk of leather from Creed's boot, plus a tiny piece of blood-soaked cotton from a sock. By the time he finished, Creed was ghost white and covered with sweat.

Neenah held Creed's hand throughout the ordeal, murmuring to him and wiping his face with a cold cloth. Cate handed Cal whatever he asked for, and then held a saucepan under the wounds while he flushed them thoroughly. She swayed once and had to look away when he began suturing, though why a needle piercing the torn flesh should make her queasy, she didn't know. She wondered when he'd learned how to suture a wound, where he'd gotten his medical training, but those were questions that could wait for another day.

Soon after that, antibiotic had been applied to the closed wounds, Creed had been made to swallow some pills, both antibiotics and painkillers, and a neat bandage was wrapped around Creed's lower leg.

'I'll splint it tomorrow, give the bone some support,' Cal said as he wearily climbed to his feet. 'He isn't going anywhere tonight.'

'I'll make sure he doesn't try,' Neenah said.

'I'm right here, and I can hear you,' Creed said grumpily, but he looked exhausted, and he didn't protest when Neenah settled beside him.

'I need a couple of hours' sleep,' Cal said, looking around for a quiet corner.

'That can be arranged,' said Cate. She and Sherry grabbed a couple of blankets and a pillow, and Cate unpacked more of the old clothes from the box Maureen had opened, arranging them to form a rough mattress. They dragged over some more boxes to form a partial shield, stacking them two high on each side of the pile of clothes, then draped an old curtain over the boxes to form an enclosure that would keep out most of the light and give at least the illusion of privacy.

Cal watched all this with weary bemusement. 'A blanket on the floor would have been fine,' he said. 'I've slept in rougher circumstances than that.'

'Maybe,' said Cate, 'but tonight you don't have to.'

'Good night,' Sherry said. 'Look, Cal, don't think you have to do everything. The other men have organized themselves to stand watch for the rest of the night. You can sleep longer than a couple of hours. They'll wake you if anything happens.'

'I'll take you up on that,' he said, and Sherry moved away to join the others.

Cate stood there awkwardly, suddenly not knowing what to say or do. She murmured 'Good night' and started to follow Sherry, but Cal caught her wrist. She froze, staring at him, unable to look away. Abruptly her heart was thudding against her breastbone. His pale gaze moved over her face, settled on her mouth, lingered.

'You're tired, too,' he said in his quiet voice, as with surprising strength he pulled her down and into his makeshift quarters. 'Come sleep with me.'

Chapter Twenty

Cate's mind went blank. 'W-what?' she stuttered, completely disoriented by the suddenness with which she found herself lying on her back on a pile of blanket-covered clothing, staring up at the underside of a curtain draped over two stacks of boxes. She felt a ludicrous moment of pride at how comfy the makeshift bed was, and how dark was the interior of the makeshift tent. Even the steady buzz of conversation from the other twenty-odd people in the basement with them seemed muted.

'Sleep with me,' he repeated softly, stretching out in the limited space and settling his head on the pillow beside hers. His voice was very low, meant for her alone. His gaze met hers, and mesmerized by the crystalline depths, she lost the ability to think, almost to breathe. She felt almost as if she were seeing straight through to his soul, and the sense of connection was more powerful than if they'd been having sex. Almost without realizing it, she reached out, lightly touching his lips, feeling the slightly damp softness of them under her fingertips. He caught her hand, his fingers cool and hard but infinitely gentle, turning it so he could touch his lips to her knuckles in the sweetest, lightest kiss she'd ever received.

The intimacy of lying here with him was staggering; she could feel him all along her body, the way she hadn't felt anyone since Derek's death. The long years alone had dimmed her memory of how it was to lie so close to a man that their breaths mingled, that she could smell the heat of his skin, feel his heart beating with strong, solid thumps. They were fully clothed – well, she had on flannel pajamas, as well as the thick cardigan she had pulled on before starting the trek to the Richardsons' house, but she was covered – yet she felt as vulnerable as if she were naked. She was

184

acutely aware of their neighbors outside this little enclosure, watching and speculating, wondering what was going on between the handyman and the widow.

Her cheeks heated as she wondered that herself. Things had changed so fast that she wasn't certain how or why, or even *what* had changed. All she knew was that shy Mr. Harris seemed to have disappeared as if he'd never existed at all, and in his place was Cal, a shotgun-toting, wound-suturing stranger who looked at her as if he wanted her naked.

Duh, her brain whispered. He was a man. Men wanted women naked; that was who they were and what they *did*. Simple as that.

But the way she felt wasn't simple. She felt confused, upset, worried, and turned on all at once. Nor was Cal a simple man. A lot of people had hidden depths, but his hidden depths evidently rivaled Loch Ness's. She should crawl out of here, and sleep alone. He wouldn't stop her; he would accept her decision. But telling herself she *should* do it and telling herself *to* do it were two entirely different things, and while she could do the first, the second was evidently beyond her ability.

'Stop thinking,' he murmured, touching one finger to her forehead. 'Just for a little while. Sleep.'

He was serious. He expected her to sleep beside him with everyone outside watching their feet to see if their toes remained pointing in the same direction. Fatigue dragged at her bones, but she didn't think she could even close her eyes. 'I can't sleep here!' she whispered urgently, finally getting her voice to work. 'Everyone will be thinking—'

'There's something I should tell you about that later.' His voice sounded drowsy, and his eyelids looked heavy. 'For now, let's just get some sleep. I'm still cold, and tomorrow will be a bitch. Please. I need you beside me tonight.'

He was cold, and tired. The plea went straight to her heart, arrowed through it. 'Roll over,' she whispered, and with a grunt of effort he did, turning his back to her. She pulled the second blanket over both of them and straightened it, leaning out of their enclosure to tuck it around their protruding feet. Her own feet were freezing, and she instinctively tucked her feet against his sock-clad ones as she curled against his back.

He was already half asleep, but he gave a contented sigh and nestled closer. Cate curled one arm under her head and the other

185

over his waist, and tucked her thighs snugly against the curve of his ass. Belatedly she remembered that the cuts on his shoulders and arm needed tending again, but his breathing had gone slow and deep just in the last thirty seconds and she didn't want to wake him.

Warmth began to steal through her, and with it came drowsiness. Beyond the wall of boxes, voices were going silent as people settled down for what rest they could get. The men had organized a guard system, Sherry had said; tucked underground here, no bullets could reach them. They were relatively safe until morning, when they could find out exactly what was going on. There was no reason why she shouldn't sleep.

She snuggled closer to his back and moved her free hand, sliding it from his waist, up his abdomen, to his chest. Feeling his heart beating under her touch, she went to sleep.

Long moments after he'd been hit, Teague struggled to a sitting position. He couldn't see; blood was pouring from the wound at the top of his forehead, getting into his eyes and blinding him. Agony pounded in his head with Satan's drumbeat. What the fuck had happened? He didn't know where he was; his searching hands couldn't find anything familiar, just rocks and more rocks. He was outside, he knew that much. But where, and why?

He waited, experience telling him that memory would return as he came to full consciousness. Until then, he pressed his hand over the jagged cut to slow his blood loss, ignoring the pain the pressure caused.

The first thing he remembered was an ungodly bright flash of light, and a boom as a giant fist punched him in the head.

Shot, he thought, then discarded that idea. If he'd been shot in the head, he wouldn't be lying here wondering about it. The shot had missed, then, but not by much. His face felt on fire, as if all the skin had been stripped off. The slug must have hit the boulder right below him, blasting him with pieces of rock.

As soon as the word *slug* formed in his mind, he thought 'shotgun' and the pieces of his memory fell into place. That was the boom he'd heard, following so closely on the heels of his own shot that the two sounds had overlapped.

He wondered if anyone else had heard the shotgun; why hadn't someone called on the radio to check on him? His thoughts were still so sluggish that several moments went by before he realized he'd been unconscious and wouldn't have heard the radio even if someone had tried to contact him.

Radio. Yeah. He reached for it, found it clipped to his belt right where it was supposed to be; he unclipped it, fumbling because his hands were wet with blood, and then sudden caution made him freeze. If he dropped the radio, he might not be able to find it. Carefully, making certain he had a solid grip, he started to key the 'talk' button – and stopped.

He could call for help. Hell, he needed help. *But* – he wasn't helpless. He could do this on his own. When you ran with a pack of wolves, you didn't show weakness or you could find yourself eaten alive. Billy wouldn't turn on him, and neither would Troy, but Teague wasn't so certain about Blake. He was damn certain about Toxtel and Goss – certain they'd turn on him in a New York minute. If he couldn't make it off this damn mountainside by himself, if he had to be carried out instead of walking under his own steam, they would view him as weak, and he couldn't afford that.

Okay. He had to do this on his own, then. He took a few deep breaths and forced himself to concentrate, to get past the pounding agony in his head, the dizziness and sense of panic. He had to be operational.

The first, most important thing he had to do was stop losing blood. Head wounds always bled like a bitch anyway, so he could lose a significant amount in a short time, probably already had. He had to put pressure on the wound, a lot of pressure, no matter how much it hurt.

He knew he had a concussion, maybe brain damage that would only worsen with time, but his exploring fingers told him the area around the wound was swelling rapidly. That was good, from what he'd heard. If the swelling was on the inside of his brain, that was bad. He could deal with a concussion; he'd done it before.

Teague braced his back against the rock behind him and drew his legs up, planting his feet as solidly as possible. Leaning forward, he braced his right elbow on his knee and put the heel of his palm against the wound, using his entire body to apply more pressure than he could have accomplished using just arm strength. He ignored the pain exploding in his head, holding firm and steady while he concentrated on breathing and getting through the agony.

While he sat there, he started swiping his left forearm across his face, trying to wipe the blood out of his eyes. The thing about blood was, the shit congealed, then it dried, and it was hard as hell to get off. He needed water to clean his face. There was a ton of it at the bottom of this fucking rock pile, but getting down there was something he'd think twice about attempting in broad daylight *without* a concussion. No, he had to get back to the road.

Other than applying pressure to the wound, he was limited in what he could do for himself, so that would have to be enough. The good news was, the longer he sat there, the more his head cleared. It still hurt like a son of a bitch, but he was thinking better.

The bad news was, the longer he sat there, the colder he felt. If the blood loss caused him to go into shock, he was screwed. On the other hand, the temperature had to be in the thirties, maybe even below freezing. Of course he was cold, but hypothermia wasn't good, either. He had to get off these rocks, the sooner the better. His head was going to hurt worse when he tried to move, but what the fuck, hurting was better than dying.

He moved his hand, waiting to see if blood poured down his face again. He felt a trickle and immediately wiped it away, then pressed his hand back over the wound. The bleeding hadn't stopped, but it had definitely slowed.

His rifle. Where was his rifle? He couldn't leave it here. For one thing, that damn expensive thermal scope was mounted on it. For another, his fingerprints were all over it. If it had slid down the rocks toward the stream, he wouldn't be able to retrieve it and someone else would have to come back for it, which right now meant they'd have to leave one firing position unmanned, and he didn't want to do that.

Something about the firing positions bothered him, but he couldn't think what it was. It would come to him, though. Forget about it for now – concentrate on finding the rifle.

Using his left hand, he felt around on the ground, but came up empty. He'd have to use the flashlight. He didn't like doing that, didn't want to give away his position to the fucker who'd shot him ... okay, the fucker already *knew* his position, otherwise how could he have shot him? Big question: How had he known?

Teague stopped searching for the rifle to concentrate on this question, because it seemed vitally important that he think it through. He hadn't used a flashlight to move into position, so did the shooter have night-vision goggles? The devices weren't that hard to come by, but what were the odds that somebody in Trail Stop, of all places, would have them? Creed, maybe; he could see Creed having all kinds of shit. But Creed hadn't shot him; Creed had been hustling some woman to cover –

Ah, fuck. The answer bloomed in his mind. That hadn't been Creed leaving the house with the woman. Creed had already gone out the back and moved into position to provide cover for the other two. When Teague had pulled the trigger, his muzzle flash had given away his position and Creed had fired. Simple as that. No night-vision device needed.

Creed could still be out there, waiting for someone to show himself.

But he'd be on the other side of the stream, because crossing it in this area was impossible. The slope down to the river was steep, so the water roared down, strong enough to sweep even the strongest man off his feet and slam him into the boulders that dotted the streambed. *Stream* was really a misnomer in this case, because that brought to mind a slow, peaceful flow of water, which this definitely wasn't. It was like a mini-river – and a bad one. Plus it was as cold as a well-digger's ass, because it was fed by snowmelt from the mountains.

Teague assessed the situation. He was behind solid cover, surrounded by rocks, his head lower than the boulder in front of him. He had to risk turning on the flashlight so he could locate the rifle. He could minimize the risk, though, by covering most of the lens.

Laboriously, using his left hand, he pulled the flashlight from its loop on his belt and carefully positioned his fingers over the lens, parting two of them to allow a very thin sliver of light to pass. He had to release pressure on his wound then, using his right hand to press the button on the cylinder, but he didn't feel any fresh blood flowing, so he didn't bother reapplying pressure.

The amount of light was slight, barely enough to make a difference, but it made him feel better to be able to see *something* and reassure himself that his eyes were still functioning. The first thing he noticed was the amount of red around him: streaks of it running down the boulder in front of him, on the smaller rock he sat on, spattered on moss and fallen leaves. His clothes were wet and sticky with blood. He'd left a shitload of DNA evidence here, but he could hardly scoop it up and put it back into his body.

This raised the stakes. He couldn't let the smallest suspicion fall on him now, or he was screwed. He'd have to clear out for a while, afterward, and that pissed him off.

That fucking Creed. He'd come out ahead in their first encounter, but damned if he'd do it again.

The frail light finally hit a glint of metal, and Teague played it across the site just long enough to verify he'd located his rifle; then he turned off the light. When he'd been knocked back, the rifle had been sent up and back a few feet, coming to lie wedged in the rocks above him. To reach it, he'd have to leave his protected position, but it wasn't as if he had a choice. He couldn't move very fast, either. He thought about it a minute, then figured, what the hell, and went for it.

Overall, moving ranked right up there with getting hit in the head with a hammer. Felt a lot like it, too. Pain exploded in his head; he was puking before he even got his hand on the rifle, but he forced himself to keep going because waiting a few more minutes wasn't going to make it get any better. As soon as his hand was on the rifle stock, he collapsed against the rocks, gasping.

No shotgun boomed at him, but right then being put out of his misery sounded like a good idea, so he didn't know whether to feel relieved or sorry.

After a few minutes, he straightened. It was time to get off this pile of rocks, regardless of what it cost him. Pushing himself to his feet, he swayed unsteadily; then he took a step. The pain wasn't quite as bad as when he'd lunged for the rifle, but it still wasn't a picnic.

He could do this, though. And before this little dance was over, he'd pay Creed back – big-time.

Chapter Twenty-One

When Teague was near the road, he pulled the radio off his belt and keyed it. 'Falcon, this is Hawk.' *Falcon* was Billy. He'd assigned bird-of-prey designators for no reason other than that was what had first come to mind. He was *Hawk*, Billy was *Falcon*, Troy was *Eagle*, and Blake was *Owl*. Come to think of it, he hoped Blake wasn't insulted by being *Owl*, because owls had the best eyesight – shit, he was worse off than he'd thought if he was worrying about this stuff.

'Go ahead, Hawk.'

'Shotgun blasted the rock right in front of me, and I'm cut to hell and back. I could use some help here. Meet me at the bridge.' Billy was the closest, and the one it was safest to pull in. The two farthest positions were now the most critical, because they overlooked the most likely escape route. Teague had no doubt someone, maybe several someones, would get around to trying to outflank them. Maybe not tonight, but soon.

'Ten-four,' Billy replied, and Teague replaced the radio. God, he was about out on his feet, but he had to keep it going for a few more minutes, at least. He had to walk out there where Toxtel and Goss could see him, so that meant he needed to suck it up. He hadn't given them radios because he didn't trust them as far as he could throw their asses, plus he didn't want them to hear everything he and the guys said. He'd be walking in on them without warning.

The bad thing was, even after he was away from them, he wouldn't have a chance to lie down until he felt better; about the best he could do was swallow some aspirin and hope the headache eased.

191

Right before he emerged from the trees and underbrush, he called softly, 'Incoming.' Made them feel like they were on some military op, or something. Pitiful. He'd been on some fucked-up ops in his time, but nothing as harebrained as this.

Toxtel and Goss had taken up positions within five yards of each other, which was another dumb-ass thing to do, but since Teague hadn't figured there would be any action at the bridge, he'd let them do what they wanted, let them think they were still in charge.

Neither of them turned to look at him as he approached; they were still wired on adrenaline, muscles tight, as they waited for someone to try to sneak across the stream. He couldn't fault them on that, though someone more experienced would have learned to relax somewhat.

'Did you get anybody?' Goss asked. 'I heard a shot.'

That confirmed Teague's impression that the shotgun blast had followed his own shot so closely they were almost simultaneous.

'I maybe got someone, but someone else got a lucky shot off at me.'

Goss glanced over his shoulder and, even in the dark, could tell that Teague's face was mostly obscured by blood. 'Fuck!' He jumped to his feet, whirling around and causing Toxtel to start in alarm. 'You got shot in the fucking *head*?'

'No, it's cuts, not a bullet wound. Someone with a shotgun blasted the rock in front of me, blew shards everywhere.' He managed to sound nonchalant.

'Shotgun?' Toxtel asked grimly, also getting up and coming over to stand with them. 'I wonder if it was our boy,' he said to Goss, confirming Teague's suspicion that one of those tough old boys over there had gotten the jump on them.

'I know who it was,' Teague told them. 'A guy named Creed. Tough son of a bitch, ex-military, does some guiding around here.'

'What does he look like? Not too big, maybe five-ten, six feet, on the skinny side? Longish hair? Spooky eyes, like they're made of glass or something?'

Huh. Teague didn't remember anyone answering that description. One thing was for certain, though, their boy wasn't Creed. 'No. Creed's a big, muscled guy. Short dark hair going gray. Looks like he should still be in uniform.'

'That's not him. You sure this Creed is the one who shot at you?' Toxtel asked.

'Almost certain.' He said 'almost' because he hadn't actually seen Creed, but his gut told him it couldn't have been anyone else.

'But you said it was a shotgun,' Toxtel persisted.

Teague barely held on to his temper. Here he was standing in front of them covered with blood, and all Toxtel could think about was the guy who'd got the jump on him. 'There's more than one shotgun in the world,' he said shortly. 'And I'd guess at least ten of them are on the other side of that stream, plus assorted rifles and pistols.'

Toxtel turned back around, evidently pissed that Teague had been shot by someone other than Toxtel's personal nemesis.

Goss looked at Toxtel, then back at Teague, and offered a shrug. 'You look like shit. Need any help?'

'Nah. I'm going to the camp to clean up.' At least Goss had offered to help, which was more than that asshole Toxtel had done. Teague turned and carefully headed back up the road and around a curve. Billy stepped out of the foliage on the other side of the road and silently joined him. Once they were out of sight of Toxtel and Goss, Billy helped him the rest of the way, pulling one of Teague's arms around his own shoulders and taking half of Teague's weight. Since Billy wasn't a big guy, getting to the camp was a struggle.

They had set up a small tent about a hundred yards from the bridge – or where the bridge had been – in a small, protected hollow that couldn't be seen from the road. Common sense had said that they'd need a place to rest, to make coffee, and to eat, especially if this went on for longer than a day, which Teague sort of expected. Billy released him long enough to duck inside and light the lantern, then returned to get Teague inside, which involved bending his head down, which made the world spin even more sickeningly than it already was.

'Shit,' Teague said wearily as he sank down on the camp chair, too sick to think of a curse more inventive.

'Maybe you should lie down,' Billy suggested, busy opening a plastic sack that contained their first-aid supplies, which either Goss or Toxtel had gathered up, so he had no idea what was in there.

'If I do, I won't be able to get up.'

'So don't get up for a few hours. There's nothing going on. I haven't seen anyone moving for about an hour. They've pulled back and hunkered down, waiting for daylight. Nothing's gonna happen until then. Diaper wipes,' he mused, throwing Teague into confusion until he blearily made out the plastic box Billy was holding. 'I guess they got 'em to clean up with. Reckon this'd be okay to clean cuts? There are a few alcohol wipes but not many. Not enough to clean you up, anyway.'

Teague started to shrug, thought better of it. 'Don't see why not. Any aspirin in there?'

'Yeah, sure. How many you want?'

'Four, to start.' He didn't think two pills would make a dent in this headache.

'Aspirin's a blood thinner.'

'I'll take the risk. I need something.'

Billy got a bottle of water and opened it, then shook four pills into his palm and gave them to Teague, who cautiously swallowed them one at a time, trying to move his head as little as possible. Then Billy set to work with the diaper wipes, cleaning the blood away so he could see the damage.

As he carefully wiped around the big cut at the top of Teague's forehead, he murmured, 'This is the most dumb-ass stunt I've ever seen. Tell me again why we're doing this.'

'Money.'

'Yeah, but it's not enough to risk getting our asses thrown in the pen for life. Blowing the bridge, holding the whole town hostage – this can go to hell so many different ways it ain't funny. Without even thinking hard, I can come up with four or five better ways of getting what those boys want, less risk all the way around.' Billy kept his voice low, so low it wouldn't carry beyond the confines of the tent.

They were getting paid very well. Teague intended to take something off the top, but the others didn't need to know about that. *Honor among thieves* was a myth, and he wasn't about to start perpetuating it. As far as the other guys knew, they were getting a cool one hundred thousand, to be divided four ways, twenty-five for each of them for a few days' work, with Toxtel picking up all the expenses for this massive charade.

'The risk to us is minimal,' he said. 'We don't let ourselves be seen, and none of those people over there have any idea we're involved.'

'Those two yahoos from Chicago know we're involved.'

'You're assuming they'll be alive to tell.'

A quick grin crossed Billy's face, then just as quickly faded. 'They're not alive, they can't pay us.'

'It's choreographed. We'll get paid when the woman over there makes arrangements to give them what they want. Toxtel wanted to wait until he actually had whatever it is to make payment, but I nixed that. He has what he wants, he'd put a bullet in all of us without blinking an eye, to keep from paying. So we get paid first.'

'He trusts us to stay around after we get paid?'

'I doubt it, but he doesn't have a choice.'

'When you gonna do it?'

When did he intend to kill Toxtel and Goss? Teague thought about it. 'After they get what they want. If they're willing to pay so much money to get their hands on whatever it is, we might be interested in it, too. See, a time will be set for the handover, because we'll have to get everything packed up and cover our tracks so we can get the hell out of Dodge as soon as it's done. It'll take a while for those people to work their way across the stream and get help, and in the meantime, we're busy vanishing. Once Toxtel has what he wants, they'll pull back, too, and we'll be waiting for them. Pop them, leave their bodies. They're the only two known to be involved. We're clear.'

'So who killed them, then, if they're the only two?'

'Most logical assumption is they had a third partner who double-crossed them. It'll work. Trust me.'

Billy was silent then as he examined Teague's wound. 'This needs stitches,' he finally said, 'but it's stopped bleeding. Come morning, you want to take a trip to the clinic in town? It's not a bullet wound, so it won't be reported.'

'I might do that. I'll decide then.' Some antibiotics might come in handy, plus the doc could give him some real painkillers. People took falls in these mountains all the time; nothing unusual there.

Billy dabbed some antibiotic ointment on the cut, taped a pad over it. 'I hope we haven't bit off more than we can chew. People died over there, Teague; when the lid blows off and the cops get in here, they'll pull in every state investigator on the job, plus some Federal ones if they need to. This will be big news, and there'll be some big dogs on our asses.'

'They may figure out more people were involved, but I've been careful not to be seen with those two guys, and nothing is written down, no phone records to worry about. If they're dead, they can't involve us. We're getting paid in cash. Unless we screw up and let ourselves be identified, we're home free.'

Billy thought it over, then nodded. 'I can see that. But – damn! Who thought of this shit to begin with?'

'Toxtel. He and Goss went in thinking they were the toughest guys around, and found out they weren't. Toxtel has a real hard-on for some guy over there who pulled a shotgun on him. Don't guess he's ever been on the losing end before, because he's got a big ego and he can't see around it.'

Billy grunted. They'd both seen it before, and nine times out of ten the situation turned into a clusterfuck. If Teague hadn't seen a way he and his boys could dance their way out, he wouldn't have touched this with a barge pole.

'How long you think this will take?'

'I'm figuring four or five days, at least,' Teague said. Toxtel might think the locals would quickly fold and throw Cate Nightingale to the wolves, but Teague knew better. These people were stubborn, and they would close ranks around her. At some point, though, the price of continued resistance would become too high – and then Ms. Nightingale herself would give in and give these boys whatever it was of theirs that she was hiding.

The only possibility of a fast outcome that he saw was that she might cave first thing, but in his experience, people who tried to screw someone else in the first place weren't real big on civic duty, or whatever you wanted to call it. No, if she was trying to score on something crooked, she wouldn't give up right away. She would lie, she'd deny, she'd stall, until she thought she'd gone as long as possible without her neighbors turning on her – then she'd start making excuses, trying to explain and make herself look as good as possible, and ultimately she'd cave.

Teague hoped she'd hold out for a while, though – just long enough for him to get to feeling better and get that bastard Creed taken care of.

Creed was going to regret pulling that trigger tonight. Payback was a bitch.

Chapter Twenty-Two

Cate sleepily opened her eyes and found herself staring at the back of Cal's head. There was no moment of incomprehension; she knew immediately where she was and who was lying beside her. A confusing rush of emotions swamped her, impressions and feelings and thoughts, all coming so fast she couldn't sort them out. Events were sweeping her along, not giving her time to analyze or think about her decisions; the resulting sense of losing control was both terrifying and exciting. Something was happening between her and Cal when she wasn't ready for anything to happen, with anyone, but now that the change had started, it was like a snowball gaining momentum as it plunged down a mountain.

She didn't think he'd moved at all since going to sleep, and this evidence of his exhaustion filled her with both tenderness and a fierce sense of protectiveness. She wanted to lay her head against his back, but she remembered the cuts he'd suffered and didn't want to hurt his wounds. She stared at his shaggy hair and wanted to run her fingers through it, but he needed all the sleep he could get and she didn't want to wake him. She wanted to slide her hand inside the too-big waistband of his borrowed jeans and explore the bulge she'd seen in his underwear when he changed clothes, and the abrupt sharpness of her own sexual need was devastating.

She hadn't wanted to have sex with anyone since Derek's death. She had wanted sexual release, yes, but not *with* anyone – and for a long time she hadn't even wanted that. Shock and grief had killed her sexuality, and she'd been so numb, so focused on the herculean task of getting through each day, that she hadn't even mourned the loss of that part of herself. After a year or so, though, her physical needs had slowly resurfaced – muted, disconnected, but at least they existed. As far as having sex went, though, she hadn't wanted that, hadn't wanted the physical reality of touching and being touched. To so suddenly want – *need* – the rawness of penetration made her feel as if she were being unfaithful to Derek, as if she had completely let him go.

Perhaps she had. Perhaps time had so gradually moved her beyond him that she hadn't noticed the moment when he faded from view. Not from her heart – she would always love him, but that love was static now, the details forever frozen and unchanging. Life wasn't static; it moved on, it changed, and what had once been so immediate instead became a dearly beloved memory that was part of the fabric of her being. Because she had loved Derek, she had become the person she was now. And that new woman was poised on the edge of something frightening and exciting and possibly life-changing. She didn't know what would happen, but at least she was willing to find out.

Assuming she and Cal both lived, that is. For a few sleepy moments, pondering the resurrection of emotion and need, and the delicious unknown of a possible new relationship, she had forgotten their bizarre, frightening situation. Reality came crashing back; yet at the same time, the whole night seemed surreal. Things like this just didn't happen. This was so far outside her experience that she had no reference point, no clue as to what she should be doing or what would happen next.

She listened intently; if dawn had arrived yet, she couldn't tell. Everyone around them was asleep, or at least trying to be. Several different snores punctuated the silence, and every so often she would hear someone shifting position. Once there was a quiet murmur that she thought might belong to Neenah, who was taking care of Joshua Creed.

Cal reached back under the blanket and put his hand on her hip, silently pulling her even closer to him.

Tears stung her eyes as she nestled close, as close as she could get. *This* – this was what she'd missed most, the quiet companionship in the night, the knowledge that she wasn't alone. They hadn't so much as kissed, yet somehow, on some level, they were already linked. She felt it as surely as she knew when the twins were all right, or when they were getting into trouble. She didn't have to see them; she didn't have to hear them; she just knew.

198

'Go back to sleep,' he whispered softly. 'You'll need all the rest you can get.'

She wanted him to hold her, wanted to feel his arms around her. When he'd held her and Neenah after the frightening episode with Mellor, for the first time in a long while Cate had felt ... safe. Not just because Cal had protected them, though she was bemused to realize that was indeed part of her response; some primitive reactions evidently didn't go away. The biggest part of it, though, was that suddenly she hadn't felt so alone.

The words asking him to hold her trembled on the verge of being spoken, but she held them back. If he held her, if he put his hands on her body, she suspected more than just holding would occur. He was a man, and he wanted her. A thrill of delight went through her as she fully acknowledged that startling fact. He might be shy – no, she wasn't even certain of that anymore, because a shy man wouldn't have dressed in front of everyone the way he'd done. He was definitely considerate, in the way he was keeping his back to her. They were surrounded by people, and while the arrangement of boxes and the curtain might give them a little privacy, it certainly wasn't enough to have any sexual intimacy. Their feet protruded beyond the boxes, and if Cal suddenly moved behind her, she knew the speculation that would go on. Others in this basement were awake, too, listening to rustlings and murmurs.

Public sex – or even semipublic sex – wasn't her thing, so she was grateful for his circumspection. She wanted to feel him behind her, to feel his arms around her, but she knew that if he held her, his hand would soon be sliding down the front of her pajama bottoms.

The thought sent her nerve endings into a spasm of delight, making her jerk against him. Oh, God, she wanted him to touch her, wanted to feel his long fingers sliding into her, wanted it so intensely she had to bite back a whimper.

He reached back once again, gently patting her butt.

The agony of desire instantly morphed into a choked-back laugh. He couldn't know what she'd been thinking, what she'd been feeling, but that gentle pat had almost seemed to say, 'Hold on. We'll get to it.'

Then she remembered that telltale jerk, and her cheeks heated. Maybe he knew after all. A little bloom of contentment unfolded

199

inside her, and she was smiling as she drifted back to sleep.

Goss watched the sky to the east slowly begin to lighten. He was tired but not yet sleepy; he figured the sleepiness would hit at some point.

Last night had been pretty damn impressive, and intense. These boys were deadly. To a man, none of them gave a rat's ass whether someone lived or died. He could see it in their eyes, and he recognized the expression because it was the same one he saw whenever he looked in a mirror.

Teague had looked pretty bad last night, but he'd been on his feet, so it must have looked worse than it was. What interested Goss was the shotgun; that had taken Toxtel's interest, too. Teague had been certain this guy Creed was the shooter, but he hadn't seen him, so what it came down to was that Teague was guessing – and Goss's gut said that Teague was guessing wrong.

This Creed was supposedly pretty good, but Teague admittedly knew nothing about the handyman or how good he was. Goss and Toxtel both had had firsthand experience with the bastard, though. Goss knew his limits, knew he was no outdoorsman, but at the same time, he was damn good at what he did and he had excellent hearing. No one – *no one* – had ever successfully sneaked up behind him before, especially when he was already alert and on watch. Yet that damn handyman had done it. Goss couldn't remember anything, not the slightest sound or warning, no sense of the air moving; it was as if he'd been attacked by a ghost.

Toxtel was just as spooked. Granted, he'd been occupied with the two women, but his instincts were as well developed as Goss's. He hadn't heard the handyman moving up a flight of old creaky stairs, just turned around and found himself looking down the barrel of a shotgun. In a very un-Toxtel-like admission, he'd said, 'You're a cold bastard, Goss, but this guy ... this guy makes you look like the Easter Bunny.'

Shotgun ... the shooter being where he wasn't supposed to be ... What were the odds that Creed and the handyman would have those things in common? *He'd* been out there last night, closer than Goss liked to think. He wanted the guy close, because he owed him for that knock on the head, but he wanted to *know* he was close. Thinking of him sitting out there, somehow invisible to Teague's precious thermal scopes, gave Goss an uneasy feeling.

Teague had been fixated on Creed, like Creed was some sort of bogeyman, but this other guy was the wild card in the deck, someone Teague hadn't factored into the equation.

All in all, though, Goss was pleased with the way things had kicked off. Some people over there were dead, enough that a huge furor was going to be raised over this. Sooner or later someone or several someones from the surrounding ranches would need something from the hardware store, and while they might buy the 'bridge out' excuse for a little while, eventually they would say something to someone, and word would get out, and next thing they knew the real state highway department would be stopping by. Then everything would go to hell. The only way that wouldn't happen would be if the Nightingale woman gave up right away and gave them the flash drive.

Regardless of what happened, Yuell Faulkner was going down. The killings last night had guaranteed that. By losing his perspective and letting things go so far, Toxtel had set in motion a chain of events that couldn't be halted or deflected. To give him credit, even though Toxtel's plan was overkill, he had every expectation of winning and getting away clean, since their real names weren't known and they would be long gone before the locals could go on foot to get help. The credit card Faulkner had used for the B and B was a dead end; Goss knew that much. He also knew that he himself was the reason this would blow up in Faulkner's face; a crucial piece of evidence 'accidentally' left behind, an anonymous phone call to the authorities, would guarantee that. He didn't see any way Toxtel wouldn't go down, too, and while he had nothing against Hugh, he wasn't sentimental about him, either. Toxtel could be sacrificed. And Kennon Goss would disappear forever; it was time for another name, another identity.

The first thing Cal did when he woke was lace on his boots. 'It's almost daylight,' he said to Cate, who had sat up when he left their makeshift bed. Several other people in the basement were stirring, too.

Maureen moved to turn up the oil lamp so they could have more light.

'I'm going out to look around, see if I can find anyone else,' Cal said

Creed was awake, propping himself up on his elbows. He had

dark circles under his eyes, but they were clear. 'I've been think-ing,' he said to Cal. 'We'll work on the plan when you get back.'

Cal nodded and slipped out the basement door. Outside he nodded to Perry Richardson, who was sitting in a corner of the retaining wall, a deer rifle cradled in his arms. 'Seen anything?' he asked, though he knew damn well there hadn't been any trouble.

Perry shook his head. 'I was hoping some of the others would make their way here, but so far it's been quiet.' His worried expression said that he was afraid no one had shown up because the rest of the inhabitants were dead.

'It's bad enough,' Cal said grimly, 'but it isn't that bad. People will have gone to ground wherever they could rather than take the risk of getting out in the open.' His task this morning was to find those people, and safely get them here.

'How many—?' Perry couldn't complete the question, but Cal knew what he was asking.

'I saw five last night. I hope that's all.' Five friends, lying where they'd fallen. He hadn't been able to get to them last night, didn't know who they were, but regardless of their identities, they had been friends. He'd be able to tell more in the daylight, though he might not be able to get to them until tonight.

'Five,' Perry murmured, shaking his head as grief entered his eyes. 'What in God's name is going on?'

'I don't know, but my guess is it has something to do with those two sons of bitches who roughed up Cate and Neenah.' If it was them, they'd brought in help. Cal had counted four different firing positions, including the one beside Neenah's house.

'But what do they want?'

Cal shook his head. Cate had given them Layton's belongings, so the only thing left was revenge, which, as far as he was concerned, was a piss-poor reason for attacking an entire commu-nity. Come after him if they felt they had to prove their balls were bigger than his; he was the one who'd gotten the better of them, not those poor people lying on the ground. This whole thing was so over the top it didn't make sense.

And if those two guys had nothing to do with this, then it *really* didn't make sense and he was completely in the dark.

Chapter Twenty-Three

Cal worked his way under the Contrerases' house, crawling on his belly through mud, debris, and spiderwebs. All sorts of bugs love the dark, damp protected spaces under a house, and this one was no different from most, in that it offered lots of darkness and dampness. Good thing he wasn't bothered by bugs and spiders.

He paused at every ventilation grate, cautiously peering through with quick movements of his head, in case one of the shooters was scanning with a thermal scope and just happened to notice that one of the grates in the foundation was glowing brighter than the others. Catching him looking would be nothing more than luck – bad on his part, good on theirs. Scopes didn't have a wide field of vision, so they couldn't get a good overall view; the shooters would be scanning, constantly moving, which upped the odds in Cal's favor. A fixed thermal-image camera would have been much more difficult to evade.

The shooters were still firing off the occasional shot to make the inhabitants keep their heads down, keep them from moving around. Head games. At some point, though, they would have to stop shooting and try to make contact, establish what it was they wanted, otherwise there was no point that he could see to this whole damn disaster.

Coming in from behind the house, he'd caught a glimpse of Mario Contreras lying half on, half off the front porch, on the left side. What he hadn't been able to see was any sign of Gena and little Angelina, nor had they answered when he called their names. Now he was trying to see if they, too, were lying on the porch, out of his previous field of vision.

He felt sick – sick and furious. Mario's brought the number of bodies he'd visually identified up to seven. Norman Box was dead, and so was Lanora Corbett. Mouse Williams would never again rattle on and on in the squeaky voice that had given him his nickname. Jim Beasley had died with a rifle in his hand, trying to fight back. Same with Andy Chapman. Maery Last, a sweet little woman in her seventies, was lying in the road in front of her house. Slowed by arthritis, she hadn't been able to move as fast as the others. Friends, all of them, and he was afraid he'd find more. Where were Gena and Angelina? God, if that cute little girl was dead –

He pushed the thought away, not wanting to anticipate the worst. Thank God the twins had gone home with Cate's mom. If they'd been here, if anything had happened to those two little imps, he'd have gone nuts.

He continued crawling from grate to grate, but he couldn't see anyone else in the yard. No Gena, no Angelina. That didn't mean they were okay; they could be in the house, dead, or lying on the porch where he couldn't see them.

He'd found several people alive; terrified, bewildered, but alive. Two people here, four there, a few who were alone – he hadn't bothered to keep count of how many, because that would come later. He'd sent them all toward the Richardsons' house, telling them the safest way, and how to get across the clear areas. Everyone needed to be in one place, so they could get organized. Several plans were formulating in the back of his mind, and he knew Creed was working on a course of action; when they knew exactly where they stood, then they'd decide what to do.

He worked his way out from under the house and tried to brush the worst of the mud off his clothes. He was wet and cold again, though the sun was now working its magic and the day promised to be considerably warmer than the day before. His boots were still wet from his soaking in the stream, and his feet were freezing. He could make do with whatever clothing the Richardsons could find for him, but he needed to get to his place if possible for another pair of boots. First, though, he had to finish locating everyone.

He picked up his shotgun, which he'd left propped against the house next to the crawlspace opening, and eased up the back steps, taking care to stay low in case one of those random shots came his way. Testing the back door, he wasn't surprised when the handle turned easily; most people in Trail Stop didn't bother locking their doors. Cate was one of the few who did, but she had adventurous young children and she was careful they didn't get it into their heads to wander at night.

He was in the eat-in kitchen, a room he knew well because he'd helped Mario install Gena's new cabinets and countertop. She'd been as excited as a child at having more storage room, at having the kitchen looking nice. 'Gena,' he called softly. 'It's Cal.' Again, there was no answer.

A belly crawl was safest, so he dropped to the floor and cradled the shotgun in his arms as he moved into the living room. He'd half expected to find their bodies there, but the room was empty. The windows had been shot out, and he had to be careful not to slice himself to ribbons on the shards as he looked for blood on the floor. None. He checked the front porch. It was empty.

Next he checked the bedrooms. Mario and Gena had slept in the front one, Angelina in the smaller back bedroom. Both were empty. Again, in the front room, the windows were out. Between the two bedrooms was the bathroom, and he found himself hoping he'd find them huddled in the bathtub or something. No luck there, either.

Where in hell could they be? The only place he hadn't looked was the attic. He hoped to hell they weren't up there, because it was so damn dangerous, but some people, when faced with danger, automatically went as far up as they could get. He studied the ceiling, and there it was, right above his head, in the little hall between the two bedrooms: the pull-down attic stairs. If they were up there, Gena had pulled the stairs back up after them.

The ceilings were just eight feet high, so he easily reached the cord and pulled the folding stairs down. 'Gena?' he called up into the darkness. 'Angelina? Are you up there? It's Cal.'

The silence was broken by a little voice saying tremulously, 'Daddy?'

He felt quick relief. Angelina was alive, at least. He cleared his throat. 'No, sweetheart, it isn't Daddy. It's Cal. Is your mommy up there?'

'Uh-huh,' she said. There were scrambling noises; then her small tearstained face appeared at the top of the stairs. 'But Mommy's hurt, and I'm scared.'

Ah, shit. Grimly Cal started up the stairs, almost certain he'd find Gena lying in a pool of blood. If she'd been shot, it had happened while she was in the attic, because there was no blood anywhere downstairs that he'd seen.

Angelina scrambled back when he reached the top of the stairs, giving him room. She was wearing her pajamas and was barefoot, which alarmed Cal until he saw the pile of old clothing that had been dragged out of a box; she had been using the clothes as covers.

The attic wasn't finished; plywood had been placed over the floor joists of about half the space, while the other was just bare joists with insulation batting laid between the two-by-sixes. The floored space was crammed with stuff: a neatly taped Christmas tree box, old toys, a dismantled baby bed, boxes of discards. Staying bent over, he picked his way through the clutter to where Gena was sitting propped against an old chest of drawers. Angelina scrambled to her mother's side, and Gena put her arm around her, holding her close.

Gena was ghostly white, but as Cal went down on one knee beside her, he checked for blood and didn't see any. The attic was dim, the only light filtering through the cracks in the ceiling and the vents, too dim for him to tell much. He took her wrist and checked her pulse; it was too fast, but strong, so she wasn't shocky. 'Where are you hurt?'

'My ankle.' Her voice was restricted, her tone almost soundless. 'I sprained it.' She took a deep, shuddering breath. 'Mario. . .?'

Cal gave a little shake of his head, and her face crumpled at having her worst fear confirmed. 'He – he told us to hide up here while he found out what was going on. I waited for him all night, expecting him to c-come get us, but—'

'Which ankle?' Cal asked, cutting her off. She had a lifetime to mourn her husband, but he had a lot to do and a short time in which to do it.

She hesitated, her eyes filling with tears, then indicated her right ankle. Cal swiftly pushed up the leg of her jeans to see how bad the ankle was. The answer was: bad. Her ankle was so swollen her sock was tightly stretched, and dark bruising extended above the fabric. She hadn't yet gotten ready for bed when the shooting started, so she was wearing jeans and sneakers, and because of the cold she hadn't removed the shoe. That was good, because if she had, she wouldn't have been able to get it back on. This would slow her down big-time.

'It was cold,' Angelina put in, her big dark eyes solemn as she rested her head against her mother. 'And dark. Mommy had a flashlight, but it went out.'

'It lasted long enough for us to find that box of old clothes we used to keep warm,' said Gena, drawing a shuddering breath as she tried not to break down in front of her daughter.

Cal was wordless with dismay. She had turned on the flashlight and left it on? She was damn lucky both she and her daughter were alive, because if sunlight could get in through cracks, light from inside would show through those same cracks at night. The fact that the attic wasn't shot full of holes confirmed for him that the shooters were using thermal instead of night-vision scopes; night vision would have magnified the faint light coming through those cracks, lighting up the attic like a neon sign saying, 'Shoot Here!'

They had done everything wrong, but somehow they were still alive. Man. Sometimes it just worked that way.

'All of us are gathering at the Richardsons' place,' he said. 'Their basement is completely protected. It's too small for everyone to stay there, but it'll do until Creed and I get something figured out.'

'F-figured out? Call the cops! That's what you do!'

'The phones are out. No electricity, either. We're stranded.' As he spoke he looked around, trying to see if there was anything useful up here that she could use as a crutch. Nada. He'd have to think of something, but first things first. 'Okay, we need to get out of this attic; there's no protection up here. Angelina needs to put on some warm clothes and some shoes—'

'I can't walk,' Gena said. 'I've tried.'

'Do you have an Ace bandage I can wrap around the ankle for support? I'll find something you can use as a crutch, but you have to walk. You don't have a choice. It'll hurt like hell, but you have to do it.' He kept his gaze steady on hers, telling her without words how dire the situation was.

'Ace bandage? Ah . . . I think so. In the bathroom.'

'I'll get it.' He was down the ladder in a matter of seconds, jerking open the drawers in the bathroom vanity until he found the rolled Ace bandage. While he was in the bathroom, he looked in the medicine cabinet and found a bottle of aspirin, which he pocketed; then he returned to the attic.

'Take a couple of aspirin,' he said, handing the bottle to Gena.

'There's no water, so chew them up if you can't swallow them whole.'

Obediently she chewed, making a horrible face, while he swiftly and efficiently wrapped her ankle. 'Here's the plan: I take Angelina down first, and put her in the kitchen to change clothes—'

'Why the kitchen?'

'More protection. Just listen, and do what I say, because I may not have time to explain every detail. I'll come back and get you, and once you're safer, I'll look for something you can use as a crutch.'

'Mario has his father's walking stick.' Her lips trembled as she mentioned her husband, but she sucked it up and went on. 'In the living room closet.'

'Okay, good.' Not as good as a crutch, but better than nothing, and he wouldn't have to use up valuable time fashioning something. Rising to a crouch, he took Angelina's hand. 'Come on, cricket, let's go down the ladder.'

'Cricket?' She giggled, diverted. 'Mommy, he called me a cricket.'

'I know, honey.' She stroked her daughter's hair. 'Go with Cal and do what he says, change clothes in the kitchen while he helps me down the ladder. Okay?'

'Okay.'

Cal positioned Angelina between him and the ladder, so she wouldn't be afraid of falling, and guided her down the wobbly steps. When she noticed the living room windows had been broken, she said, 'Look!' indignantly and started into the room, but he intercepted her. The last thing he wanted was for her to look out the window and see her father's body, nor did he want her to cut her bare feet on the broken glass.

'You can't go in there,' he explained, herding her toward her bedroom. 'That glass on the floor would cut your feet even if you were wearing shoes.'

'It would cut through the shoes?'

'Right through them. That was special glass.'

'Wow,' she said, wide-eyed, as she peered back at the glass in question.

Little-girl clothing, he found, was basically the same as little-boy clothing, just pink. He found jeans and a pullover shirt, little sneakers with pink shoestrings, socks with flowers on them, and a pink fleece hooded jacket. 'Can you put these on by yourself?' he asked, guiding her into the kitchen.

She nodded, looking confused. 'I put my clothes on in my bedroom, not the kitchen.'

'This one time Mommy wants you to change clothes here in the kitchen,' he replied. 'She told you about it, remember?'

She nodded, then said, 'Why?'

Oh, hell, now what did he tell her? Recalling experiences with his own mother, he pulled out an old standby: 'Because she said so.'

Evidently Angelina had run into that edict from on high before. She sighed and sat down on the floor. 'Okay, but you can't watch.'

'I won't. I'm going to get your mommy from the attic. Don't leave the kitchen. Stay right where you are.'

Taking another long-suffering sigh as agreement, he went back to the ladder and looked up to find Gena sitting in the opening. 'I scooted,' she explained, experimentally setting her left foot on the second rung down and bracing her arms on each side of the opening so she could turn around. He'd been thinking of lowering her with a rope, but what the hell, she was already on the ladder.

There was no way she could come down without using her sprained ankle. The first time she put weight on it, she couldn't hold back a sharp cry of pain that she quickly muffled. The next time she tried, she bit her lip and simply forced herself to bear the pain for the brief time it took her to step down with her good foot. She rested there, waiting for the pain to recede, then did it again. Cal steadied the ladder as much as possible, but he couldn't go up it to help her because the flimsy ladder wasn't built to hold that much weight. When she was far enough down that he could reach her waist, he simply plucked her off the rungs and carried her to the kitchen, where he sat her in one of the chairs at the table.

Angelina was in the process of putting on her shoes, and she jumped up to run to her mother. Gena gathered her close, her blond head bent down to Angelina's dark one. 'I'll get the walking stick,' he said, and went into the living room. The stick was shoved in the very back of the closet, but he found it in short order and took it back to Gena.

'We'll go out the back door. I'll carry Angelina. I know your ankle hurts, Gena, but you have to keep up with me.'

'I'll try,' she said, still so white-faced she looked as if she'd faint at any moment. She hadn't let her gaze so much as flicker toward the living room, as if she was afraid she would see Mario and she knew she couldn't bear that.

'Sometimes we'll have to crawl. Just do what I do.' He didn't have time to explain the tortuous angles he'd worked out that would keep them mostly hidden from the thermal scopes. Infrared didn't work as well during a warm day anyway, because the temperature difference between the ambient air and a human wasn't as great. After two unusually chilly days, today was noticeably warmer. That, together with the fact that the human eye couldn't see everything at the same time in such a wide radius as the shooters would be scanning, would help him get them to the Richardsons' with minimal exposure. There were a couple of places where there was simply no structure available for shielding movement, and then Gena would have to hurry as best she could. The second person crossing was always in more danger than the first.

He had a lot to do, more people to find, but he put that out of his mind and simply concentrated on the task at hand. It took time – too much time, but Gena was doing the best she could. Finally he got them to a place where he could send them on without him. 'You're leaving us here?' Gena gasped, when he told her he was going back.

'You can make it; it's just a couple hundred yards. I haven't found the Starkeys yet, or the Youngs.' Despite her protests, he sent her on, then doubled back.

Before continuing his search, he worked his way to the feed store. Pressed against the back of the building, he darted his head around for quick looks as he studied the stairs leading up to his place, and the angles that would expose him to rifle fire. The stairs were just too risky, and that was the only entrance; there wasn't one from inside the feed store.

Yet.

Using the butt of his shotgun, he beat the lock off the door to the back storeroom; the residents of Trail Stop might not lock up their houses, but that didn't mean they left their businesses unprotected. Inside the storeroom was the chain saw he'd been using to cut firewood for the winter – there was already a sizable stack just outside the door – as well as the small ax he used to split the smaller pieces of kindling.

Taking the ax, he went into the main room of the feed store and

210

studied the ceiling, mentally mapping out his apartment overhead.

He wanted to stay away from any plumbing, so that meant the left side. His bathroom was directly above the feed-store bathroom, which was only logical. His tiny efficiency kitchen, if it was big enough to qualify as an efficiency, was also on the left. Unfortunately, so was the checkout counter, which would have been the sturdiest, most stable platform for him to climb on.

He eyed the ceiling and did the math. The ceiling here on the first floor was ten feet high. He was just under six feet tall. That meant he needed to get about three feet off the ground in order to have some leverage with the ax. Well, hell, all those sacks of feed might as well do some good instead of just lying there.

He got busy hefting those fifty-pound bags. Each layer was stacked in the opposite direction as the one below it, providing stability. By the time he finished, he was sweating and thirsty, but he didn't pause. Instead, he jumped onto his platform, braced his feet, and started swinging the ax upward.

The stack of feed wasn't completely stable, and his balance was a little precarious because he couldn't move his feet, which meant he couldn't put all his power into his swings. With those constraints, it took him half an hour to chop a man-size hole through the ceiling and the flooring above. When he judged it was large enough, he knelt to carefully place the ax against the stack; then he stood, bent his knees, and jumped.

He caught the rough edge of the hole and hung there for a few seconds, getting the swing of his body under control, then flexed the muscles in his upper arms and shoulders and pulled himself up. Under the strain, the cuts Cate had so gently tended the night before stung as they began bleeding again.

When he was high enough, he gave a surge of effort that shot him upward, enabling him to wedge one arm on the floor. Planting the other arm, he pushed and lifted himself through the opening, and rolled onto the floor of his own bedroom.

Swiftly he stripped naked, leaving his wet and dirty clothes where they lay.

When he dropped back down into the feed store, he was dressed for hunting.

Chapter Twenty-Four

Every time the outside door opened, Cate's stomach would tighten and her heart would give a little leap as she looked up, hoping to see a lean, shaggy-haired man coming in. When time after time it wasn't him, she felt her nerves wind tighter and tighter, until she had to distract herself or go crazy.

She tried to keep busy, but there was only so much to be done in a basement with so many people who were hungry, thirsty, and in need of a bathroom. The thirsty part, at least, was easily taken care of by Perry and his water bucket. Cate and Maureen did their best with food, but Maureen hadn't been prepared to feed that many people; she didn't even have a full loaf of sandwich bread on hand. They heated soup and stew on top of the kerosene heater, and slathered peanut butter on a mound of crackers for a quick protein fix. Other than that, without electricity, they were limited in what they could do.

The bathroom situation was more iffy, since it involved leaving the secure basement and going upstairs, where there wasn't as much protection, but desperation eventually sent every person up. With no electricity to run the water pump, flushing involved carrying a bucket of water up with you to pour in the toilet, which meant Perry was kept busy drawing water from the well. Even Creed managed to hobble up the stairs, to Neenah's consternation, using Gena's cane.

'Last night was a lucky shot,' Creed said, pausing on his way up when Neenah mentioned Maureen's close call. 'They were firing for effect, in the dark, keeping us off balance. They haven't been shooting as much today, because now they have to factor in how much ammunition they want to waste. Of course, they can always go get more, while we can't. I figure they've been shooting whenever they get a glimpse of Cal.'

A sort of charged silence fell over everyone, and Creed looked around. He saw Cate standing at the foot of the stairs, white-faced and feeling as if she'd been punched in the stomach.

She knew that everyone who had arrived that morning had told of being located by Cal, rescued by Cal, taken care of by Cal, sent over by Cal. She had pictured him as a sort of shepherd, rounding up the flock. Instead, he was out there *getting shot at*.

Creed winced when he saw the look on her face, muttering, 'Shit,' under his breath. Then: 'Cate, he'll be all right. Better men than those yahoos have tried to kill him.'

She felt light-headed as she put out a hand for balance. Creed winced again, evidently realizing his last statement hadn't been exactly reassuring, and backtracked. 'What I mean is – I was in the Marines with him. He knows what he's doing.'

She didn't feel any better. Presumably Creed had also known what he was doing, but he'd gotten shot anyway. Maybe if she hadn't already been widowed once, she would have had a more noble outlook, but she *had* lost her husband suddenly at a young age. Untimely deaths happened – and doctors had been fighting to save Derek. Now people were actively *trying* to kill Cal; how could she possibly be reassured?

She felt as if she had just met him, and something was bursting to life between them. Everything was new and exciting and trembling with promise. She couldn't lose him now.

Forgetting about his errand for now, Creed hobbled back down the stairs and gently took her suddenly cold hands in his. His rugged face was kind, his hazel eyes full of understanding as he warmed her hands in his. 'He'll be okay. I don't know who those guys shooting at us are, but I promise you none of them is even close to being as good as he is. Cal wasn't a regular Marine, he was Force Recon. I don't know if you know what that means—' He paused, and she shook her head no. 'Well, it means he's an expert at a lot of things, and high on that list is not getting killed.'

Emotion roiled in her, terror and anger and even embarrassment that she was falling apart like this. But she couldn't help herself; she clung to his hands for support, looked up at him for even more reassurance. 'Mr. Creed, I—'

'Call me Josh,' he said. 'I think everyone here is on a first-name basis, don't you?'

'Josh,' she said, vaguely ashamed because she had kept him, too, at a distance. 'I – you—' She stopped because she was stammering and had no clear idea of what she wanted to say. *Go get him? Bring him back safe and sound?* Yes, that was what she wanted. She wanted Cal to walk in that door.

'Listen.' He squeezed her hands, then patted them. 'He's doing what he does best, which is finding out what's going on.'

'It's been hours—'

'People are still coming in, aren't they? He sent them, so you know he's okay. Roy Edward,' he called, raising his voice. The elderly Starkeys were the most recent to arrive. 'When did you last see Cal?'

Roy Edward looked away from Milly Earl, who had been cleaning his face. He and Judith, his wife, were bruised and scraped from falling. They weren't nimble on their feet; both had taken some bad tumbles, but, by some small miracle, hadn't broken any bones. 'No more'n an hour,' he replied. The old man was exhausted, his voice thready. 'We were the last ones, he said. He was going to gather some things before he came back here.'

The last ones. Stunned out of her own misery, Cate looked around at those who were here, and those who weren't. Everyone in the basement was doing the same thing, because no more neighbors would be arriving to cries of relief and welcome. Mario Contreras. Norman Box. Maery Last. Andy Chapman. Jim Beasley. Lanora Corbett. Mouse Williams. They'd lost seven people – *seven!*

Silently Creed made his halting way up the stairs. Tears streaked Neenah's face as she went with him, lending him support so he wouldn't damage his leg more.

'We can't let 'em just lay there,' Roy Edward declared, something fierce entering his cracked old voice. 'They're our people. We have to do right by them.'

Again there was silence as, one by one, they realized the enormous responsibility that lay before them. Retrieving the bodies would be a daunting task, and even then, without electricity, there was no way to preserve them. Still, they had to do something. The weather was warm today, which meant the need for action was extremely pressing.

'I have that generator,' Walter finally said. 'We all have freezers. People, we'll manage something.'

But Walter's generator was on the side of the community closest to the shooters – and moving chest-type freezers around was a two-man job that would require them to be in the open.

Gena couldn't bear up any longer, not even for Angelina's sake. She buried her face in her hands, sobbing in great, raw sounds, her entire body heaving. Cate remembered when she, too, had cried that way, and she crossed to Gena, sat down, and put her arms around her. There were no words that would make the pain less, so she didn't say anything. Angelina's face crumpled and her big dark eyes began swimming with tears. 'Mommy, don't cry!' She patted Gena's leg, both giving and searching for comfort. 'Mommy!'

Cate gathered Angelina close, too. Her babies had been too young to know anything when Derek died, too young to miss him and cry for him, but Angelina wasn't. When she understood that her daddy was gone and was never coming back, nothing in the world except time would give her solace.

'How do you do it?' Gena sobbed, the words so thick with tears and choked out through sobs that Cate barely understood her. 'How do you manage?'

How do you function when your entire body has been overtaken by searing emotional pain? How do you function day to day when a huge hole has been ripped in your life? How do you ever smile again, laugh again, feel joy again?

'You just do it,' Cate answered quietly. 'Because you have no choice. I had my babies. You have Angelina. That's why you *have* to do it.'

The door opened and Cal came in.

He'd changed clothes. He was wearing what she thought of as deer-hunting clothes: a pair of woodland-pattern camouflage cargo pants, an olive-drab T-shirt, and an unbuttoned shirt in the same woodland pattern as his pants. He also had on flexible Gore-Tex boots, a hunting knife in a scabbard on his belt, the shotgun with its sling hooked over his left shoulder, and a rifle with a big scope mounted on it in his right hand. If he'd been going deer hunting, though, he'd have been wearing either a cap or a hunting vest in bright orange.

The bottom dropped out of her stomach. What he was wearing

215

told her louder than words that he intended to go after the men who were shooting at them. She released Gena and stood up, galvanized by the sheer, icy terror that seized her. She wanted to scream; she wanted to tackle him and tie him up so he couldn't go. She refused to let him do this; she couldn't watch him walk away knowing there was a strong possibility he wouldn't come back –

His gaze snagged hers. She saw him take in her white, strained expression. Carefully he stood both weapons in a safe place where they couldn't be knocked over and then threaded his way across the crowded, cluttered room to her side. People spoke to him, patted him on the shoulder, and he nodded and spoke and traded greetings, but he never paused, never wavered from his course.

When he reached her, he touched her hand and said, 'Are you okay?'

She felt as if she would choke if she tried to utter a word. She gave a fierce, single shake of her head.

He looked around, saw there was no privacy to be had for even a moment. 'Follow me.'

Numbly she did, scarcely aware of anything around her as she trailed in his wake, seeing nothing but his back. He led her outside, into the warm sunshine, but stopped while they were still protected by the downward curve of the land. Turning to study her with his pale, steady gaze, he said, 'What's wrong?'

What was wrong? 'Your clothes,' she blurted, unable to formulate a more coherent reason.

Bewildered, he looked down at himself. 'My clothes?'

'You're going after them, aren't you?'

Understanding dawned. 'We can't just sit here,' he said quietly. 'Someone has to do something.'

'But not you! Why does it have to be you?'

'I don't know who else it would be. Look around you. Mario was the youngest man, and he's dead. Josh could have done it, but he's got a cracked bone in his leg. Everyone else is older and out of shape. I'm the logical choice.'

'Screw logic!' she said fiercely, grabbing his shirt with both hands. 'I know I don't have the right to say anything because we aren't – we haven't—' She shook her head, fighting a sudden rush of tears. 'I can't lose . . . not again—'

He stopped her incoherent babble by dipping his head and putting his mouth on hers.

His lips were soft, so soft. The kiss was gentle, questing. His lips moved against hers, learning and asking, and she tilted her head up to answer.

'You have the right,' he murmured, and framed her face with his hands, his fingers sliding into her hair as he took her with a series of tender, hungry kisses, as if he were eating her mouth. She gripped his forearms, digging her fingers into the hard muscles and tendons, holding on for dear life as she sagged against him. His tongue made leisurely forays, touched and stroked and enticed as though he had all the time in the world and couldn't think of a better way to spend it.

She had never before been kissed so . . . contentedly.

He was aroused; she could feel the hard bulk of his penis against her. She expected to feel his hips move, but he remained still except for his tongue and those soft, soft lips. Warmth glowed to life within her, pushing away her fear, her anger that he would take such a risk when they were hovering on the verge of something that felt so wonderful she could scarcely believe it.

Leaving her mouth, he pressed kisses on her cheek, her temple, her eyes, then went back to her lips for more.

If he made love as leisurely as he kissed – oh, dear God.

'We should go back inside,' he whispered against her mouth, then rested his forehead against hers. 'I have a lot to do.'

She pulled back and looked into his blue eyes. They were as calm as always, but now she recognized the steel core of this man. He wasn't dramatic; he wasn't someone who demanded attention – because he didn't need it. He was supremely certain of himself and his capabilities. He would risk his life for them without a moment's hesitation.

She would have stayed out there and argued until they were both drawing their social security checks, but he turned her and somehow herded her back into the basement. A lot of smiling, knowing looks were directed their way, but that wasn't a surprise, considering how he'd acted last night, and that they'd just now been kissing outside the door. What did surprise her was that no one, absolutely no one, seemed surprised. Apparently, she was the only one who was having trouble coming up to speed on this, but then, she was the only one who had deliberately worn blinders.

In the irritating way that most men seemed to have, he'd already reverted completely to business mode, gathering with Creed and the other men. Creed even had a notebook and was mapping out something with swift strokes of a pen. Everyone crowded around to hear what was being said.

'The bridge is out,' Cal was saying. 'That was the explosion. The electricity went out right before that, which means they cut the wires. The phones are out, too. From the way the shooters have positioned themselves, their intention is to keep anyone from going for help through the cut in the mountains. They wanted to cut us off and hem us in.'

'But why in hell are they doing all this? And who are they, anyway?' Walter growled, running his hand through his thinning hair in frustration.

'I haven't seen anyone, but my guess is those two guys from last week brought in reinforcements, and as for what they want—' Cal shrugged. 'I'd say they want me.'

'Because you got the drop on them?'

'And bashed one of them in the head,' Neenah added. She was sitting on the cold concrete next to Creed. She hadn't strayed far from his side since the night before.

'I didn't say it was reasonable,' Cal said. 'Some people let their egos get involved, and they turn vicious.'

'But this – this is so far over the top, it's insane,' Sherry protested. Seven people were *dead*. This was way beyond squashed egos. 'If they're that mad, why didn't they just catch you out somewhere and stomp your ass?'

'I'm hard to stomp,' he said mildly. 'Maybe this is the mob way of saying, 'Mind your own business.' I just don't know.'

'Mob? You think it's the mob?' Milly put in.

That question earned another shrug. 'I'd have to say it's possible.'

'The geography works against us,' Creed said, pulling the conversation back on subject. He indicated the map he'd sketched. 'The river makes it impossible to operate on this side. The current is too fast to ford the river anywhere around here, and those rocks would bash any boat to pieces in seconds. Upriver is a vertical canyon that you can't go around, so that direction is a no-go.'

'The land peninsula Trail Stop is on is shaped like a paramecium,' Cal continued. 'The bridge was at the tail, and on this side of the tail is the river. We have no land there to work with, and the river is a natural barricade. Right here' – he touched Creed's sketch – 'are mountains only a goat can negotiate. So that funnels us down this side of the paramecium, toward this cut in the mountains, and they've sealed that off with shooters. They have thermal scopes, which work best at night, but during the daytime they don't need the scopes to see. I'll have to wait until night, and go into the water to dissipate my heat signature.'

'How long would it take you to get through the cut?' Sherry asked.

'I don't have to go through the cut. All I have to do is get by one of the shooters, then I'm behind them and can follow the road.'

Cate sucked in her breath with an audible gasp. She wasn't a tactician, but she knew how cold he'd been last night, how close to hypothermia. And the water hadn't gotten any warmer since then. Who knew how long he'd have to stay in the stream, waiting for the right moment? Then he'd have to walk miles in those cold, wet clothes, and he'd be losing more body heat every moment. And if he was seen by any of them on the other side of the stream, they would be hunting him as if he were an animal, and he would be too cold to evade them. Why wasn't anyone saying no, this was too dangerous? Why were they so willing to let him risk his life?

Because, as he'd pointed out, there was no one else. Creed was hurt. Mario was dead. All the others were middle-aged and out of shape, or elderly and *really* out of shape.

Except for her.

'No,' she said, because no one else would. '*No*. It's too dangerous, and don't try to tell me it isn't,' she said violently when Cal opened his mouth to do just that. 'Do you think they won't be waiting for someone to try that? You could barely walk last night, you were so cold from being in that water. And what happens to us if you get killed?'

'I imagine they'll go away, since I'm the one they want.'

His calmness made her want to scream, to grab him and shake him for daring to be so casual with his life. She stood with her fists clenched while all those damned men stared at her as if she just didn't understand. She understood, all right, and she wasn't going to live through that again.

'You don't know that. We don't know for certain who they are or what they want. What if it has nothing to do with you? And even if it did, what makes you think they'd just pack up and leave? They've killed seven people, and we're all agreed that's a drastic

219

action to take just because you got the better of them. It's something else, it has to be. We just don't know what.'

He regarded her thoughtfully, then nodded. 'You're right. It has to be something else.'

'Can you guarantee you'll make it past them without being spotted?'

'No, I can't guarantee it.'

'Then we can't risk losing you, Cal. We can't. We aren't helpless, but we *are* cut off, and they have the upper hand.' Desperately she searched for inspiration, some way out that didn't involve Cal risking his life against odds that were weighted against him. He was right, in that the most direct way was through the shooters. If they could somehow go up and over –

'We can't just sit and wait,' Creed said. 'We aren't prepared for a siege, and that's what this is—'

Cate felt as if her voice were coming from outside her. 'There's another way,' she heard herself say. Everyone shut up and looked at her, and she found herself moving forward. Deep inside her a panicked little voice was saying *no, no,* but somehow she couldn't stop her feet from moving as she pushed her way through the knot of people to jab her finger hard on the mountains Cal had judged goat-worthy. 'I can get up those mountains. I've *been* up those mountains. I'm a climber, you know that, you saw my gear. It's safe when you tie off' – that wasn't quite the truth, but she was going with it – 'and they won't be expecting us to try that route, so they won't be watching. No one will be shooting, no one will be sticking his neck out like a sacrificial lamb.'

'Cate,' Cal began. 'You have two kids.'

'I know,' she said, tears gathering in her eyes. 'I *know.*' And she wanted to see them grow up. She wanted to take care of them and hold her grandchildren and have all the million other things parents dreamed of. But she couldn't shake a sudden certainty that he wouldn't make it through if he went with his plan, which would leave them even more vulnerable. Everyone here could end up dead, and her kids would lose their mother anyway. As dangerous as it was, she didn't think going up the mountains was as dangerous as what Cal was proposing.

'She's right,' Roy Edward interrupted.

They all turned toward the old man. He was sitting on one of the dining room chairs that they'd brought down the night before.

220

His left arm and the left side of his face were colored a deep purple from a fall, but his mouth was a grim line. 'What you're wanting to do is dangerous, boy, and I don't see why you'd think we'd be willing to sacrifice you to save ourselves.'

There was a murmur of agreement. Cate was so grateful to the crusty old man she could have hugged him.

'Going over the mountains in that direction will take too long,' Cal pointed out.

'If you kept on in that direction, yes, but these mountains are riddled with abandoned mines.' Roy Edward hauled himself to his feet and unsteadily made his way over to them. 'I know because my daddy worked in some of them, and I played in 'em when I was a sprout. There used to be trails from the cut that wound all over, because every one of them started from there. Makes sense they weren't going to climb up from the other side, don't it? As I remember, one or two of those old mines go completely through a fold in the mountains. Don't know what kind of shape they'd be in after all these years, but if you could get through one of them, that could save considerable time.'

He traced a shaky forefinger across the mountains to the cut and looked up at Cate. 'Even if the mines are blocked, which I expect they are, you could work your way over to the cut. You'd be way above where these bastards would be looking, and the cover is dense up there. Once you got to the cut, you'd be behind them.'

She wiped the tears from her face and turned to face Cal. 'I'm going,' she said shakily. 'No matter what you do, I'm going.'

He was silent a moment, his pale gaze searching her face and reading the desperation there. He glanced at Creed, and she couldn't read the message that passed between them.

'All right,' he finally said in that calm way of his, as if she'd said she was going to the grocery store. 'But I'm going with you.'

Chapter Twenty-Five

Cate was astonished – you didn't just 'go' rock climbing; it was something that took conditioning, preparation, and experience – but then she recalled a conversation they'd had when Cal opened the door to the attic stairs after she broke the key to it, just days ago. Days. Dear God, so much had happened it seemed as if weeks had passed. 'You said you'd done some mountaineering.' Mountaineering was different from rock climbing, but a lot of the equipment was the same. She supposed it was basically the same principle, too, just some different techniques.

'Mostly mountaineering,' he corrected. 'Some climbing.'

Creed spun the notebook around in that decisive way he had and took up the pen. 'Okay, let's make a list of what you'll need so nothing is forgotten. How long do you think it will take you to get through the cut and to a phone?' He looked at Cate as he spoke, because she had been on climbs here.

All the climbs she'd done had been day climbs, but she knew the terrain they were talking about. The mountains loomed behind her house, and she saw them every day. She could look at several of the rock faces and think, *I climbed you*. She knew how long it took to get to them, and how long to go up them. In some places the ascent might be easier than the climbs she and Derek had mapped out, because a challenging climb had been what they were there for. Memories flooded back, crystal-clear mental pictures of exactly what she was proposing to do, the climbs and hiking they would face.

She finally said, 'I'm thinking a day and a half, maybe two days, to get to a point where we can start hiking. How far would it be to the cut, Roy Edward?'

He snorted. 'As the crow flies, maybe five miles, but you're not a crow. With all the up and down, I'd say you're looking at fifteen, twenty miles.'

'Daylight hours only,' Cal said. 'We won't be able to use lights. So ... two days of hiking, and that's a hard pace. Four days total to the cut.'

Four days. Cate felt sick to her stomach. That was too long, way too long. So much could happen in that length of time –

Neenah reached out and took her hand. 'We'll be all right,' she said firmly. 'We'll hold out, no matter what they want or what they do.'

'Damn right,' Walter said. He looked tired, they all did, but there was also an undiminished fury in his eyes. They had been attacked, friends had died, and he didn't look inclined to throw up his hands in surrender. 'Just about all of us have some sort of rifle or shotgun; we have ammunition – and more of it in the general store if we need it. We have food, and we have water. If those sons of bitches thought we'd be an easy target, they can just think again.'

A muted chorus of 'yeahs,' 'damn straights,' and 'that's rights' filled the basement, and heads nodded.

Cal scratched his jaw. 'Along that line – Neenah, you have a good many fifty-pound bags of feed in the back of the store.'

'Yes, I've started stocking up for the winter. Why?'

'Not even an armor-piercing bullet will go through bags of sand, which is why the military uses them. We don't have sand, but we do have those bags of feed. Feed won't be as good as sand – it isn't packed as tightly – but stack 'em two deep and you've got an effective barricade.' He paused. 'By the way, I chopped a hole in the ceiling.'

She blinked, then smiled. 'Of course you did. I wondered how you got to your rooms.' She indicated his clothes. If having a hole in the ceiling of her store bothered her, she didn't show it.

Cal looked around the basement. 'All of you can't stay here; it's too crowded, and it isn't necessary. We'll pick out the safest houses, the ones with the least exposure, and spread out. We can use the feed bags to fortify the walls exposed to gunfire. That way you can function better and keep a better watch. Get some trenches dug, too, so you can move from place to place in safety. They don't have to be deep and they don't have to be long, just long

223

enough to cross some open areas and deep enough for a belly crawl.'

'We need food, too, and blankets, and clothes. Some people need their medications,' said Sherry. 'Show us how to get from place to place without getting our asses blown off, so we can start gathering stuff.'

'I'll get most of it—' he began, but she raised her hand to stop him.

'I didn't say do it, I said show us how to do it. If you don't, we'll be pretty useless without you. We have to be able to hold down the fort.'

'I have a lot of extra blankets and pillows,' Cate said. 'Food, too. And a bunch of mattresses that could be used for protection, if those are any good. If not, then drag them down and sleep on them.'

'Mattresses are a good idea,' Cal said, 'for sleeping. Don't sleep in a bed. Drag the mattresses down on the floor.'

'What else can we use to barricade the walls?' asked Milly.

'Things like boxes of old magazines, if you keep things like that. Books, packed tight in a box. Cushions aren't any good; they aren't dense enough. Furniture's no good. Think of things like rolling up your rugs as tight as you can, tying them so they'll stay rolled, and standing them at an angle against the vulnerable wall.'

'Does anyone have a pool table with a slate bed?' asked Creed.

'I do,' someone said, and Cate looked around to see Roland Gettys raise his hand a little. He seldom said much, usually just listened to conversations with a slight smile on his face, unless someone asked him a direct question.

'A slate pool table is an excellent shield, if you can get it turned on its side.'

'Weighs a ton,' said Roland, nodding his head.

Creed looked at Cal. 'I'll take care of getting this organized. You and Cate go get what you'll need.' He looked down at his notepad. 'I've written down exactly nothing. Do you need to make a list?'

'I don't think so, not for the climbing gear,' Cate said. 'I could pack that with my eyes closed.' She also needed something to wear besides pajamas, but she wasn't likely to forget clothes.

'That's it, then,' said Cal, holding out his hand to her. 'You handle the climbing gear, and I'll handle everything else. Let's get moving.'

Getting back to her house seemed easier, in one way, than her desperate flight the night before – she didn't have to run. Flimsy bedroom slippers didn't provide much protection for her feet, so she was glad to take more care as she and Cal slipped from cover to cover. Taking more care, however, meant taking more time, and the longer they were out there the more exposed she felt. It was incredibly creepy, knowing someone sitting on the side of a mountain over half a mile away could be watching her through a scope, tracking her every move, easing his finger to the trigger –

At that thought, she stopped where she was, shuddering. As if he were aware of her slightest movement, her position, at all times, Cal stopped and looked back at her. 'What's wrong?'

Cate looked around. They were, for the moment, completely protected. Cal used every bit of possible cover, from rocks and trees and buildings to low places in the ground. Right now they were behind some waist-high rocks. This wasn't the same as the night before, when she and Maureen had been on the first floor of the house, with only wooden walls between them and a bullet. 'I just felt as if someone was watching, as if the shooters could see us.'

'They can't. Not right now.'

'I know. But last night – when Maureen and I were upstairs – I felt the bullet coming, and I panicked and tackled her. It was so *eerie*. I could actually feel it, like something tickling between my shoulder blades. The window blew in, and after that we heard the shot. I just now had sort of the same feeling, but there's no way a bullet can go through these rocks, is there?'

'No, we're safe here.' He worked his way back to her and crouched there, looking around, an intent expression in his eyes. 'But don't discount that feeling, especially in a combat situation. I get 'em on the back of my neck. I always listen. So we're going to change course a little. It's longer this way, but if you've got the willies, we aren't taking any chances.'

She nodded, absurdly pleased that he knew what she was talking about. He studied the ground for a moment, then got on his belly and began slithering away from the rocks at a ninety-degree angle, following a slight indentation that she hadn't noticed. Her pajamas would be beyond saving, she thought, and went down on her belly, too, to follow him.

Billy Copeland carefully scanned with his scope, back and forth. He thought he'd seen a flash of cloth around some rocks. The distance was at the far end of his skill, but a lucky shot was just as good as a skillful one, and in any case, as Teague had explained, they were now in the psychological phase of this operation: Work on their nerves, wear them down. He didn't have to actually hit his target to remind them that they could be touched from a frightening distance.

The decision he had to make was whether or not to fire without having a clear target. On the one hand, they had fired a helluva lot of rounds last night, and his instinct now told him to make every shot count. On the other hand, it would be fun to make someone piss their britches when they thought they were so well hidden.

His finger began tightening on the trigger, but then he eased the pressure. Not yet, not unless he knew for certain he'd seen something. No sense in wasting a round.

Her house was totally silent. Even at night when the boys were in bed asleep, Cate could hear the faint hum of appliances, feel a vague sense that the house was alive. Not now. It was empty and curiously dark and cold, despite the sunshine, because she'd pulled all the curtains against the night at sundown the day before. The curtains had not only kept the light at bay, they also had prevented the house from warming.

'Give me the key to the attic door,' said Cal. 'I'll bring down all the climbing gear while you're changing clothes.'

'I thought I was going to get the climbing gear.'

'You've been having the willies. Stay where it's safer. The attic has no protection at all.'

She raised her eyebrows. 'That makes me feel better, how? *You'll* be up there.'

'That's right. And you'll be in your room. Just a little while ago you looked ready to fight half the state to keep me from going out by myself tonight, and I listened to you. That's the way I feel right now, in this situation, and you're going to listen to me.' His voice was firm, the expression in his eyes cool and clear.

Putting it like that had just frustrated all her objections. She made a face at him and went to her desk in the foyer to get the key. 'Does anyone ever win an argument with you?'

'I don't argue. Waste of time and effort. I do listen to opinions, though.' He was right behind her and reached out to take the key.

She gave it to him without objection, but as he started up the stairs she asked, 'Don't you ever get mad?'

He paused, looking down at her. In the gloom his pale eyes looked like crystal, without any hint of blue. 'Yeah, I get mad. When I found that asshole Mellor threatening you with a gun, I could have torn him apart with my bare hands.'

Her stomach tightened in a knot of shock, because she believed every word he'd said. She reached out and grasped the newel post, her fingers clenching on the wood. She remembered the look in his eye, the way his finger had begun tightening on the trigger. 'You were really going to shoot him, weren't you?'

'No point in aiming a weapon at someone if you don't intend to pull the trigger,' he said, and went on up the stairs. 'Stay down while you're changing clothes,' he called back.

After a moment Cate followed him up the stairs, then turned to the right to go to her bedroom. Obediently, she bent as low as she could manage and still walk. She didn't have the willies now, but that didn't mean anything. Nothing had happened out by the rocks; the night before had been a freaky coincidence, nothing more.

If she kept telling herself that, she might one day believe it. The spooky sensation had been too strong, too immediate.

She shook away all thoughts except those about preparing for the grueling challenge ahead of her. A recreational climb was hard work, but fun, and she'd always known that at the end of the day she would have a hot shower, a hot meal, and sleep in a nice comfortable bed. She'd gone camping once, and hadn't liked it.

When she had been climbing, she usually wore spandex pants and a snug tank top with a sport bra underneath, and her climbing shoes. Her first consideration was her shoes, because climbing shoes weren't for walking. Conversely, walking shoes weren't good for climbing. She had always worn athletic shoes to the site, then changed into her climbing shoes. That wouldn't work this time, because they weren't coming back down. They had to carry their food, water, and blankets as well as their climbing gear, plus whatever weapons Cal thought he needed.

She took a deep breath, not letting herself think how impossible this was. They wouldn't be tackling the vertical climbs; they would be looking for the absolute easiest way up – which would still be hell, but not quite the same degree of hell.

She didn't have any hiking boots, so her only other choice was her athletic shoes. Instead of choosing spandex pants, she prepared for spending probably three or four nights in the mountains, at an altitude that often got chilly at night even in the middle of summer; that meant sweatpants. She had a pair with pockets that zipped, so that was the pair she chose, and laid them across the bed. She added several pairs of socks, plus clean underwear. Maybe she was being silly, but she couldn't face wearing the same pair of underwear for four days. She put both pairs on. A silk T-shirt, tucked in. A hooded sweatshirt jacket, which could be tied around her waist. She tucked lip balm into one of the pants pockets, then fished around in her underwear drawer until she found her old Swiss Army knife; it went in another pocket.

Next she brushed out her hair and pulled it back in a snug pony-tail to keep it secure; getting hair caught in any of the gear was painful. She stood there a minute, trying to think if she'd forgotten anything. Maybe her silk long johns, in case the nights got really cold? They would be too hot to wear during the day, but they weighed nothing and took up practically no space. In fact, they would fit in the pouch pockets of the sweatshirt jacket.

When she thought she had everything, she got dressed. Two pairs of socks, one thin and one thick. The extra two pairs also went into her pants pockets. Then the pants, then her shoes, and finally she tied the jacket around her waist. Experimentally she stretched and twisted, seeing if her clothing hampered her move-ment in any way. It didn't, so she was good to go.

Next stop: kitchen.

Cal entered the kitchen while she was dividing muesli into zippered plastic bags. He was laden with gear, all the harnesses and belaying devices, the biners and pins and anchors, the chalk bags, plus coils of thin rope. 'How old are these ropes?' he asked.

Just like that, her heart dropped into her stomach. 'Oh, no,' she said softly. 'They're over five years old.'

Synthetic rope deteriorated over time, even if it had never been used, and these ropes had been used. She and Derek had taken very good care of their ropes, hand-washing them in the bathtub, keeping them out of sunlight, but she couldn't stop the march of time. They couldn't climb with these ropes; it was as simple as that. A rope as old as these could be used for top-roping but not leading, but she didn't want to use them, period.

'Walter has some synthetic rope in the store,' he said. 'Maybe not exactly what we want, but newer than this. I'll get it now. How long?'

'Seventy meters.'

He nodded. He didn't ask what thickness, so she guessed that Walter had only the one roll stocked. They would use whatever was there.

He disappeared out the front, and she left the food to inspect the gear. She hadn't touched it since putting it in the attic three years ago, when she moved here. He hadn't brought down the helmets, but she understood why: they were brightly colored, easily visible. A lot of climbers didn't wear helmets anyway, but she and Derek always had.

The old fascination returned as she sorted out the gear, and for a minute she felt the tug of excitement, the lure of sun and height, her skill and strength pitted against the rock. She had fallen, of course. So had Derek. So had every climber she knew. But that was what the ropes were for, and that was why she wouldn't climb with old ones.

She forced herself to turn away from the gear and go back to food prep. Water would be a big problem, because it was so heavy. A gallon of water weighed eight pounds, not counting the weight of the container. She had some bottled water, but no convenient way to carry it. They needed a waterskin that could be slung on the back, but she couldn't think of any way to improvise one.

Maybe Roy Edward would know if there was running water on the mountains. There was, surely, aside from the bigger stream that formed part of Trail Stop's boundary before joining with the river.

Cal returned with coils of rope over his shoulders. He looked over her preparations and nodded. 'I helped myself to some things while I was getting the rope. I have matches in a waterproof box, some things like that. How about blankets?'

'The ones I have are thick,' she said. 'I was going to take some back to the others, but they're too thick to carry while we're climbing.'

He nodded. 'I have a couple of thin blankets at my place, and a sleep pad that rolls up tight. Okay, that's it. We could use more stuff, but we can't carry it. Let's go. By the time we get ready to leave, we won't have much daylight left.'

'What are we going to do? We can't climb in the dark.'

'We're going to get into position, which could take a couple of hours. Whatever we can do tonight, that's time we'll save tomorrow.'

He was right about that, and he had a brisk discipline to every movement, even his tone of voice, that told her he knew exactly what he was doing. He'd done this before, probably in circumstances just as dire.

When they made it back to the Richardsons', they found that Creed had organized the others with the same sort of crispness Cal displayed. While Cal took some of them out to show them the safest ways to move around, the angles they should use, and where they should be wary, Creed worked on the water problem.

According to Roy Edward there were several streams in the mountains, which helped, but they still had to solve the bottle problem. Creed looked thoughtful. The next thing Cate knew, Maureen was cutting the legs out of some of Perry's thermal-knit underwear. She tied off the end of one, and loaded bottles in the cutoff leg as if putting torpedoes in a firing tube. When each leg was full, she tied off the other end, then fashioned slings that could be worn across the shoulder and chest, with the weight of the water on their backs. Cate tried it out. There was more weight than she was comfortable with, but that would lessen as they drank.

Cal returned with two blankets and what she supposed was a sleeping pad, which looked much like a yoga mat. One of the blankets was rolled up and strapped to her, while he carried the mat and the other blanket. He put on his sling of water, grinning at the solution, then looked at Creed.

'What's the closest place we can go for help, after we get through the cut?'

'My place,' Creed said. 'From my back porch, I can see the cut. Other than that, there's a dude ranch about six or seven miles off the highway, and Gordon Moon's place is a little farther than that in the opposite direction. If you can find my place, you can use the phone there, but you'd have to use some dead-on course plotting, Marine.'

Cal grinned. 'If you happen to know the coordinates, I have a handheld GPS unit.' He tapped the cargo pocket on his right thigh.

A slow answering grin spread across Creed's face. 'Imagine that. It happens I have one, too. Wouldn't look good for the guide to get lost, now would it?'

'You remember the coordinates?'

'Does a kitty cat have an ass? Know 'em like my birthday.'

Chapter Twenty-Six

'What the hell are they doing over there?' Toxtel muttered to Teague when the latter walked by on his way to relieve Billy. Goss was taking a break back at the tent, since he was due to relieve Toxtel at midnight. Now was when they settled into routine, and now was when staying alert would become harder and harder.

Teague looked like hell and felt worse, but he was walking, and he intended to take his shift. The lump on his forehead was so big he couldn't get a cap on, but the slightest pressure made him feel as if his head were exploding anyway, so he was just as glad to do without one. The pain had kept up a steady pounding all day, but he'd checked his pupils in his rearview mirror and they were both the same size, so he figured he was okay; he'd just have to tough it out through the pain. He popped a couple of ibuprofen every four hours and that took the edge off, which would have to do.

Teague glanced across at the seemingly deserted community. From where he stood, he could see a couple of bodies lying where they'd fallen. If anything much had happened over there today, he couldn't tell. 'What do you mean?'

'You'd think they'd at least try to find out what's going on, but no one's stuck his nose out or yelled.'

'Give 'em until tomorrow,' said Teague. 'I figure Creed is getting them organized to try something. They may not wait until tomorrow; they might try something tonight. We'll have to stay alert.' He stared across the wreckage of the bridge; he wouldn't have been surprised to see Creed on the other side, shotgun to shoulder and sighting down the barrel at him ... Shit, he had to stop thinking about Creed, stop letting himself be mind-fucked. He wasn't stupid, he wouldn't discount Creed, but the bastard wasn't a superman. He was good at what he did, period. Well, Teague thought, so am I.

'I don't like it,' said Toxtel. He, too, was staring across the bridge. 'They should have been asking what we want.'

'Don't forget, my boys have been shooting at 'em every so often. They're probably not all that anxious to stick their heads up. Tomorrow, we shoot only if we see a target.'

'Then how in hell are we going to talk to them?'

Didn't these city boys know anything? 'As soon as one of them ties a flag to a stick so we know he wants to talk, that's when we talk.'

He left then and climbed to where Billy was positioned, the movement made more tortuous because he knew damn good and well that some of those old deer hunters could have their scopes on him, waiting for a good shot. He had to make certain they didn't get the chance, even though he didn't think it likely any of them would have the firepower to reach out this far. But then, he'd been surprised by how close Creed had managed to get last night; he wouldn't let himself get caught twice.

Billy was exhausted, since Teague hadn't been able to relieve him any during the day; he rolled away from the prone rest position he'd held for hours and lay sprawled on the rough ground. 'Thank God. You feeling any better?'

'I'm here. Seen anything interesting?'

'I get the feeling there's been a lot of movement going on behind cover. Blake and Troy think the same thing. Sometimes I'd catch a glimpse of something, but never enough to tell what it was. And always behind good, solid cover, so I know I wasn't looking at a dog or a cat.'

'You fire to make 'em keep their heads down?'

'A couple of times yes, a couple of times no. Goes against the grain to waste ammo.'

Teague knew what he meant. He settled with his rifle on the blanket Billy had spread on the ground over some leaves and pine needles to make the long watch more comfortable. His spare battery for the thermal scope was at hand, as well as a thermos of coffee and a pack of snack crackers if he needed to keep his energy up. At least tonight wasn't as cold as last night had been, so he wouldn't be shivering and shaking, which would play hell with his headache.

'Nobody tried to retrieve the bodies,' Billy said, sounding troubled. 'That bothers me.'

'If they're going to, it'll be tonight. They'll have waited for dark.'

'They have to have figured we got special scopes, that's how we could hit 'em last night.'

'Yeah, but maybe they've worked out something movable they can hide behind. We'll see.'

'You going to shoot if they go after the bodies?'

Teague considered the question. 'I don't think so. Is Blake already in position?'

'He relieved Troy about half an hour ago.'

'I'll radio him. Let them get the bodies. I don't know what they'll do with them, but I don't think it'll be pleasant, having all those dead people lying around attracting flies and turning black. Put a little more pressure on them.'

'That it will.' Billy stretched, then got into a crouch and worked his way behind Teague, heading toward the tent. 'Have fun tonight.'

Teague carefully braced his rifle, then turned on the thermal scope and put his eye to it. Last night Trail Stop had been lit with thermal signatures; tonight there was nothing. The houses didn't glow with heat, and none of the brightly lit little figures were running around making perfect targets of themselves. Considering how his head felt, he hoped the night stayed just as quiet as it was now.

Cate checked the glowing hands of Cal's watch, which he'd lent her, since hers wasn't luminous. Eleven thirty. She pulled her blanket more securely over her shoulders and stared up at the cloudy sky, glad the night was cool but not cold. She would have preferred a nice bright moon, too, but her eyesight had long since adjusted to the darkness, which wasn't total. She wouldn't want to walk anywhere; she couldn't see *that* well, but she could make out darker shapes and shadows. So long as nothing moved, and she didn't hear any crashing sounds, she was good.

Cal slept on his side on the thin pad he'd brought, blanket pulled up to his chin. They were keeping watch, for this first night at least, since they could have been seen working their way toward this location. Cate had the first shift; since the midnight to dawn shift was the hardest, he'd said, he would take that one.

234

He'd fallen asleep so fast, so easily, that she'd been disconcerted. She wished the light had been sufficient for her to watch him, but she'd had to content herself with listening to him breathe. He'd shifted position once or twice, but for the most part he'd been very still. As nothing happened to keep her alert, after a while she stopped starting at every rustle, every tiny scratch and scurry, as the night animals and insects went about their business. Instead, she thought about him.

Cal had said Trail Stop was shaped like a paramecium. The odd word had gone around and around in her brain as she followed him down the steep slope toward the river. Cate remembered what a paramecium was, from high school biology, but the word choice alerted her to yet another facet that made up the complicated whole of the man.

The past few days had been one revelation after another, until she felt as if she had to be the blindest, most oblivious person in Trail Stop. Until just a few days before, she had seen him as a sort of nonentity: painfully shy, inarticulate, but able to fix just about anything. He was definitely a jack-of-all-trades, but she'd discovered that while he might be a quiet man, he wasn't shy at all; in fact, he was well-spoken, educated, and decisive. He'd been in the military, about which she knew next to nothing, but evidently he'd been in some kind of exclusive unit.

Everyone else in Trail Stop seemed to have known all this. How could she not have noticed the disparity between the way she had looked at him and the way they saw him? Of course, they had known him far longer, but still – she felt as if she were still missing some big piece of the puzzle, some magic piece that would bring everything into focus.

The thick end of the paramecium slanted downward, which was good for two reasons: it provided cover, and the sharp slant down to the river wasn't as high. On the highest side, the bluff was sheer and a good seventy feet, but here at the eastern end it decreased to a mere forty feet, at a lesser angle, which meant they were able to get down without rappelling. Cal used a short-handled trenching tool to cut footholds in the dirt, and they both went down in a mostly upright position.

That close to the river the roar of the water had made conversation impossible unless they shouted, so she'd concentrated on not falling as they negotiated over jagged boulders. There was no riverbank, not in the sense that people usually thought. At the water's edge were rocks, period: big ones, little ones, rounded ones, and sharp ones. Some were solidly placed, some rolled underfoot. Some were slippery. Some were slippery *and* rolled, and they were the most treacherous. She'd had to make certain she had a secure grip with at least one hand before placing her weight on any rock. The pace was necessarily slow, so slow that she had begun to worry they wouldn't be able to get to more hospitable ground before dark, but they'd made it to the base of the mountain just in time. Cal had found a protected slope and that was where they'd stopped.

There was no semblance of camping. It was just the two of them, sitting on the ground in the dark, eating muesli from a plastic bag and drinking a little water. Then he'd unrolled the pad and lay down to sleep, leaving her alone with her thoughts.

At midnight she said, 'Cal,' and just like that, he was awake, without her having to shake him or repeat his name. He sat up and stretched, yawning.

'How did you *do* that?' she asked, pitching her voice low because sound carried at night.

'Do what?'

'Wake up that fast.'

'Practice, I guess.'

She gave him his watch, and he strapped it back on his wrist while she stretched out on the pad. She had wondered if it would be as comfortable as it looked. It wasn't. It was a thin pad on the rough ground, and she could feel every root and rock; still, it was better than sleeping on the ground, because it kept the chill away.

She spread her blanket over her as he took a drink of water and sat down where she'd been sitting. She tried to doze off, if not immediately as he'd done, at least within five or ten minutes. Fifteen minutes later she was still fidgeting.

'If you're not still, you won't ever get to sleep,' he said, sounding amused.

'I'm not a good camper; I don't like sleeping on the ground.'

'In different circumstances—' He stopped.

She waited for him to say something else, but he seemed inclined to let drop whatever he had been about to say, rather than rephrasing it. 'In different circumstances – what?' she prodded.

More silence, broken only by a slight breeze soughing through the trees. He was just an indistinct shape in the darkness, but she could tell he'd raised his head, listening for something. He must not have heard anything alarming, because his body posture soon relaxed. His words came softly. 'You could sleep on me.'

The rush of blood through her body made her feel light-headed. *Yes.* Yes, that was what she wanted, what she craved. She heard herself saying, just as softly, 'Or vice versa.'

He inhaled raggedly, and she smiled in the darkness. It was good to know she could do to him what he'd just done to her.

He shifted his legs, as if he was uncomfortable. Finally he muttered something, stood, and made some adjustments before cautiously sitting again. Cate smothered a giggle. 'I'm sorry,' she made herself say, though she wasn't at all sorry.

'I doubt it.' His tone was wry. 'You should have one of these for a little while, just to see how inconvenient they can be.'

'If *I* had one, *you* wouldn't be uncomfortable.'

'I said for a little while. I definitely wouldn't want you to have one permanently.'

'I don't need to have one at all.' A tiny devil prodded her to add, 'Because you'll let me use yours, won't you?'

Another sucked-in breath, and some rough breathing. He said, 'Damn it,' and stood again.

This time she couldn't hold back a tiny hiccup of a laugh.

'Tucker sounds just like that sometimes,' he said. 'They don't look like you very much, but sometimes the way they'll say things, or hold their heads – that's when I see you in them.'

Just like that her heart squeezed. She hadn't seen her babies since Friday morning, and it was now Sunday night. They were okay, though; that was the main thing. They were safe. And Cal was the only person who had ever said they reminded him of her. If he wanted to change the subject by talking about her boys, she was willing.

'I have a confession to make,' he muttered.

'About what?'

He cleared his throat. 'I'm the one – uh – I said some things I shouldn't have in front of them.'

Cate sat up on the pad, glad he couldn't see her face. 'Such as … damn idgit?' she asked suspiciously.

'I hit my thumb with the hammer,' he said, sounding incredibly sheepish. 'I – uh – said a whole alphabet soup of things.'

'Such as?' she asked again, somehow managing to keep her tone stern.

'Well, I – Cate, I was a *Marine,* if that gives you any idea.'

'Exactly what should I be prepared to hear my children saying?'

He gave in, his shoulders slumping. 'Do you want the words, or just the initials?'

Uh-oh. If she could recognize what he'd said by the initials, she knew it was bad. 'The initials will do.'

'It started with g.d.'

'And then what?'

'Um . . . m.f. and s.o.b.'

She blinked. She could just hear those words coming out of four-year-old mouths – probably when her mother was in the grocery store with them.

'I heard a giggle and looked around, and there they were, all ears. I couldn't think of anything else to do, so I threw the hammer, jumped up, and yelled, "I'm a damn idiot!" They thought that was hilarious, especially when I told them "damn idiot" was a really, really bad thing to say and they should never say it, and I should never have said it in front of them, but that was what you said when you were really mad.' He paused. ' guess it worked.'

'I guess it did,' she said faintly. He certainly knew how little boys' minds worked. They had promptly forgotten the words deemed not as bad, and concentrated on what he'd told them were really bad words. She should count her blessings.

She clapped a hand over her mouth as she shook with laughter, giggling and snorting. In that moment, listening to the sheepishness in his voice, delighting over the mental picture of him swearing a blue streak and suddenly looking into the fascinated faces of two little boys, she tipped over the emotional edge she'd been hovering on – and fell.

Chapter Twenty-Seven

When morning came, Teague sat up and rolled his shoulders, glad the night was over and nothing had happened. He'd forced himself to stay alert through the graveyard shift, knowing that if Creed had planned anything, that was when it would take place; a person's natural circadian rhythm was at its lowest point in those hours – at least for those who waited and watched. Teague had expected something, anything, even if just a few experimental forays. But hour after hour he'd scanned with the scope, without seeing the bright flare of a human thermal signature. Blake had been on edge, too, getting on the radio way too often to ask if Teague saw anything, but nothing had come their way.

Dawn was overcast, with sullen, low-hanging clouds that wreathed the tops of the mountains in mist. The warmer temperatures had held during the night, but now a chilly wind was beginning to blow. September weather could be iffy, as the seasons transitioned. Teague checked the level of coffee in his thermos; it was getting low. He'd need more if this wind kept blowing.

He glanced across at Trail Stop. It looked like a ghost town, with no one moving around. No, wait – he was certain he saw some smoke rising from the far side. It was difficult to tell, because the sky was so gray and, with the clouds hanging low on the mountains, everything sort of blended together, but – hell, yeah, that was smoke. Someone had a fire going in their fireplace. That was where the people would be, where they could get warm, maybe heat some soup, make some coffee. He keyed the radio. 'Blake. Check toward the river, the houses farthest away. Is that smoke?' Blake's eyes were younger than his, more reliable.

Blake came back with an answer in just a few seconds. 'It's

smoke, no two ways about it. Want me to try getting a shot in there?'

'I don't think you have a clear shot, too much structure between here and there. I know I don't.'

A minute went by, and Blake was on the radio again. 'Negative on the clear shot. Used my binoculars to check it out.'

'What I figured.' Teague settled back on the blanket, once again studying the road and the houses closest to him. An uneasy feeling skittered up his spine. There was something spooky about the place today, but it could have been the grayness of the morning and the low clouds that made him feel sort of hemmed in. The empty road was somehow wrong. He froze, staring. The road *was* empty, completely so.

The bodies were gone.

He couldn't believe his eyes. He blinked, stared, but they didn't magically reappear. The bodies were fucking *gone*.

He picked up the radio. 'Blake,' he said hoarsely.

'Come back,' said Blake.

'The bodies are gone.'

'Wha—?' Blake must have then looked for himself, because he said, '*Shit*.'

Teague kept staring, unable to quite take it in. How in hell – ? Creed. Fucking Creed. He'd figured out they had thermal scopes instead of night vision, and devised some way for the locals to move around without being detected. Thermal imaging wasn't foolproof; going into water to mask your thermal signature was the best-known trick. But if they'd gone into the stream to the right, the water was damn rough from all the rocks and practically impassable; then they would have had to walk a good distance to get to the bodies, and by then they would have been showing a thermal signature again. Likewise, they couldn't have gone to the left, because that would have put them right in Blake's front yard, and he'd have seen them way before they got to the stream.

Some other way, then.

He narrowed his eyes, studying the place, then picked up his binoculars and made a slow sweep from house to house, pausing at what, from this distance, looked like a low block wall. There hadn't been a wall there before. He'd have noted something like that when he made his reconnaissance. Besides, the top wasn' level. Instead of a wall, it looked more like sandbags.

Well, son of a bitch. The locals had been busy during the night. He felt perversely pleased that they hadn't just rolled over and played dead; he'd have been embarrassed in front of the city boys if they had. He'd said they were tough, and they'd just proven him right. They were fortifying their positions and providing themselves with a safe way of moving about. Behind those bags, no bullets could reach them.

He got on the radio again. 'Blake. Take a look at those sections of low wall. Those aren't walls. Looks like sandbags to me.' Even as he said it, he realized they wouldn't have had access to sandbags. Something else, then, something in bags. Feed, concrete mix, something like that. Didn't really matter; the principle was the same.

Blake looked. 'What're we gonna do?' he finally asked, evidently agreeing with the sandbag assessment.

'Nothing we can do, other than what we're already doing. Don't let anybody get by you; keep them hemmed up until they're ready to give the city boys what they want.' Could take longer than what he'd planned on, though, which wasn't good. This whole house of cards could come tumbling down at any time if the wrong person decided to come poking around. That was a risk he'd accepted, but he wasn't going to let this situation drag out indefinitely. He'd stay with his own timetable, regardless of what the city boys thought.

'Belay on?'

'Belay on.'

At Cal's quiet reassurance that he had her if she fell, Cate stretched for a grip on the rock. Cal had searched for a better route, because scaling rock was time-consuming, but he hadn't found anything that wouldn't have left them exposed to rifle fire. Going up this rock face was the safest, most direct route. She was glad it wasn't one of the tougher, higher climbs, since neither of them was in practice, and neither was wearing climbing shoes. She wasn't in good shape to be climbing, either; her leg muscles were strong, from climbing the stairs she went up and down every day, but her upper-body strength was probably half what it had been when she climbed regularly.

The weather wasn't great for climbing, either; the wind was picking up, and the clouds were pressing lower and lower. If it started raining, they wouldn't be able to go back down and wait for better weather; they'd have to press on, even though rain would make the rock more slippery. They'd just have to be extra careful. She thanked God this was what she would have considered an easy climb, back in the day. It was about a hundred yards, maybe a hundred and twenty, to the top – and it wasn't vertical.

Other climbers had been there before them; bolts and anchors were already hammered into the rock in various places. Some climbers removed them as they went, leaving the rock as they'd found it, others didn't bother. Generally Cate didn't like trusting a bolt she hadn't set herself – or that Derek hadn't set – but in the name of speed she was prepared to use some of the presets if they felt sturdy.

Both of them were harnessed and securely roped together. Because she had the most experience, she was the lead rope; she set the way, and when she reached, literally, the end of their rope, she would stop and he'd follow. With the belay set, he would catch her if she fell. When she stopped, she became the belayer and would catch him if he fell.

Part of her was exhilarated to be back on the rock, even an easy rock. It was the stretch and play of muscle, her strength and skill against the rock. At the same time, she knew deep down in her bones this would be her last climb – at least until her boys were grown – and the only reason she was doing it now was because of the severity of the circumstances. Because she knew this was the last time she'd experience this particular thrill, she paid attention to every second, every scrape and smell and sound, the whisper of the ropes, the wind in her face, the cool, rough rock beneath her fingertips. Every time she looked around and saw how high she'd climbed, she felt intense satisfaction.

She gained a solid foothold, set a chock, and securely clipped herself to the rock. At her signal, Cal began climbing toward her following her established route. She watched his every move, he brake hand ready on the rope in case he slipped. The boots he wore were even less suitable for climbing than her sneakers, so every move he made was risky. His upper-body strength compensated somewhat for his boots. Despite the chilly wind, he'd taken off his jacket and rolled it up before adding it to the supplies strapped to his back, so she could see the flex of muscle and tendon in his bare arms. A climber's strength was sinewy and flexible, like a steel coil, not bulky in the way of bodybuilders'. Cal's arms looked as if he'd been climbing all his life.

A cold mist swept over them, and in a matter of seconds, visibility was down to about zero as the cloud engulfed the mountain.

She knew he was still there, she could feel him on the rope, but she couldn't see him. 'Cal!'

'I'm still here.'

He sounded as calm as if they were out for a stroll. One day soon she needed to have a talk with him about this; it wasn't natural. 'I can't see you, so talk to me, damn it. Tell me everything you do, every step. I have to be able to anticipate.'

He obliged, talking steadily to her until the wind blew the mist away and he once more emerged into sight. That was the way it went for the next hour, with the mist blowing in and out as the low clouds engulfed them. At one point the mist was like a heavy fog, and they both stopped to put on thin, cheap ponchos that would at least keep most of their clothing dry. That was the rain gear they'd brought, because the ponchos weighed so little, but climbing was impossible with them on. So they simply waited for the mist to clear again. When they could take the ponchos off, they climbed.

The weather slowed them considerably, and it was just after ten in the morning when they finally reached the top of the rock face, which was nowhere near as high as they needed to get ultimately. Stretching ahead of them was a thickly treed slope; the geography would take them due north instead of northwest, the direction they needed, but they had to follow the land and its restrictions.

After sipping some water and eating more muesli, then stepping away from each other to answer nature calls in private, they carefully coiled the ropes, slung them over their shoulders, and set off again, this time with Cal in the lead. A light rain began to fall. They put the ponchos on again, and kept hiking.

'Let's talk!' Toxtel boomed out, cupping his hands around his mouth to make the sound carry.

The hell of it, Goss thought, was that he didn't know if anyone was within hearing distance. All those damn people had disappeared, dropping out of sight as if they'd never existed. Even the bodies were gone. When he and Toxtel had first noticed that this morning, they'd been a little unnerved, because Teague had put such faith in his fancy thermal scopes and now, somehow, the yokels had outsmarted him. It was time for the next step, before these people had a chance to come up with something else.

Toxtel had been bellowing for a good fifteen minutes, and there hadn't been so much as a flicker of movement on the other side. He might as well have been farting in the wind, for all the effect he was having.

After half an hour, Toxtel's voice was hoarse, but finally a hand waving a white piece of cloth appeared out the front door of the first house. Toxtel shouted again, then waved his own flag, and an old man shuffled out onto the porch.

The old guy looked to be close to ninety, Goss thought in disbelief, watching as he laboriously made his way down the steps and tottered the hundred yards to the mangled wreckage of the bridge. Was this the best they had to send? But then again, why send the best? Why take that risk? Come to think of it, the old guy was a damn smart choice.

'What do you want?' he demanded querulously, looking disgruntled at having to go to all this effort.

Toxtel went right to the point. 'The Nightingale woman has what we're after. Tell her to hand it over, and we'll pull out and leave.'

The old guy stared across the ravine separating them, working his jaws as if he were chewing the idea over. Finally he said, 'I'll pass the message on,' and turned around, retracing his steps as if uninterested in anything else they might have to say. They carefully placed themselves behind cover, then watched until he was once more out of sight.

'What the hell do you make of that?' Toxtel asked rhetorically.

'They're pissed' was Goss's reply.

Chapter Twenty-Eight

The first snowflake drifted down just after five that afternoon. Cate stopped in her tracks, staring at it in consternation. Several more flakes followed the first one; then they all disappeared in a swirl of wind.

'Did you see that?' she asked Cal.

'Yep.'

It was early in the season for snow, though not unheard of. With any luck, those few flakes didn't have any buddies. Rain had started falling in earnest several hours ago. As cold as the temperature had gotten, though, falling steadily through the afternoon hours as they climbed higher and higher, they had to assume a real snowfall was possible.

Snow wasn't good for a couple of reasons, the biggest one of which was that they wouldn't be able to continue. The footing was treacherous enough when they could see where they were stepping; if the way was covered with snow, they would be risking life and limb. Nor were they dressed for snow, or for weather this cold. They'd left the ponchos on as protection against the wind and rain, but they didn't have the layers necessary to keep them warm. She'd been shivering for some time now, even though she'd put on her sweatshirt jacket and pulled up its hood as well as the hood of the poncho.

Cal pulled out the rough map Roy Edward had drawn of the abandoned mines. 'Are we close to one of them?' Cate asked, moving to his side to look at the piece of paper. She hoped so; they had to get out of this weather before nightfall, which was only a couple of hours away. They would freeze if they had to stay out in this all night.

'I don't think so,' he said. He pointed to an X. 'That's the closest one, and by my reckoning we're about here.' He indicated another spot. 'If Roy Edward was anywhere near accurate with his guess, we're at least a mile from there, plus another five hundred or so feet in altitude. At the pace we've been traveling, we wouldn't make it by dark. Even if we could, we need to stop now, and get dry and warm. Your shoes are soaked.'

Unfortunately, he was right. Her feet were so cold and painful she was already hobbling. If getting anywhere required any climbing, she couldn't do it. 'What are we going to do?'

'You're going to get somewhere out of the wind and stay there while I scout around. Here's where I earn my keep.'

Since the wind was swirling from every direction, she didn't know where that would be. But he found a big fir with branches so thick the ground beneath it was dry, and she sat down there, with her knees hugged up under the poncho to preserve her body heat. She looked up at him through the rain, seeing how reddened his face was from the cold and wind, and remembered that he wasn't dressed any more warmly than she was. His only advantage was that his boots were waterproof, so his feet were still dry. 'Be careful,' she said, because that was the only thing she could think of.

'If I can't find an overhang, I'll make us a lean-to.' He began removing all of his climbing gear, putting it beside Cate and placing the coil of rope on top. He gently touched her cheek, then was gone. All he took with him was his trenching tool. She watched him stride off through the rain with as much energy as if he had steel springs inside his legs, while every muscle in her body was aching, not just from the rigorous exercise she'd given them that day but from shivering for so long.

Tiredly she pulled the front of the poncho up over her nose so the air she was breathing would be warmer. Instantly she felt better able to endure the cold, though wind still whistled through the trees and rain dripped all around her. The sloping branches of the big fir created a natural runoff, like a living umbrella spread over her head.

They had been gone from Trail Stop for twenty-four hours. What was going on there now? She and Cal hadn't been able to talk, because they had spent the day either strung out across a rock face or hiking uphill, neither of which made conversation easy.

They had stopped when they had to, then pressed on, always aware of time slipping away.

Half an hour later, the rain became mixed with snow. Cate stared out at it, willing the white flakes away. She didn't mind snow flurries, though she wished the weather had stayed as warm as it had been the day before; she just didn't want snow on the ground. Down in the valley, they probably weren't getting any snow at all.

As the flakes became larger and the ground began taking on a white tint in the growing gloom, she wondered where Cal was, and what he was doing.

Cal had picked up a broken limb as thick as his thumb and was using it to poke into any clump of undergrowth that looked as if it might harbor a small cave, an overhang, anything that would provide them sufficient shelter for the coming night. He was acutely aware that bears wouldn't have gone into den yet – the season was still too early – so he'd hung the trenching tool back on his belt and instead unbuttoned the right pocket of his camouflage jacket, pulling out his holstered nine-millimeter automatic. Normally he would have worn the holster on his belt, or strapped to his thigh if he'd been on a mission, but while climbing rock, he hadn't wanted to wear it where it could become snagged. Instead he had secured it in his coat and made certain the pocket was buttoned. When the jacket had been rolled and secured on his back, the automatic had been snugged against his body. The pistol wasn't the best weapon for facing a bear, but it was a hundred times better than a trenching tool.

He was allowing himself only so much time to find a rock shelter. There were plenty of overhangs, but they were either too shallow or the rock was cracked or the ground beneath them didn't seem stable. Some of them had water running out of them; since one of his requirements was that their shelter be dry, that eliminated those possibilities. If he didn't find one soon, he'd have to use the remaining light, poor as it was, to build a lean-to. Since the ground wasn't exactly level, he hoped it wouldn't come to that.

Finally he saw something that had possibilities. A prow of granite jutted out at a slight upward angle, balanced on another giant slab. These weren't going anywhere – they'd been there so long they were mostly buried, with mature trees growing on top of the prow. Another of those giant firs grew on the south side of the opening underneath, partially blocking it. Brushing aside the limbs that hung almost to the ground, he squatted and surveyed the interior. It was about ten feet long and shallow, no more than five feet deep, and the highest point in the opening was about the same. That was good, because small spaces were easier to warm than large ones.

He'd brought a small flashlight, so he clicked it on and swept the light into every corner, looking for snakes, dead rats, live rats, anything with which he wouldn't want to spend the night. There was debris, of course, and some insects that scurried away from the light. The fire would take care of them.

He broke a small limb off the fir and used it to sweep out his chosen sanctuary, then used the trenching tool to gather more branches from the surrounding trees, not taking too many from any one tree, and laid the limbs in a crosshatch pattern on the floor of the opening. Not only would the evergreen freshen the musty smell, but the limber branches would provide something of a cushion for the sleep mat. He could sleep on the ground, rolled up in his blanket, but Cate would be more comfortable on the rough mattress.

At least they could have a fire tonight. The slope they were on faced east, away from the shooters. The trees overhead would filter the smoke through their branches, breaking it up so it didn't form a plume, and the weather would dissipate it anyway. A little light and a lot of warmth would go a long way toward making them more comfortable. Besides, he had to get Cate's shoes dry.

The rain had changed completely to snow, and it began swirling down fast enough that the ground began turning white despite being so wet. He didn't like that, not just because of the snow, but because after dark the temperature would plummet and whatever was wet would develop a slick coating of ice. Their only hope was if this was a fast-moving front, with warmer rain behind it.

He had other things to do, but he didn't want to leave Cate sitting alone in the cold any longer than he had to. The sooner she got into their little shelter and he could get a fire started, the sooner she could pull off her wet shoes and socks and start warming her feet. He could finish securing the shelter afterward.

There was about twenty minutes of light left by the time he could make his way back to her; the thin layer of snow was incredibly slippery. Several times he had to use the trenching tool to catch himself. The drops of water still on the tree branches were beginning to freeze, making a faintly clinking sound in the wind.

'I have us a place,' he said, and she looked up from where she'd buried her face against her knees. The poncho was pulled up over her nose to warm the air she breathed, and her eyes were more alert; they had begun to take on the dullness of suffering, which had worried him a lot more than he'd let her see. 'It's dry, and we can build a fire.'

'You said the magic word.' She crawled out from under the sheltering branches with more energy than she'd shown crawling under them. The rest had refreshed her. She would have been in much better shape if he'd insisted she wear boots, but he hadn't expected rain and snow. He didn't have arthritis to warn him of changing weather, and he hadn't been able to watch the Weather Channel for the past couple of days. For all he knew, a record-breaking early-season blizzard had been predicted.

'The rain has started freezing,' he said. 'Getting back is going to be tough, because the ground is so slippery. Don't take a step unless you're holding on to something.'

'Got it.' She pulled out her hammer and gripped it in her left hand as he loaded himself down with all the gear he'd earlier removed. He started out, moving as easily under the weight as he had without it, and she carefully followed.

Cate's feet were still miserably cold and wet, but while she'd been resting, she had constantly flexed her toes to increase the blood flow in them, so she wasn't as clumsy as she'd been before. Still, she hoped the shelter he'd found wasn't far, because light was fading fast and the snow was getting heavier, filtering down through the trees in eerie silence.

She hoped the valley was getting snow. She hoped the shooters staked out on the mountainside were getting ten feet of snow dumped on their asses. She hoped they'd been in the rain all day, and were now frozen into human Popsicles. The mountains often got snow when the valley didn't, but she hoped this wasn't one of those times.

'We'll have to turn back, won't we?' she asked softly.

'Probably.' He didn't sugarcoat it. She was glad. She could deal better with reality than with rosy pictures that dealt more in wishes than fact. 'Unless it's so bad we have to wait it out.'

He paused on a particularly slippery patch and used the trenching tool to hack a stepping place in the ground. With his poncho covering the supplies on his back, he looked like some misshapen monster, but she figured she looked the same.

Physically she was as miserable as she could remember ever being. Steam puffed from her open mouth, and she made an effort to close it and breathe through her nose, which gave her a dragon effect. She distracted herself by thinking about how she could show this to the boys this winter. They would love playing dragon.

'Here it is,' he finally said, sweeping aside the branches of a giant fir and using his flashlight to show her the interior of a slanted overhang. 'I swept it out and laid down those fir limbs for a cushion. Crawl in and get comfy while I gather firewood.'

She didn't ask where he intended to find dry wood; she had absolute faith that if there was any out there, he would find it. She stopped at the entrance and pulled off her wet poncho, reaching out to hang it on one of the fir branches, then quickly ducked inside. An extra flashlight would have come in handy, but she didn't have one.

'Here,' he said, pulling a thin green tube out of his pack. As soon as she saw it, she knew what it was, having seen them in stores that carried outdoor gear. He bent it to start the chemical reaction and the tube began to glow.

Light was a wonderful thing. She immediately felt better, even though she was just as cold and miserable as before.

He knelt at the entrance and began shedding supplies and gear, trying to wiggle out of most of it without pulling off his poncho, though he especially didn't want to get his blanket and the sleep pad wet. All of the climbing gear went at one end; she pulled hers off and placed it down there, too.

She had become used to the weight of the water in the improvised sling, but as soon as she took it off, she breathed a huge sigh of relief as her back and shoulder muscles relaxed. The water was a big part of their burden, each of them carrying about twenty pounds of it, or two and a half gallons.

'Do you have dry socks with you?'

'In my pocket.'

'Before you do anything else, get those wet shoes and socks off, dry your feet, and put on fresh socks.' Then he was gone, ducking back into the night. She watched the bob of the flashlight for a moment, then did exactly as he'd said. He was the survival expert, not she.

She put aside her wet shoes and with difficulty peeled off the two pairs of socks. Her feet looked dead white. She cupped her hands around her toes, but her hands were also cold and that didn't give her much relief. Briskly she began rubbing her feet, both to get them dry and to get the blood flow going again. What she needed was a pan of hot water to soak them in, but this over-hang didn't have plumbing, so she kept rubbing and chafing, and slowly began to warm both her hands and her feet.

The light the chem tube gave off was dim and weird green in color, so she couldn't tell if her toes were getting a little pink or not, but they felt somewhat warmer. Quickly she pulled the fresh socks out of her pocket and put them on. Joy of joys, they had absorbed some of her body heat; it was almost like wrapping her feet in heated towels. The sensation quickly faded, but it was wonderful while it lasted.

Her sweatpants were wet from the knees down, but she didn't have another pair of pants to put on. Then she remembered the silk long johns she'd put in her jacket pocket. She got them out, then swiftly shucked the wet sweatpants and pulled on the formfitting long johns. They were dry, but felt too insubstantial in the cold, so she pulled her blanket around her, then started arranging the meager space in their shelter.

That consisted of rolling out the sleep pad on the layer of tree limbs he'd put down, then placing his blanket roll on top of it. She moved their slings of water to the back of the space, where she hoped they wouldn't freeze, and got out a bottle of water for each of them. Their available food was more muesli, some individual boxes of raisins, and miniature PayDay candy bars. To her surprise, his pack yielded some corn chips. She shrugged; maybe he was a corn chip fanatic. She could understand that. For a few days every month, she would kill for chocolate – perhaps not liter-ally, but she would certainly knock down old ladies in the grocery store parking lot to get to any Hershey's bars they might have in their shopping bags.

A smile touched her lips. Tanner had once offered her a Hershey's Kiss to make her feel better. She'd burst out laughing and hugged him exuberantly, confirming in his mind that chocolate could heal all woes.

Cal reappeared, carrying an armful of sticks and twigs under his poncho. He dumped them in a dry spot, then took the trenching tool and swiftly dug a small pit at the inside edge of their enclosure. When he was finished, he said, 'I need some rocks,' and he was off again. Finding rocks didn't take as long as finding dry wood. He made a couple of trips, lining the bottom of the pit with the rocks. Then he arranged a layer of twigs, then the sticks on top. 'This is just to get a fire started; then I'll look for more wood,' he said as he seized the bag of corn chips and tore it open. He popped one chip into his mouth, then took out another one. Laying it aside, he got the waterproof box of matches and lit a match, but instead of holding the flame to the twigs, he picked up the corn chip and delicately held it to the match.

To her surprise the chip began to flame, fire sitting in the curve of the chip like a baby in a swing. 'I'll be damned,' she murmured.

'High oil content,' he said, sliding the chip under the twigs.

She leaned forward, watching the corn chip in fascination as the twigs began to catch and smoke curled upward. 'How long will it burn?'

'Never timed it. Long enough. Don't let the fire get too hot; feed it just enough to keep it going until I get back with more wood.' He went back into the night.

The fire was engrossing, and the warmth that began to bathe her face was pure heaven. She watched the corn chip until it was no more and was tempted to light another one, but instead she carefully monitored the little fire and let it die down before she fed it another small stick.

He amassed what looked like a small mountain of sticks and dry bark in the far end of their shelter before he deemed it enough. Then he cut young, limber branches from the nearby trees and sat just under the overhang while he quickly lashed together a frame, using long strips of fiber pulled from the branches themselves to tie everything together. He began weaving the remaining branches in and out of the frame, overlapping and interlocking. When he was finished, he propped one end of the frame against the outside edge of their enclosure and drove a stick into the ground to prop up the other end. He'd made a screen that blocked most of the opening, to hold in more of their precious heat and keep out the wind, and he'd done it in little more than half an hour.

Then he sighed and rubbed his hands over his face, and she saw how tired he was.

'Sit down,' she said, moving over on the pad to give him room. She handed him a bottle of water and a bag of muesli. 'I also have raisins and PayDay bars, if you want them.'

'Both,' he said. 'We've burned a lot of calories today.'

They were silent while they ate, so tired they had to concentrate on the act of chewing. When she ate the raisins, she could almost feel the sugar in them racing through her bloodstream in a rapid burn. She laid the little cardboard box beside the fire, to feed to it later.

He noticed her shoes and moved them closer to the fire, as well as her socks. That was when he saw her sweatpants. He froze for a moment, then slowly reached out and drew them closer to the fire, too, arranging them so the wet parts were nearest the heat. He darted a quick glance at her, clearly wondering if she was naked under the blanket.

Smiling, she parted the edges of the blanket to show her silk long johns. Some of the tension went out of his shoulders, and he gave her a rueful smile in return. 'You nearly gave me a heart attack.'

After they ate, nothing seemed as interesting as getting some sleep. He pulled off his boots and dropped the light stick down in one of them, effectively turning out the light except for the green glow coming from his boot and the much more comforting light from the fire. Wrapping himself in his blanket, he stretched out between her and the opening to the shelter.

Cate lay down on the pad and pulled her blanket around her. 'Aren't we keeping watch tonight?'

'No need.' His voice was a sleepy murmur.

'We'll take turns on the pad.'

'I'm fine here. I've slept on the ground more nights than I can remember.'

She started to protest, but her eyes were too heavy. Instead she sighed and dropped off to sleep.

She woke sometime later – could have been an hour, could have been several hours – shivering as cold air crept under the edges of her blanket. She opened her eyes to find Cal sitting up and feeding another stick to the fire, so evidently the cold had awakened him, too. Light flared brighter as the stick caught and began to burn, but she couldn't tell any difference in the amount of heat.

The night had grown a lot colder. She could feel a difference in the air that came around and through the screen he'd built. How much colder would they have been if the screen hadn't been there? She curled on her side, pulling her knees up in an effort to conserve her body heat. He glanced at her, saw her eyes open.

'Cold?' he asked, and she nodded. He added another stick to make the fire hotter.

She squinted at her watch but in the uncertain light couldn't make out the time. 'What time is it?'

He must have already checked his watch, because he said, 'Just after midnight.' They had been asleep a couple of hours, at least.

'Is it still snowing?' She was thirsty, so she sat up to take a quick sip of water, then swiftly snuggled back under the blanket.

'Yeah. There are three or four inches on the ground.'

Three or four inches wasn't a vast amount of snow, but under the circumstances, it might as well have been a blizzard. They simply weren't equipped to handle snow; they weren't dressed warmly enough, plus the underlying ice made even the simplest task dangerous. And it was still snowing.

He lay back down, too, his back to her, the way they had slept in the basement, except now they weren't cuddled together. Of course, the pad was barely wide enough for one, but there were other options.

She considered those options, wondering if she was truly ready to take such a step. She looked at the back of his head, at the shaggy dark blond hair, and the answer was a simple *yes*. Yes, she could very happily wake and see that head on the pillow beside her for the rest of her life. She wanted him. She wanted to explore the mysteries of who he was, what had made him, every complicated detail of him. She wanted to make love with him, laugh with him, share her life with him. Whether he was interested in taking on a widow with two children was something she would have to find out, but she knew he was interested in her on at least one basic level.

'Cal,' she whispered, reaching out to touch his back.

That was all. He rolled over and looked at her, his gaze crystal clear and direct. The moment stretched between them, a fine tension pulling tight every muscle in her body, which was humming with a need that silently asked and was answered.

He tossed aside his blanket and crouched beside her, reaching under her blanket to peel the silk long johns and underwear down her legs and place them on top of the piles of gear. Her sudden nakedness made her heart thunder in her chest, made her clench her legs together to contain the sudden jolt of heat and sensation. Abruptly she felt so aroused she was afraid she might come at his first touch. She didn't want that, she wanted to feel him inside her, feel the deliciousness of hard strokes that built and built until she couldn't take any more and broke.

On his knees beside her, he unfastened his pants and pushed them down. His penis thrust up and out, blue veins prominent and the head dark with engorged blood. She reached out to grasp him, and he caught her hand, the move so fast she saw only a blur. 'No.' His eyes were narrow as he lifted the blanket and moved on top of her, kneeing her clenched thighs apart and pushing his hips between them. 'I've waited so long to make love to you; I don't want to come in your hand.'

She knew, oh, she knew. She wanted to relax but she couldn't, her entire body was coiled and tense. Her legs clamped around him, pulling him to her. Her hips lifted, seeking, but the angle was wrong and his erection was a stiff rod between them, pushing and making her gasp with pain. He fought her grip, levering himself away far enough to get his hand between them while she desperately tried to pull him back.

'Jesus,' he said between clenched teeth. 'Cate – God! Let me—' He dragged the head of his penis into place and worked it inside her, then pushed hard.

She heard herself taking ragged breaths, almost sobbing. It hurt. She was surprised by how much it hurt. She was wet and aroused, but almost locked with tension. She wanted to cry. She wanted to scream. She wanted to buck him off and be rid of this hot, full, stretched sensation, and at the same time she wanted him to thrust hard and fast until this horrible tension was gone and she could relax again. Her fingers dug into his back, found his muscles as tight as hers.

He was sucking in deep breaths, too, his entire body shaking as if he were straining against some irresistible force. She turned her head and saw his fingers sunk into the web of branches beneath the pad, the muscles in his forearm standing out and quivering.

He made a raw sound, and pressed his forehead against hers. 'If I move, I'll come.'

If he didn't move, she would die.

They strained against each other, desperately fighting to control the savage urgency that gripped them. She whimpered, feeling as if she'd been caught in some great vortex that was about to tear her to pieces, whirling her closer and closer to some unbearable destruction. She gave a small scream and her inner muscles clamped convulsively around him. Her sight dimmed, the world went away, and she began coming.

His control broke and he braced over her, his whole body surging, flexing, thrusting, pushing so deep she screamed again. He shook with the force of his climax, shook and cursed and groaned so harshly the sounds seemed to tear from his chest.

Slowly, so slowly, he collapsed onto her.

She became aware that he was incredibly heavy, for someone who looked so lean. And he was hot, his body heat counteracting the frigid air creeping into their little enclosure. She was still clutching at his back, and she forced her hands to relax. They slid down his back, brushed over the smoothness of his bare buttocks.

Her cheeks were wet. She didn't know why she was crying, and she really wasn't; she was gasping for breath and trying to slow her galloping heartbeat, but the tears kept leaking from her eyes. He kissed them away, nuzzled her temples, her jawline, and finally settled on her mouth. She felt the stickiness of his semen leaking out of her, but he didn't withdraw even though she could tell that he'd softened. Staying inside her saved time.

The second time was much, much slower. She came again, but though he got hard, he couldn't climax, and he didn't seem to care. He just kept moving against her like the ripple of wind on a lake, riding her to a third climax before she begged him to stop. She was going to be sore and she suspected he would be, too, but still she hated that moment when their flesh separated, and she had to bite her lip to keep from crying out in protest.

They managed to clean up, using some of the bottled water; then he pulled up his pants and with a groan collapsed back onto the sleep pad, pulling her down on top of him. With both blankets over them and sharing their body heat, she was much warmer than before and quickly dozed off, to waken when he shifted beneath her.

She touched his face, loving the stubble that scraped her palm, loving, too, the way he pressed a light kiss to her palm before closing his eyes again.

'You stopped blushing,' she murmured, tracing her fingertip over the curve of his upper lip. Suddenly the subject seemed important. 'Why did you stop blushing?'

He opened his eyes, his gaze steady on her face. 'Because you started.'

She *had* blushed around him lately; she'd been so confused by the abrupt change in her feelings for him that she'd felt completely unbalanced.

'When you moved here,' he said, 'I knew you weren't ready.' His quiet voice wrapped around her like a touch. The snow outside had muted all other sounds except the gentle crackling of the fire, and his voice. 'You were still in shock from losing your husband, still grieving. You had a wall around you that didn't let you see me as a man.'

'I saw you,' she protested. 'You just seemed so shy—'

A faint smile quirked his lips. 'Yeah. The whole town got a kick out of watching me blush and stammer like a schoolkid when you were anywhere around.'

'But that was – From the very beginning? Three years ago?' She was surprised. No, she was astounded, and completely shocked. She couldn't have been so totally oblivious, so blind to something a thirteen-year-old would have noticed.

'From the first time I saw you.'

'Why didn't you say something?' She felt indignant that everyone else knew and she'd been completely in the dark.

'You weren't ready,' he repeated. 'There were only two men you addressed as "mister" – Creed and me. Think about it.'

She didn't have to think about it. The truth was there like a highway billboard. They were the only two truly eligible men in Trail Stop – Gordon Moon didn't count – and she had firmly put them at a distance.

'When you called me by my first name, I knew the wall was down,' he said, lifting his head to kiss her.

'*Everyone* knew.' She couldn't get over that.

'Not only that – uh – I guess I have another confession. Your house didn't need that much work. They would sabotage it, do things like cutting a wire or loosening a pipe fitting so you'd have a leak, just to throw us together. They thought it was funny to watch me fall all over myself if you spoke to me.'

She stared at him, trying to decide whether she should laugh or get angry. 'But – but,' she sputtered.

'I could take it.' He smiled at her. 'I'm a patient man. And they were doing what they could to get us together. They didn't want to lose a good handyman.'

Okay, now she was completely at sea. 'Why would they lose you?'

'I'd been out of the Marines a month when you came to Trail Stop. I was cruising around the country, not sure what I wanted to do, and I came to visit Creed. He was my commanding officer in the Corps, and we became friends. He got out ... oh, eight years ago, I guess, and I hadn't seen him since, so I looked him up. I'd been here a couple of weeks and was getting ready to move on when you moved in. I saw you, and stayed. Simple as that.'

What was simple about it? 'I thought you lived here! I thought you'd been here for years!' She was almost wailing, though she didn't know why, other than because she felt like such an idiot.

'Nope. I've been here two weeks longer than you.'

She stared down at the tender expression in his eyes, saw the toughness and completeness of him as a man, the utter strength, and she wanted to weep. She opened her mouth, intending to say something important and meaningful, but the words that came out were neither.

'But I have a mouth like a duck!'

He blinked, and in complete seriousness said, 'I like ducks.'

Chapter Twenty-Nine

They were lying on their sides facing each other, talking and kissing, letting the newfound sense of familiarity settle in. There was nothing they could do at the moment about the situation in Trail Stop, nowhere they could go. Snow was still coming down, but here, in this hole in the ground, there was light and warmth and a sense of completion. They couldn't stop touching each other, each led by the desire to absorb as much detail as possible of the other. Cal's questing fingers found the scar low on her abdomen and paused, tracing it. 'What's this?'

Some scars might have bothered her, but not that particular one, because it meant she had two living sons. Cate put her hand over his, loving the tough, sinewy strength that could touch her so gently. 'C-section. I carried the boys until eighteen days short of their due date, which is good with twins, but then I went into labor. As it progressed, the first twin, Tucker, went into fetal distress. His umbilical cord was caught. The C-section saved his life.'

Cal looked alarmed, even though those events were more than four years in the past. 'But he was okay? You were okay?'

'Yes to both questions.' She chuckled. 'You've known Tucker most of his life. He's been pedal-to-the-metal from the day he was born.'

'He is that,' Cal agreed, and mimicked Tucker's piping voice: *'Mimi shoulda watched me better!'*

Cate had to laugh. 'Not one of his finer moments, I admit. I've been so terrified since Derek died, afraid I wouldn't do a good job raising them, afraid I couldn't support them. Since our good neighbors were "helping" you by sabotaging my house, I was actually

259

considering cutting expenses by offering you free room and board in exchange for repairs.'

He laughed, too, shaking his head. 'That's the same deal I have with Neenah. Well, not the food. Food *was* part of the offer, right?'

'It was, but now I know the truth.' She kissed him, reveling in her freedom to do so. 'You'll do my repairs for free anyway, won't you?'

'Depends. I prefer trade.' He moved his hand down to her butt, squeezing it to let her know just what sort of trade he preferred.

Something curious occurred to her. 'Just how *did* you learn how to do all those repairs? You'd just got out of the Marines.'

He shrugged. 'I'm just good with my hands, I guess. I signed up on my seventeenth birthday—'

'Seventeen!' She was horrified. Seventeen was ... seventeen was a *baby*.

'Well, I finished high school when I was sixteen, and nobody wanted to hire a sixteen-year-old full-time. I didn't want to go to college because I was too young to fit in. I didn't fit anywhere, except the Marines. I got a degree in electrical engineering while I was in, plus I'm a master mechanic, and, hell, anyone can hammer some nails and slap on paint. What's so hard about it? I'm reading up now on how to reenamel an old tub. What?'

He didn't get it, she thought. He truly didn't get it. She kissed him again. 'Nothing. Just that you're the handiest handyman I've ever met.'

'It's not like jobs are thick on the ground in Trail Stop, and I knew I'd never see you if I went off to work somewhere and came home only at night. Besides, I like being my own boss.'

She knew what he meant. As stressful as it was being out on her own, at the same time, owning the bed-and-breakfast, and sinking or swimming by her own effort, was particularly satisfying.

He lifted his head, looking a little concerned. 'Would it bother you, being married to a handyman?'

Marry. There it was, the big word, the Big M. She had barely gotten her mind around being in love with him, and he was already moving to the next step. To him, though, this was nothing new; he'd spent the last three years getting accustomed to the idea. 'You want to marry me?' she squeaked.

'I didn't wait three years for you just for sex,' he pointed out with stunning practicality. 'I want the whole enchilada. You, the twins, marriage, at least one kid of our own, *and* sex.'

'Can't leave out the sex,' she said faintly.

'No, ma'am, you can't.' He was firm on that point.

'Well. In that case. In reverse order, though you really didn't ask a second question: yes and no.'

'The answer to the question I didn't ask is yes?'

'That's right. Yes, I'll marry you.'

A slow smile started in his eyes, crinkling the corners, spreading to his mouth.

'As for the first question, I'd marry you no matter what your job was, so I guess the answer to that one is no.'

'I don't make a lot of money—'

'Neither do I.'

'—but when you add my military pension, I do okay.'

'Plus Neenah will have to start paying you for her repairs, once you move into the B and B.'

'I'll have to fix her ceiling for free, though, since I'm the one who chopped the hole in it.'

'That would only be right.' Their lighthearted mood dimmed then, as they were reminded of the situation they'd left behind, the people who were dead. She snuggled closer to him, feeling suddenly chilled and needing to cling. 'It makes no sense, what those men did.'

'No. There's nothing reasonable about it. You gave them Layton's things, they had what they wanted, there was no reason to—'

He stopped, frowning, and she saw his gaze turn inward. After a minute it was her turn to say, 'What?'

'You gave him a suitcase,' he said slowly, 'but I carried two pieces upstairs.'

'A suitcase was all Layton brought in—' Now she stopped and stared at him with dawning horror. 'The shaving kit! I couldn't get it in the suitcase because of the shoes. I forgot about it.'

'I would have noticed if there weren't any shaving things in the suitcase. So whatever it is they want, they must think you still have it.'

All the pieces snapped into place, and suddenly everything made sense. Tears stung her eyes, dripped down her cheeks. Seven people had died because she forgot to give Mellor a damn shaving kit. She was both furious and devastated, because if he'd bothered to pick up the phone and call, she'd have mailed the damn thing to him. Hell, she'd have sent it express!

A cool, decisive look entered Cal's eyes. They lay awake talking for another hour while he formulated his plan. Cate didn't like it; she argued and begged that they go back together, but this time he was impervious. He held her and kissed her, but he didn't change his mind.

'I have a better angle on them now,' he said. 'You were worried about me going into the water; now I won't have to. Well, except for crossing the stream. I won't have to stay in it.' That slightly distant look remained in his eyes, and she knew he was mentally working out the details, weighing the odds, developing a strategy.

Finally, worn out, she slept, and woke at dawn to Cal making love to her. He loved her long and carefully, holding back as if he couldn't bear to let the moment end. She *was* sore, but if the pleasure was mixed with discomfort, she didn't care. Terrified that she might lose him so soon after finding him, she held on tight and prayed.

Over fifteen hundred miles away, Jeffrey Layton stood at the sink in a ratty motel room in Chicago and shaved with a disposable razor. He was in a shitty mood. This should have worked. He'd been certain it would work. But this was the eleventh day, and still the money he'd demanded from Bandini wasn't in his numbered account.

He'd told Bandini he had fourteen days to transfer the money, but Layton had never intended to wait that long. He knew Bandini would be doing everything possible to hunt him down, and he had no intention of helping the odds in Bandini's favor. Before he'd ever started down this road, he had decided that ten days was it. If he didn't have the money in ten days, he wasn't going to get it.

Okay. He wasn't going to get it.

He had deliberately left a trail to Podunk, Idaho, calculating how long it would take for someone to trace his credit card charges there. His intention had always been to drive back to Chicago and hide in plain sight, in the one city in which Bandini would never think to look for him, effectively hiding right under his nose. He still had no idea whether the nonlocal he'd heard in the dining room at the B and B was someone Bandini had hired, but that wasn't a risk he'd been prepared to take. The accent had been totally different, that was certain, with a sort of fake heartiness that he'd been able to tell the locals despised. Rather than risk being seen, or alerting the guy with the opening and closing of the front door, Layton had elected to leave the cheap stuff he'd bought behind in the B and B, climb out the window with the flash drive in his pocket, and get out while he could.

He'd ditched the Idaho plates and replaced them with Wyoming plates; then, when he'd gotten back to Illinois, he drove around until he found a vehicle identical to the rental he was driving and replaced the Wyoming plates with ones from Illinois. He'd paid for this sorry room in cash, giving a fake name, used only drive-through burger joints for his food or had Chinese delivered, and every day he'd checked his account with his BlackBerry.

It wasn't going to happen. The tenth day had been yesterday. He should have gone to the FBI then, but he'd decided to wait the full day. Today he'd teach Salazar Bandini he should have paid more attention when Jeffrey Layton told him something.

It never pays to dis the man who does the books.

He had his story all worked out, what he'd tell the FBI. When he'd found the hidden files he'd been alarmed, especially when he saw the names there. He'd downloaded the files to a flash drive, but Bandini had found out, and since then Layton had been running for his life. He'd finally shaken Bandini's men off his tail, and he was certain the FBI would be very interested in what was on the flash drive. They might wonder why he hadn't simply picked up a telephone and asked to be taken in, but he had an answer for that: he'd heard Bandini had a source in the FBI, and he couldn't be certain that whoever arrived to pick him up wasn't the source. He had actually heard that, so he wasn't lying. He'd figured that if he turned over the flash drive in front of several agents, that would prevent the evidence – and him – from disappearing.

Not that he didn't plan to disappear anyway. They'd probably figure Bandini had gotten to him. He didn't care, didn't care if they needed him to give a deposition or anything like that. What they did with the information on the flash drive was up to them; Layton figured they could get a conviction on several counts even without his testimony.

Not his problem.

He would love to be a fly on the wall and watch Bandini go down, but he had to protect himself. He had his spot all picked out. He had his new identity set up. Life would be good – not as good as it could have been if Bandini had come through with the money, but good enough.

After shaving, he dressed in one of his suits, very precisely chosen for the middle-of-the-road, nonentity persona they projected. They were good suits, but not expensive. Tasteful, but not stylish. Those suits allowed him to blend in, to become almost invisible. He hated them.

At precisely ten o'clock he checked out of the motel and drove to the local FBI office on Dearborn. He should have known better; he should have taken a taxi, so he didn't have to look for parking. He hated looking for parking; it was such a waste of time. He drove around for several minutes, looking, passing by several parking lots with 'open' signs because they were farther away than he liked. He didn't want to park so far away that the walk would make him sweaty, because that wasn't the impression he wanted to give. Wait, maybe it was. Maybe sweating was a good idea. Maybe that would make him look nervous.

Yes. That *was* a good idea. With that in mind, he took the next parking opportunity that presented itself.

He had a two-block walk to the Dirksen Building, where the FBI was located. The warm, humid September air brought out an immediate sweat. Then he had to go through security, then reception proved a roadblock. By the time he got what he wanted, which was at least two special agents from the racketeering division or whatever they called it, he had almost stopped sweating, and he was annoyed. All that effort, and the effect was lost.

He took the flash drive out of his pocket, held it up to show them what it was, then tossed it to the nearest agent. 'Salazar Bandini's private books,' he said brusquely. 'Enjoy.'

There were about seven inches of snow on the ground, but the weather had cleared and the air was like crystal. To the right they could see the far mountains and part of Trail Stop's paramecium shape. The snow line was about a thousand feet down; the valley was still snow-free.

Cate had given up trying to convince Cal to return with her. His reasoning was sound. The snow and ice had changed everything.

The trip they had estimated would take them four days would now take at least six, and that was if they had no trouble along the way. They couldn't take any route that would go over rock because of the ice. The ice might or might not melt; they didn't know the weather forecast. And if the weather warmed and the ice and snow did melt, it would cause another problem.

They had brought enough food and water for only four days, for two people, and a day and a half of those provisions were already gone. If they continued, they would run out of food about two days before they reached Creed's cabin.

Their lack of sufficient clothing was also a problem. They had gambled and brought only the minimum because of the load they were already having to manage while climbing, and they'd lost. There was no way they could continue.

Cate agreed with all that. It was Cal's solution that worried her.

He was sending her back alone. Going back would be much faster than climbing up, because she could rappel down the rock. She could easily be back in Trail Stop in a few hours.

He was going after the men with the rifles.

She'd pointed out that he would be traveling alone through some very rough country, that he would be in snow, that he didn't have the right clothing, and that the dangerous conditions still existed. At some point he would have to cross the stream and he would get wet and cold; all her original objections still applied.

He didn't agree. He said that knowing Mellor was after something specific, something he thought Cate had, made all the difference in the world. If Mellor was willing to go to these extreme lengths, then they had to assume he would stop at nothing and neither would he be willing to wait very long. He couldn't afford to wait very long, because keeping an entire community isolated and under attack was an iffy thing; he couldn't control chance or outside interference. Marbury could return with more questions. A repair crew from the power company could show up. Anything could happen.

By now Mellor had probably made his demand. If what he wanted wasn't forthcoming, he would have no reason to be patient. He could start shooting incendiary rounds into the houses and burn them out. Mellor could do this. Mellor could do that. Cate was astonished that Cal had such an encyclopedia of violence and destruction in his head. The bottom line was that he thought there was little time left before the situation exploded and even more of their friends were killed.

She couldn't reach him. He had pulled inside some fortified mental position; his focus was on what he needed to do. Finally she sat in despairing silence, watching as he fashioned some rough snowshoes, which would allow them to move faster over the snow and keep their shoes dry.

Her sneakers hadn't completely dried, and the leather was stiff from being so close to the fire, but he'd kept the empty plastic bags their rations of muesli had been in and had her put her feet inside them before putting on her shoes. The bags fit awkwardly, and he'd had to cut out the zipper because they kept rubbing her heels, but the plastic would keep the dampness from soaking through her socks. The snowshoes would keep her from sinking into the snow over the tops of her shoes, which would promptly have gotten her feet wet again.

He sat on the pad with his legs crossed, his expression intent as he worked. He'd cut some saplings about the width of his thumb, trimming them with his big multipurpose utility knife. He'd also cut some smaller lengths and notched each end, as well as a two-foot section from one end of his rope. He had then unbraided the rope fibers, separating them into individual cords.

Next he bent the saplings into a U shape, pulling the ends together and securely tying them with a piece of cord. The notched sticks were fitted inside the U to form bracing crosspieces and tied on each end to the sapling. The resulting snowshoe was crude but durable. He cut more rope, then laced the snowshoe to her right foot. In a matter of minutes he constructed the left snowshoe and had her walking around experimentally.

She had never worn snowshoes before, and she quickly found a normal gait wasn't possible. You didn't *walk* in snowshoes, you sort of waddled and shuffled, because you had to either keep your legs straight like cross-country skiers or lift your knees high to keep the front end of the snowshoe from digging in.

Nevertheless, the improvised shoes worked. She stayed on top of the snow instead of sinking into it.

Awkwardly, she crawled back into their shelter where Cal sat working on his own set of shoes. Eyes narrowed, he surveyed her shoes to make certain the bindings and laces were holding. 'When you get out of the snow,' he instructed, 'just cut the bindings. You have a knife, don't you?'

'In my pocket.'

'Work your way back to the Richardsons' exactly the way we came. You'll have a protected route the entire way. Tell Creed right away what we've figured out; he'll need to know because the situation could change at the drop of a hat.'

'I will.' She was chilled, as much from fear as from the weather, and she carefully placed another stick on their little fire. She wasn't afraid for herself, even though she was going back alone, rappelling down a rock face alone. A hundred things could happen to her, but all of those possible calamities were accidents. Cal was deliberately going into a situation where people would actively be trying to kill him. She had never been so terrified in her life, and she couldn't protect him any more than she'd been able to protect Derek from the bacteria that ravaged his body.

If anything happened to Cal, she would be emotionally destroyed. She couldn't go through that again, couldn't lose the man she loved and emerge in any way whole. Part of her would be dead, her capacity for love permanently stunted. No new people would be taken into her heart. She knew that, but she didn't say it, didn't lay that guilt trip on him. He was a hero, she thought painfully, a true hero, risking his life to save the world. Well, not the entire world, but people he cared about. Wasn't that just her luck? Why couldn't she have fallen for a math teacher or something?

'Hey,' he said softly, and when she looked up, startled, she found he was watching her with an expression of such tenderness she almost burst into tears. 'I know what I'm doing, and they don't. They're good shots, maybe good hunters, but I'm better. Ask Creed. I'll be fine. I promise you – I *promise* – that we're going to have that wedding, that new little kid we talked about, and a lot of years together. Have the same faith in me that I have in you.'

She managed to glare at him through the tears that blurred her vision. 'I can't believe you're so underhanded when you argue, pulling that line on me.'

'I don't argue,' he said.

'Right.'

Too soon, all too soon, he put out their fire by dumping snow on it, then scattered the ashes. She almost cried again, seeing the coals die. He was leaving most of his climbing gear behind so he could travel faster. He took his rope and trenching tool, and that was it as far as equipment went. She was slightly comforted by the big automatic weapon and holster that he slid onto his belt, and the knife in its scabbard. He put some food in his pockets and took one bottle of water. Then he used the knife to cut a hole in the middle of the blanket, which he then dropped over his head.

He cut strips from the bottom of the blanket and motioned her over. Gently he held her hands and tied the strips around them to form makeshift gloves. Then he cut two sturdy limbs for her to use as walking sticks, to keep her balance on the snowshoes. Until she gripped the sticks, she hadn't realized how much she needed the protection for her hands.

'I love you,' he said, leaning to kiss her. His lips were cold and soft, his bristly cheeks were rough. 'Now go.'

'I love you, too,' she replied, and went. She had to force herself away from him, and she'd gone only about fifty yards when she stopped to look back.

He had already vanished.

Chapter Thirty

Once he was safely out of Cate's sight, Cal used the walking sticks he'd cut for himself, digging them in and propelling himself forward almost as if he were on skis, looking for every bit of speed he could muster. He wasn't hiking across miles of mountainous terrain, wasting precious time; he was going down in as straight a line as he could manage, as fast as he could manage without turning cartwheels and landing headfirst on a boulder. He wanted to be in the valley while there were still hours of daylight left.

He'd used thermal scopes himself. They were heavy, and during the day the images blurred, lost their distinctness. He'd bet his life – he *was* betting his life – that those guys put the thermals aside during the day and used normal scopes and binoculars for surveillance. That's what he would do in a situation like this, where they were dealing with normal, mostly middle-aged people, men who occasionally went hunting but for the most part farmed or worked in shops. Against people like that, regular surveillance would be good enough.

But they didn't know about him. He wasn't normal, and no way in hell would they spot him with a pair of binoculars, much less a magnification scope with such a narrow field of vision. He wasn't waiting for the cover of night. By the time twilight came and they switched back to the thermals, he'd be in their front yard, practically under their noses, and they wouldn't know a thing until it was too late.

Cate was their target – *Cate*. He didn't care what their objective was, what they wanted; as far as he was concerned, they had signed their own death warrants.

*

Cate was in the valley by noon, her muscles shaking with fatigue. The unfamiliar gait forced on her by the snowshoes had left her thigh muscles sore and trembling. At the first rappel she'd been forced to make she was still inside the snow line, so she'd had to leave the damn snowshoes on, which had made for an interesting experience. She wasn't fond of rappelling anyway and had never done it alone. A rappel looked like easy fun to the casual observer, but it wasn't. It was a demanding physical maneuver, and if she slipped, if she did it wrong, she could maim or kill herself. To make things even more interesting, her arms and shoulders were sore from the unaccustomed climbing.

When she was finally out of the snow, she cut herself out of the improvised snowshoes – and promptly fell, tumbling several feet and banging her right knee hard against a large rock. 'Son of a *bitch*!' Swearing between her clenched teeth, she sat on the wet ground and rocked back and forth for a few minutes, holding her injured knee and wondering if she'd be able to walk on it. If she couldn't, she was screwed.

When the pain lessened from agony to merely severe, she tried to pull up the leg of her sweatpants and long johns so she could see her knee, but the long johns were too tight. She tried to get to her feet, and the knee gave out in the middle of the first effort. Oh, shit. She had to be able to walk. The joint had to support her, because she had another rappel to make, longer than the first.

She grabbed one of her walking sticks and jammed it into the ground, using it as leverage to swing her body around so she was closer to a skinny tree. Seizing one of the lower branches, she pulled herself to a standing position and swayed there for a minute; holding on to the limb for dear life, she gradually eased her weight onto her knee. It hurt, but not as badly as she'd feared.

The only way to inspect the knee was to pull her pants down, so she did. The skin was broken, and a huge knot was beginning to swell and darken just below her kneecap. At least it wasn't the kneecap itself.

An ice pack that she could strap on would be nice right about now. She turned and looked up at the snow, and shook her head. Not even for the joy of packing snow on her knee could she climb back up that slope.

Holding the tree for balance, she took a tentative step. Again, it hurt, but the joint held and felt stable. The injury was nothing more than a severe bruise, then, no torn ligaments. When she could put all her weight on the leg and walk normally, she continued down the slope, swearing every step of the way because going downhill was hard on the knees anyway.

The last rappel, the longest one, was a nightmare. She had to stay squared off on her legs or she would fall sideways into the rock. Her right knee didn't want anything squaring off on it, didn't want to absorb any impact. It was so swollen now that she could barely flex it. When she was finally on the bottom, she was bathed in sweat.

The air in the valley was cool, but pleasantly so. She looked up at the towering mountains around her, at the white caps they now wore, the dusting reaching halfway down the rugged slopes. That was where she'd been, all the way up there.

Cal was still up there, but he would be farther to the west, toward the cut. She sent a brief but fervent prayer for safekeeping winging his way, then turned and began the long trudge around the land spit to where she and Cal had climbed down the bluff. She remembered that the base of the cliff was nothing but rocks, and she almost burst into tears. She couldn't depend on the knee on that kind of footing, and she certainly couldn't crawl over the rocks because she couldn't bear to put her weight down on the swollen part of her knee. The only way she could negotiate those rocks was sitting down and sliding from rock to rock. Oh, joy.

She didn't have to, at least not the entire trip. In the two and a half days she'd been gone, the townspeople had organized watches so they wouldn't be caught by surprise. Roland Gettys spotted her and came down the cliff to help. Getting over the rocks and to the top of the cliff still took time and considerable effort, longer than she had expected – almost as long as it had taken her to get off the mountain.

Roland took her to the Richardsons, since their house was closest. He left her at the door and hurriedly returned to his watch. To Cate's surprise, the basement was nearly empty, at least in comparison to the crowd that had been there when she and Cal left. Gena and Angelina were still there, because Gena still couldn't walk on her sprained ankle; she could barely hobble. Creed and Neenah were there – same reason for him – and Perry and Maureen. Someone had strung ropes across the basement and draped sheets across them to create a little privacy.

Creed gave her a sharp look when she staggered in alone. 'Where's Cal?'

'He's gone after them,' she gasped, sinking down on a chair Maureen hurriedly shoved at her. 'He's going to try— He said they wouldn't be looking for him from that direction.'

'Do you want some water?' Maureen asked in concern. 'Or something to eat?'

'Water,' Cate said. 'Please.'

'What happened?' asked Creed, iron in his tone. 'What changed?'

'Joshua,' said Neenah, softly chiding.

'It's okay,' Cate said. 'Cal remembered . . . He put the things in the attic for me – Layton's things. There was a shaving kit. When those men – Mellor – when Mellor said he wanted the suitcase, I grabbed the suitcase and gave it to him, and I never thought about the shaving kit. It's still in the attic. What they want must be in the kit. That's why they came back.'

'I'll get it,' said Perry, at a glance from Creed. 'What does it look like?'

'It's just a brown Dopp Kit. It's sitting on the floor.' Cate closed her eyes, visualizing the attic. 'When you get to the top of the stairs, turn to your right. You'll see two rock-climbing helmets hanging on the wall. The kit is on the floor somewhere in that vicinity, unless Cal shoved it aside when he was getting the climbing gear.'

Perry left, and Cate took the cup of water from Maureen, gulping thirstily. 'What happened to your leg?' Maureen asked, looking worried.

'I fell on a rock, landed on my knee. I don't think there's any structural damage, but it's swollen and sore.' That was an understatement. What she wouldn't give for an ice pack and two aspirin.

'You came to the right place,' said Gena, trying to sound chipper and failing miserably. Her face was pale, her eyes sunken. 'This is the orthopedic section.'

'She's right,' said Neenah, leaving Creed's side to come to her. 'Let's get you cleaned up and see how that knee looks.'

'I don't have any clothes to change into,' said Cate, too tired to really care.

'I'll take care of that,' Maureen said as she helped Cate to a chair in another section of the basement where she could pull a

272

sheet across for privacy. 'Tell me what you want, and I'll send Perry back for it.'

'The poor man. He'll be exhausted from running back and forth.' Cate closed her eyes and let them undress her down to her underwear, standing on one leg when they helped her up so they could remove both pairs of pants. It was soothing to feel a cool washcloth being stroked over her face, arms, and hands.

'The swelling is really bad,' Neenah murmured. 'You probably shouldn't be using this knee at all.'

'I didn't have a choice.'

'I know, but you do now. We'll arrange some cushions to prop up that leg and support it, so you'll be more comfortable.' The cloth was dipped in cold water again and laid across her knee. It wasn't an ice pack, but the cold water was soothing. Maureen appeared with two tablets in her palm; Cate took them without asking what they were, without caring.

Together Neenah and Maureen moved some cushions, boxes, and piles of folded clothing, making a sort of recliner on the floor, then they helped her to it. She sat on the cushions, leaned against the boxes, and the piles of folded clothes were placed under her knee. The support was wonderful. They covered her with a blanket and left her alone.

She went to sleep immediately, not hearing Perry when he returned.

Creed woke her a short time later, hobbling to her 'room' with the aid of a cane and dragging a chair with him. Neenah followed, holding the Dopp Kit and giving him an exasperated look. 'He won't listen to me,' she complained to Cate, though beneath the exasperation she looked strangely content.

'I know the feeling,' Cate said wryly.

'Is this the right shaving kit?' Creed asked, taking it from Neenah.

Cate nodded. 'There isn't another one in the house. Did you find anything?'

'Nothing. I dumped everything out, opened everything that would open—'

'And some that wouldn't,' interjected Neenah.

He slanted a quick look up at her, a glance so laden with intimacy that Cate almost sucked in an audible breath. When had this happened?

Well, the answer to that was obvious: the same time it had happened for her and Cal.

'There's nothing here,' said Creed. 'I've felt the seams, the zipper, practically ripped the damn thing apart. If there was anything valuable, incriminating, or remotely interesting in this kit, I haven't found it.'

Cate stared at the kit, forcing her tired brain to work. 'They only think it's here,' she said slowly.

'Think what's here?' Creed's tone was sharp.

'I don't know. But whatever it is, they think it's here because when they checked Layton's suitcase his shaving kit wasn't in it. Layton has it – the thing, it, whatever. He took it with him. When he climbed out the window and left, he was running, so of course he took whatever it is with him.'

'Do they know he climbed out a window and took off?'

Slowly she shook her head, mentally going over what she'd told the mystery man when he'd called that day, pretending he worked for National. 'At the time, I thought Mr. Layton must have had an accident somewhere. When some man called looking for him, I told him Mr. Layton had disappeared, that he hadn't checked out or returned for his things, and I thought he must have had an accident in the mountains. I didn't mention that he'd left by way of the window.'

'Which puts an entirely different outlook on Mr. Layton's disappearance,' said Creed. 'If they'd known about the window, they'd have realized he bolted, and logic says he took what they're looking for with him. So now they think you still have it, and even if you tell them differently, they won't believe you, not after all this.'

All this. Seven people dead. Creed wounded. An untold amount of damage to houses and vehicles, all for something that wasn't even here. Suddenly overwhelmed, Cate buried her face in her hands and wept.

Yuell Faulkner was more worried than he'd ever been in his life. He hadn't been able to get in touch with either Toxtel or Goss for three days now. He'd sent them on a simple retrieval, but they'd been gone a week. They should have been back days ago.

Bandini would be expecting to hear from him, and Yuell had nothing to tell him. He couldn't say they'd recovered the flash drive or that they'd found Layton – nothing.

He was spooked; he admitted it. He left a light on in his office to make it look as if he were still there, in case anyone was watching the window, and left by a basement exit that put him in an alley. Fine with him. He wasn't getting in his car and leading any watchers to his home, anyway.

He walked a couple of blocks and hailed a cab. After thirty minutes of aimlessly driving in circles, he got out, walked another couple of blocks, and got another cab. He watched carefully both times. No one appeared to be following. He took the precaution of exiting that taxi several blocks from his home and waited until it was out of sight before he turned in the correct direction.

At last he let himself into his house. The dark, familiar spaces enfolded him. Usually he could relax here, but until he heard from either Toxtel or Goss he wouldn't be able to relax anywhere. Damn it, did he need to go out to Idaho himself? If they'd screwed up, why hadn't they just called and admitted it? He'd think of something, some way to fix the situation, but he had to know what was going on.

He turned on a lamp and thought longingly of a nice stiff drink, but he needed to be in top form if anything went down. No drinks at all for him until he heard –

'Faulkner.'

Yuell didn't turn toward the voice, the way most people would have. He dove to the side, toward the doorway.

It didn't work. The cough of a silenced weapon only slightly preceded an explosion of pain in his back. He forced himself to keep rolling, moving through the pain and shock, and felt another bullet enter. His legs jerked wildly, spasming out of control, and he crashed heavily into the wall. He tried to reach for his weapon, but nothing was where it was supposed to be and his hand sort of floated in the air, grasping at emptiness, which was damn stupid.

A dark, faceless shape loomed over him, but Yuell knew who it was. He knew that voice, had heard it in his nightmares.

The shape pointed at his face, and there was another cough, but Yuell didn't hear that one – or anything else, ever again.

Chapter Thirty-One

Cal lay on his stomach to the north of where he'd mentally marked the location of the farthest firing position. It was a good place. Strategically, it was where he would have placed a shooter if he wanted to prevent someone from coming down that side of the land spit and either making it into the cut or slipping behind him. The long, narrow groove was like a bowling alley lane, without a lot of great cover – for thermal scopes, that is. He'd guessed right about them switching to regular scopes and binoculars during the day, though, and it took a sniper a helluva lot more skilled than these old boys to spot him when he didn't want to be spotted.

Creed had always called him a naturally sneaky son of a bitch. Nice to know some things never changed.

He had waited, wanting to see when the shifts changed. The first night he had counted four different firing positions, but after that only two – the two most strategically placed to knock off anyone trying for the cut. No one could man those positions nonstop for three and a half days without being relieved and do any kind of a decent job. Not only did you need sleep, you needed food and water and the occasional trip behind the bushes. If you popped enough speed, you could stay awake that long, but you'd be hallucinating, shooting at ghosts, so paranoid you'd shoot your own self for spying, so he discounted that possibility. Either the shooters were asleep during the day, or someone was relieving them. Four shooters the first night, two after that. The math was simple. They were splitting shifts.

That left a big gap in coverage over toward the bridge, and Mellor had gone to too much trouble to make that kind of mistake. There would be another guard positioned at the bridge, armed with shorter-range weapons; that meant continuing with the two-shifts per twenty-four hours theory, two more men, for a total of six.

Six men, six civilians, meant at least two vehicles, probably more. They would be parked nearby, but off-road where they couldn't be spotted in case anyone going to Trail Stop came along. Likely someone would, if they hadn't already. Conrad and Gordon Moon really liked Cate's muffins and usually made the drive at least once a week. Maybe Cate had guests scheduled to arrive. There could be a big pretense about the bridge collapse, the power and phone lines being out because of it, but that charade wouldn't last for long.

These guys had to know they were hard up against the wall, time-wise, and they would move against the people in Trail Stop soon, against Cate, because they thought she had what they were looking for. He would have preferred not to send her back to Trail Stop, but there had been no other place. She couldn't have come with him, and she couldn't have stayed on the mountain; she had to have food and shelter. At least if she was in Trail Stop, Creed would look out for her.

Night would be the best time for these men to move. They had the thermal scopes; they could see what they were shooting at. But they'd made a tactical error by blowing the bridge, and the difficultly in crossing the stream went both ways. He'd had to go half a mile upstream to find a place where he could cross without being swept off his feet. They'd made another tactical error by waiting; now the townspeople had organized some barricades where Cal had shown them, they had spread out, and they were mad as hell.

Still, when shooting started, anything could happen, and Cate was over there.

He had two choices: slip by the three on watch, locate their vehicles, take care of the three who would probably be there resting, and go for help; or take out all six, one by one, make it look as if they'd turned on each other, and *then* go for help. He could do it; he could set that scene with no problem at all. He really liked that idea a lot. He didn't want a single one of these bastards getting out alive.

Generally he was an easygoing guy, but you didn't want to piss him off. Right now, he was pissed off, big time.

He kept an eye on his watch. The shift changes wouldn't be at dumb-ass times like nine AM and nine PM; they would be straight-up-and-down times like noon and midnight, or six AM and six PM. If he didn't see any movement at six PM, that meant each shooter had been on watch since noon and was tired, but would be on duty for another six. A smart tactician would have staggered them, had one position swapping out at noon and midnight and the other swapping on the sixes, so one was always fresh while the other was tiring, but most people went for simplicity – and predictability. It boggled the mind.

At six PM, all was quiet. He didn't detect any activity.

Too bad. If a fresh shift had come on at six, he'd have waited until midnight, let them get tired, and they would all have lived a little longer.

As silent as a snake, each movement slow and deliberate, Cal crawled higher on the mountain, above where he'd marked the shooting locations, and began a meticulous grid search, looking for the first shooter. Cal had taken care to disguise his silhouette, with the olive drab blanket draped around him. He'd cut strips off the blanket and tied them around his hands and fingers, both for warmth and to keep him from leaving any telltale fingerprints on anything. Another strip was tied around his head, and small branches and leaves were stuck under the strip. When he was still, the naked eye would pass right over him.

Time passed and he didn't see anything. He began to wonder if either he'd mistaken the location or they'd moved around; if the latter, he might well be screwed and someone was drawing a bead on his head right now. But his head remained unexploded, and he continued his painfully slow crawl, looking for something, anything, that would betray the shooter's position.

There was a faint glint of metal about fifteen feet ahead and to the right, then a tiny green glow that immediately winked out. The stupid asshole had lit up his watch to check the time. *Dumb*. You didn't wear a watch that had to be backlit; you wore one with luminous hands and covered the face with a peel-back flap. The devil was truly in the details, and that little detail had just betrayed the shooter. Otherwise it was a good position; the guy was prone, which made a more stable platform for shooting, and he had good cover in the rocks. His head didn't stick up above the rocks, which was why Cal hadn't spotted him before.

The guy was totally focused on a slow, continuous sweep with the scope, even after all these hours. He didn't sense Cal's near ness, even when Cal was just a whisper away. He died without even knowing Death had come calling, his spinal cord snapped at C-2.

It was a difficult maneuver to perfect. It required skill, technique, and a lot of strength. Another obstacle to mastery was that not many people were stupid enough to let you practice on them. For that reason, it was often practiced in real-time situations, where a mistake could be costly.

The guy just went limp, the stink telling Cal he was dead, though the audible snap had been proof enough for him. He patted the body until he found the hunting knife on the man's belt, which he'd known would be there. He drew the knife and inspected it as much as he could. It would do. He slipped the knife inside his belt and hoped to hell he didn't accidently stick himself, then quietly heaved the guy up and over the rocks, as if he'd slipped. It happened. Too bad.

He picked up the man's rifle and put it to his shoulder, his eye to the scope as he scanned the mountainside, looking for the bright glow of thermal signatures. Aha. The next position was a hundred yards away and somewhat lower, for flatter, more accurate shooting. Farther still, about where he judged the bridge to be, was another flare of light. That was it. Three, just as he'd thought. He scanned higher and lower, making certain. Nothing, except for some small animals and a couple of deer.

The rifle was a fine piece of work; it felt like magic in his hands, the balance perfect. Regretfully, he held it over the rocks and let it join the guy who had owned it. Now it really did look like an accident, as if the guy had stood up to take a piss, tripped, and went headlong down the rocks, taking his rifle with him.

Silently, he began stalking the next shooter.

Goss could feel it all going to hell. He sat in the tent playing Texas hold 'em with Teague and his cousin, Troy Gunnell, but his mind wasn't on the game and he was losing regularly.

Toxtel was on the verge of a nervous breakdown. After telling the old guy what they wanted, they had heard ... nothing. Not a peep out of them. You couldn't negotiate with people who wouldn't talk. They hadn't seen any movement over there lately, either, but Goss knew damn good and well they were moving around behind those fortifications they'd thrown up. They had somehow retrieved their dead. Teague had said they'd either drenched themselves with icy water or somehow mounted some kind of rolling barricade they could hide behind, which sounded like something out of a movie about a medieval war, so Goss went with the simplest explanation: water.

Teague was so proud of those fucking scopes, and they could be fooled by cold water. Great.

Teague was sort of losing it, too. He looked like hell, and he was popping ibuprofen as if they were candy. But he was functioning, and except for being obsessed with this guy Creed, he made sense when he talked. His three pals didn't seem to notice anything funny about him, so maybe it was only that he was still dealing with the effects of a concussion. Having been there himself just a week ago, Goss could sympathize.

Today two guys had come blowing down the road as blithely as if they hadn't driven around the fucking Bridge Out sign back at the highway. Yeah, they'd seen it, but thought it could have been there by mistake. Any idea how long it would take to repair the bridge? A couple of days, maybe?

They were just the sort of dimwits, Goss thought, who would complain long and loudly to anyone they thought could get the bridge fixed. Any day now, someone with the highway department would show up.

Maybe there was some sort of cosmic soup from which they all drew the same thoughts, because Teague suddenly said, 'Your guy looks ready to flip out.'

Goss shrugged. 'He's under a lot of pressure. He's never failed to deliver before, plus he and the boss go back a long ways together.'

'He's let his ego get involved.'

'I know.' He had quietly helped that by spurring Toxtel on at every opportunity, agreeing with the most asinine of ideas, putting the most extreme twist on any view Toxtel came up with. Toxtel wasn't an idiot, far from it, but his pride was at stake and he didn' know how to back down because he'd never *had* to back down before. An unbroken string of successes could become a handicap if it went on too long, because a guy lost perspective.

Toxtel had definitely lost perspective.

Maybe it was time to end this and move on, Goss thought suddenly feeling cheerful at the idea. There was no way the li

280

could be kept on this fiasco. Too many people had died, too much damage had been done. All he had to do was make certain this blew back on Faulkner, and that was the easiest thing in the world to do.

'That's it for me,' he said, yawning, when the current game ended. 'I think I'll go talk to Hugh, maybe relieve him early if he's tired.'

'It's a couple of hours yet until midnight. That makes for a long shift for you,' said Teague.

'Yeah, well, don't tell him I said it, but I'm younger.' He stood and stretched, and pulled on his heavy coat, made sure he had gloves and a watch cap. The weather here could change in the blink of an eye. It had gone from clear and cold to warm and cloudy, then to cold and cloudy, then cold and rainy, and now back to clear and cold – all in as many days as there were changes. This morning the mountains had been snowcapped. Winter was coming, and he wanted the hell out of Idaho.

Good old Hugh. He'd miss him.

Not really.

He had to make certain this pointed back to Faulkner. Maybe plant a note on Hugh that said, 'Yuell Faulkner paid me to do this'? Yeah, right. It had to be something the cops would catch, but not so obvious they would discount it as a plant. Tying Bandini in would be a nice touch, too, guaranteed to bring a shitload of trouble down on Faulkner's ass, from both the good guys and the bad.

He pulled on his gloves as he went over to the Tahoe, opened the door, and fished Toxtel's cell phone out of the glove box. The phones were useless out here in the mountains, but he wasn't interested in making a call. He turned on the phone, then entered Faulkner's number in the address book. No name, just a number. The cops would run it down. He turned the phone off and replaced it in the glove box, then on second thought got it out again and slipped it into his pocket. Then he had a third thought, smiled, and once more put the phone in the glove box. Yeah. That would work even better.

There was a pile of papers in the Tahoe, maps and lists and sketches. One of the sheets of paper had fallen to the floorboard, been stepped on, and was generally dirty. Goss grabbed a pen, clumsily scribbled Bandini's name on the dirty sheet of paper, put a question mark after it, then marked through the name so it was almost illegible – almost, but not quite. He dumped all the papers on the back floorboard, and dropped the pen between the driver's seat and the console.

Then, whistling, he walked down the dark trail to where Toxtel stood – or rather, sat – lonely vigil, waiting for someone on the other side to talk to him.

Cal melted into the shadow of a tree, making himself part of the undergrowth. He was no more than five feet from the third guard, whom he recognized as Mellor, when he heard someone coming toward them, *whistling*.

He stood motionless, his head down and his eyes narrowed to mere slits. He'd smeared mud on his face to break up the pattern of pale features, but he'd slid effortlessly into the zone he reached when he was hunting, and if instinct prompted him to duck his head and close his eyes, he did. He was so close, the gleam of his eyes might give him away.

The second shooter was lying motionless in a pool of his own blood, the first guy's knife in his throat. Two down, four to go. He was tempted to take these two at the same time, but he ignored the idea. Controlling the noise, the scene, would be too difficult. He'd stick to his original plan and take them one at a time.

'You're early,' said Mellor, standing up from his protected posi-tion. He was wearing a heavy coat and was holding a pistol instead of a rifle. Cal mentally shook his head at the way the guy was exposing himself to possible gunfire. He must feel safe at night, thinking no one in Trail Stop could see him.

'Thought I'd give you a break,' said the other guy. Cal recog-nized him, too. Huxley. 'Teague and his cousin are playing Texas hold 'em in the tent if you want to relax before turning in.' As he spoke he leaned down and picked up a blanket, shook it out, started folding it.

'I don't play cards,' said Mellor, turning to stare across the water at the dark houses. 'What's with these people?' he asked suddenly. 'Are they nuts? I'd have been trying to find out what wa going on, what we want, anything. They just pulled back an locked down.'

'Teague said they were—'

'Piss on Teague. If he'd known what he was doing, we'

already have the flash drive and be back in Chicago.'

Flash drive. So that's what they wanted. But Cate had a computer; if there had been anything electronic in Layton's belongings, Cate would have recognized it, realized that was likely what they wanted. She hadn't, because it wasn't there. It had gone out the window with Layton.

'I thought you said he was highly recommended.' Huxley had draped the folded blanket over his arm. Something was funny about the way he was holding it, with his hand inside the fold.

'I called a guy I know,' Mellor muttered, turning back. 'I trus—'

Huxley fired three shots, the sound muffled by the blanket, so it wasn't much louder than if it had been suppressed. Mellor jerked as two shots hit him in the chest, a double tap, then the insurance tap to his forehead. He went down like a sack of feed. Huxley didn't check to see if he was dead, didn't spare his erstwhile partner a second glance; he simply turned and walked away, back the way he'd come.

Now, wasn't this interesting? A falling out, or a hidden agenda? Silently Cal followed, blending with the shadows, a part of the night itself. Huxley made no attempt at silence; he strode up the road as if he were on a sidewalk in the city. Around a curve he left the road, took a newly beaten-down path to the left. The vehicles would be tucked back in here, Cal thought; the flattened bushes looked as if something wide had been over them.

There was a tent set up in a clearing, with five vehicles parked around it: four pickup trucks and one Tahoe. A camp lantern hung inside the tent, shedding its less-than-sufficient light on two men playing a halfhearted round of poker. Through the opened flap, Cal could see sleeping bags rolled up on the floor of the tent.

'Toxtel in love with standing watch?' a big man with a huge, vivid bruise on his face asked, looking up. 'Or does he think they'll suddenly start talking tonight?'

'Just conscientious, I guess,' said Huxley, who brought his arm up, started pulling the trigger. Either he had given a lot of thought to how he was going to do two men, or he'd practiced until it was second nature. There was something almost mechanical about him: no hesitation, no excitement, no emotion at all. Two shots here, to the big man first, then two more to the other man, following so swiftly the second man had no time to react. Then the barrel swept back to the big man, the motion perfectly controlled, and he delivered the insurance tap. Back to the other man, once more, without feeling. *taptap, taptap, tap, tap.* Almost like a dance.

Huxley squatted beside the big man's body, stuck his gloved fingers in the right pants pocket, and came out with a set of keys. He tossed the pistol on the ground between the two bodies and walked out of the tent to one of the pickups.

Cal watched him drive away, his gaze narrow and thoughtful. He could have taken him at any time, but the guy was doing his work for him and at the same time effectively putting him completely in the clear, so this seemed best. Let the cops figure out what happened. Whatever Huxley's agenda was, it hadn't included his partners.

Cal went into the tent and took a set of keys from the second body. Glancing down at the key, he saw it was for a Dodge, and without hesitation he walked to the big four-wheel drive Dodge Ram and climbed in. He would be at Creed's place in fifteen minutes.

Neenah stayed with Creed at the clinic the next day while his leg was X-rayed and Cal's handiwork examined. When the doctor asked who did the suturing, Creed merely said an old buddy who'd had some medical training in the Corps, and left it at that. It was enough; the doctor immediately assumed 'medic' and was satisfied.

Turned out he had a hairline fracture – like Cal hadn't already told him that – and they put him in a soft cast instead of a plaster one. He was to wear the cast until he came back in two weeks for more X-rays, but the doctor thought the fracture would be healed by then. All in all, good news. They gave him a pair of crutches; the doc ordered him to use them and give his leg as much rest as possible, and said that if he did what he was supposed to, in two weeks he'd be walking on his own two feet again.

Neenah smiled in relief when she heard Creed's prognosis. 'I was afraid you'd done some sort of permanent damage, hobbling around the way you did,' she said as he got into her rental car. How she'd gotten a car so fast, he didn't know. Maybe someone in the sheriff's department had helped. She had driven up to the clinic steps to pick him up, to keep his walking to a minimum.

'That's the only way I know how to hobble,' he retorted, making her laugh. He loved her laugh, loved the way she tilted her head back and her eyes sparkled. The tension and strain of the past few days had left dark circles under her eyes and occasionally he'd seen grief etched in her face, but for a moment all that was gone. He'd like to keep it that way, keep the pain away from her. He knew he couldn't, knew everyone who had been in Trail Stop would have to deal with what had happened, each in his own way. He hadn't escaped unscathed himself, and he wasn't thinking about his leg. Old memories had resurfaced, brought back by the violence that had touched their lives. He'd dealt with them before and he would this time, too, the memories shared by all men who had been to war. The details differed, but friends had been lost.

The Trail Stop Massacre, as it was already being called by the bloodsucker press, was big news right now. A steady stream of reporters was flowing into town, which created an instant motel-room shortage because the Trail Stop inhabitants were already here and needed places to stay.

Eventually everything would settle down, but now the sheriff's department was taking statements from everyone and scrambling to find accommodations for so many people until the electricity and phone service could be restored to the community, which some people were saying could take until the bridge was rebuilt. Bridges weren't thrown up overnight, not even small bridges. The word was they might not be back in their houses by Christmas. Creed knew better. He'd already made some phone calls to some people who knew some people, and red tape was being sliced through, the Trail Stop bridge shoved to the front of a list of projects. Creed expected the new bridge would be ready within a month.

Things would still be a mess in Trail Stop, though. Food in refrigerators and freezers would be spoiled, rain would have blown in through broken windows and damaged floors and walls, plus there was the little matter of all the bullet holes, damaged or destroyed possessions, vehicles that had been damaged ... the insurance adjusters would be busy for a while.

At least the cops seemed to be leaning toward the scenario that there had been trouble in the bad-guy ranks, and one of them had turned on the rest. Unless Cal spoke up and said otherwise, that was the theory Creed was publicly buying.

Privately, Creed knew otherwise. He'd been on too many missions with the cunning bastard not to recognize his handiwork. Cal had always gotten the job done. No matter what that job was, he'd been Creed's go-to guy in tougher situations than this. He was never the biggest guy around, never the fastest or the strongest, but by God, he'd always been the toughest.

'You're smiling like a wolf,' Neenah observed, which might have been a caution that people could be watching.

The comparison startled him. 'Wolves smile?'

'Not really. It's more a baring of teeth.'

Okay, so the comparison was an apt one.

'I was just thinking about Cate and Cal. It's nice to see them together.' It was only half a lie. He'd been thinking about Cal. But, damn, it *was* nice the way he'd seen Cate three years ago and hung in there all this time, waiting for her to notice him – and while he was waiting, quietly bonding with her kids and inserting himself into her life so completely she wouldn't know what to do without him. That was Cal. He decided what he wanted, then he made it happen. Creed was suddenly glad Cal hadn't wanted Neenah, or he'd have had to kill the best friend he had in the world.

Creed directed Neenah to his house, and for the first time in his life he suddenly wondered if he'd left underwear lying on the floor. He knew he hadn't – his military training was too deeply ingrained – but if ever he had, it would probably be when Neenah would see the house for the first time.

He made it to the front door and started to unlock it, then noticed where Cal had knocked out a window. He laughed, reached inside, and unlocked the door, then maneuvered his crutches to the side so she could precede him inside.

He liked his place. It was rustic, small enough for him, but not too small, since there were two bedrooms. The kitchen was modern, not that he used it a lot, the furniture sized to fit him and comfortable enough to sleep on. The decorating was plain Jane, if you could call it decorating. The furniture was put where he wanted it, and the bed was made up. That was the extent of his domestic abilities, or inclinations.

She didn't have a place to live, he realized. Her house had taken a lot of hits, plus she couldn't even get to it right now. The sheriff's department had brought in a helicopter to airlift the stranded inhabitants to town, because that was deemed the fastest, easiest way.

'It looks like you,' she said with her serene smile. 'No nonsense. I like it.'

He touched her cheek with one finger, lightly stroking her

smooth skin. 'You could stay here with me,' he offered, going straight to the heart of what he wanted.

'Would you want me to have sex with you?'

He almost fell, the crutches suddenly becoming unmanageable, but he found he was incapable of lying to this woman, incapable of looking into those blue eyes and uttering anything except the absolute truth. 'Hell, yes, but I want to do that regardless of where you live.'

'You know I was a nun?'

How could she be so calm when his heart was suddenly beating so fast he thought he'd pass out. 'I heard. Are you a virgin?'

She smiled, a tiny curve of her mouth. 'No, I'm not. Does it matter?'

'It matters in that I'm relieved as hell. I'm fifty years old; I can't take that kind of stress.'

'Don't you want to know why I'm not a nun anymore?'

He bit the bullet and hazarded a guess. 'Because you liked sex too much to give it up?'

She burst out laughing. She seemed to think that was so hilarious, in fact, that she ended up sitting on his couch laughing so hard she cried. He began to get the idea she hadn't liked sex that much. He bet he could change her mind. He was slower now, and he knew a hell of a lot, and when it came to sex that was a good thing.

'I became a nun because I was too afraid of life, too afraid to live,' she finally said. 'I left the convent because those were the wrong reasons for being there.'

He eased down beside her and put his crutches aside. With one arm around her he tilted her face up. 'Do you remember where we left off right before the bridge exploded and your house got shot up?'

'Vaguely,' she said, the twinkle in her eye telling him she was teasing.

'Do you want to pick up there, or do you want to go to bed and make love?'

Her cheeks turned pink and she regarded him with absolute seriousness. 'Bed.'

Thank you, Jesus. 'Okay, but first there are two things I want to get clear.'

She nodded, her clear blue gaze locked with his.

'I've had the serious hots for you for years, I love you, and I want to marry you.'

Her mouth fell open. She turned white, then pink again, he hoped with pleasure. She said, 'That's three things.'

He thought about it for a split second then shrugged before scooping her onto his lap to kiss her. 'Actually, I think it's just separate parts of one big thing.'

'You know, I think you're right.' She wiggled against him, and ended up sitting astride his lap with her arms looped around his neck while they kissed each other crazy. After a while she was half naked and his pants were unzipped, and she was all but panting as she lay against his sweaty chest. Her hand was inside his pants and she was stroking up and down and his spine was so rigid he thought he could do a good imitation of a plank. Bed was the last thing on his mind.

'This had better be good,' she said fiercely.

'It will be,' he promised as he eased her into position.

'If I've gone all this time without having sex and if this turns into another dud, I—'

'Honey,' he said clearly, getting out his last lucid thought for the next twenty minutes, 'Marines don't fire duds.'

'Cate!' Sheila flew out of the house, sobbing in relief even though Cate had called her mother immediately on reaching a phone two days ago. She had been anxious to speak to her mother before the news hit the wire services, and she'd wanted to talk to her boys. They'd been in bed asleep, but Cate had insisted Sheila wake them so she could hear their sleepy protests that faded when they realized Mommy was on the phone.

With all the police questions Cal had been obliged to answer, they hadn't been allowed to leave until just that morning. Until the electricity was on and the bridge rebuilt, they couldn't go home, and Cate's parents had invited them to stay with them in Seattle until that was possible.

Cate was engulfed in her mother's arms, tightly hugged, kissed, then hugged again. Her father came out of the house and hugged her, too, very tightly, and was followed closely by two jumping, shouting, very dirty little boys who couldn't decide if they wanted to shriek 'Mommy!' or 'Mr. *Hawwis*!' so they did both.

Cal swiftly shook hands with Cate's father, then went down on one knee and the boys all but swarmed him. After three years of it, she was accustomed to being abandoned in favor of the handyman, who, after all, had taught them how to cuss. How could a mother compete with that? She found herself grinning like an idiot at the sight of him with two sets of little arms wrapped tightly around his neck while they both vied to tell him all the news of their visit with Mimi. He looked as if he were being choked, they had such tight and enthusiastic grips on him.

'I see I was right,' said Sheila, looking down at him with satisfaction.

'Right about what?' he managed to gasp out.

'That there was something going on between you and Cate.'

'Yes, ma'am, you were. I've been after her for three years.'

'Well, good job. Are you getting married?'

'Mom!'

'Yes, ma'am,' said Cal, without a hint of a blush.

'When?'

'*Mom!*'

'*As soon as possible.*'

'In that case,' said Sheila, 'I'll let you stay here with her. But no hanky-panky with my daughter under my roof.'

Her dad looked as if he would choke with laughter. Cal was close to being choked by the twins. Cate thought she might choke on indignation. 'I wouldn't think of it, ma'am,' Cal assured her mother.

'Liar,' Sheila said briskly.

Cal winked at his future mother-in-law. 'Yes, ma'am,' he said very definitely, and she grinned.

A couple of weeks later, the man who used to be Kennon Goss, who used to be Ryan Ferris, walked casually through a cemetery outside Chicago. He seemed to walk without purpose, pausing to read names, then meandering on.

He passed by a new grave. There was a temporary marker up, and the name on it was Yuell Faulkner, with the dates of his birth and death listed. The man didn't stop, didn't appear to pay the grave any attention. He went by it to study the old tombstone of a child who had died in 1903, and from there to a veteran's grave decorated with two small American flags.

One of life's ironies, the man thought. Faulkner had already been dead that night, by a few hours. Good old Hugh Toxtel hadn't had to die; his involuntary sacrifice hadn't been necessary, after all. The others, either, but he didn't care about Teague and his cousin Troy. He did wonder about Billy Copeland and that young guy, Blake, though; he hadn't killed them, so who had?

Thinking back on that night, sometimes he thought he remembered a hint of a breeze, as if something or someone had moved close to him. Other times his common sense told him that there *had* been a breeze – a real breeze, caused by the movement of air. That didn't explain why several times since then he'd bolted upright in bed, startled out of a sound sleep by this weird sensation that his dreams had conjured up, of being watched.

He was glad to his bones to be out of Idaho, but he couldn't stay in Chicago. It was time to move on. Maybe someplace warm. Maybe Miami. He'd heard on the news there had been a series of vicious murders down there. The killer was evidently collecting eyeballs.

What were the odds?

Also available by Linda Howard, published by Piatkus:

ICE

Gabriel McQueen has only just arrived home on holiday leave from the service when his county-sheriff father sends him back out again with new marching orders. A brewing ice storm and a distant neighbour who's fallen out of contact have the local lawman concerned. So he enlists Gabriel to trek to the middle of nowhere to ensure Lolly Helton is safe and sound. It's a trip the younger McQueen would rather not make given the bitter winter weather – and the icy conditions that have always existed between him and Lolly – but there's no talking back when your dad's the town's top cop.

Despite the treacherous weather conditions, Gabriel gets to the house but, on approach, spots strangers in Lolly's home – one of them carrying a weapon. His stealth training is all he needs to extract Lolly from the house without alerting her captors. But when the escape is discovered, the heat – and the hunt – is on. And the winter woods are not a place to be once the ice storm touches down, dropping trees, blocking roads, and trapping the fleeing pair in the freezing dark.

978-0-349-40011-2

DEATH ANGEL

A striking beauty with a taste for diamonds and dangerous men, Drea Rousseau was once content to be arm candy for Rafael Salinas, a notorious crime lord. Seeing that a break with Rafael is coming, Drea makes a fateful decision and a desperate move to escape, stealing a mountain of cash from the malicious killer.

Though Drea runs, Salinas knows she can't hide – and dispatches a cold-blooded assassin in hot pursuit. Left for dead, Drea miraculously returns to the realm of the living a changed woman. Both humbled and thrilled with this unexpected second chance, she embraces her new life. But in order to feel safe and sound, and stop nervously looking over her shoulder, she will need to take down those who marked her for death.

Joining forces with the FBI, Drea finds herself working with the most dangerous man she's ever known, yet the closer they get to danger, the more intense their feelings for each other become, and the more Drea realises that the cost of her new life may not just be her heart, but her life itself.

978-0-7499-0911-6